Burning Sky

a novel

John Darnton

Arcade Publishing · New York

Also by John Darnton

Almost a Family
Black and White and Dead All Over
The Darwin Conspiracy
Mind Catcher
The Experiment
Neanderthal

Arcade Publishing books may be purchased in bulk at special discounts for
sales promotion, corporate gifts, fund-raising, or educational purposes. Special
editions can also be created to specifications. For details, contact the Special
Sales Department, Arcade Publishing, 307 West 36th Street, 11th Floor,
New York, NY 10018 or arcade@skyhorsepublishing.com.

Arcade Publishing® is a registered trademark of Skyhorse Publishing, Inc.®,
a Delaware corporation.

Visit our website at www.arcadepub.com.

10 9 8 7 6 5 4 3 2 1

Library of Congress Cataloging-in-Publication Data is available on file.

Jacket design by Brian Peterson
Jacket painting by Zdzislaw Beksiski with permission of the Historical Museum
of Sanok, Poland

Print ISBN: 978-1-64821-024-2
Ebook ISBN: 978-1-64821-025-9

Printed in the United States of America

For Nina
and
Kyra, Liza, and Jamie
and
Zachary and Ella
and
Asher and Adara
and
Lucy, Benny, and Calvin

For many years, I have been moved by the blue at the far edge of what can be seen, that color of horizons, of remote mountain ranges, of anything far away. The color of that distance is the color of an emotion, the color of solitude and of desire, the color of there seen from here, the color of where you are not. And the color of where you can never go. For the blue is not in the places those miles away at the horizon, but in the atmospheric distance between you and the mountains . . .

Blue is the color of longing for the distances you never arrive in, for the blue world.

—Rebecca Solnit
A Field Guide to Getting Lost

I had a dream, which was not all a dream.
The bright sun was extinguish'd, and the stars
Did wander darkling in the eternal space,
Rayless, and pathless, and the icy earth
Swung blind and blackening in the moonless air;
Morn came and went—and came, and brought no day,
And men forgot their passions in the dread
Of this their desolation; and all hearts
Were chill'd into a selfish prayer for light . . .

—Lord Byron, *Darkness*
July 1816, "the year without summer"

Prologue

THE SPOTLESS WHITE UNIFORM DOESN'T FIT HER. IT BALLOONS around her elbows and knees, and the trousers would sweep the metal floor had she not folded them into double cuffs. Clearly the flight engineers, charged with anticipating any and all contingencies, did not envision this one: suiting up the gawky frame of a sixteen-year-old adolescent female.

Not that she is just any adolescent. It's hard to carry that anonymity when you're the daughter of a scientific dynasty and the offspring of the most powerful man in the Northern Hemisphere in 2076. Usually she tries to disavow her privileged status but now, in order to do this, she has embraced it.

She had shamelessly pleaded with her father to get aboard the ultra-supersonic jet, displaying her inquisitive, adventurous side. That spirit was their bond.

She did not tell her father why she is so compelled to fly on the Launch. It isn't just to circumnavigate the globe in a matter of hours, though that is part of it. It is to experience, to understand . . . what, exactly? Well, she will have to see. She will know what the allure is when she gets there.

The plane's support crew treats her with studied indifference, all but the thin-lipped copilot whose resentment she feels speaks for the others. He and the pilot escort her to the plane and show her where to sit—strapped into a remarkably confined spot behind their cushioned seats.

Not much room, the pilot acknowledges. "That's because of the payload. You can imagine how big it has to be and how much fuel we use. We've got one hundred drones to release."

"And no one figured we'd be carrying a passenger," puts in the copilot.

They slip on their headphones and turn their attention to the crescent-moon console of dials, switches, and blinking lights. After a rondelet of indecipherable exchanges with the control tower, the plane shoots down the runway. Her spine presses into the seat back as they lift off with a happy bounce.

They take a steep path that feels almost vertical. They go up and up, all the way into the stratosphere. There, where no other plane dares venture, they reach the operative altitude. The plane vibrates and her stomach lurches. She hears a grinding of the bay doors opening behind her, then the whoosh of the aerosol sulfur being released. She imagines the wake washing through the stratosphere, widening and thickening, replenishing the Cocoon.

She looks out the windows at the opaque grayness. She can't see anything. It's like flying through dirty dishwater. When they're halfway over the Pacific, she taps the pilot on the shoulder for him to remove his headset and asks: can you take it any higher?

He shakes his head no. We have to stick right here.

"What," says the copilot. "You wanna see what's up there?"

Her unspoken answer is *yes, yes, yes. I want to see what's up there. More than you can possibly imagine.*

All that she's read, all her learning about the way the world used to be, makes her long to see it.

What was it like, the blinding sun, the playful colors of the crystalline dome? What was it like to live under the glutinous overload of glittering stars? What was it like, for those astronauts one hundred years ago, to peer down at the beckoning azure marble Earth? And to look up and experience the blackness of the universe?

The only answers during the forty-five hours of flight come from her imagination. She falls asleep and wakes when the wheels hit the runway.

When they step out of the plane, she unzips her white uniform and thanks them and goes out to her car in the parking lot. Under the gray miasma that hangs low like an oppressive ceiling, she still wonders: *What was it like before they stole the sky?*

PART I
DARK DAYS

2085
(YON)

I

THE BOY HEARS THEM COMING BEFORE HE SEES THEM. HE RUNS deeper into the wild, away from the thunderous sounds pursuing him; the gnashing of the rooter machines upending bushes and trees, the eerie scream of the blast guns that obliterate birds in midair.

The Color Guard. The Boy detests them. He has been raised to do so. But he also fears them.

Just that morning, before breakfast, Grampa warned that they were due for the sweep.

"Make sure you keep outta their way," he said, raising his crusted head from the sick bed that has become his prison. "They're not after you but you bother 'em, they'll mess you. They're heartless bastards." He paused to catch his breath, wiped his chapped lips. "You see 'em, you run. Fast as your legs carry you. Hear?"

Yon nodded. He had received the warning countless times.

He runs faster, branches tearing at his arms, ripping his clothes. Soon he'll hit the deep woods. He figures that'll slow them down. Trees ten feet tall, ferns up to their shoulders, leaves the size of lily pads drooping from the branches.

Yon and his grandparents live in a cabin in deep woods of

northern Canada, the area left after the fires leveled the boreal forests. Each year the Guards shrink the wild zone, picking and choosing the bushes and birds to kill with a cold eye. Now the zone is less than half what it was a hundred years ago and the flora has changed in the dwindling sunlight.

* * *

The woods are Yon's world. Ten years old, he loves to gallop through them, climb trees like a squirrel, swing from the vines. Burning up energy. Free . . . but not free as a bird. That's wrong, the birds are anything but free. They're being hunted down mercilessly, some of them. Why only some? He doesn't know.

He is a cat perhaps, moving stealthily in the yellow haze. Or a wolf, which he has read about in books. Wolves no longer exist either.

Caw-caw, the blackbirds call. They're still around. No more jays. Very few robins. They've been marked for extermination.

He makes forts, lean-tos small as nests. He sleeps curled up inside, gathering leaves about his slender body. His dog lies just outside, his nose resting on his forepaws, pointing toward him.

His grampa named the big mongrel Shadow, says he's a sly hunting dog. To the boy, the name Shadow doesn't make sense, since he's never seen a real shadow under the sunless sky. He's only seen vague silhouettes on the floorboards cast by candles at night.

When he leaves the forts he disguises them with branches and underbrush, turning back to imprint the location on his memory. He builds them on a zigzag path deeper and deeper into the wilderness. That way he can stay out for a long time.

He hunts small game for meat and pelts with his old squirrel gun, but he would never trap them. He reveres animals too much for that. Once he came upon a deer no bigger than Shadow, a leg crushed in the metal teeth of a trap, and he tried to free it while it bucked. He finally pried the trap open and it bounded away on three legs, leaving a trail of blood.

He especially loves birds, loves to watch them glide through the trees and fly high, disappearing into the dirty fog of the Cocoon. His grampa'd raise his busy eyebrows in delight whenever the Boy was the first to hear the song of a robin.

Yon has nightmares, vivid ones, about crawling through tunnels, escaping monsters, falling into crevices. During the day he talks to himself, in his mind at least, not a narration but a random flow of phrases to keep him company. He walks through the bush quietly, light on his feet and bending his knees to muffle the sound.

He examines a new nest of wasps: crawling out a hole at the bottom, shaking their wings, and flying off. At times he feels like that, newly created, without a past, as if he sprang fully formed into this singular life. At other times he feels a heaviness, a burden, like Shadow when they leashed him as a pup to keep him from wandering. But what is holding him back and where does he want to go?

He tells himself it's Grampa's doing. When the old man took him camping he filled his ears with stories about the old days when game was plentiful and "the trees'd reach up to the sky." Back then, people could do as they chose. They were free.

The two would sit around the campfire and the old man would sip fermented cider and talk. He pushed concepts like freedom and heroism into the Boy's young mind the way he'd take a stick and push half-burnt twigs into the center of the blaze. *You're a child now but someday you'll be a man and you'll see. You're destined for greatness.* Destined? To do what? *You'll know when it happens,* Grampa'd say, staring into the fire.

* * *

Yon runs with the machines behind him thrashing and crashing.

He passes the demarcation line where the Color Guard stopped last year and keeps on going. He comes to a clearing. There! One of his forts, dug halfway into the ground, the roof branches resting upon a tree stump, surrounded by ferns. He slips inside, pulls leaves around the entrance. He digs his fingertips into the dirt and darkens his cheeks and forehead and lies in wait.

In time they come. Six of them, men and women, dressed in the camouflage green uniform. The machines are deafening. They march into the clearing and stop and look around. They cut the machines off, a sudden silence. He peers out.

No more than a dozen feet away they are sitting on tree stumps and rocks, opening lunch pails.

"Same old shit," says one, holding up a sandwich. He takes a bite, ripping the crust. After chewing it, he wipes his mouth with his sleeve. A slightly older man sits off by himself, silent. The others taunt him. One throws a piece of bread that strikes him on the chest.

Yon watches every move. He has never seen them this close. Before he had imagined resisting them, maybe even blocking their machines somehow, but this is impossible now. They are so large. He can see the bulge of their arm muscles and their wide black boots.

A woman stands and wanders close. She lowers her pants, kneels down, and takes a pee. The Boy holds his breath, doesn't move. He hears the stream of urine strike the leaves, then break into shorter spurts and finally stop.

"Fiona," yells a Guard. "Woods everywhere and you take a piss right in my face."

"Lucky I didn't shit." She stands, zips up, and walks back. The Boy still holds his breath, releases it slowly.

The afternoon seems hot and silent and they relax in the heavy air, lulled by a chorus of cicadas. Three of the Guards close their eyes and seem asleep. Then one of the women barks out a command and slowly they drag themselves to their feet.

The older man exclaims and points. They look up. Yon looks, too. He sees a bird weighing down a thin branch. A robin, his red breast puffed out. The Guards move quickly but noiselessly. Two of them pull out nets. Another pulls out a blast gun, slowly raises it, and points. The sound, a deep throat-clearing *Ka-voom*, echoes through the woods. The robin breaks apart into pieces, blood splashed against the trunk, two feathers spiraling to the ground.

The men barely react. They must have done this a thousand times. The commander pulls out a computer, punches in something. They gather their things and put away the nets and start up the machine and with a thrashing and crashing they move on.

Yon waits a long time before he comes out of his hiding place. He looks at the pile of feathers. He is amazed that something so alive can be gone so quickly. But he has seen something the men did not see—or at least did not understand. The bird was carrying a worm in her beak. She had a nest.

He looks around, on all sides, up in the air, and it is not long before he finds it, on the top branch, eight feet high. He climbs up and looks in. There are three eggs. He handles them carefully— they are warm to the touch—and carries them to the ground one by one. He removes his shirt and swaddles them.

Grampa will be pleased.

He takes them home and walks into the bedroom and lays them on the bed. The old man is sleeping but one touch and he wakes. He sees the eggs and smiles, looks at the boy, back at the eggs again.

"Robins," he says. His voice sounds like rustling leaves. The Boy fetches him a glass of water.

"Where did you get them?"

The Boy describes his encounter with the Color Guard, leaving out the part about the woman peeing.

"You did good," says Grampa, leaning over to pat him on the sleeve. "Someday you'll get the bastards." He falls back in a

7

coughing fit, making sure the eggs are safely cradled in a depression in the blanket between his legs.

* * *

They keep the eggs in a makeshift incubator near the fire. From his bed the old man gives Yon instructions on how to care for them. He is failing quickly, a little weaker every day. He says he doesn't know if he'll live to see them hatch.

"You know how much he loves those damn eggs," says Gramma. "Sometimes I think they're the only things keeping him going."

The old man's last day comes. By coincidence two of the three eggs hatch that very morning. Grampa dies between the two hatchings. He holds the first newborn in his wizened hand and smiles and then picks up the broken eggshell. He falls into a deep sleep and slowly expires, giving a slight spasm at the end. He crushes the broken shell in his fist.

Yon's gramma leaves the room and goes outside and looks at the trees. She isn't crying. Shadow is pacing around the front door, softly moaning.

Yon stands there, shaken. He has seen animals die but this is different. Grampa looks like himself but not really. Nothing moves, not a single thing. Something has gone out of him. His skin looks like wax. It's horrific.

He picks up the baby bird and puts it in a shoebox that's been prepared with cotton wool. Then he opens his grandfather's fist, suddenly cold, and picks out the bits of shell.

The old man seemed to love the eggs every bit as much as the chick. Maybe even more. Why? Once Yon asked him and the old man said, "The color. You can't see it but I can. It's the most beautiful color in the whole world."

The Boy looks at the pieces and holds them up to the light.

What's so special about the color? They are regular robin's shells like any other, thin with jagged edges—and creamy white.

2

THEY BURY GRAMPA ON THE HILL BEHIND THE CABIN. SITTING at the table afterward, Yon reaches over to hold his gramma's hand but she places hers on top of his. Giving it a squeeze, she rises from her seat and cooks breakfast—two tiny eggs from the scrawny chickens out back.

"I always hoped he would go first," she says. "I worried about him without me—how he would get on." She forks two pieces of toast next to the sunny-side eggs and slides the plate before him.

Yon has a sudden realization: Of the two, she was the stronger. He wonders if she's pulling herself together for his sake, because he still needs looking after. He's not used to thinking of them like this, at a distance.

In the weeks that follow he devotes himself to hunting. More than ever he feels the obligation to provide meat. Now that the coyotes are almost all gone, the stripped carcasses of the rabbits and squirrels hang undisturbed in the smokehouse. Once a month Gramma trades the pelts for canned food from the cinderblock trading post ten miles away. The owner holds a shotgun under one arm and never asks who she is.

To find the animals he has to wander farther and farther afield.

John Darnton

When he's far away he constructs lean-tos and sleeps there. There is a large lake to the east and to cross it he uses an old rowboat and rigs it up the way Grampa showed him, with an old sheet for a sail. He gets good at maneuvering it and catching the wind.

He misses Grampa, thinks often of their overnight camping expeditions. The old man would sit back against a tree trunk and tell stories. Sometimes he would act out the Greek myths, including one that petrified Yon—about the Minotaur, the half-bull, half-man monster. He'd hoist his shirt over his head like a shroud and lope around the campfire, throwing off shadows, to hunt down children in his labyrinth.

Yon is anxious about leaving Gramma alone. Their cabin is isolated and far from any road but still he worries that bands of thugs might somehow happen upon it. He tells her about this. She takes an old shotgun down from a crossbeam and goes out back to show him what a good shot she is. Still, he's not sure she could bring herself to use it against a person.

Sometimes, returning from a hunt, his imagination turns fearful. He breaks into a run and doesn't stop until he sees the wisp of smoke rising from the chimney and Shadow, asleep by the door, hauling up his old bones to greet him.

Now that Gramma's eighty, she begins having mental lapses. One evening she is telling him about "a ruckus in the henhouse." She begins, "I go out to see what's going on and . . ." She falters. She casts a panicked look around, as if she could retrieve the memory from the metal sink or the thin white curtains hanging languid in the heat.

In the past she was taciturn, but now when the mood takes her she talks a lot. She rattles on in a litany about unimaginable things—the sun and the sky and the seasons of bygone days. Sometimes she describes a scene so vividly, Yon can close his eyes and almost be there.

"You can't imagine snow. It's like diamonds, little diamonds

10

falling from the sky. I'd wake up and run to the window and see the whole world different, all white and sparkling, every tree, branches hanging to the ground. It made my heart leap up."

"What happened to it? Where did it go?"

"You know that. We told you. Everything changed. The whole world—it got hotter and hotter."

"Yes. Because of people. But why didn't they stop doing all those stupid things? What were they thinking?"

"Ah . . . If only I could explain that."

Sometimes she reminisces about "the old days," before the Cocoon. She sits on the edge of her chair in a characteristic pose, her legs spread wide, and talks about all sorts of things that no longer exist—cell phones and computers and something called the internet, which he can never quite grasp.

"What happened to them?"

"They just collapsed when everything fell apart. They weren't maintained." She pauses. "Maybe some of it was intentional. Maybe the Power didn't take kindly to things that could help people organize."

But she never answers personal questions. *Who was my father? My mother? What happened to them? Why are we living in Canada in the middle of nowhere?* No electricity. No car. No neighbors.

"Because there's no way to track us," is the most she says. Then abruptly she stops talking, turns away, and sinks back into her shell.

* * *

Five years pass. She becomes quiet and increasingly disoriented. Moments of lucidity are becoming rare. Senility is gradually stealing her soul.

Yon is growing quickly, tall but thin as a cornstalk. He's in his fifteenth year. His body is doing unusual things. Hair sprouts in new places. He grows a scraggly beard to cover his hollow cheeks. He feels vague yearnings. He wants something but doesn't know what. He's eager to leave, he aches for adventures, but of course he can't abandon Gramma.

Sometimes he has visions. They begin on an ordinary day when he is tracking a rabbit that leads him on a wild chase, all the way up a promontory. He climbs to the top and comes to a plateau. Behind him is a grove of tiny pines that protect him like a sanctuary. He sits down and looks out. The land extends for miles until it disappears in the fog, an expanse he has never seen.

He lies spread-eagled upon the rock and closes his eyes. He can almost feel the Earth spinning. He opens his eyes. A bird is circling just above. He imagines rising up to meet it. He closes his eyes again and feels he *is* rising up. He perceives something high above the Cocoon, something far away. An ineffable sense of lightness permeates his being. It passes through him like a beam of light and then leaves him drained and calm, serene.

He returns to the spot many times but only rarely does he undergo the same experience.

* * *

Gramma keeps a treasure. A rock kept in a pouch at the bottom of a closet. He knows it's important—it's been there as long as he can remember—but he doesn't know why. Sometimes, when she's out working in the garden, he steals in to examine it. He slips it out of the pouch, weighs it in one hand, holds it up to the light. What's so special about a gray rock? But sometimes, if the light strikes it, it *does* look special.

One afternoon she retreats to a corner of the cabin and turns a table into a makeshift workbench. She wields pliers and small hammers and twists of metal, hunched over the table for hours. Yon leaves her alone and goes hunting.

When he returns, the table is back in its usual place, the tools put away. She greets him with a wry smile and cooks him a tough piece of chicken and a small pile of wrinkled peas.

"Tomorrow's your birthday," she says. This he knows well—he's been thinking of little else since that morning. "Sixteen. Almost a man," she continues in a spry voice. "I got something for you."

She goes to the closet and pulls out a package wrapped in old paper. She places it ceremoniously before him.

Lying in the cradle of the paper is an amulet holding some sort of object. He stares at it. The amulet is made from the chain of Grampa's old canteen. The object is set inside a circle of silver. It's a sculpted stone, rounded and smooth, and it takes him a moment to recognize it: a piece of the mysterious rock from the pouch.

"Put it on," she commands.

He drapes it around his neck, feeling the weight of the stone against his breastbone.

"It's beautiful," he says. "But . . . why?"

"Go outside and look at it."

He does. He peers at it close up and at arm's length. It's slightly brighter than the usual gray but not much, a little richer in white perhaps. He sees her observing him through the window and feels a little ridiculous.

He goes back inside the cabin. "I don't understand," he says. "What's it supposed to do?"

She stays with her back to him, pouting. "The damn Cocoon."

"What is?"

"Why you don't see it."

"But I do. I just don't see . . . whatever it is I'm supposed to."

"You will. Someday. Meanwhile, make sure you don't let anybody else see it. That could bring trouble. Real trouble."

"And here—"

She reaches into the pouch and pulls out a slip of paper and hands it to him. A single line of letters and numbers.

13

"What is it?"

"A place to go. An address in New York City."

"New York City! Why?"

"Just in case."

"In case?"

"You never know. You might need it. If something happens."

He can't imagine New York City. The mere thought of going there is overwhelming—but also exciting.

She starts sweeping the floor and refuses to answer any more questions. They don't talk about the amulet or New York again.

* * *

Several months later, on a day when he is unable to find any game, he ranges farther afield than ever before. It's evening, the rust color in the west is disappearing, and he builds a lean-to and tries to sleep. His eyes are just closing when he hears the yipping of dogs. Louder and louder. A patrol of some sort—heading in his direction.

He leaps up, grabs his rifle, and runs away from the barking. He smashes into branches that tear his face and clothes. He's gone only a short distance when he runs into a barrier—a cyclone fence. He hears a humming sound. Floodlights flash on. His hands feel a searing pain. He wrenches them away, turns and gallops through the brush.

He runs and runs, pulling great gulps of air into his lungs, his legs leaping over bushes, arms flailing, faster and faster. He runs until he can run no more, then collapses under a tree. He listens. No more yipping dogs.

He has a moment to think. He saw a sign on the fence: CLEN. Crop Lighting Enclosure. It must be one of the reserves for artificial cultivation of crops that his grandparents told him about—the reserves that are off limits and patrolled by special security guards.

What should he do? He remembers hearing them say that the Power employed satellites to track people. Would they be up here in Canada? Can they see at night?

He finds a muddy stream to soothe his hands. They are black-ened but not seriously burned. He walks until the pale gray morning comes up. Then he hides and sleeps until afternoon. He wanders for another day and a half, glancing up at the Cocoon, wondering if there's a satellite up there somewhere. When he finally judges it safe, he returns home, rushing into Gramma's arms.

She doesn't seem to notice that he was away.

* * *

Shadow is behaving oddly. The old dog whines and scratches to go outside. Once there he circles the cabin, sniffing. He raises his head, trying to catch a scent. Back inside, he settles down for a moment, turning around and around before curling into a ball, then rouses himself and paces and whines again.

The dog's behavior worries Yon. His gramma doesn't notice it or if she does, she doesn't mention it. For the most part she falls back into her pit of silence.

Except for one evening.

Once dinner is over and the dishes put away, she appears unusu-ally alert. Her eyes glimmer in a way he hasn't seen for some time, and she begins to talk. She sits at the table opposite him, cradling a steaming cup of tea in her hands. Her hair hangs down in strings but somehow she looks younger.

"Did I ever tell you about the time . . ." she begins. She recounts a distant memory. She does this over and over, each time reach-ing her mind further back in the past. When Shadow was a pup. When they built the cabin. When they made "the trek" up here. She describes a house in Washington, DC. She speaks about his mother.

15

"My mother!"

For years he has asked about his mother, never before with the glimmering possibility of an answer. Gramma looks down, as if a painful memory lay on the floor.

"Tell me. Tell me."

"Ah, poor woman."

"What happened to her?"

Gramma turns silent for a moment.

"And your father, my God."

"My father! You knew him too?"

"Well, no, not directly. But I knew *of* him, of course."

"But Gramma—"

"I'm not your grandmother."

"But you . . . Grampa—"

"He wasn't your grandfather."

"What do you mean?" He's almost shouting.

"It's a long story." She grasps the cup of tea, takes a sip, and wipes her lips.

He urges her to continue. But she just shakes her head and says, "Somebody had to take you in."

Yon feels the foundation of his world crumbling, his past collapsing like the walls of a house falling outward. His grandfather . . . not really his grandfather. And this woman before him . . . He looks at her, her white hair a nimbus in the light, so familiar and suddenly so unknown. Not his grandmother.

"Please. Tell me."

No answer. It is as if a battery were slowing down.

The light dims in her eyes. She stops drinking her tea and stops talking.

That evening Yon can't sleep. The world has slipped its axis. So many questions, so many secrets. His thoughts tumble. Who were his parents? His grandparents? What happened to them? What did she mean—*somebody had to take you in?*

16

Dread steals over him. It is a dread he has often felt, ever since he heard the yipping dogs and ran from the CLEN patrol, the fear that he has brought danger to their cabin.

* * *

Returning from a four-day hunt, the first thing he sees is Shadow lying on the ground. He knows instantly that his dog is dead but it's not until he stands over him and sees the pool of dried blood that he realizes he has been killed. His back is bent, caved in. An axe lies five feet away.

The cabin door is open.

He doesn't run toward it. Something tells him not to. He makes his way slowly, even though he doesn't think the killers are inside. His judgment is based on clues: Shadow's blood was dry, there's no smoke from the chimney.

He steps across the threshold, his rifle raised. Flies buzz in a spiral in one corner. A stench strikes him. It takes only a moment for his eyes to become accustomed to the dimness.

She is lying across the bed on her stomach, her legs resting on the floor, as if in prayer. But her head is on its side, cracked open. A pool of blood is curdled on the floor. He backs away but stops himself and forces himself to approach her.

He straightens her out on the bed, on her back, and folds her hands across her chest. He goes outside, finds some tiny wilted leaves, and places them around her. Her body is cold and lifeless. His eyes fill with tears but he stops himself from weeping.

He buries her two hours later, in a hole next to Grampa. He has to drag her up the hill to the grave, holding her from behind, under her arms. He wraps her body in sheets and lowers it awkwardly into the hole and covers it with dirt. The first shovelful lands on her, black against the white sheet.

He buries Shadow in a shallow grave near her feet. He places a small round stone above Gramma's grave, a marker known only to him. Better not to leave anything for them to find.

He goes back to the cabin and packs a few belongings into a small case. He takes his squirrel gun and a paper bag of cash. Opening the pouch, he retrieves the amulet and the paper with the New York City address.

He goes out the door and looks back. He thinks of burning the cabin but decides not to. The smoke might draw attention. They will surely come for him. Why give them a head start?

3

THE FIRST DAY, YON FOLLOWS THE PATH HIS GRAMMA TROD TO the trading post—so faint that three times he has to double back to find it. When he arrives, he walks quietly through the trees to give the squat cinderblock structure a wide berth. With narrow slits for windows and a roof fitted with wooden barricades, it doesn't look friendly.

No one is around. The ground on the far side is marked with half a dozen paths and he chooses the one that looks most traveled. He doesn't want to take a dead end, arriving at the door of some rifle-packing stranger, especially with his own squirrel gun slung across his shoulder.

When it gets dark he finds a cluster of evergreens and bundles down in a cradle of pine needles, waking every few hours. It doesn't feel as safe as his lean-tos. He is up and off before the day arrives with its customary pallid light seeping down like swamp mist.

The next day he walks thirty miles and the one after that thirty-five, until he arrives at a ragged town of dirt roads and wooden shacks. It centers on a train depot but the ticket window is shut. Two days he waits, sleeping in a shed and scrounging food from a frightened family of Mexicans in a boarded-up house. He slips money under the door and they leave a plate of beans and stringy beef outside.

The train creeps into town so stealthily he almost doesn't hear it. He has to run a whole block—his rifle banging his tailbone—and he jumps onboard just as it pulls out. He buys a ticket from a shifty-eyed conductor. It costs $1,800. He hesitates—he's not accustomed to counting out money—and the conductor grabs the bills and moves on without giving change.

The car has eight other people in it. Two men sitting side by side and whispering, a woman in a bonnet traveling with a chubby boy, and four other passengers sitting alone. Most have their eyes closed, rocking to the pendulum swing of the train.

He turns to look out the window at the trees moving past. He feels a sudden stab of longing for Grampa and Gramma. At sixteen, he thinks, he is an orphan—although he knows they weren't his parents nor, as he reminds himself, even his grandparents. His eyes glide back to the interior of the car. He's never seen so many people—and he's never felt more alone.

Thirty miles down the line, the engine gives out. The passengers clamber down with their baggage and set out through a waist-high meadow. Each one leaves a wake of trodden grass and disappears quickly into a wall of woods beyond.

He is the last to leave. He walks through the woods for several hours and comes upon a deserted road. He follows it until he comes to a clapboard roadhouse at a crossing. When he enters, half a dozen people sprawling at a counter turn to stare at him. No one speaks. He makes his way to an empty stool and orders a ham sandwich. Five minutes later the waitress slides a plate in front of him. As he eats he looks out a dirt-encrusted window.

Broken-down cars litter the parking lot. Some are rusted heaps, others metal skeletons with weeds growing out the windows. He remembers how Grampa used to rant against the internal combustion engine. "People talked about doing away with them but never did," he would say. "Some switched to electric cars but not enough. Mostly what they did was talk, talk, talk."

He finishes the sandwich. Next to the door is a blackboard with notices. One offers to sell a ride to New York City. He writes his name beside it and waits in a corner. Some three hours later a man in his twenties walks in, wearing filthy jeans and a camouflage T-shirt. He checks out the board and bawls out his name. Yon raises his hand. The man looks him up and down, gives a wet cough, and motions him outside with a sharp nod of his head. They negotiate the price—twice the cost of the train ticket—and the man insists on half payment up front. Yon turns his back to fish through the wad in the paper bag.

The man eyes his rifle. "Fucking thing better not be loaded." Yon opens the breech to assure him.

The road is pockmarked with gullies and littered with debris. They come to a paved highway. The asphalt is riddled with large potholes and chunks that rise up like miniature volcanoes. From time to time there's a downed tree across the road, sometimes sawed in half but more often not, forcing them to detour around it.

They hit a smooth stretch and Yon glances over at the driver squinting through the windshield. His long hair is greasy and rises up in a clump to meet the breeze through the window. The sleeves of his T-shirt are rolled up and his left arm rests on the window frame. His right arm sports a tattoo of a grinning skeleton in a billowing dress.

"No one's on the road," Yon says. "We've been going an hour and we haven't seen a single car."

"So?"

"I thought there'd be more."

The man looks at him, frowning. "Where the fuck you been?"

When Yon doesn't answer, the man gives a wet cough and spits out the window. "Been like this since the world went to shit." He shakes his head once.

By evening they come to a sign, riddled with bullet holes, that says, US BORDER AHEAD. The man pulls off onto a dirt track.

"Black Guards at the border. Can't stand those fuckers."

Yon doesn't say anything, doesn't ask what the Black Guard is. Instinct tells him to suppress his ignorance.

The car bumps so violently Yon's head grazes the ceiling. The man drives for several miles, turns left and drives several miles more, turns again and climbs an embankment to slip back onto the highway.

They're in the US now. The road here is even more chopped up.

They drive deep into the night, sleep briefly in the car, and eat a quick breakfast at an outdoor grill. They drive all the next day and on the following morning come to a populated area. More and more buildings crowd the road, some old and dilapidated, others new and made of slapdash materials. A river floods the deserted streets on both banks. Not many people are around.

"Hartford," says the man, with another wet cough. "Bad fucking place."

They continue south and pass more and more houses and eventually cars appear, moving in both directions. Now there are people on the sides of the road. Yon sees three boys tossing a ball around. A man is giving another man a haircut under a tree. A number of people traipse along the edge of the road, sometimes not bothering to step out of the way. Drivers honk continually.

The signs are mostly down, so Yon doesn't know where they are. Hours pass and they skirt vast stretches of water that reach all but the high ground. It smells foul. Between clumps of trees he sees a river. Could that be the Hudson that Gramma talked about?

Soon the buildings are three and four stories high and made of brick or cement. They're packed in side by side. Many look unoccupied, with smashed windowpanes and holes in the walls. From time to time the car slows to a crawl because so many pedestrians press close. Yon is astounded: so many different types of people, varying skin colors, young and old, wearing odd assortments of clothing, shabby and colorful and everything in between.

They come to a wide boulevard crammed with cars, carts, bicycles, and motorbikes.

"Here." The driver stops the car and points with a grimy finger across the street to a staircase into the ground. "There's the subway."

Yon pays him, grabs his rifle and case, and opens the door. The man's gaze seems suddenly intense. "Good luck, Little Red Riding Hood," he says.

Yon watches as the car pulls away. He feels he's stepped from the shore into a swirling river of humanity. There are people everywhere, a roaring tide of faces and bodies.

He moves slowly, looking at the surroundings. On closer inspection, most of the buildings are falling apart. Some are halfway demolished, their bricks tumbling into the gutter and their front walls missing, displaying sad interior settings of pipes, stained wallpaper, and oddly intimate arrangements of chairs and tables. Outside, mountains of garbage lie beside the doorways.

In front of him the sidewalk is lined with tables piled with merchandise. Behind them sit vendors, their faces illuminated in a ghostly glow by flickering candles. He walks by the tables. There are all kinds of things arranged in pyramids—cans of olive oil, kerosene lanterns, knives, flashlights, batteries, tin cans and other goods. On the ground are jackets, boots, and used tires. The vendors don't hawk their wares but sit sullenly close to them.

He goes down the subway staircase into a dimly lit station. The walls are streaked with leaking water, tiles are missing, wires hang down. A booth is dark. A man ahead of him climbs over the turnstile. Yon does, too.

On the platform a jumble of people sleep under blankets or in sleeping bags. All around are rusted shopping carts, colored bags, pots and pans, small stoves and other detritus. One man sits leaning against the wall, smoking.

"When's the next train?"

The man gives him a bloodshot look and doesn't reply.

Yon settles in at the end of the platform. He's so exhausted he falls asleep and wakes abruptly when he hears someone rifling through his belongings.

"Hey!"

The figure flees. Yon sees he's carrying something and it takes him a few seconds to realize it's his bag and rifle. He leaps up to race after him, but at that moment a train screeches into the station and he runs back to board.

He upbraids himself. A few hours in the city and already he's lost everything he has. He might need that rifle.

He gets off the train at the last stop, joining a throng of riders. When he walks outside, the people seem to melt away. He breathes deeply in the night air. Gray shapes and shadows abound. Buildings jut up into the darkness. No windows are lighted—must be no electricity.

* * *

Almost no one is around. The stores are empty, their display windows smashed or sealed with plywood. In one, a door hangs from the hinges. Four junked cars lie at odd angles near the sidewalk. A burnt-out traffic light droops almost to the middle of the street, swinging slightly.

He walks two blocks and approaches a large building with two stone lions flanking the door. He tries the front doors, which don't budge. He walks around to the rear, where he comes upon an open area. It is teeming with life. A jumble of sounds and smells—spirals of smoke, snatches of music and the indistinct murmur of a hundred conversations.

It's a shantytown of jerry-built wooden shelters, tents, hovels under tarps, and tin-roofed shacks. Two men sit on a wall at the entrance—perhaps they're guards—but they look at him and keep talking. He enters.

Inside it's a rabbit's warren of alleyways. Everywhere he looks there are people, all ages and colors, leaning on windowsills, sitting on stoops, playing cards on barrels, lying on plastic lounge chairs.

They cast casual looks at him, not hostile, not friendly. He walks deeper into the labyrinth, turning so many corners that he's soon lost. The alleys get narrower as the shacks squeeze together. A trench with fetid water runs down the center, and smells of food and spices and smoke permeate the air.

A soccer ball rolls at his feet, followed by a boy of about ten who skids to a halt and throws his head back to look up in surprise. Yon taps the ball back with his foot. The boy spins around, plucks it up with his feet, and disappears into a side alley.

"Play him one-on-one and you'll lose," says a voice. Yon looks over. A man in a flowered shirt leans back in a chair propped against a wall. He grins, showing a mouth with no teeth.

Yon walks over. "Hello."

"Hello."

"Can you tell me . . . what is this place?"

"You not from here?"

Yon explains he's come from Canada and the man nods, looks him over, then offers his hand.

"You're smack in the belly of Bryant Park, the oldest, baddest homeless settlement in the city of New York."

Yon shakes his hand willingly.

"Reggie."

"Yon."

"What kind of name is that?"

"Short for Yolander."

Reggie asks him about his trip and introduces him to his son, Billy, still bouncing the soccer ball. Yon asks about the settlement—"been here as long as anyone knows"—and how they survive—"day to day, mouth to mouth, like anyone else."

"You got your ID?" asks Reggie. Yon looks puzzled. "You know, your papers."

Yon shakes his head no.

"Not good. Without them, they stop you, you're a marked man."

Yon pulls out the slip of paper with the address and shows it to Reggie. "I've got to get there," he says. "Can you help me?"

"Too late for that. You can walk it tomorrow. Better bed down with us."

They go around the corner to his shack. Reggie plops a mattress down on the floor of the cramped front room, hands Yon a hunk of cheese and some bread, and he and Billy go into the room behind.

Yon eats, undresses, and puts his amulet in his pants pocket. His head is heavy with fatigue but he's burning to ask a question before he falls off to sleep. He raises his voice to be heard through the open doorway. Tell me, he says, what is the Black Guard?

Reggie comes in. "Not something you want to yell out loud." He makes a *tut-tut* sound. "You really are from another planet. Let me tell you, the Black Guard is the worst of the worst. You don't want to tangle with them. They roam the streets, they've got serious weapons, and they get a kick out of beating on innocent people. They pick you up on the street, you're liable to never be seen again." He pauses. "I guess you heard the rumor, huh?"

"What rumor?"

"They come in here from time to time and bust our butts. Word is we're about due for a visit."

4

YON WAKES WHEN HE FEELS SOMEONE ROUSING HIM. IT TAKES him a moment to remember where he is. The night before comes back all at once. It's Reggie, shaking his shoulder, whispering something, sounding urgent.

"They're here. Quick, get up. You got no ID. You got to get out." He pushes his son forward. "Billy'll take you."

Yon throws on his clothes and follows the boy outside. The day's sallow light is just coming up and it's hard to see in the dimmed alleyways. All around people are beginning to stir.

Billy darts ahead like a bullet, taking corners quickly, ducking under overhangs and leaping over puddles. Yon runs as fast as he can but continually falls behind. From time to time the boy stops to wait for him, looking back with exasperation.

They come to the back end of the settlement, to a wall of thick planks eight feet tall. Before it are stacks of used tires. Billy goes to the stack in the middle and pulls the tires off one by one, tossing them behind him. Yon helps him.

When a path is cleared Billy bends down and smacks a board with the side of his fist. It moves. He sits and bangs it with both feet, dislodging it. He turns on his side and wriggles out headfirst.

His small hand motions Yon to follow. It's a tight squeeze and he rips his shirt and scrapes his ribcage but he manages to force his body through. Billy lets the board fall back in place. Yon looks up the street. Forty feet away, he sees figures in black uniforms massing in a line. To one side are four vans, disgorging more of them, their black helmets glinting in the arc light from a stanchion.

Billy runs and Yon follows him. They pass the two lions, enter a back alley, open the door of a building, and climb to the fourth floor. Through an empty ramshackle office they stop at a window. The boy points down below at the settlement's main entrance.

Yon sees the Black Guards closer now. There are more than a hundred of them on the street below, circling around like angry wasps. They're outfitted in bulging black uniforms and carry thick plastic shields, guns and nightsticks strapped to their sides. Their helmets have mirrored visors so their faces are invisible behind silvery masks.

But Billy can pick some out. He's looking around avidly.

"That one," he says abruptly, pointing to a man in the center strutting around and barking orders. His visor is pulled down and his helmet is the only white one.

"He's the worst. Name's Vexler . . . Vexler Tigor. He's the leader and he's famous."

"What's he famous for?"

"Evil. Pure evil. He hurts people just for the sake of it. Sometimes he comes in with a small gang and they'll pick one or two of us kids and chase us down."

Billy seems to be getting upset just talking about it. "You seen where we live. It's a maze. But he always catches us. He outsmarts us. He gets you and you disappear. Your body is apt to be found in the river."

He looks away, as if the sight of Vexler would turn him into stone. Yon stares down at the Black Guard below—they seem to be mustering for an attack.

"That Vexler," Billy says, "he's got some kind of scar on his face." He touches his left cheek. "They say you see that scar, it's the last thing you see in this world."

"What did you say?" asks Yon, his attention focusing on the movements of the troops below.

Before he can answer, the Black Guard come alive. The figure in the white helmet yells out a command; the men don gas masks and suddenly rush the entrance to the settlement. Sounds of wood smashing and guns firing rise up. A contingent outside lobs in tear gas canisters in long hissing arcs.

From their vantage point Yon and Billy see tents buckling and shacks collapsing and falling down and sending up clouds of dust. In the closest alleys they can even see the tops of nightsticks crashing down.

After a short while they turn away and retreat to the center of the empty office. They sit on the floor. Billy is silent for a while, then looks at Yon and asks, "What's that thing you wear around your neck?"

"It's a good luck charm."

Billy pauses a beat, then says, "Can I have it?"

Yon doesn't even consider the request. No, he says, but I can give you something else. He reaches into his other pocket and hands over a jackknife.

When he leaves many hours later, when the sounds outside are beginning to die down and some injured people are being carried out, Billy is still playing with the knife, throwing it spinning through the air into the back of a wooden chair and opening the blades one by one.

Yon puts his arm around him. "I'm sure your dad's okay. He knows his way around."

Billy just nods.

* * *

Yon walks down Fifth Avenue, counting down the blocks and guided by an occasional street sign. Thirty-Ninth Street . . . Thirtieth . . . Twenty-Second . . .

New York is less creepy in the daytime but still feels as if violence could erupt at any time—a monster could just fall out of the sky or rise up out of a manhole. So many strange-looking characters roam the streets. Some are in rags, talking to themselves loudly, waving their arms and cursing.

He passes two men sitting on the sidewalk and a woman lounging against a car. Their heads are nodding and their eyes are half-closed. Syringes and a rubber hose lie at their feet.

None of the traffic lights are working. Most of the stores are closed or boarded over but he comes to a stretch where they're open. They're dark inside, like caves, and when he peers in he sees beefy men and women peering back behind thick transparent barricades. The items for sale are mostly survival gear.

Below Twentieth Street water begins to intrude on the right side. The overflowing river is sending its dirty fingers over the street, covering everything in its path. The water is ankle deep nearby but down the block it looks to be eight feet, as tall as the no-parking signs. The farther he walks, the closer it comes.

When he reaches Twelfth Street he turns right and heads toward the flooding. He spies a number, 200, and the next, 202. He is approaching a narrow lake. Tiny ripples lap at the near edge. Ahead the murky water covers hydrants and stoops and even the first-floor windows. Farther ahead, between the shoulders of the distant buildings, he sees the open expanse of the river and, way on the other side of the river, a wall of bleak gray towers.

He comes to a brownstone and looks over the double doors encasing two dirty stained-glass windows. On the transom, the number is painted: 240. That's the one he wants.

The windows are dark. The water has reached the second step

of the stoop. He leaps up to the third step and tries the front door. It's locked. He steps across to a ledge, lifts a window, and enters.

"Hello!" he yells. "Anybody here?"

No answer. The hallway is bare.

The rooms on the ground floor are sparsely furnished, with mismatched chairs and a couch with a gaping hole shedding a wad of cotton padding. Everything is covered in dust. He mounts the stairs without touching the wide peeling banister. The beds are mussed, blankets and sheets are heaped in a corner, and more mattresses lie on the floor, but it's impossible to say when they were last slept on.

The other floors are similar. In one room there are piles of papers and a filing cabinet. He returns to the ground floor. In the kitchen he finds a bottle of water in the refrigerator and a food container with rice and a single spare rib.

He goes back to the top floor and sits at a desk to read the papers. They seem to be from a child's course at school, nothing interesting. He opens the filing cabinet; it's empty. He searches the closets, which contain only a few old clothes of varying sizes, mostly for adults.

As he closes the last closet door, he hears a noise downstairs. Sounds like boards creaking, someone walking.

He hurries down the three flights, sticking close to the wall. At the bottom of the ground floor he trips and goes flying, stumbling onto the floor. His amulet has broken its chain. He searches for it, finds it, and grabs it. He lifts his head just as a figure reaches the window ledge outside. It's a boy, who looks down at him in alarm.

Yon jumps up but his right knee gives way. He feels a stab of pain. He looks out the window. The boy is gone. He sees him running down the street—too far ahead to catch him.

He sits, rubs his knee until it feels somewhat better. And wonders: What should he do now? Is he safe here?

He traipses back to the kitchen—relieved that he can walk—and finishes off the rice and rib. He goes upstairs and lugs a mattress into a small alcove. He's too tired to think straight. He places his arms behind his head and his eyes close. He falls into a deep, dreamless slumber.

* * *

He awakens before the footsteps reach his floor. He slips into a closet and looks out through a crack. The boy is back and this time he is with a large man, dressed in a long leather trench coat.

The man is about fifty, with black hair speckled with gray swept back, steel-gray eyes, and a forehead riddled with creases. Crow's feet and hollow cheeks make him look a bit ravaged.

"Well he's sure as shit gone now," the man says.

"He surprised me," the boy says. "Just came out of nowhere."

"You should have done something, Bevin. Grabbed him."

The two look around, go from room to room. Yon silences his breathing, his heart thudding, and waits until the sound of their steps recedes and everything falls silent again.

He waits five minutes and goes outside. It's a gray morning. No one on the street. His stomach is rumbling. For twenty-four hours he's only eaten a rib and bits of rice. He walks back to Fifth Avenue and turns right.

There is a store advertising "gas" a block away. Outside are jerry cans smelling of gasoline and a picnic table at which two old men sit drinking. Nearby half a dozen motorcycles are parked. Yon peers through a dirty window at a bar. A sign promotes gen-modified beef burgers for $110. He counts his money—only $250 left—but he's hungry. He pushes open the door and steps inside.

Four pairs of eyes lock onto him. Hostile. The men lounge on chairs and the rim of a pool table. Smoke circles in a cloud over their heads. They're dressed in some kind of uniform, tight pants and shirts with high collars, gaudy orange. They swivel to face him as he approaches the bar. He orders a beef burger from a woman with green hair. Her black tights have thick runs so that slabs of white flesh show through.

"You in the right place?" she murmurs, one eyebrow cocked.

He shrugs. The bar is silent.

She goes to a stove, slaps a burger onto a bun and plate, and hands it to him. He pays her, leaving a $25 tip, then takes the plate to a table in a corner.

Behind him he hears the door open. Someone slips into the room, quiet as a shadow. Yon glances over. It's the man in the leather trench coat. The boy is not with him.

The man orders a large beer, takes it outside, and sits at a card table. Yon can see him through the window. The room remains quiet as Yon eats. From time to time a gang member turns to stare at him. One of them is swinging his leg. Another rolls a pool cue back and forth on the table.

Two of the gang exchange looks. One of them, a thin man with a scraggly tuft of a beard, stands slowly, moving one leg at a time. He rolls his shoulders and saunters over to Yon.

"Where you from?"

"Um . . . up north."

"Shit. The North. You boys up there, you been taking all our good stuff."

Yon remains silent. No one moves.

"You don't share. They don't teach you manners there?"

"Pardon?"

"Betty here, she served you nice. I didn't hear you say thank you. All you did is shrug."

Yon doesn't react. His pulse is racing.

"'Nother thing. You eatin' in front of us and you don't offer us fuck all. No manners." The man reaches over and lifts up the empty plate. "I'd say that's straight unfriendly. Wouldn't you?" He drops it on the floor. It shatters.

The leader looks around. His mates nod and chuckle.

Yon hears the door open. Should he make a run for it? He sizes up the situation: he'd have to get by the table where the gang is. Three of them stand up and walk over. The leader reaches down and pulls Yon up by his collar.

"We can teach you to share. We're good at that."

Yon balls a fist recklessly. He's about to try to break loose when a deep voice comes from the front of the room. It's the man in the trench coat.

"Let him go."

Everyone turns to look at him. Yon steps back and moves to one side and slips across to the front door. The man in the trench coat is holding something in his right hand—a beer glass. He tosses it onto the gang. It splashes on their orange uniforms. The smell of gasoline permeates the room.

The man holds up one hand, palm outward. With the other he brandishes a lighter, clicks it open and strikes a flame. The gang members freeze.

"Nothing hurts like fire, so I'm told," he says. "I believe it, though I can't say I've experienced it firsthand. Not like you're going to."

They stand there, dripping gasoline. The leader holds his hands out, palms down. His eyes are burning and he's trembling.

"So you boys just sit back down," the man says. "And you stay there. You come after us, you'll go up in flames."

He motions Yon outside, follows him, and slams the door shut. Looking back, they see the gang ripping their orange shirts off.

"Quick," says the man.

They duck down an alley, then cut into a back door through a railroad apartment, past empty rooms, emerging on the avenue, where the man resumes a normal pace.

"Why did you go there?" he asks.

"I was hungry."

"Picked a hell of a place for a burger."

"Why did *you* go there?"

"Looking for you."

They hear the roar of motorcycles approaching. The man hurries Yon to a parked Chevy and opens it. They slouch down as the bikes thunder past and disappear around the corner.

The man holds out his hand. "Quinlin," he says.

"Yon."

"Good to meet you, Yon."

Quinlin starts the car.

"Where are you taking me?" he asks.

"Somewhere safe."

"But where?"

"You'll see. All in good time."

"But . . . why did you go looking for me?"

"'Cause of that." Quinlin points to Yon's chest. He suddenly understands. It's the amulet.

5

QUINLIN AND YON DRIVE UP TENTH AVENUE. THERE ARE MORE people here but many of them look threatening. They pass another gang of young men.

"Who are all those guys?"

"Bangers," says Quinlin.

"And what . . . do they do?"

"Same thing they do everywhere. Hang out. Cause trouble. Mug people."

Yon looks out the window, quiet for a moment. Too many questions are bouncing around in his head.

"What is that place? Where you were looking for me."

"A safe house. We don't use it anymore. You're lucky we found you."

"When you say *we* . . . who are you?"

"All in good time."

Yon touches his amulet gently. "And what is it about this?" He raises it outside his collar.

"All in good time."

Quinlin looks back at the road and frowns in concentration. Yon is quiet a moment, then says, "What's happened to this city? Half of it's underwater."

"Been that way for decades."

"But what happened?"

"Don't tell me you don't know. The hurricanes, the seas rising."

"But I thought the Cocoon—you know—was supposed to save everything."

Quinlin shoots him a look. "Does it look saved?"

They come to Thirtieth Street. Quinlin parks the car in front of a clothing store. Its protective gate is smashed open, inside shelves are empty, a few shirts and shorts scattered on the floor.

The boy from the house on Twelfth Street is already there.

"Bevin," says Quinlin. "Take a look."

The boy nods and goes to the corner, looking in all directions. He signals: all clear. Quinlin leads Yon to a demolished lot, surrounded by a fence. He fusses with a lock on a gate, curses, finally opens it, and closes it after them. Through a patch of weeds and trash he goes to a small dark building with windows painted black. He knocks at a rear door. The sound of locks slipping open.

It's dim inside. The man who let them in turns and lies down on a mattress. Another man is sleeping on another mattress.

Quinlin leads the way down a narrow hall to a thick metal door. He gives it a heave and slides it open. He switches on a flashlight. Yon sees a huge black hole in the ground. A metal bucket is suspended over it. Cables and pulleys are attached: a makeshift elevator.

"Where are we?"

Quinlin's face relaxes into an almost smile. "Safest spot in the city." He steps into the bucket through a narrow half door and holds it open for Yon.

"This was built by sandhogs, long time ago. They used it to work on what was called the third water tunnel. They never did finish it. Which is lucky for us."

"*Us?* Who's us?"

"You know what I'm going to say."

"All in good time?"

"Fast learner."

He turns a lever that unlocks a cable winding through a winch above them. A brief plunge makes Yon's stomach jump. Quinlin presses a brake handle so the elevator continues its descent more slowly. Light from the surface slips away.

They go down lower and lower. Yon feels a coldness emanating from the black rock less than an arm's length away. He feels goose bumps in the engulfing half darkness.

"How far down we going?"

"Six hundred feet."

Four minutes later the bucket slows and comes to a jolting halt. Quinlin opens the door and they step out. He leans down to a box and comes up with two miners' helmets. "You'll need this," he says, switching the lamp on and handing the other over. He leaves the flashlight in a crevice and leads the way through a massive tunnel twenty feet high. Outcroppings of rock line the ceiling. Water runs down the walls and pools on the floor. Yon feels it seep into his shoes. They arrive at a raised path of planks. A musty smell permeates the air.

After a quarter of a mile, the tunnel widens into a cavern. It's lighted by overhead cables, so they turn off their lamps. They pass half a dozen people—some of them wave at Quinlin, others stare at Yon—and come to what looks like a construction shed. Quinlin raps on the door, tells Yon to wait, and enters. Several minutes later he emerges and motions to him to come in.

Inside is a woman sitting behind a desk. She looks to be any-where between thirty and forty. She has high cheekbones, accen-tuated because her long hair is pulled back in a bun. Against the walls are a ragged couch, a file cabinet and three folding chairs. Papers and books are piled everywhere.

The woman smiles and stands—she's a good six inches taller than him—and offers her hand.

"I'm Sessler."

Yon shakes her hand. He starts to speak but she interrupts him.

"Quin tells me he found you wandering around downtown. Not a place you should be, you know, if you're not from around here— or for that matter, even if you are." She gestures to a wooden chair. He sits down. "He tells me you have something interesting." She points to his chest.

Yon nods. He hesitates only a moment, then reaches inside his shirt and lifts the amulet into full view. She stands and leans over to inspect it.

"May I?" She lifts the stone delicately, balancing it on her fingertips, appraising it like a jeweler. "Genuine. And good quality." She sits back down.

"Why is it so precious?" he asks.

"Because of its beauty. And because of its special quality—its color." She looks into his eyes. "I imagine you're too young to perceive it. Most young people are. It's called lapis lazuli."

"That boy Bevin, back in that building, he saw something special in it."

"Yes. That's because he's not from here. He comes from the South. We have a number of so-called refugees here." Her voice assumes a commanding tone. "Now tell me—where did you get it?"

"I inherited it. My grandmother. She told me to be careful with it and not show it to people, but I have no idea what she was talking about."

"She's right. And who are your parents?"

"My mother, I never knew. My father disappeared when I was young. So I can't say exactly."

"How old are you?"

"Sixteen."

"What's your name?"

"Yon."

Sessler's mouth drops open. She freezes.

"Your family name?"

39

"Zeger."

She stares at him for a long while. She seems to be struggling to maintain her composure. Then she leans back in her chair and faces the ceiling. She remains quiet for a moment, then abruptly sits upright. She opens a drawer, takes out a stone, and places it carefully on the desk. He sees it's grayish white, like his.

"You have one, too," he says.

"Yes."

She peppers him with questions. Each question spawns more questions: Where did he grow up? What did he know about the Color Guard? How did he get here? And why did he come, precisely? What happened to the people who raised him?

"They're both dead."

"Are you sure?"

"I buried them."

He answers the questions as best he can. Something about her makes him want to confide. He tells about his upbringing in Canada, the cabin in the woods, the people he thought were his grandparents. His shock when he learned they weren't. It's the first time he has told anyone his story. When he talks of the attack on his cabin and finding his gramma dead, his throat tightens. It's difficult to talk. He quickly passes over it and tells about his trip to New York. He talks for twenty minutes. She seems to hang on every word. Unanswered questions are in the air.

When he finishes, she rubs her chin and says, "Can you prove you are who you say you are?"

His mouth drops open. He leans forward, looks around helplessly, and shrugs. "I don't know."

"How did you know to go to the house on West Twelfth Street?"

He pulls out the slip of paper with the address and shows it to her and explains it was in the pouch with the rock.

She is startled, then softens. "I'm sorry. But we have to be careful. We have enemies and they try to infiltrate our ranks."

"Enemies?"

"The Power."

Yon knows that word from his grandparents.

"I've heard of them. They control everything. They run the country."

"Not just this country. The whole world—at least in the North."

She keeps staring at him intently.

"You were raised off the grid?"

He nods.

"Home schooled, I suppose."

He nods again.

"How much do you know about politics and things? How the Power operates. How it crushes dissent?"

"I just know they're bad. That's what my grandparents . . . these people . . . kept saying. I believe them."

"Do you know how the world got into this mess?"

"Not much, I guess. I know there were storms and droughts and when things got even worse, these people running things, they came up with the Cocoon—"

"Exactly, the Cocoon."

She falls silent, deep in thought. Already she is hatching a plan for him. Finally she rouses herself and thumps the desk.

"We need you," she says.

"But tell me," he says. "Who are all of you? What are you doing?"

She smiles—for the first time, a truly warm smile. "Simple. We are the Resistance."

She leads him out of her office and tells Quinlin to take him to the kitchen for something to eat.

Yon isn't really hungry but he goes along anyway. He's dazed. Everything is so strange. Fighting the Power? How is that even possible? He decides the best course is to trust them. There's really no alternative.

6

YON STAYS WITH THE RESISTANCE UNDERGROUND FOR NEARLY two weeks.

He sleeps in a side room off the main tunnel that has twelve beds, seven of them occupied, mostly by young people.

On the afternoon of the third day Quinlin comes for Yon.

They head north through the tunnel. Quinlin says it extends through a bedrock of granite, which has preserved the tunnel from flooding. They follow a decline leading to a lower level where rooms were blasted out of the rock by the sandhogs. Yon looks in. Some are furnished with desks and chairs and even bookshelves. One room, off by itself, lies behind a wooden door.

"Go inside," Quinlin commands. "Lie down. Relax. Think of nothing. Let yourself go. I'll be back in two hours."

Yon does as he's told. He lies down. The bed is unusually comfortable. Soft music. Not a sound from beyond the door. Nothing to do but let his mind wander. He thinks of all that has happened in the past few days.

But the ceiling is impossible to ignore. He has the sensation that he is not looking at it so much as looking inside it. It's white, but more than white—luminous. When he stares at it, it seems to pulsate.

He looks away but he's drawn back to it. He stares. It seems to surround him, encircle him. He sits up and stares at the floor. The sensation ceases. But the moment he lies back and looks at the ceiling, it resumes, stronger than ever.

He tries to sleep but suddenly bolts up, his eyes open. The room is peculiar. He gets up and checks the walls, actually touching them. Nothing has moved. It's an illusion, some trick of the mind. He lies back down and begins counting by sevens backward from 1,000. That used to make him sleepy but not this time. His heart races, his mind jumps around. How long before Quinlin comes for him? There's still a lot of time left. He falls into a kind of daze. Eyes open, lying there. He feels pleasant, a warm feeling deep inside. Time slips by.

A knock at the door. He shakes himself awake. He slings his feet to the floor, steadies himself, and walks over, opening the door to find Quinlin looking at him—curiously.

"You alright?"

Yon nods slowly, uncertainly. Outside the room he feels better, things falling into place.

"What was that?"

"Meditation. It's good for you. Stretches the mind."

"But the ceiling—it's strange. It does strange things."

"You recognize it?" Quinlin pulls Yon's amulet out of his shirt collar. "The same."

On the walk back they say little, but this time the silence doesn't bother Yon. He can't help but notice that for some reason he's feeling unattached to everything—almost serene.

He is allowed to spend as much time in the meditation room as he wants and soon he goes there every day. He begins to crave the experience. It reminds him of when he was young, way up North, and spent hours sprawled upon the rock, daydreaming.

* * *

One day Sessler summons him to her office. As he enters, he notices an open door. Beyond it is some kind of small laboratory—a table with bottles and test tubes and beakers.

He's about to remark on it but Sessler speaks first. She says they discussed him at a "plenary meeting" of the leaders. They've decided to send him on an important mission—in fact, it is absolutely vital to their survival. He'll be going to the South to bring back something essential.

"What?"

"It's best you not know until you get there. For your own safety."

"Where will I go?"

"You'll go with Quinlin. He will get you there."

"But . . . why me?"

"You're not known to the authorities. They have no record of you."

She looks at him for a long moment. When she speaks she has a different tone. Not so distant. She appears to be struggling to maintain her composure. Her gaze drills into him.

"Listen, Yon. Listen closely. You come from a family that's very important. It's important and divided . . . two sides, good and bad." She pauses. "Do you have any idea who your grandfather was— your *real* grandfather?"

"No. Not at all."

"He was a great man. A scientist. He was among the first to raise the alarm over our failing planet. That's why he was killed."

"*Killed?* Who killed him?"

"That's a long, long story, and there's no clear answer. Let's just say that he died trying to raise the alarm about global warming."

"How did he die?"

"He was doing research in the Arctic and his project was sabotaged."

"Was his name Zeger?"

She shakes her head and continues. "No. These people who

raised you, they were telling the truth. They were good people. *Their* names were Zeger, Suzanne and Kurt Zeger. They took you away and saved you when you were an infant—"

"Saved me?"

"From the Black Guard."

"But how do you know all—"

She cuts him off. "Wait. Listen. That's enough for now. You have to concentrate on the mission ahead."

"And what did you mean when you said my family was half bad?"

She looks deeply into his eyes. "Let's just say you are a child of destiny."

He is lost in a fog of confusion. "What does that mean?"

She looks down and fiddles with a pencil. "I'm sorry. I can't explain everything."

His mind leaps around. "The people who killed my gramma . . . Were they after me?"

She pauses. "Good question. I think not. I hope not. You said you blundered into a prohibited agricultural zone. Maybe that was it."

He remains silent, feeling the weight of guilt.

She looks into his eyes again. "You better go."

"But where am I going?"

"To a country in the South. We've got allies there. They're going to give you something we desperately need."

He protests. "But I don't know what to do. I don't know if I can do whatever it is you want."

"You will. I know you will."

She turns toward the wall for a moment. When she turns back he sees her eyes are filled with tears.

"Be careful," she says softly. " Quin will look after you. He knows what to do."

She rises and hugs him tightly before he leaves.

Quinlin has been waiting for him outside the shed.

"Come with me while I pack," he says happily. He slaps Yon on the back. "Where we're going we'll need different clothing."

"Why?"

"There'll be downpours and storms and all kinds of things. Maybe even seasons."

"What are seasons?"

Quinlin laughs. "You have no idea."

* * *

Minutes later, a tall, lithe Black woman knocks gently on Sessler's door, bringing two cups of tea. It is Gabriella—Gabe—Sessler's top lieutenant, best friend, and lover.

She stares at Sessler, who sits pale and frozen in place.

"You okay?"

Sessler nods.

"Did you tell him?" Gabe asks, placing one cup on the desk and sitting down with the other.

"No. I figure he's got enough to deal with."

"Meanwhile, we've got a problem." Gabe blows on her tea with forced nonchalance.

Sessler surfaces. "What?"

"A runner's gone missing. No one's seen him for eight days."

"Who?"

"Bevin. He covers lower Manhattan. Runs messages to the Midtown contact. Keeps an eye on Twelfth Street from time to time."

"I know who he is. Yon mentioned him. He met him the day he came down to the tunnel—and Quinlin did, too. You think he's been picked up?"

"It's possible. Word on the street is that Vexler Tigor is running sweeps."

"Tigor . . . he's—"

"Top cop. Black Guard. A real bastard."

"Has Bevin been down here? Does he know our location?"

"Not clear."

Sessler runs through the possibilities. "We have to find out. See if anyone knows. In the meantime, make sure the warning sentries are up there twenty-four hours a day."

"Okay." Gabe finishes her tea and lets the empty cup dangle from her finger. "Something strange about Tigor. They say he has a scar on his left cheek. A perfect X."

"What's so strange about that?"

"They say he did it to himself."

PART II
BEGINNINGS
2025
(LESLEY)

7

Lesley Kyserike ignored the .375 H&H Magnums in the rifle rack of the outer entryway. They were there for quick access in case a polar bear, desperate for food, came prowling around. She couldn't imagine killing a polar bear—unless it was practically on top of you, about to rip you to pieces.

She was nervous but excited, too. For the second time, she examined the arctic suit and white outerwear, looking for rips. Once more she went through the knapsack, checking the instruments they would need to probe the secrets of Greenland's mammoth Petermann Glacier.

She'd carry the instruments for Henry Messian until they reached the site on the ice sheet. Then she'd watch from the shore as he maneuvered himself out on the "high wire" above the rushing melt water to take the readings—its speed, temperature, and depth—as it made its dash to the sea.

Yesterday he had told her he had done it twice several years back, and both times he hated it. Glaciers that grow normally, with snow falling and freezing over eons, were as stable as ponies, he had said. But glaciers in the throes of melting were wild broncos.

"It's not just the risk," he continued, sitting next to her on the

51

LC-130, strapped to the skin of the plane as it crossed into the Arctic Circle. "It's the landscape. It's enough to break you. A goddamned moonscape . . . crumpled hillocks and hollows. White as far as you can see. Nothing else. Just whiteness. It makes you feel your insignificance. Makes you *live* your insignificance."

He undid his seat belt and stood to look down through the small window and cursed. The glacier had visibly diminished from last time. He said it must have calved half a dozen times and retreated twenty miles. When they flew low, she stood on the other side and saw melt water everywhere, bright cerulean rivers cutting through the pristine white crust like gash wounds.

"A fucking disaster," he murmured.

They set down on a small landing strip near a cluster of structures covered in ice and snow. It was a radar and satellite station, whose mission was to track Russian shipping through the Northern Passage, looking ahead to the day when the unfrozen Arctic water routes would be crisscrossed by rival vessels. A Washington budget item allowed the ecologists to use the station.

The worse Messian had made the expedition sound, the more she looked forward to it. She was like that—adventurous almost to the point of foolhardy, drawn to the edge, restless at the age of twenty-four.

Her accent was confusing—East Coast with an overlay of British—and so he had asked her where she was from. She gave a capsule summary: an only child in Vermont; a troubled home, but she didn't elaborate; dance as a ticket out, a scholarship to Julliard in New York City; and then a stint in England to answer the siren call of Science.

Now she was a researcher and strategist for a nonprofit, STE, Save the Earth, located with the lobbyists on K Street in Washington.

* * *

She headed for the station's kitchen galley but stopped off at the women's room, crossing to the sink to wash her hands. The face that greeted her did not satisfy her—it never did; she thought it too angular with a nose too large—but now her features looked drawn. There were shadows under her hazel eyes. She had her auburn hair, normally down to her shoulders, in a ponytail.

She went to the kitchen, where she saw Messian sitting alone. She poured two cups of coffee, joined him, and slid one across the wooden table.

Messian shook his head. "Thanks but no."

"Go ahead. Last one of the morning."

"It'll make me piss. And I'll be in the outfit."

She asked if he had slept okay. He said no, not at all. He felt claustrophobic in his narrow room in the radar station.

She agreed. "I kept imagining that I could feel the whole glacier moving. It was like being in a berth on a giant freighter."

"Except it's a massive chunk of ice 10,000 feet thick and 1,000 miles from land."

She gave a half smile and looked across at him. Lesley didn't have many idols in this world, but he was one of them. Harry Messian had practically invented the field of paleoclimatology. He was one of the first to document climate change, the Earth's inexorable march toward hellfire.

He was much admired by his fellow scientists, but not liked. He yelled at his assistants, rarely said *thank you,* and expected everyone to wait on him. Behind his back they called him "Saint Harry," a curmudgeon with a penchant for bombast that came from the conviction he was always right.

Trouble was, he *was* always right. For fifty years he'd been the voice in the wilderness, crying out about the perils of the ever-expanding carbon footprint. He built ever more accurate and frightening computer models projecting the irreversible effects of climate change brought about by our idiotic, befouling species.

A raging Jeremiah, way back in the late 1970s. He'd courted controversy, and controversy accepted him with open arms. The "establishment"—that conglomeration of oil, mining, and electrical interests, assorted lobbyists, and right-wing think tanks and their paid scientific goons—turned on him.

Fifteen years ago he had lost his job with the EPA. He scrambled for years until he found a perch at Georgetown University. And now, according to the scientific grapevine, a move was afoot to remove him from that. He'd lately had trouble getting papers published. Lesser colleagues poked holes in his research.

All this coming down on his head, just when, rumors had it, he'd finally got his personal life in order. After two divorces and a debt load of alimony, he had met and married a young woman, Maria. They were happily ensconced in a town house in Washington, DC, with a two-year-old son, Paul, whose bright eyes—in a photo he had shown Lesley two nights ago—peered at the strange big world over the rim of his stroller.

"Sure you don't want the coffee?" she asked.

He shook his head.

Kyserike examined Messian as he pulled out a checklist and ran through the protocol. He'd keep his all-weather notepads in his outer pockets. The basic measurements would come first, the depth speed of the melt water and the width of the river. Then the temperature and the samples.

He rubbed his stubble and confessed he couldn't shake a bad feeling—not a premonition exactly, something more vague. A nagging.

"It's like that mental mosquito when you board a plane: maybe this is the one that will go down . . . maybe the fact that I'm *thinking* it could go down is a sign that it actually *will* go down."

"Sometimes your mind is your own worst enemy," she said.

He checked his watch. It was time.

They walked to the entry chamber and donned their arctic

wear, adding the layers slowly and methodically: the thermal underwear, the middle layer of lightweight down, the neck gaiter, and the skull-hugging fleece hat. Then the waterproof outer shell with hood and goggles. For the feet, they pulled on mukluks. For the hands, two pairs of gloves.

Messian opened the thick front door and stepped out. Kyserike followed. For a moment she carried the warmth with her, like an inner glow. But a dozen crunching steps on the frozen snow with frigid air pressing in and the glow began to dissipate. Soon she would feel the cold like tiny bites at her elbows and knees.

Up ahead was the helicopter, its blades already whooshing and raising a whirlwind of snow.

She heard Messian muttering as the arctic wind raged around them. "What am I doing here? What's an aging father of a toddler and a loving young wife doing in a godforsaken place like this?"

* * *

Two nights ago it had been Lesley who suggested they "go for a pint" in Reykjavík. She had picked up that particular British colloquialism during her time at Cambridge. Like the Brits, she drank a lot during her university years.

She had even picked out the bar, a small place on a grungy back street called, appropriately enough, Hole in the Wall. Good blues, played loud. They took a table in a corner nook. The room wasn't crowded but the waitress took her time coming over. She cocked her left hip, sultry, and took their order. For Messian, a straight vodka. For Lesley, Jack Daniel's.

Lesley looked around, in her element, and when the drinks arrived gave that slight smile.

"Let me ask you something," she began. "You're the bête noir of the oil companies. They hate you so much they barely utter your name. But you used to work for Exxon, didn't you?"

55

"Yup. It was called Humble Oil back then."

"So what happened?"

Messian finished off his vodka and ordered another. She resisted. He didn't answer right away, so she repeated the question and waited expectantly until he spoke.

"This was a long time ago, back in the '70s. I was young—'bout your age. I studied geology and climatology. I became an intern at Exxon. They offered me a staff job. Thought I'd make some money—and I did for a while, good money. Then I was hit on the head." He paused.

"By what?"

"An epiphany. Pumping all that carbon dioxide into the atmosphere is dooming our planet. Our planet and everything on it—including us. It's so simple, so fundamental, it can't be denied. And yet it is denied."

"So your employer didn't like that."

"Wrong . . . at least, initially. It sounds strange but back then, Exxon was a different outfit. It was at the forefront of climate research. It had top scientists . . . allowed us to do real science. We rang the alarm bell. We drew up climate change models that scared the shit out of everyone. Disaster ahead! The *greenhouse effect*, we called it. We were on committees, spread the word, even published three important peer-reviewed articles."

"I read them."

"So you know about the supertanker they gave us. It was fitted out with custom-made instruments to take samples of CO_2 in the air and water. The *Esso Atlantic*. We went from the Gulf of Mexico to the Persian Gulf. Best time of my life. Lolling about on the open sea, doing research on the cutting edge. The samples showed we were right to panic.

"As you might expect, somebody high up realized we were giving away the store. Not too smart—the largest oil company in the world proving that its own product was consigning us all to perdition. We thought we'd take the company in a new direction, get a jump on the fossil fuel problem, maybe go into alternate sources, sustainable energy."

He shook his head. "How goddamn naïve we were." He looked off toward the bar. Three young women were dancing to an Otis Redding song.

"They dropped that idea like it was radioactive. A complete about-face. This was in the '90s. Exxon began sabotaging its own research. They insisted the dire climate models were out of whack. They funded the global warming deniers. Some of their scientists did a 180 without a backward look."

He took another gulp of vodka. He talked as if his tongue had turned thick. "The barking dog turned into the chicken thief. Nobody came out covered in glory."

"What about you?"

"What about me?"

"Well, you left, didn't you?"

"Yeah. But I was no hero. They made my life miserable, so I quit."

He got up, went to the bar, and came back with two more drinks. The waitress leaned over to the bartender and pointed to a sign: NO SELF-SERVICE AT TABLES. He ignored her.

"I don't want to talk about Exxon anymore," Messian said.

Lesley cleared her throat. "Let me ask you something."

"Stop saying that, for Christ sake, just ask it."

"Okay." She paused a beat and the ends of her lips turned up. "Why are you so hard on people?"

Messian seemed taken aback. He stared at her, first in shock, then in anger, then as if seriously considering the question. He looked off again, then back.

"Simple reason. They don't like me. I tell the truth. We're fucked. They all know it but they don't want to admit it, so they come after me because I won't shut up about it.

"The Paris Agreement fell apart years ago. Nobody abides by the pledges, not India, not China, not the US. Especially not the US.

"Temperatures are rising. Our oceans are dying. Acidification. Coral bleaching. Fish disappearing. Forests burning. Species going extinct. We're getting killer storms. Droughts that haven't been seen for millennia. Low-lying islands washed away."

Messian got up, started walking nervously around the bar floor. She realized he was drunk. He was muttering to himself, like a crazed prophet. He stalked over to a blackboard fixed to a pillar wrapped in rope. It had the day's specials chalked on it. With one sleeve, he wiped it clean and picked up a piece of chalk. He steadied himself. His hand drew close to the blackboard, then he quickly scribbled a number.

2050.

The chalk hit the edge of the board and broke. A piece skipped across the floor. People stared. He shouted.

"That's it. A quarter of a century from now. The big year. The tipping point."

He twisted his face and lapsed into a Porky Pig *Looney Tunes* imitation. "Bluh-bluh-bluh . . . That's all, folks!"

He waved his left hand in the air, a cartoonish salute.

The bar fell mostly silent. In a corner, two people giggled.

The waitress walked over and pushed the bar bill into his shirt pocket. She put her arm in the square of his back and pushed him, none too gently, toward a burly cashier.

"And that's *all* for *you*, bub."

Lesley helped him out of the bar and walked him, arm in arm, back to their hotel. At one point he stopped and stared at her, rocking a bit but suddenly appearing sober.

"You don't know what you're getting into, do you?" His voice was clear, his words coming out in clouds of steam. "This so-called radar station in the godforsaken Arctic. Keeping an eye on the Ruskies. You believe that crap?"

* * *

In their arctic wear, Messian and Kyserike waddled clumsily to the helicopter. The pilot wore dark aviator glasses and a headset. He had a thermos in a holder fixed to the instrument panel. He grunted hello as she climbed into the chopper, his eyes lingering on her.

She crammed into the back with the packs. Messian occupied the front passenger seat and pulled the door closed. The chopper lifted so quickly her stomach lurched. Then the pilot slapped the joystick and it swerved and caught the wind and flew off like an angry hornet.

Messian was hunched over. She touched his shoulder and he half turned, his ear tilted toward her.

She shouted over the screaming engine. "You know, you don't have to do this." He didn't answer. No reaction. "I can take this one," she yelled.

Messian shook his head no.

"I mean it. I'm happy to. I've got to learn anyway, sooner or later."

Messian shook his head again, violently this time.

"Why not?" she persisted.

He didn't answer. She yelled even more loudly. "Think about it—I can do it. I want to."

He shook his head a third time.

She turned away and looked out the frosted window at the everlasting whiteness. The blades churned up the snow beneath them. It rose wildly and pursued them, like a white tornado. They rode the fifteen minutes to the site in silence.

The landing was rough. The wind rocked the copter and it landed hard, jolting them. The pilot thrust open a side window. Flurries flew in.

"You better work fast," the pilot yelled. "Fucking storm's

coming." They nodded. "I mean it. I can't wait around. Thirty minutes tops, got it?"

"We work until we're finished," insisted Messian.

"Don't worry," she said. "We'll hurry. We don't like this any more than you."

They lumbered out, steadying themselves and unloading the backpacks. The pilot didn't help, just sat in his seat sipping coffee from his thermos.

They lugged the equipment thirty yards along what they thought was once a path. It led to the bank of a roaring river, the ice melt. Twenty yards downstream it plunged through an icy sinkhole in the middle of nowhere. It dropped through the glacier thousands of feet below.

"The moulin," shouted Messian through the wind.

Lesley stared at it. The water rushed down a slope and then began swirling rapidly until finally it dropped down into darkness. Looking at it was almost hypnotic—it was like the slurring, insatiable mouth of some primeval beast.

He squeezed her arm for emphasis. "The asshole of the Arctic. Fall down there and you won't last a minute. There's one consolation, though."

"What?"

"You'll never rot. You'll freeze solid. In 50,000 years, when a different kind of creature walks this world, they'll find you and wonder what the hell you were."

He opened his pack and pulled out the instruments. He donned the "straight jacket," a vest festooned with clips, and attached the instruments one by one. He straightened up and walked in a circle, weighted down. He turned toward the river, looked back at her, and shook his head.

"I can tell just by looking at the melt water, the damn thing's bigger. It's wider and it's moving like a son of a bitch. Lot faster."

He walked off toward the river, tottering from side to side like a laden astronaut. She followed. They reached the staging area, a wooden ladder leading up to a fifteen-foot-tall metal tower. Its base, a tripod, was sunk deep into the ice. Two cables swung out across the river, a thick one to walk on and a narrow one higher up to cling to for balance. Both were attached to a similar tower on the other side. The distance across was about forty feet.

She contemplated the rushing river. How much longer until it spread so wide it would reach the base of the towers? They'd need a work crew to reassemble them farther apart.

Messian climbed the ladder to the top. He attached a clip on his vest to the upper cable, looked down, and waved at Lesley. Then he pushed off, sliding down the cable like a zip line, the instruments dangling wildly, until he came to a halt, hanging six feet or so above the raging torrent. He stood on the support cable and pulled himself forward until he reached the stop point halfway across. It was marked by a yellow band. To return—that would be the agonizing part: he would have to pull himself along the upper cable by his arms, keeping most of his weight on the support cable.

He unclipped an instrument from his jacket—from where she stood, it looked like the flow meter. She wiped her goggles with the back of her glove to get a better view.

Then she gasped. Something was wrong.

The tower opposite was bending with his weight. He didn't see it. It bent more and more, like a tree in a hurricane. Suddenly it sprang. The cable had snapped. The wire end was whipping wildly. She looked at Messian. He slid forward smoothly, almost gracefully, into the water, as if he were going down a chute. The cable thrashed into the current, unspooling slowly, a metal snake. He made not a sound. She yelled into the wind, a brief sharp cry. He slid quickly along the cable moving toward the open end. He left it, now free of it, bobbing in the current. The water carried him along swiftly. He looked small—a twig in a brook. He held both arms straight up, as if he were balancing. He struggled. The current

61

swept him onward, farther and farther, toward the horrible dark hole. He spiraled around the opening, then was sucked down into the mouth of the moulin.

That was it. He was gone. One moment he was there, the next not. It took less than a minute for him to disappear. Nothing left. Just the howling wind and the swiftly moving water.

She was riveted in place by the horror of it. She tried to think, to figure out what to do.

She turned and ran to the chopper. The pilot had the door open and was standing on the landing skid, his head barely beneath the whirring blade. She could read the shock in his posture. His dark glasses were off, his mouth open.

"Christ Almighty," he yelled when she reached him. "What happened?"

"I don't know. The cable broke. He's gone."

The pilot climbed into his seat.

"Get in. There's nothing we can do. We've got to leave. Storm's coming up."

His voice was shaky, uncertain.

"Not a chance." She sat down and closed the door. "Fly over there. To the other side."

"Why?"

"That's where the thing broke."

"We don't have time."

"You do it. Or I'll report you. To Washington."

He looked over at her, sitting next to him rigid and implacable. He grabbed the joystick and pulled it back. The chopper lifted. Crossing the river took two minutes. When they landed, she hurried to the tower. The short end of the cable was buried in the snow. She pulled it up and examined the metal tip.

She could see where the break occurred, a narrow frayed bit. It gave way to a smooth cut more than three-quarters of the way across.

She understood instantly. This was no accident.

She tugged at the cable. It was unmovable.

The pilot ran over and grabbed her.

"We gotta get out of here."

"One minute."

She unzipped the white jacket, reached inside and pulled out a small camera. "Hold this." She handed him the cable. She snapped a photo of it, another and another and another.

They trudged to the chopper, already hard to see in the blizzard, and took off.

8

THE CHOPPER BUCKED AND KICKED AS IT PULLED AWAY BUT
Lesley barely noticed. Her mind was turning somersaults.

Messian was *murdered*. Who could have done it and why? Had
the killer targeted him directly or booby-trapped the apparatus to
get rid of the next person using it? Who knew the protocol for the
field study? Who had access to a plane? Had they crossed overland
on snowmobiles?

Once they landed at the base, the pilot sank back in his seat.
He looked sick. Lesley told him to switch to a prop plane and fly
her right away to Thule so she could catch a plane to the capital.

"Not on your life. Not in this fucking storm."

She opened the door and walked briskly to the radar station,
not even pulling up her hood. Inside she took off her outer gear,
went into the office, and sat at the desk. She pulled out her cell
phone and examined the photos of the cable. The cut halfway
through was clearly visible.

She put both palms on the desk, tried to calm herself, to ignore
the thudding inside her head. She reached for the desk phone.

It took five minutes to place the call to Felix Besermann at the
Energy Department in Washington and another three minutes for

64

him to come on the line. Besermann ran the Arctic study from a distant desk. She thought of him as a careerist, someone on the right side of the issues but vain and ambitious. Still, he was smart and connected and she needed someone outside to talk to.

His "hello" had a calming effect.

She drained her voice of alarm and told him Messian had died at the site without going into details. She could practically feel his shock over the line.

"They'll say it was an accident," she said.

"Jesus Christ! What do you mean, *they'll say*? What kind of accident?"

"That's hard to say—right now."

He paused. "An accident bound to happen?"

"Yes. Something like that."

"I see."

"Is this line secure?" she asked.

"Not really. Place is a snake pit of conspiracies and climate deniers."

He was quiet for a full five seconds. She imagined he was trying to figure out what this might mean for the program, for himself. When he spoke next, he was in executive mode.

"Come to Washington. Gather as much material as you can and get out as soon as you can. Don't talk about this to anyone. We'll get the department to release a statement. It'll just say he died in an accident, it's being looked into, nothing more."

"How about the police? The authorities here. Shouldn't I notify them? See if they want to investigate?"

Again, a pause while he thought. "Notify them. But don't tell them too many details. And don't tell them everything you may be thinking."

They talked a few more minutes. He asked her how she was holding up. She said okay.

"I'll have to tell his wife," he continued. "They have a

two-year-old, you know. A son. He was starting a whole new life, getting it right this time. And then this happens. Christ."

"I know. He talked about her. He was head over heels."

"Maria will want to know that. She'll want to know everything. Do you think . . . could you meet with her? That might help her."

"Certainly."

"Good. I'm glad—don't take this wrong—but I'm glad in a way you're there. I can't think of anyone better. You'll know what to do."

Before hanging up, he said, "Um, and one more thing: be careful, will you? Don't take any chances."

"Don't worry."

"And don't tell anyone we've talked."

"I won't."

"Is there anyone in the room with you? Anyone listening?"

"No."

"Keep it that way. And don't mention my name."

When she put the receiver down the reality—or *unreality*—of what had happened struck home, not quick and hard like a slap but slow and all engulfing, like the ice water that rose around Messian.

She entered the communications center where the radar operators and auxiliary crew members were. She knew by looking at them, by their awkwardness, that they already knew about Messian. Only a few of them asked questions, not very probing ones. She figured they knew how dangerous the site work was and weren't surprised that an accident had occurred.

"What happens now?" asked one of the operators. "They going to shut down your project?"

"I don't know. That's a decision for Washington. But whatever happens, I would think they're going to keep this station operative. It's too important."

She hadn't seen the pilot since they returned. She asked about him and was told he was in bed resting up from the ordeal.

* * *

Lesley spent the next four hours going through the logs and files in an attempt to discover who had been to the station. The records were shockingly incomplete. Some planes were logged in without a manifest of the passengers. Others were missing call numbers or exact times or had been marked down as arriving but not departing.

A dispatcher told her that meticulous records were kept only for the equipment because it was so expensive.

She tried sleeping, without success. As she tossed in her bunk, she couldn't fight down the images—the cable snapping, the stanchion beginning to buckle, Messian smoothly slipping into the water, then rushing downstream and disappearing into the swirling hole, into darkness.

She took a sleeping pill, which worked for three hours. When she awoke it was dark outside but the storm had abated. She went to the galley and made a strong cup of coffee. She came to a decision. She had to go back to the site. A photograph was not evidence enough. She needed the cable.

A bearded man, the comptroller, walked in rubbing his eyes. He grunted hello and reflexively filled a coffee mug and slumped into a chair. She asked him about the pilot—had he seen him?

"I saw him earlier. He just fell into bed. Man, was he zonked. It's more than upset. I think he's ill."

She vowed to wake the pilot in the morning. She called Besermann and left a voice message explaining her plan to return to the moulin. When he called back, she'd already be gone. Good. That way he couldn't dissuade her.

* * *

At 6:00 a.m. she barged into the pilot's sleeping quarters and got him out of bed. She had to pull the covers off. She was surprised to see he was still in his clothes.

At first he refused to fly back to the site. He raised all kinds of objections, including the inclement weather—and in fact, as the meteorologist had informed her, the storm was coming alive again. But then, rubbing his chin and shaking his head slowly as if to rid it of cobwebs, he finally relented.

"One condition," he said. "We stay half an hour and that's it."

"An hour."

"Forty-five minutes."

"Okay."

She met him in the antechamber, where they donned their outerwear. This time he wore a thick purple parka. She was lugging a long-handled heavy-duty cable cutter that she had retrieved from the tool room.

"I'm not even gonna ask what that's for," he said.

"Good."

No one saw them leave. Outside the wind was biting. She saw small white funnels of snow. The sky was gray, a heavy blanket of roiling clouds ready to drop its payload.

They flew to the site quickly. From above, as they circled, she got a bird's-eye view. The metal stanchion still standing on the near side, the balance cable extending across the rushing stream, the other cable missing and the other stanchion partially collapsed.

She shouted over the engine and motioned to the far side. "That's where I want to land."

"I figured." He wasn't smiling.

They set down no more than ten yards from the broken equipment.

"I'll keep this running," he said. "Look over there." He pointed west. She did. She saw a gray curtain raining down from the sky to the ice sheet. "If it gets close I'm outta here—whether you're back or not. You hear me?"

She nodded and left. Her feet sank six inches in the snow, which made for hard going. She was perspiring after only a dozen or so steps. The equipment was much as she had left it, at least as far as she could tell. The base of the stanchion was set solidly in the ice. A metal beam was hanging to one side and another one, about four feet long, was on the ground nearby. The top of the tower was bent halfway over and listed toward the river, pulled down by the cable that had failed.

She trudged closer with the cable cutter. Her footsteps from the earlier visit were obliterated. Nothing but steel and snow all around. But the cable? Where was the cable? She was sure she had dropped the end close to the stanchion. It wasn't there.

She walked to the base and turned, holding her arms straight ahead. She walked along the right-side vector to a distance of twelve feet, then returned and did the same on the left. She moved five feet from the base and connected the two paths. Halfway across she felt something under her left foot. She stopped, reached down and scooped out armfuls of snow. There it was, buried.

She held tight and pulled. It was resistant. She pulled harder and as she did so, she raised her head and looked dead ahead. She saw the storm cloud moving closer. She pulled some more, with all her strength, and the cable loosened and rose up from the snow. She held the end and stared. Her breath caught.

Something was wrong! The half cut was gone. Instead, there was a complete cut. Someone had sliced it smooth. Someone had been there since Messian's death. Someone who knew she had taken a photograph.

She turned to look at the chopper just as its blades began to whirl. Of course. The illness was a ruse. The pilot had slipped away and returned to destroy the evidence. But then why bring her back, unless he was planning—

She dropped the cable cutter and tried to run to the chopper. Her feet sank with each step and she waved her arms for balance.

The helicopter shuddered and began slowly to rise, to leave her. She grabbed the metal beam and ran with it, slowing her even more.

The chopper was having trouble ascending. The wind had picked up speed and was forcing it down. The pilot was trying to balance it for liftoff. She struggled, tugging the beam, pushing through snow up to her knees . . . one step, another, moving closer.

The helicopter was righted now. She could see through the window, the pilot's face glancing back at her, a curiously bland expression, showing only a hint of urgency. The craft hovered above the ice. He thrust the joystick and it began to levitate. Two feet off the ground it turned away from her, slowly, with an oddly smooth robotic movement.

At that moment she struck. She hoisted the metal beam waist high and swung it toward the copter. It struck the blade of the tail rotor. The searing sound of metal striking metal, sparks leaping up. The copter lurched in its assent, destabilized. It leapt in the air like a wounded animal and spun in a low arc. The arc became a loop. It shuddered and turned upside down and fell into a downward trajectory. It smashed into the ice. She felt the shock wave of the crash against her cheeks and stared, aghast. Sounds of crunching metal and twisting plastic and breaking glass. The heap broke, bounced in the snow, tumbled and collapsed. A geyser of oil and smoke shooting into the air.

He was dead, she thought. No way he could survive that. Still, she waited until the beast settled down. It expired gradually, as bits of smoke and small explosions rent the air. A heavy, acrid smell— was it oil or burning plastic?—filled her nostrils.

She approached and looked inside. The pilot was motionless and upside down, squeezed into an unnatural position with his head bent almost backward, pressed against the cracked windscreen. Next to him was a tangle of instruments, wires, broken glass, and leaking fluid.

She unlocked the door, which swung open by itself. She struck the side. There was no give. It was solidly lodged in the ice. No smoke inside. She scanned the instrument panel. It was badly damaged. The radio looked smashed. She tried it. It was dead. Shit. That was her best hope. She stood back and heaved a deep breath. Behind her was the sound of the wind, picking up. The storm was gaining. She had to move fast. She extracted some items.

* * *

The first problem was getting across the river. She was stranded on the wrong side. The moulin that had swallowed up Messian was not far away but trying to skirt it was dangerous. She had seen from above that it was fed by melt water from both directions. Trying to negotiate the thin crust around it would be treacherous.

She would have to cross on the only remaining cable, the one for balance. Would it hold? Was she strong enough? She carried the metal beam to the stanchion and struck the cable. It reverberated but held fast. It appeared secure. She walked over to the bent tower, reached up, and hung from a crossbeam. She raised her legs and swung back and forth. It didn't dislodge. For additional support she propped the metal beam against the tower.

She walked around to the ladder side and scrutinized the items she had salvaged from the plane: snowshoes, a compass, four flares, an ice pick, and a bottle of water. She pulled the pilot out of the cabin and laid him on his back and took his parka. She glanced at him. Lying on the ice, looking almost peaceful, he would freeze and be preserved. Whoever found him would wonder how he managed to get out.

She put the small items in the parka, rolled it into a bundle, and fastened it with the drawstrings. She slung it onto her back and tied the arms around her neck. She attached the snowshoes to her belt. She climbed the ladder, tested the staying power of the tower by shifting her weight from side to side, and lay down upon the cable. She reached out with both arms, grasped it, and pulled herself forward like a caterpillar on a stem.

It was harder than she expected. She moved ahead two yards. The tower was now behind her. The cable pressed between her breasts and against her abdomen. She crossed her ankles on top of it. She lowered down the snowshoes as balancing weights, one on each side, and pulled herself ahead once more.

She was now over the raging river. She looked down. The water below was closer than expected. It tossed up cold splashes of spray that struck her face. The river thrashed and rose and dodged like an angry creature, heartless and hateful. She understood why Messian had dreaded venturing across it.

Again and again she pulled herself forward, a few inches at a time. Her goggles steamed over and she felt claustrophobic. She wiped them. She tried to divert herself, counting the inches, reciting verses, calculating the time to reach the opposite shore.

Halfway across she paused to catch her breath. Abruptly the wind picked up, whipping her from one side, almost pushing her off the cable. Panic seized her. Crossing on it was a mistake. She wasn't going to make it. She moved ahead only a few feet before she had to stop again. She felt the blood rushing in her ears and looked down at the raging water. Maybe the river wasn't so cruel. Maybe she should give up. Just let go and fall and drift down the river like Messian. It would be quick—freezing to death.

She thought of the moulin with a shudder. Dropping down into that black hole. What had Messian called it? The asshole of the Arctic. She would continue. She squeezed her fingers to get the circulation going and pulled herself ahead again.

At that point she fell. How it happened, she didn't know. Perhaps she lost her focus. Or her muscles gave way. All she knew was that she was suddenly upside down, holding on to the cable from below. She clung tight with both arms and feet. She lifted her body and cradled her knees around it. The snowshoes were dangling, pulling her downward. But she couldn't reach to cut them loose. And if she did, how would she travel?

She paused to collect herself for a second. Already her arms were tiring. The effort to stay aloft was straining her biceps and back muscles. She couldn't see. She raised her head and nudged it against her right elbow, pushing her goggles onto her forehead. She could see again. That was better.

She extended her arms until they straightened, then thrust herself upward and swung to one side, hooking the cable with her elbow. Without missing a beat, she twisted her legs into position, hooking one knee over, and gave another heave. She spun on top. She lay there, catching her breath, shivering suddenly.

Clutching the cable with her right hand, she used the left to pull up the snowshoes. She untangled them and dropped them down again, one on either side for balance. Then she raised her head to look ahead, replaced her goggles, and resumed her crawl, inches at a time. Four times, stop to rest. Five times, stop to rest. Six times, stop to rest. She looked down. Beneath her was ice. No more river. She had made it. She climbed down the tower. Now all she had to do—*all she had to do*, she thought with a bitter laugh—was make it back to the base.

* * *

That night the sun lingered on the horizon but was soon extinguished by the storm. She had prepared for it. She stopped walking after six hours and found a deep patch of snow and dug a small hole. She used one of the flares to melt snow and ice. She collected the water in the goggles and poured it into the bottle. She drank greedily and sprinkled some over the parka. It quickly froze. She propped it across the snowshoes like a dome, piled a foot of snow on top of it, built walls, and dug down and settled inside. She blocked the entrance with packed snow.

Her cave was surprisingly warm. Outside she heard the wind scream. The parka seemed to shiver but it held. Before long she fell asleep.

She awoke to silence. She checked her watch. Six hours. She pushed away the snow and felt a rush of cold air but no storm. It was over. Everything was still. She pushed away the roof and sat on the edge of the dugout.

It was dark but something caught her eye and she looked up. The sky shuddered with light, seeming to crack and crackle. A magnificent deep green quivered and danced. The horizons seemed to move toward her and lift her up to the heavens. The green rained down on all sides, then sprang up again like fountain spray and turned into a velvety ribbon that wove back and forth across the sky. The green gave way to waves of purple and then back to green and streaks of black and explosions of pink.

Nature's fireworks. Aurora borealis. The northern lights.

She stood full up and marveled. Everything dropped away, the cold, the fear, pushed aside by the giddy display. She had this flash of insight into . . . what? . . . a kind of grandeur, an all-encompassing majesty. Here she was, a tiny being, a small rational creature no bigger than a log, and the unfathomable universe was turning tricks and jumping through hoops for her to witness. She was the lone spectator as Nature spread her peacock feathers.

Three hours later, trekking monotonously in the same direction, her legs aching, she heard the plane in the distance. Its propellers set up an unmistakable droning. They were looking for her. The sound got louder and louder. When it was within range, she fired off a flare, then another.

The plane circled and came down lower and lower. She knew that she had been spotted but she set off the last flare anyway—just for the joy of it.

9

EVEN ON THE VERGE OF COLLAPSE, LESLEY INSISTED ON WALKING into the station unaided. As she crossed a path through the snow one of her rescuers reached over to steady her and she shook his arm off. She needed to remain strong and vigilant; the pilot might have a confederate, maybe a whole group of them.

Once inside the compound, consuming a bowl of hot soup before a gallery of onlookers amazed that she had survived her ordeal and eager to hear about it, she dispensed with the truth. She said the pilot had died in a horrible accident caused by the storm.

The resident medic gave her a quick exam and some pills, which she surreptitiously dropped in a wastebasket. She pleaded exhaustion and went to her bunk, but she remained awake for hours. Her pulse wouldn't stop racing.

As she returned to the commons room, the prop plane pilot who had found her and another man came in, stamping their feet and rubbing their hands for warmth. They had flown back to the site and retrieved the pilot's body, storing it in a shed out back.

He described what he found—the tower half collapsed, the balancing cable, the wreckage of the chopper with the dead body nearby. The storm had apparently obliterated Lesley's footprints and other signs of the fatal struggle. A piece of luck—Nature had become her accomplice.

Half an hour later she left the group and returned to her bunk. Still in her clothes, she fell into a profound sleep. Six hours later she awoke, her cheeks burning and her thighs and back aching. She showered, put on clean clothes, and left for the kitchen. She was ravenous.

The dimmed hallways and cramped offices were deserted. In the communications center there was a single officer, who sat transfixed before a computer screen. He looked up and gave her a thumbs-up without removing his headphones. As she passed behind him, he hit two buttons and the screen changed to a video game. She motioned him to remove the headset, which he did with obvious reluctance.

"Where is everyone?" she asked.

"I'm here."

"I can see that. Where is everyone else?"

He shrugged. "Welcome to the late shift."

"Is the galley open?"

"Maybe."

"Shouldn't you be spotting Russian subs or something instead of playing *Grand Theft Auto?*"

He looked nonplussed. "Well . . . yeah. We don't monitor every second." He put the headset back on and she left.

She went to the neon-lighted galley, microwaved a pre-cooked meal of chicken drums, and ate slowly.

Her next step was clear. She needed more information. She took her tray into the scrub room, washed it, returned to her bunk for warm underclothes, then went to the outfitting chamber to don her arctic wear. Outside it was disconcertingly bright, the early morning sun reflecting off the snow and straight into her goggles. She closed her eyes and stood motionless for a while, securing her balance. Then she trod on the flattened snow, skirting the compound to the hangar and shed behind.

The door was hard to open. She shoved it with her shoulder until finally it gave ground. Inside it was dark and she didn't move until her eyes adjusted. Gradually objects emerged from the Stygian gloom and assumed their proper shape. A pile of tools, a metal tower of drawers, swirls of wire on the walls, a snow blower in a corner, and a workbench littered with airplane parts. And along the far wall, on the ground, was what she had come to see, covered by a green tarp. She approached and pulled the tarp off.

Oddly, he was not badly disfigured. His head was twisted at a grotesque angle but it was not crushed or bloody. She stared closely. The hair was plastered down and lying with a flap of skin over a two-inch wide hole. She squeezed around to get a good look at the face, cold and gray. She pulled out her cell phone and snapped half a dozen photos. She pulled down the tarp and reached around his rigid body into his pockets until she felt a bulge. His wallet.

The name on a Virginia license was Henry L. Bloggert. Thirty-four years old. His tiny photo showed an unsmiling man with thick lips and long, girlish-looking dark hair. His eyes had a suspicious glint. She took more photos, searched him, and found a Bowie knife fitted in a slit on the outside of his left trouser leg.

She put the knife and wallet back and pulled the tarp back over him.

Back inside the station she went into a rear office, closed the door, and called Washington. Besermann picked up on the third ring. As soon as he heard her voice he started in. "I called and they said you'd gone back out there . . . that was thirty hours ago. I've called three times."

"No one told me."

"I didn't leave my name."

She didn't tell him about her attempts to secure the cable or the pilot's treachery or her long trek back on the ice, just hinted that odd things had been going on and that she wasn't safe.

"I want you to leave," he insisted. "Right away. I've been hearing some weird stories."

"What stories?"

"Just come out as soon as you can. Come straight to Washington."

Before they hung up, he told her that Messian's obituary had run on the front pages of most papers. His death was being called an accident.

"His obit got big play. You should be aware of that. I don't know if it's going to affect anything up there. But be careful."

* * *

The next morning Lesley reported to the medic's office with an excruciating pain in her lower right abdomen and a slight fever, courtesy of a spare thermometer she had held up to a light bulb.

"Appendicitis," pronounced the medic, a goateed, silver-haired man. He told her she had to be flown out immediately.

"Unless, of course, you want me to try the procedure."

"No, thanks," she said, grimacing.

She was ready to leave three hours later, a bit fed up from having to walk nearly doubled over. The prop pilot was loading her bag in the plane when two helicopters appeared out of the sky and landed on the runway, sending up billows of snow. Four policemen in thick white overcoats emerged.

They accosted her. Did she know anything about the death of the famous American scientist? She said she did not. They ordered her back inside but she politely explained that she was being evacuated because of a medical emergency, and the pilot verified her story.

Moments later, she pulled one policeman aside. "As I said, I don't know anything. But I hear there's a body in the shed out back. Maybe that'll help your investigation."

With that, she mounted a small ladder to board the plane.

10

FELIX BESERMANN LISTENED TO HER STORY, HIS BUSHY EYEBROWS furrowed low. They were walking along the Mall—he said he hadn't felt secure talking at his office—and when she finished, they found a bench and sat for several minutes, looking off toward the Washington Monument. Four large elms were lying on the ground nearby, their roots upended in mini-mountains of earth—the latest casualties of the most recent hurricane.

"I had no idea," he said finally. "I mean, I know climate change deniers have their radical fringe. And they hated Messian, sure. But murder . . ."

"Who are they?"

"As best we know, a shadowy group. People connected with oil and gas. They joined up over the invasion of Iraq and grew more powerful ever since Trump. They've infiltrated a lot of the agencies. DOE is riddled with them."

"What's their objective?" she asked.

"I keep wondering. At first it was to scuttle the environment regs. Then to kill the Paris Accord. But now, who knows? These people aren't fools. They have to be thinking over the long term."

A man wandered over and sat on a bench nearby. Besermann looked at him and suggested they resume their walk. He rose with a grunt—he was a big man with a bureaucrat's belly.

"I feel horrible about Messian," he said. "I sent him up there."

Lesley tried to assuage his guilt. She said that no one could have foreseen what would happen, that Messian was following the dictates of his conscience, and so on—but her words seemed to have little impact.

"By the way," she said, "he was suspicious of the radar station."

"What do you mean?"

"He wasn't sure it was legitimate. That it may have had some hidden agenda. You yourself said you heard weird stories about it—no?"

"Hard to say. There're always rumors about everything."

"So you think that's what they're doing, monitoring shipping by the Russians?"

"Maybe. Preparing for the open sea-lanes. The famous Northwest Passage, suddenly realizable."

"You don't think it's a cover?"

"Who knows?"

They turned off the Mall, their footsteps echoing off the massive stones of government buildings.

"About this shadowy group," she continued. "How can we find out who's in it? How can we blow the whistle on it?"

Besermann was not encouraging. He said he had one or two secret allies in the FBI looking into it, but he was not hopeful. He had passed along the name she provided—Henry Bloggert—but it had come up empty. He had also forwarded her photo of the cut in the cable. "They weren't impressed. They said yeah, you've got a defective cable. It could be anywhere. It could have been done by anything. It establishes nothing."

There was no one to be trusted, he observed. "All of Washington's turned into a cesspool."

Through the cross streets they could see the Capitol, bathed in the gold light of the dwindling day.

Something else seemed to be on his mind. They walked a block in silence, then he took her arm and asked if she would do him a favor, if she would look in on Maria, Messian's widow.

"She seems more than . . . you know, grieving."

"What do you mean?"

"Like she's been knocked into another world. Overwhelmed. I don't think she's capable of functioning, at least not right now. At the memorial service, she was out of it."

"Like how?"

"For instance, her baby, Paul, was crying through most of the service. She just left him there, in a stroller in the aisle. Didn't even pick him up. Like she wasn't even aware. I've seen her dozens of times since their marriage, but she didn't seem to recognize me."

"Maybe she's on meds."

"Maybe. But I think she needs help. She's never been what you'd call evenly balanced. That was part of Messian's attraction to her. You know he always had a sort of rescue complex."

Slowly and sadly, they wended their way back toward his office on Independence Avenue.

* * *

Two days later, Lesley visited Maria at her town house in the southeast section. It was on a ratty block that looked ripe for gentrification, and the three-story building, from the outside at least, fit right in.

But the inside showed attempts at remodeling—a refurbished staircase with a deep mahogany banister, a marble island in the kitchen, and a living room bookcase of handsome cherry. At the same time, there were toys scattered on the floor, mail tossed into

81

one corner, dirty dishes piled in the sink, and ashtrays overflowing on a coffee table.

Maria was wearing an old nightgown when she opened the door. She seemed to have forgotten that Lesley was expected, then tried to cover up her surprise. She moved slowly to sit down and seemed in a fog. She vaguely offered food or drink, wandered off to see what was available, and minutes later emerged from the kitchen to suggest tea.

They talked for a while. Maria spoke as if through a sheet of glass. Her pupils were dilated. All the signs were there—medication or doping, not that it made a big difference which one.

Lesley asked, gently, if she wanted to know more about Harry's death. The question seemed to stump her for a moment, then she rubbed her eyes and said, "You were there, right?"

"Yes."

"I would like to know something." Her voice took on an angry edge. "I'd like to know he didn't suffer."

Lesley assured her that he didn't, that his death was quick and painless and that he had died doing the work he loved. The remark struck a nerve in Maria.

"Don't feed me that crap. He hated going there and no one valued what he did."

The teakettle screamed, making Maria start. As she left for the kitchen, Lesley asked if she could use the bathroom and went upstairs.

It was even messier here. In one room she saw a crib. The toddler, Paul, was asleep wearing a diaper and nothing more. The smell of soiled diapers rose from a nearby white container. She went into the bathroom and checked the medicine cabinet. A vast assortment of pill bottles: Oxycontin, Ambien, Xanax, and a host of others she couldn't identify.

Lesley knew well the not-so-subtle signs of a household skidding into an abyss. She made a vow then and there that she was not going to let that happen to Paul.

82

* * *

For three months she was life support to the mother and child. She brought them food, got their clothes washed, hired people to clean the house. She took Paul out for long walks in the stroller—he was a delightful child, eager to learn and seemingly advanced for a two-year-old. His vocabulary was multiplying by the day.

But she could do nothing to help Maria crawl out of the hole of her depression. She convinced her to attend an Alcoholics Anonymous meeting—finding one in a church only three blocks away—but the third time, when she went to pick her up, Maria was missing. She was in a bar up the street.

"She has to hit rock bottom," said her AA sponsor. "And there's nothing you can do to catch her. It's got to come from her."

Maria, it turned out, had no family. Both parents were deceased. Strangely, she seemed to have no friends.

She had taken to watching dark television series and reading dense, melancholy books. She didn't talk very much.

* * *

Lesley came to take Paul out for the day at Maria's pleading. Maria had called her the night before saying she had an important appointment. Was it about a job? Lesley asked. Something like that. Please come, please.

Lesley took a day off work at Save the Earth. She wondered: where do you take a two-year-old for hours on end? She arrived in her car, a somewhat beat-up Nissan with a new car seat in the back.

Maria was not dressed for a job interview but she appeared appropriately nervous. She checked her watch several times. Lesley heard a bath running upstairs. That was reassuring. Maria kissed Paul not once but three times and deeply inhaled his infant smell, nestling into the folds of his neck.

Lesley found Paul's warmest coat—a padded gray jacket—and carried him outside. She strapped him in the infant seat, making sure his favorite object—a soft, soiled hand puppet of a lion—was within reach. They set out.

For quite a while she just drove around, past the White House, up Connecticut Avenue to Rock Creek Park almost to Bethesda. She turned around and headed back downtown. Now Paul was getting restless, whining and arching his back against the restraints.

Amazingly, she found a parking space near the Mall. She took him to a deli and fed him egg salad. She tied a cloth napkin around his neck as a bib but it didn't work well and he got bits of yellow on the new flannel shirt she had bought him.

They went out. She retrieved the stroller and they walked to the National Gallery, patrolling the rooms, the stroller gliding almost effortlessly across the shining floors. Next stop was the cafeteria. Coffee for her, milk for him. She looked at her watch—two hours to go—and was contemplating the next move when her cell phone rang. It was Besermann. He sounded upset but she couldn't really hear him. She went to a corner near a window where the reception was better, keeping her eyes cocked on Paul. She had a bad premonition.

He told her that Maria was dead. Had just died. Cut her wrists in the bath. It was horrible. He had just been informed. The mailman had heard the water falling through the ceiling. But the child was missing.

Lesley couldn't talk right away. She gasped for air, stared ahead, then desperately scanned the room. Paul was still seated in a highchair at the table, cuddling his lion puppet. She told Besermann she had him. Thank God, he said.

But what was she going to do with him? Where would she take him? Who would she leave him with? Besermann asked her where she was. He said he'd come right over.

She went back to the table. Paul was delighted to see her. He smiled and held up his puppet to her, arm fully outstretched, ready to share.

II

PAUL WAS FIVE YEARS OLD NOW, AN UNUSUAL CHILD, SILENT IN his own world, headstrong and vulnerable.

Lesley had decided to take him to the conference on global warming. She didn't want to spend time away from him. She was bringing along Alicia, the young Australian au pair she had hired after combing through dozens of applications. Solid and unflappable, Alicia was able to handle him.

They were almost to the mountain house in the Adirondacks. She was driving up the steep road, Paul asleep in the back—thankfully—and Alicia staring quietly out at the scenery. The car was in the outside lane and there was no guardrail to save them from the drop-off of a sheer cliff. At times the edge looked dangerously close, which made her stomach knot up. She gripped the steering wheel tightly.

After Maria's death, she had become Paul's guardian and fierce protector. Somehow she had managed. They moved into a small apartment in Bethesda. She left the nonprofit and with Besermann's help had gotten a top job at a scientific foundation, the Climate Research Institute. It had a decent salary, and she used it as a perch from which to carry on Henry Messian's work. She felt herself an inadequate proxy.

By now Paul had outwardly adjusted to life without his mother—at least as far as she could tell. After about a year he had stopped asking for "Mama," but there were still troubling signs. He was subject to inconsolable rages, slept badly, and didn't eat much. She was worried about weight loss and tried every trick and every bribe to get him to eat anything other than noodles and white rice.

Raising a child drew on every resource she had. When she had mused about it years ago, she imagined doing it with a partner, if not a husband. Now she was alone, except for Alicia—and thank God for her. But hired help was not the same. You couldn't easily ask her to stay late or pitch in with things outside her normal duties. And there was something else, which shamed her to admit: the relationship between Paul and Alicia was seemingly so smooth, at least by comparison, that at times she felt jealous.

She couldn't remember actually reaching a decision to take on Paul. It seemed he had simply been thrust upon her by fate. And now between her job and her day-to-day parenting, life was an exhausting act of juggling with one hand and spinning plates with the other. But she could no longer imagine life without him.

This was the first trip they had taken in over a year.

She came to another curve and slowed the Volvo to a crawl to take in the view. In the distance the mountains were wrapped in a faint haze. A carpet of evergreens covered the valley below with only a few signs of human intervention—peaked rooftops, barns and silos, planted fields following the contours of the land. No birch trees. They had all died out years ago.

She thought of the conference ahead. How strange that Besermann had emerged as the prime spokesman for the cause, that he should be the one to organize it, almost as if he were trying to assume Messian's mantle. She knew he was a weathervane spinning in the political currents. That fed her disturbing sense that unnameable forces were working on a hidden agenda.

To hear Besermann tell it, the idea for the climate conference had come six months earlier when two men called upon him at work. They introduced themselves—Jeffrey Slatter and Maximus Dodd—with business cards that carried the logo of the International Climate Control Agency, which grew out of the United Nations Framework Convention on Climate Change.

They said they represented an assortment of major businesses and enterprises: big tech, Silicon Valley, energy companies, major universities, and nongovernmental organizations—a sort of consortium of interests, driven by an emerging consensus that now, in the year 2028, something must finally be done about global warming.

They wanted Besermann to head up an assembly of thirty or so US and international scientists—"the best brains in the world"— to come up with a solution. They would provide the funding.

"You know what they said?" Besermann had told her. "They said it'll be like the Manhattan Project." He tried to hide a smile. "They said I'll be the new Oppenheimer."

* * *

She came to the mountain house overlooking a glacial lake, with resplendent gardens and curving walkways. It was called Tiger's Nest after a mountain monastery in Bhutan. She checked in, settled Paul and Alicia in an adjoining room, and headed for the first plenary session, held in a large ballroom flooded with light. She walked in as Besermann took the stage to address the fifty or so participants, seated in folding chairs. He whipped the cord of a handheld microphone as he paced back and forth.

A series of photos flashed onto a screen. Flooding in Miami. St. Mark's Square with boards to walk on. The Mississippi breaking its banks. The Great Coral Reef bleached. Thousands of dead frogs. Collapsed beehives. Bodies piled in makeshift morgues during a pandemic.

Things were deteriorating faster than anyone predicted, he declared. By mid-century the warming effects of fossil fuel pollution would reach a climax. He spun on his heels and walked to a blackboard, drawing a rough graph: years along the horizontal, carbon measurements on the vertical. Then a line on the chart, ascending more and more sharply over time.

"Since the Industrial Revolution, we've burned 365 billion metric tons of carbon into the atmosphere. Every year we burn another nine billion tons."

He traced the rise carefully. The line rose steeper and steeper. He stopped and circled the highest point.

"Here it is. The year 2050." As he spoke, Lesley had a vision of Messian in that bar years ago.

"Less than twenty-five years from now. The year of destiny. Projections show that's when we hit a two-degree rise Celsius. We all know it'll be more. What it's going to be like?

"For one thing, 80 percent of our sea ice is gone. The North and South Poles lose their ice sheets, so they no longer reflect back sunlight. Greenland is a heap of rock. Alaska is a dry plain.

"Half of all species are extinct. Central America is devastated by drought. Much of Southern Africa is covered by sand dunes. North Africa is a desert. The oceans rise five feet, ten feet. Millions die in Bangladesh, India, Indonesia, and elsewhere. Extreme weather events become the norm. I mean really extreme—storms with high winds never before recorded, tidal surges, mega tornadoes.

"Okay, it's a big deal. It's a catastrophe. But, you know, we could probably adjust, some of us. Life would be hard but somehow some of us would survive. Millions along the coasts would have to evacuate. There'd be refugees, riots, food shortages, epidemics, famine—all that—but, taking the long view, humanity would continue. Or so you might think." He paused. "But you'd be wrong."

He stopped pacing.

"Here's the kick in the head. It's called negative feedback. With negative feedback the carbon cycle is reversed. Instead of absorbing carbon dioxide, the planet releases it. All that peat moss and vegetation that died and stored carbon over millennia now sends it back into the atmosphere. The warming oceans can't absorb any more and they, too, start releasing it into the environment.

"In simple terms, we cross a Rubicon. The carbon release feeds on itself and becomes an irreversible spiral. The mechanisms that used to wash it out increase it. The concentration of carbon and global warming mounts so quickly and irrevocably it becomes inimical to human life, to animal life in any form."

He stood before the audience, staring at it.

"The ultimate destruction. Who knows when it'll happen, the final end? Extinction of humankind. Thirty years, forty, maybe even fifty or sixty. But soon enough. We used to talk about saving the world for our grandchildren. We're way past that now. It's not our grandchildren, it's our children. And not just our children—it's us as well." He laughed humorlessly and scanned the audience. "Maybe not all of you, if you're over sixty. But the rest of you, you might want to get your papers in order."

It was time for questions. Hands shot up. Many gave vent to speeches, pronouncements, finger-pointing declarations. What was to be done? How to even begin to tackle the problem? People wanted what they wanted. They wouldn't change their ways. A conscientious handful of civic-minded consumers turned their thermostats down ten degrees and wore sweaters. Or recycled and stopped using drinking straws. Or bought electric cars. How pathetic was that? And then once the price of oil dropped, people bought gas-guzzlers as if they were going out of style. They still flew jets, burned coal, cut down forests. Elected politicians who demanded nothing of them. We were all lemmings jumping off a cliff.

One man, with gray hair tied in a ponytail, delivered a short lecture of his own. He said he didn't believe you could reduce carbon by changing people's habits. They were too set in their ways—"the wagon wheels cut that rut too deep." There was only one viable path ahead. "Ge-o-en-gin-eer-ing." He pronounced the term sententiously, syllable by syllable.

"We have to come up with something immediate and drastic," the gray-haired man continued. "We have to physically reduce the temperature of the planet. We have to come up with a magic bullet. That's the only hope."

Lesley shook her head and interjected, "There are other ways. Less risky ways. We could pull carbon out of the atmosphere and send it underground. Or at the very least capture it at the point of entry, install trapping mechanisms on all those smokestacks."

The man leapt up. "That'll never work. It's gone too far. You can't just suck it out of the air. We don't live in a goddamned balloon."

They argued, fruitlessly, for half an hour. Lesley thought more people would back her but they remained silent.

Afterward, committee assignments were made, a long and tedious process. There were committees on rising seas, coral death, ocean acidification, extreme weather events, species extinction, shrinking glaciers, encroaching deserts, and other topics. The scientists argued over who belonged on what committee. They were adept at these internecine battles. It looked like a long night ahead.

Lesley collected her papers and went upstairs in the mountain house. She relieved Alicia and told her to grab a bite downstairs. Then she gave Paul a bath, tucked him in bed, and read him a chapter of *Stuart Little*. He was unusually cooperative. In hopes that he would fall asleep, she softened her voice, more and more, trailing off into silence.

A rush of joy flooded her. She sang to him softly until he fell asleep.

She stared at him, his hands with small, slender fingers, his long eyelashes, the blanket rising and falling with his breathing. So helpless, so innocent, but already knowing loss. Her joy dissipated, replaced by the storm of questions hanging over everything these days: What would become of him? What would he see in his life? What kind of world would he be living in twenty-five years from now?

She rose and went over to the desk. There was the embossed envelope that had been handed to her at the check-in table—her assignment.

She tore it open. Paragraph upon paragraph of instructions: when to meet, where to meet, nondisclosure agreements to be signed, the plenary session agenda—until finally there it was. "You are to report to the committee on volcanoes." *Volcanoes*. Here she was, a specialist on degrading ice caps, a PhD in meteorology, and she'd been assigned to a committee on volcanoes. What the hell did she know about volcanoes?

* * *

Soon Lesley knew quite a bit. At the end of three days she and her five fellow committee members were experts. They researched volcanoes online, ordered esoteric books on related topics, plunged into academic papers, and conferred by phone with specialists and volcanologists.

Her colleagues researched various eruptions, from the recent Mount Pinatubo in the Philippines in 1991 to those that erupted a thousand years ago.

Lesley's own purview was spectacular Mount Tambora, the most powerful blast in recorded history. It happened in 1815 in the lush islands of the Dutch East Indies. Three pillars of liquid flame broke out and an eruption column rose up twenty-seven miles, dropping ash and pumice stones eight inches thick and sending rivers of molten lava into the surrounding sea.

So loud was the final assault on the sky that soldiers 1,600 miles away on Sumatra thought gunmen were attacking them. The fine ash particles stayed in the atmosphere for years at altitudes as high as eighteen miles.

The ash composition, sulfur dioxide, was crucial. It created a global anomaly. The year 1816 was "the year without a summer." In June frost appeared throughout New England, snow fell in Albany, and crops failed across North America. An unidentifiable "dry fog" wrapped itself around Europe and refused to lift, ruining wheat, oat, and potato harvests. Food shortages caused riots, arson, looting, and the worst famine of the century. In India the monsoons were disrupted. In Bengal a new strain of cholera broke out. In China the Yangtze Valley flooded, forcing thousands to flee coastal areas.

All these events were caused by a phenomenon not understood at the time: Worldwide, temperatures plummeted. It happened because a veil of sulfate aerosol reflected back the sunlight and caused a drop of almost a full degree Fahrenheit. The drop lasted for three years.

Lesley read all this out to the conference members, at which point they became rapt. Some murmured or leaned toward her, others perched on the edges of their chairs. The same thought was racing around the room. It could be captured in a single word:

Geo-engineering.

She knew her committee assignment had not been randomly made. Besermann was trying to convert her to the simple solution.

* * *

Three hours later, just before dusk was falling, Lesley took Paul for a walk. They followed a path up a long but gradual climb until they reached the ridge of a small mountain. Here was a lookout, made of planks and logs, extending over a cliff so that inside looking out, they felt suspended in midair. She held Paul's hand.

The sunset was stunning, a haze of fire half hidden by a gossamer blanket of clouds. Red and yellow and purple streaks crossed the sky like vast fingers stretching around an invisible dome. Around it was a penumbra of cerulean. Off in the distance was a darker shade that seemed to reach into her soul. It veered off into black.

The trees below shimmered in an evening breeze. Nearby she saw a cluster of gnats hovering over a bush. Above, bats dove through the air currents. She heard a deep chorus of bullfrogs and in between the hard chirping of birds settling in for the night.

She almost shuddered. It was unearthly, or—the opposite— very much belonging to this earth, so very much alive. The sights and sounds buoyed her mind for a long time. Then she drifted slowly back, thinking of things she had discovered in the course of her research, things she had left out of her talk because they did not seem germane to the exigencies of science. Footnotes, really.

She thought of the aftereffects of Tambora and the law of unintended consequences. London, during that notorious missing summer of 1816, had seen sunsets that were fantastically vivid. It was captured by painters like J. M. W. Turner. Their paintings suffused realism with something new, an overlay of Impressionism, but one that glimmered with a disturbing undercurrent. The world it conjured up was bleak.

The sense of the tempestuous was everywhere that year. Crops failed. People rioted, thousands died. The time out of joint gave rise to dark fashion, apocalyptic visions, religious ecstasies, even gothic fiction. In Geneva Mary Shelley conceived the story of Frankenstein and Lord Byron plotted vampire tales and composed his ode to the apocalypse, "Darkness." Europe was in upheaval. Imaginations ran wild. So did fear.

She bent down and hugged Paul close.

That was what was missing from science: the human dimension. You never know, she thought, how a sudden change in the natural world will affect us. We are complicated beings, creators and victims of our culture. We feel we are superior to animals, placed on a higher plain, but we quake at a freak hailstorm in summer or succumb to melancholy at a week of drenching rain.

She looked again at Paul and wrapped her arms around him and felt her heart stir. The fading warmth of the sun, the cooling breeze, the blinking stars against the gathering majestic night sky.

What would the world be like were it not for these?

12

Lesley deposited Paul and Alicia at the Hayden Planetarium and walked down Central Park West. She kept to the western side of the avenue, away from the dangers of Central Park, and kept one eye out for muggers. The sweltering heat was said to bring them out of the woodwork.

She and Paul had come on a one-day trip to New York City for different reasons. He had wanted to follow his thirteen-year-old's passion: to behold the stars and galaxies in all their artificial glory. She wanted to attend a gathering of diplomats and VIPs assembled by Besermann.

He hadn't invited her—his ego had so burgeoned that their relationship was frayed these days—but when she asked him about the meeting at least he hadn't denied all knowledge. She felt she should attend; she needed to read the political winds. Seven long years had passed since the Adirondack conference, and it was still questionable whether they were blowing in favor of climate change realists or against them.

The conclave was being held at the Metropolitan Opera House in Lincoln Center. After two more superstorms devastated New York City, each of them more destructive than Hurricane Sandy twenty-three years ago, the United Nations had abandoned its waterlogged headquarters on the East River and set up temporary quarters there.

A bizarre turn of events, she thought: the arts ceding the high ground—literally—to politics.

Amazing how much resistance was being mounted by a confederation of benighted thinkers: climate change deniers, anti-science goons, mystical preachers, and superstitious healers who saw a conspiracy under every thermometer.

What will it take? she wondered. *How can you deny the effects of global warming when water is lapping around your ankles?* Still, she mused, public opinion was fickle—it could reverse course like fans in a sports stadium performing a wave.

She walked up the steps to the central plaza of cracked marble, thinking again of Besermann. This conclave was meant to be quiet, if not secret, and that did not sit well with her. She suspected it would amount to his coronation. She agreed with him that drastic action was needed to save the world, but she didn't like the direction of his thinking. And he wouldn't listen to her or anyone else who disagreed.

They often argued. At a recent dinner he had asserted that it might take a dictator to push through a plan to save the planet, "and if so, the sooner the better." She was aghast. They raised their voices to the point of shouting. "Your concern for civil liberties is going to shrivel up like a dried maggot when the sun starts burning your hair," he fumed. She countered: "What good is saving the world if the world isn't worth saving?"

She wasn't sure she even liked him anymore. She felt obligated to him, and until recently he had been a regular in her life, dropping in at their apartment unannounced, to teach Paul the latest unworkable theory on cold fusion or demand a martini or lecture her on her "chaotic lifestyle."

She was thirty-three, energetic and ambitious, but more and

more she felt burdened by the exigencies of her life. Like being nibbled to death by ducks, she thought, an expression she had heard somewhere. She remembered with a jolt *where* she had heard it: from Messian in the Arctic, describing what it felt like to be pilloried by the scientific establishment.

She arrived at Lincoln Center, dripping with perspiration. She stopped at the central fountain and sat on its circular rim. The empty basin was cracked and stained brown. It hadn't flowed for half a decade.

It was 110 degrees and the July sun was beating down mercilessly. The city was baking: tar melting on the streets, plants wilting everywhere, cars scalding to the touch, subway platforms turned into furnaces.

She worried about Paul. He was troubled. He had always been bright—super-bright, so much so that he amazed her, at times almost frightened her. He had skipped two grades, was already past algebra, and consumed scientific papers to fill a storehouse of knowledge. But he was a loner. He spent most of the time in his room and he was pale and thin because he didn't eat much.

At the quaint little day school he attended, they didn't know what to do with him. He exhausted the teachers with his aggressive questions—in studying the solar system, for example, he demanded to know the chemical composition of each planet. He sometimes frightened the other children, not physically but through sheer intellectual dominance. He had no close friends and spent recess in the school library reading books on cosmology.

A teacher summed him up at a recent conference: "Paul seems both strong and fragile. He can be hurt so easily. Something—a harsh word or an elbow in the rib that other kids would shake off—sends him into a paroxysm. It's as if the membrane between him and the outside world is too thin for his own good." She recommended therapy.

That didn't work out. Paul resented the therapist and challenged him at every turn. When Lesley paid the last bill, the therapist admitted failure.

"I tried many avenues to reach him but his defenses are unassailable. At every entrance he's posted a guard."

Writing the check, she had observed coolly that she had always thought of Paul more as a boy than an army in a fortified castle.

As Paul entered full-blown adolescence, he was increasingly prey to sudden mood changes and quick to take offense. He picked fights with her and criticized her and seemed to freeze when she went to hug him. Before, he would sometimes sit close to her and unconsciously place a hand on her arm. Now he wouldn't walk next to her on the sidewalk.

They had arguments, sometimes screaming ones, and as much as she vowed to control her temper, he knew which buttons to push to drive her up the wall. Following the perverse logic of the human heart, the more he rejected her, the more desperate was her love for him.

Recently he had stopped asking about his father. In his early years, he was obsessed with him, wanting to hear the same stories over and over, about his research, his idiosyncrasies, his mannerisms, the way he walked and talked. His hunger was so bottomless that she began making things up—after all, she hadn't known Messian all that well—and then she worried that she was painting a portrait that was too perfect. Boys who live with their fathers have the chance to see them up close; they realize they're flawed like anyone else. Boys without fathers idolize them into gods.

Oddly, Paul had never shown much interest in his mother. But even this was beginning to change. Lesley had the unnerving feeling that he was somehow blaming her for Maria's death. Just two days ago, in yet another tantrum, he had shouted, "You think you're so perfect! So self-righteous! Who asked *you* to adopt me?" It had hurt her.

* * *

She spotted Besermann walking quickly across the plaza toward the Metropolitan Opera House. She followed him at a distance.

Through the revolving door, she was struck by a blast of cool air. She watched as a young Japanese woman approached Besermann and led him to an elevator that carried him upstairs. She crossed the lobby and opened the concert hall door to look at the familiar curved seat rows of UN delegates, now mounted on a vast wooden floor that was empty.

She climbed the central staircase. The attendees were being ushered into the Grand Tier restaurant. Two uniformed officials guarded the door, one with a clipboard on which he checked off names. Hers was not on it and he motioned her away.

She spotted Besermann inside and waved him out.

"Tell them to let me in."

He had the presence of mind to not look embarrassed.

"Of course. As long as you back me up."

"Depends on what you say."

"Look. This is important. We've got the scientists on board. Now we're working on the diplomats. And by the way, it's all off the record."

She took a table in the back and surveyed the crowd. Across the room were Jeffrey Slatter and Maximus Dodd, the two men from the ICCA, who always turned up at the scientific conferences. One of them—Dodd—ducked his head a moment to speak into a cell phone.

She recognized the US ambassador to the UN, an abrasive woman in a pinstriped business suit who was a major political campaign donor. Not far away was the Chinese delegate, a stooped octogenarian whom she knew to be a party hack.

The two seemed to be working the room. Perfect, she thought: both countries were late to board the save-the-world bus and now, typically, they're trying to push their way into the driver's seat.

After a lavish meal—steak or fish, with matching wine—Besermann brought his chair to the center and settled on it casually, as if for a friendly postprandial chat.

He began with the bald truth: Natural processes remove less than half of the fossil fuel emissions each year. Even if all the emissions could somehow miraculously stop, the buildup of carbon dioxide in the atmosphere was already so vast, it would take thousands of years before the Earth returned to preindustrial levels.

The upheavals were already upon us. Things had passed the tipping point. Simply curbing emissions was no longer enough. So much CO_2 was being pumped into the atmosphere that a radical solution was called for. And there were only two possibilities—you could try to capture and sequester the carbon dioxide, or you could decrease the amount of sunlight.

Capturing CO_2 and, say, pumping it into underground chambers was difficult—after all, the gas was diffused throughout the air. The whole atmosphere would have to be scrubbed. The cost was prohibitive.

"There's only one hope," he said, fixing his eyes on the audience. "And that's to decrease the amount of sunlight reaching Earth. We can do this by increasing the amount that's reflected back into space. As you know, it's called the *albedo*. From the Latin word for 'white.'

"Our models of albedo modification suggest that significant cooling can be achieved by sending sulfur particles into the stratosphere. That would block the sunlight before it reaches us." He paused to let his words sink in.

"This is what happens naturally in volcanic eruptions. If we pump up sixty million tons, that would be equivalent to five volcanic eruptions—five Mount Pinatubos. Each one would cut global temperatures by about half a degree Celsius.

"Of course, we wouldn't have to try that much right away. Initially we thought ten million tons might be enough. Now we think we'd need more. We could start with twenty or twenty-five million tons and see how it goes. Or we might even use engineered nanoparticles, which could be dispersed with a single plane. The beauty is the amount's adjustable.

"And here are two important points to keep in mind. One, the effects are instantaneous. You'd experience the difference right away. And two, the cost is unbelievably reasonable—between five and ten billion dollars at the most. No other way to put it—it's a bargain."

At this, the delegates stirred. Some of them exchanged meaningful glances.

Besermann continued: "That means it's even within the budget of a small island nation. In fact—maybe I shouldn't say this—but that's the fear of some people in our intelligence services, that a threatened country might go rogue—do it unilaterally. We've been watching some of these places in the Pacific to make sure they don't jump the gun."

When he finished his half-hour spiel, he was peppered with questions.

"How would the sulfur seeding be done?"

"Easy. You send up a jet plane to release the nanoparticles around the world. They turn into sulfurous-like gases throughout the stratosphere. And of course the procedure would have to be done every so often—say, every two years, to keep the protective shield operative."

"So it's not permanent?"

"No."

"And what about fossil fuel emissions?"

"Well, the hope is we'd ultimately reduce them. But in the meantime, they wouldn't be cooking us to death. Think of it in terms of a thermostat system that has two knobs. One controls the emissions, the other the particles. Over time we could dial them both down."

"What would it look like, this—what did you call it?—this shield?"

"Interesting question. We can't say for sure. You might, optically speaking, generate something along the lines of a layer of cirrus clouds, though it'd be thinner than the clouds you see today. Sort of like a membrane. But light would still get through."

"So it'd look different."

"Depends what you mean. You ever been in London in the winter? Or Warsaw pretty much anytime?"

He chuckled and the audience laughed along with him. Except for Lesley. From time to time he had been looking at her, frowning.

A delegate from Norway asked how long the shield would last.

That, said Besermann, was the great unknown. It would depend on what steps were taken to curb the carbon emissions. In the best scenario, if severe measures were taken against them and if the warming stopped at its current level of two degrees centigrade, it would remain until the year 2700.

The effect was astonishment. Two or three even gasped.

"What! Six hundred and sixty years!" yelled one delegate.

"Granted, that sounds like a long time," Besermann conceded.

"And that's if we actually stop polluting?"

"Yes."

"And if we don't?"

Besermann began sweating at the podium. "Well, we will stop. We'll have to. Yes, it's a long time. But don't forget, maintenance won't be difficult. In fact, we anticipate it'll get easier as time goes on. Perhaps we could begin to taper off long before."

He was rescued by a diversion. A delegate from France raised her hand and he quickly called on her.

"I notice that the launch sites you propose are all in the Northern Hemisphere. Why is that?"

Lesley scanned the audience. She realized something that had been niggling at her: no delegates from the Southern Hemisphere were there.

"Glad you asked." Besermann said. He paused, looking at the tables around him. "In the interests of full disclosure, I'm going to be honest here. There may be a significant effect on Earth's weather system."

"Like what?" the woman demanded.

"Without going into too much detail, I'll just say the South . . . well, as you know, things are far more difficult there. Droughts. Monsoons. Vulnerable populations. That's why—and I am sorry to say this—the South is not a reliable partner in this venture.

"So for various reasons, including considerations of reliability and follow-through . . . I think it'd be wise to concentrate the remedial process in the North."

"And what happens to the South?"

"They'd go their own way."

"Their own way?"

"Basically, they'd be their own masters. They could do their own intervention or not, as they wish. Naturally we'd offer to transfer the technology to them."

The delegates accepted this without further discussion.

Lesley was increasingly upset. She blurted out a question without raising her hand: "And what are the risks? Surely there are risks. You haven't mentioned any."

He scratched his chin.

"Well, yes. Of course there are risks. There are always risks in any scientific endeavor. And something like this, albedo modification, something on this scale has never been done before—obviously. We're turning over a new leaf here.

"All I can say is we have tried to ascertain the problems. We've examined the risks as best we can. We've performed any number of computer simulations. We think the possibility of risks is outweighed by the certainty of risk of not taking action now, when we can still do something."

She was dissatisfied with his answer and showed it, so he

continued by enumerating some of the unknowns: "regional disparities, a minimal effect on crops and trees and continuing ocean acidification, which wouldn't be addressed by SAAM."

"Sam?" asked another audience member.

"Sorry, S-A-A-M. That's the technical term. *Stratospheric aerosol albedo modification.*"

Lesley still wasn't satisfied. "How about moral hazard?" she asked. "Sorry?"

"You know, moral hazard. You keep engaging in risky behavior because you believe you're protected from the consequences. The fact is we've been polluting the atmosphere almost to the point of extinction and you're putting a system in place that will allow us to continue polluting. There's a disincentive to change."

"Ah, I see," he said. "Well, now you're talking about human nature. And there's nothing we can do about that. Science hasn't begun to solve that puzzle—at least not yet."

The French delegate raised a tangential consideration.

"Why do I hear rumors about only China and the US as sites for this project? Why should the two worst polluters reap the benefits? How about us? France has excellent facilities."

People hooted and hissed. Besermann let the uproar continue long enough to think of something to say.

"Madam Delegate, think of it not as a benefit. Think of it as a fitting form of penitence by the major polluters."

This set off a round of laughter.

He smiled and the American representative stood, indicating the session was over, and led a long round of heartfelt applause.

During a coffee session afterward Besermann avoided Lesley. When he left the opera house, spinning through the revolving doors into the furnace outside, she caught up with him and tugged at his sleeve. He whirled around as if he had been accosted and declared, in a stentorian voice, "How dare you!" Then he strode off.

105

13

LESLEY WAS FLYING OVER THE YUKON DELTA, AGHAST AS SHE looked out over coastal Alaska. The rising sea level had reduced the islands and made them unrecognizable. They passed Kodiak—it had lost its genteel sprawl of slopes and glens and was little more than a brown lump rising out of the water.

She caught her breath. In places the land was crumbling into the ocean. She had seen glaciers calving—that sight had been ubiquitous on news videos for decades—but until now she had never seen *land* calving. Great slabs of green and brown permafrost peeled off and thundered into the water like bread being sliced with a knife.

"When did this begin?" she shouted to the pilot over the drone of the plane's motor.

Rowland lifted his gaze toward her. His weather-beaten face, riddled with wrinkles like cracks in a dried lakebed, was scowling.

"We've known about it for years. But to see it like this . . . in real time . . . about two years."

"How much coast has been lost?"

Rowland shrugged. "Twenty-two miles here, at the worst point. Satellite data establishes an overall average of fifteen miles." He pointed to a trail of muddy swirl in the ocean. "That's it dissolving. As far as you can see."

Lesley hadn't been eager to return to the far north—memories of Messian still rose up to attack her in nightmares from time to time—but this trip was important. The forces for tackling climate change were finally reaching a consensus, and she needed to come up with a researched article that would give them a push.

And there was another struggle underway: what to do about it. Felix Besermann's influence was growing. Geo-engineering was on everyone's lips. At first people had seemed to regard SAAM as an unlikely deus ex machina. But now they embraced it because it was straightforward, easy to grasp, and cheap.

Lesley's was a voice of opposition. Her foundation, the Climate Research Institute, had become the main challenger of SAAM. She was convinced that there had to be a better way than constructing a shield around the planet to reflect back sunlight, with all the unknown consequences that would entail.

Her foundation promoted "the sane alternative" to deal with carbon: drastically cutting emissions and then scrubbing it out of the atmosphere and sequestering it underground. To the proponents of seeding the stratosphere with sulfur particles, as Besermann put it, that was "overkill and over budget."

She hadn't seen him in four years, not since he took such umbrage at Lincoln Center. She had known he wouldn't forgive such a public challenge and she was right. The consolation was that people were beginning to listen to her. Her newsletter, *CRI Reports*, had a growing readership. More and more professionals were looking at carbon sequestration.

She was in the copilot's seat. Behind them sat a young woman named Helena, who was from London and announced she was traveling around the world to "visit all the exotic places."

Rowland didn't claim to be a scientist. He was a native-born Alaskan, an adventurer turned ecologist, but he had become an

107

expert on permafrost destruction. He had contacted Lesley and insisted she come up for a look. "A bit of disaster tourism," he had called it.

"Look out the right side," he said. "See those two bogs? They've just about doubled since I was here last month. The bogs are everywhere now. They've been around for twenty years or so. But they're immense now. More like lakes."

Lesley looked down again at the dull green and brown vegetation woven together into a tight mass like a shag rug. The two bogs were like giant black sinkholes, maybe fifty feet in diameter. The water came from below, melting upward.

She thought of all that carbon packed into the permafrost built up over the centuries during the last ice age—all those plants that had extracted carbon dioxide from the atmosphere, frozen before they could decompose, and now were expelling it.

"How much carbon is in there?" asked Helena.

"You know, the permafrost isn't just on the surface. It extends down hundreds of feet. So it's massive. Altogether, we estimate 1.8 trillion tons. That's twice as much carbon as currently in the atmosphere."

"And how much is being released every year?" asked Helena.

"Over 1.5 billion tons. That means it's more carbon than from fossil fuels. It's as if we've just doubled the number of cars and coal plants sending that shit into the atmosphere."

Rowland dropped the plane lower, setting the bog water shimmering. "Think about that. We could annihilate every car on the planet tomorrow and the temperature would still go up two degrees. And there's nothing we can do to stop it. We're locked into the negative feedback cycle. Are you depressed yet?" He gave a half smile.

"I've been depressed for a very long time," Lesley said.

"And I haven't even mentioned methane yet."

He talked to Helena over his shoulder. "When it's too wet and oxidizing decomposition doesn't take place, the anaerobic bacteria take over and produce methane—"

"Which is even more dangerous for the climate," said Lesley, "because it has far greater heat-trapping ability. It doesn't stay around as long, but it's twenty times stronger."

Helena gave a short laugh. "I heard something about methane coming from cow farts."

"Every little bit hurts." Rowland was quiet for a moment. When he resumed, his tone turned hard. "You know, I came here thirty years ago because I loved the place. I loved the tundra. I loved the expanse of it, the openness. I'm a hunter—I mean, I used to be—and I'd spend days out here in the summers. Course there's no hunting now, because there's almost no animals. No reindeer, no elk. Not to mention the polar bears. What's left? Moss and lichen. You can't really relate to moss and lichen."

He lifted the plane higher again. "And you know what? I'm beginning to detest this place. It's rotting. You can feel it. You can smell it. And it's taking us down with it."

A radio message crackled. It was from a colleague of Rowland's at the Woods Hole Research Center of the National Wildlife Refuge.

"Return to base. Immediately. Return to base."

Rowland acknowledged the call and turned the plane around.

* * *

They landed. Helen left in a waiting car to continue her trip.

"What's wrong?" Rowland asked as a young man rushed out to meet their plane once it parked on the tarmac. With a glance at Lesley, the man pulled Rowland off to one side and talked softly but urgently. His hands were turning circles in the air.

"Christ!" Rowland muttered.

They talked more. Lesley heard Rowland say, "Put her in

isolation. We'll try Harbor View again. It's not enough for them to send us a doctor."

The young man went back inside. Rowland lighted a cigarette and shook the pack toward Lesley, who shook her head.

"Sounds like bad news," she said.

"It *is* bad news. The worst. I didn't want to tell you 'cause we're not sure what we're dealing with. But what the hell, we won't know any more months from now." He gave a world-weary sigh. "Follow me."

He led the way through a back entrance and into his office. It was piled with old files, articles, and maps. He hung up his coat, gestured to Lesley to sit down, and poured two cups of bitter luke-warm coffee. He took a swig, grimaced, and sat back in his chair.

"There are some effects of permafrost thaw that were unforeseen. A few people envisioned it but they fell off the radar. It was too . . . sci-fi, if you can believe it. You scientists can be a conservative lot, you know. You don't believe something until it hits you on the head and maybe not even then. You remember hearing about a massive kill-off of reindeer twenty years ago?"

Lesley did not.

"It was 2016. Thousands of them died off in the Yamal Peninsula in the Siberian tundra. At the time it was a mystery. Turns out it was anthrax. It was released from the permafrost after a warm summer that year. A century before reindeer died of it and now their graves melted. It got into the water and the food supply. Twenty people were infected, including a twelve-year-old kid who died.

"Here's the thing. The temperature's rising here three times faster than the rest of the planet. The permafrost is cold and dark—the perfect environment for the preservation of bacteria and viruses. We've found RNA fragments from the Spanish flu that killed millions after World War I. Who knows what else is down there? Smallpox. Bubonic plague. Giant viruses."

He stood abruptly and opened the door. "Leave your coffee here," he commanded. He continued talking as they walked downstairs and along a basement corridor deep into the bowels of the building.

"In 2005, believe it or not, right here in Alaska, NASA unearthed bacteria that was at least 32,000 years old. Thirty-two thousand years. Back then woolly mammoths were running around. Woolly mammoths, for Christ's sake!

"The thing is, our immune system can only protect us from diseases it recognizes. What happens if there are pathogens that have lain dormant for 100,000 years? A million years? We'd be totally unprotected."

He gave a weak smile. "It gives new meaning to Pandora's box."

Rowland came to a closed door and punched in a code. When the door opened Lesley heard the suction of a hermetic seal. They stepped inside, into a narrow corridor, and it closed quickly behind them. A buzzing neon burned overhead. Before them was a large window, thick glass.

On the other side was a patient's room, machines beeping, lines dancing across circular green screens in pulsating movements. On a bed in the center, attached to an IV and electrodes and an oxygen feed, lay a young woman, her eyes closed. Her head was turned away so Lesley mostly saw her hair, brown with streaks of gray. In the background she saw two half-open doors, each with the foot of a bed that also appeared occupied.

"That's Linda," said Rowland. "We've had three cases so far. Vomiting, bleeding through the eyes, spiking temperatures, one with open sores. No one can identify the illness. She's the fourth. She was the doctor treating them. We've got to get her to a real hospital in Seattle."

They stood there awkwardly for a few minutes. Lesley found it hard to know what to say.

111

* * *

Flying back to Washington, Lesley added "new and unknown dis-eases" to the ever-growing litany of the dreadful effects of a planet out of control. She had her article.

She wondered, for the umpteenth time, how it had all happened.

Over the past five years disasters everywhere had ratcheted up. Powerful hurricanes came barreling up "Hurricane Alley" one after another, not just in late summer and fall. Tornadoes, flash floods, and mudslides were so common and destructive the media often didn't cover them. The South and West were scorching with tem-peratures hitting 115 and even 125—so hot in places like Phoenix that planes couldn't achieve lift-off in air that was less dense and runways had to be doubled. Deaths from heat exposure were com-mon among the elderly.

People on the seaboards rebuilt their homes the first couple of times, then gave up when their living rooms showed successive lines of high water marks. Those who could afford it fled to the mountains. Those who couldn't stayed at lower altitudes, close to their laboring air conditioners.

And the changes seemed to take place so quickly. Looking back, she felt a wave of guilt. Perhaps she should have raised the alarm more urgently, shouted out at the top of her lungs, knocked equivocating politicians off their pedestals.

The problem was that the damage was incremental. It crept up. Just when you normalized some environmental outrage, you were confronted with a new one, which in turn was soon overshadowed by yet another, and so on. You only saw the deadly progression when you looked back.

Her plane landed and she collected her luggage. Paul picked her up in the Volvo. Textbooks were scattered on the floor—he was soon to be a freshman at MIT. On the way to Bethesda, he made a declaration: Besermann had offered him a summer internship and he was going to accept it.

She couldn't suppress a wince.

"C'mon," he complained. "This is what you've always been telling me I should do—save the world."

14

A YEAR LATER, ON A STEAMY AFTERNOON, WHILE SHE WAS FIX-
ing breakfast in a rented ranch house in Woodstock, New
York, Lesley received a strange telephone call. The caller refused
to identify himself, saying only that he had met her during "those
horrible days in the Arctic."

"How did you get this number?" she asked.

"Your office."

"What do you want?"

He was silent a moment, then the words came out in a torrent. He said he admired Harry Messian, who was a great man,
way ahead of his time. The work he did in Greenland was important, he was tireless in his pursuit of truth and he sacrificed his life
because of it. A great man.

"And so?"

"I'm convinced he was murdered. And I'm on the verge of proving it."

He refused to give details over the phone. "You never know
who's listening." Instead he was driving up right away from
Washington to see her.

"I need your help," he declared breathlessly. "I know you

114

revered him. And you had nothing to do with his murder. We've got to solve this thing once and for all. We owe it to him—and to ourselves."

In that, he struck a chord. We *do* owe it to Messian, she thought. She gave her home address in Woodstock, but had regretted doing so the moment he said, "I'll be there by ten p.m." and clicked off.

She looked out the window at the humpbacked mountains.

Long ago she had given up hope of getting to the bottom of Messian's assassination. Attempts to find out who was responsible invariably ended in a blind alley. Every so often she would call the FBI contact provided by Besermann years ago only to hear that no new leads had developed; eventually the agent stopped returning her calls. The photo of the half-severed cable, which she had printed out, had sunk lower and lower in a stack of documents until finally she relegated it to a bottom desk drawer.

She loathed the thought of dredging the whole thing up again.

Lesley's professional life was so hectic that she had come to the Hudson Valley for two weeks of peace. The town's oldster hippie vibe was soothing—it was hard, she told herself, to be frightened by people in sandals. She found a ranch house on the outskirts of town. At the moment Paul was away in Geneva, attending the plenipotentiary conference of ICCA at WHO headquarters. He was accompanying Besermann—his mentor, she thought bitterly.

Lately she and Paul had arrived at something of a truce. Months ago they kept arguing about Besermann. It was as if he were a ghost in their household, showing up to rattle his chains whenever they were getting along. She winced at the memory of one fight in Bethesda, two weeks before Paul went off to MIT.

It began when he looked up from his computer and said, with excitement, that he thought the projections of aerosol particles calculated by Besermann's team were wrong. That opened a door that should have remained closed. She struck a hard tone and said, "You know I don't like you working for that man."

"*That man*. You're the one who teamed up with him."

"That was long ago."

"You're the one who introduced me to him, for Christ's sake. You made him part of our life."

"But he's against me now. He's become an enemy."

"That's so petty. How can he be an enemy when we're all working for the same thing? Isn't it important enough to forget your squabbles? At least he's doing something."

"We're *all* doing something."

"But he's far ahead. He's in the vanguard. You're just sniping and finding fault. If we don't get this right, we're all doomed—that's what you keep saying."

"He's using you to get back at me."

"What! To get back at you. That's so typical. So self-centered. Don't you see how you denigrate my intelligence?"

"I'm not doing that—I don't mean to."

Angrily, he turned off the computer.

"I worry," she said. "You're getting compulsive again."

He began to leave the room and turned back. "Me? What about you? You're in no position to criticize me. You can't tell me what to do."

"I'm not telling. I'm just suggesting."

"Like hell." He shook his head in frustration. "You're not my mother."

It was like a cold slap in the face. She decided not to answer—they had been around this boxing ring many times but he had never thrown that punch before. They didn't talk for two days.

But lately things had improved somewhat. Paul had even picked fault with the methodology of Besermann's team and shared that with her, as if he wasn't really one of them. Yesterday he had called from Geneva to fill her in on the actions of the international convention, which officially launched SAAM, and his tone made light of them.

A great compromise, he had reported sarcastically. The Chinese got to build the rocket and the Americans got to construct the launch site. "Guess where it's going to be—right in the center of Washington. And they've come up with a name for the organization—the United Nations Consortium for Life on Earth. Get it? UNCLE."

Besermann himself came up with a name for the shield. The PR people had been scratching their heads. Nothing sounded right—all the proposed names sounded too threatening.

"But as the conference ended and we all left the pavilion we ran into protesters outside. They carried signs and banged on cars. It was a little scary. Besermann was in his limo and had to be rescued by the cops. They formed a ring around him to escort him to safety.

"Later, when I saw him, he was ecstatic. He said: 'I've got it. I've got the name. We'll call it the Cocoon.' " Paul laughed. "How's that for a eureka moment?"

On her side, Lesley didn't tell Paul that her fight with Besermann had reached a new turning point. She needed something solid to cast doubt on the efficacy of SAAM, and she thought she had come up with it.

Her institute's computers did a wide-ranging analysis of the shield's stratospheric effects; the finding was so significant she gasped at the numbers. She ordered a second run and there it was again: The data suggested that the project might have a tragic flaw, that a sulfuric layer around the Earth could lead to a breakdown of the ozone that absorbs much of the sun's ultraviolet radiation.

In other words, the plan that was meant to save the earth might end up killing it.

She had written a paper raising the possibility—"Is SAAM Lethal?" She hadn't published it yet, but it was ready to go and word about it was already getting around. At the same time there were rumors that her institute might lose its funding.

She wondered if that was a coincidence.

* * *

The stranger arrived sometime after midnight. She saw the car lights shimmer across the living room ceiling as he pulled up the long dirt driveway and parked.

When she opened the door, his fist was poised to knock. He was about six feet, his hair unkempt, his eyes narrowing behind a pair of horn-rimmed glasses.

"Come in." She examined him warily. "You had no trouble finding me?"

"I used a map. Don't worry—no GPS."

He shook her hand too hard and introduced himself. Jonas Anderson. He said he was the man who was monitoring the computer screen the night she was rescued.

"I wouldn't say *rescued*," she said. "I fought my way halfway across the ice." She didn't remember him.

"You don't?" he said, disappointed. "We all remember you. After you left it was a shit storm. Cops turned the place upside down. They never did come up with anything." He looked around.

"Care for a cup of coffee?"

"Maybe a drink."

She fetched the bottle of Jack Daniel's under the sink, poured two glasses, and brought them to the kitchen table. They sat facing each other. The light reflected off Anderson's forehead. He seemed ragged, at the end of his tether.

She asked about his background. He described working as a researcher in the Energy Department, his growing alarm at global warming, and the setbacks in his attempts to do something about it. He talked of purges of people who thought like him.

"It got so you couldn't speak of the future at all unless you were willing to enter their fantasy land. To say everything was going to work out—that was the groupthink. And as things got worse, the thinking was yes, okay, so maybe we made a god-awful mess but we'll find our way out of it. After all, we're the best scientists in the best country in the world. We can do anything. Those guys, they're blind. So arrogant. It got so if you spoke up at all, you'd be axed."

"But you managed to survive."

"Hardly." He stiffened. "I mean do you call being sent to the godforsaken Arctic surviving? I don't."

"It didn't seem that bad. You were doing research."

"You don't know the half of it."

He paused, taking a deep sip of whiskey. He had lost the thread of the narrative.

"You were talking about the DOE."

"You know, they even changed the science. They doctored the climate reports. They made black white."

"I know that." She saw him losing his train of thought. "You were saying it's a fantasy land."

"Right. Well, not everyone was aboard. Turns out there were some people like me, people who objected to the way things were going. We'd meet quietly, exchange ideas, kick things around. Sort of a scientific underground. And guess what we found."

"What?"

"The people in charge weren't just a bunch of well-meaning morons. They were organized. They were planning everything out. It was all arranged."

"Who were they?"

"A whole bunch. All kinds, I don't know. Former CIA agents, war vets, private security firms, you name it. And guess who was behind it."

"Who?"

"Vested interests. Oil companies. They no longer denied global warming—I mean, that was hardly possible under the circum-stances, was it? So instead, they did a 180 and embraced it—pro-vided, of course, they could be the ones to decide what to do about it."

He stopped to take another sip of whiskey. He seemed to be enjoying laying out the story, but he was rapidly getting drunk. He wiped his mouth with the back of his hand.

"For them the question became not how do we deny it, but how do we control it. Control it by making some electric cars, appease the public, pretend things are changing, but meanwhile continue mining fossil fuels and getting rich."

"But who's in charge?"

"I can't say for sure. But if we can solve Messian's murder, we can find out."

"You're saying it's the same group."

"Absolutely. They latched onto this idea of spreading sulfur to bring the temperature down. Pay dirt! Megabucks. They worked behind the scenes, getting the scientists to sign on, then selling the idea to the public. Why do you think there's no opposition? I mean, the scheme's bonkers—right?" He took a deep sip. "You remember the conference in that old mountain house in the Adirondacks?"

"Yes."

"Shortly after that, Besermann turned. Fell right into their pocket. Became a shill. Promoting a scheme to keep them in business."

She grunted, noncommittal. "You said you were close to solving Messian's death."

"His *murder*."

"I believe that. But I can't prove it."

"That Arctic operation was a sham. Officially they were there to keep an eye on Russian shipping. That was a cover. Their real job was to search for oil. They found it. They have plans to drill it."

"How do you know?"

"Because I was one of them. Or pretended to be. That whole group up there was part of it. Including that guy Henry Bloggert who tried to kill you. Turns out he was a sniper for Special Forces in Baghdad. Real bad guy. You're lucky you're not dead."

"How'd you learn that?"

"Like I said, contacts."

"So what about Messian?"

"They killed him because he was on to them. Now we just have to figure out who ordered it."

Anderson was slowing down. The drink was beginning to hit him.

"You don't know?" she asked.

"No."

She looked at her watch. She felt tired. "Look," she said, "I don't mean to be rude. But I've left that world behind years ago. A lot of this is intriguing, but it's hard to prove. It's late and I've got to do some writing tomorrow."

"No you don't."

"What do you mean?"

"You're coming with me. I've located a guy who's willing to talk. You met him up in the Arctic. One of the pilots who brought back Bloggert's body. A communications officer. He'll talk if you come with me. *Only* if you come with me."

She raised her eyebrows. "What makes you think he knows anything?"

"He just does." He continued, "Don't ask me why, but he trusts you." He finished his glass with a quick swig. "And guess where he is. That very same mountain house. The Tiger's Nest. He's waiting for us. Noon sharp. You in?"

"Let me sleep on it."

But she knew she wouldn't get much sleep that night.

* * *

They left early in the morning. Anderson asked her to take the wheel since she knew the way and he was adamant about not using GPS, but she suspected he was too hung over to drive.

121

It took her a while to get accustomed to the car, which was electric with a self-driving mode, which she had no interest in using. She couldn't bring herself to trust a computer-run hunk of steel and glass.

A few hours later, they were winding up the long, treacherous mountain road. Anderson slept next to her, snoring with his mouth open.

From a distance the mountain house looked the same, but as they approached it was apparent that it had weathered badly. The gardens had gone to weed, the windows were filthy, and one of the slate roofs was sagging in the middle. There were fewer than a dozen cars in the parking lot.

Oddly, the desk clerk held a room in their names. He insisted they sign the register.

"But we're not staying," said Lesley.

"I'm sorry, it's required, even for a short visit," he insisted.

They did.

"We're looking for someone by the name of Victor," Anderson said.

The clerk had not heard of the man. He had no message for them.

They sat in the lobby and waited.

"Keep an eye out," said Anderson. "You know what he looks like."

"It's been a while. I'm not sure I'd recognize him."

After two hours, they had lunch in the restaurant and went back to the lobby and waited some more. Anderson began pacing. From time to time he took a walk outside, and each time he returned looking more distressed.

"I can't figure it out," he said. "I'm sure I got it right."

An hour later, he gave in to a darker theory. "They must have got to him. They knew he was going to talk."

An hour after that, he said, "I don't like this. Somebody knew we were coming. They had us down for a room. And why did we have to sign the register?"

At six they decided to give up. Anderson was shaking his head and cursing as he walked to the car and opened the passenger door. She slid into the driver's side. She wanted to get home before it got dark.

The sky was black with clouds and the wind was up. The leaves were showing their pale underside. It was going to rain soon. She sped down the mountain.

As they came around a corner, she spotted something off to one side—a man, sitting there, holding a device of some kind. Maybe a portable computer. She couldn't get a good look. She had to keep her eyes on the road.

"Christ," yelled Anderson. "Slow down!"

But she couldn't. She hit the brake and nothing happened. The car was no longer under her control. She clasped the steering wheel tightly and tried to right it as it began to veer left. It moved, inexorably, stronger than she was, swinging into the oncoming lane and then toward the shoulder of grass and then across the grass toward the abyss beyond.

She fought it. The car shimmied a bit, skidded, then made up its mind. It swerved decisively and went sailing off the cliff, toward the tops of the pines fifty feet below.

They were in free fall. Silence at first, then floating down. Anderson screamed. She remained quiet, frozen, then felt her stomach rising up and her arms going weightless. A thought was trying to fight its way through the panic but it barely had time to take form. She had no chance to wonder about Paul.

What would happen to him without her?

PART III
THE ROAD SOUTH

2091
(YON)

15

DRIVING SOUTH OUT OF NEW YORK CITY, YON AND QUINLIN take an inland route because, Quinlin explains, the roads along the coast are liable to collapse.

The windows are open so a cross breeze cuts the heat. They go for hours on end without stopping.

Yon gapes at everything on both sides of the road, drinking it all in: the straggly trees—he thinks they're perhaps even shorter here—the junked cars, occasional piles of rubbish, odd things like an old washing machine that must have fallen off a truck.

The towns appear to be uninhabited, the houses collapsing against one another like drunks. Two cars pass them, crammed with gang members dressed in their distinctive colors—Bangers. Heads swiveling, they stare.

The silence begins to weigh on Yon.

"Tell me about Sessler," he says.

"What about her?"

"I mean, who is she exactly?"

"She runs the Resistance."

"Yes, but—"

"She does a good job."

Quinlin focuses on the road.

An hour later Yon spots a road sign depicting a car in front of a barrier. "What's that?"

"Roadblock."

Quinlin flashes a confident smile. He's already told Yon that their documents, expertly forged, are in order. They are traveling as the Brewsters, father and son, to visit relatives in Louisiana.

"This roadblock's official," he continues. "They might harass you, just for the hell of it. But they have their weak spots. It's the unofficial ones I don't like."

As he slows down, he rolls down the sleeves of his jacket so that both wrists are covered.

Four concrete booths spread across the road. Their windows are filthy and the frames are peeling paint. Between them, red and white striped bars block the lanes.

They stop before a bar. None of the booths are manned. From a blockhouse nearby come sounds of people talking. A man in a cap looks through a window at them but doesn't make a move. Five minutes pass, then ten.

Quinlin presses the horn, which gives a loud blast.

Yon jumps. "Is that wise?"

"Main thing is to act natural. A normal person sitting here would get angry."

Two Black Guards come out. Their uniforms are the same as those Yon saw at the homeless settlement but they are not wearing helmets and have no shields. One goes to Quinlin's side, the other to Yon's, placing his hand on the window frame. Yon sees thin black hairs sprouting up from his fingers.

"You in a hurry?" demands the one on the driver's side.

"My apologies, officer," says Quinlin. "My son is sick and I need to get him to a doctor." Taking the cue, Yon half closes his eyes, leans his head back against the seat.

The Guard near Yon removes his hand. The other one grazes a palm against a blast gun tucked into his belt.

"No reason to be disrespectful," he says. The other one walks around the car, then steps inside a booth and emerges pulling a wheeled mirror. He slides it under the chassis and begins to circle the car.

Quinlin watches until he's out of view. He hands the papers to the commanding officer and as he does, his left sleeve rises up, revealing a watch. With one hand the Black Guard takes the papers and with the other he lifts Quinlin's arm, raising the watch within a foot of his face.

"What time is it?" he asks.

Quinlin removes the watch and holds it out. "I can't read it from here."

The man takes the watch and slides it into a side pocket. He returns the papers. "It's late. You better fuck off."

Quinlin nods. The other man goes to a booth, puts away the mirror, and presses a button to lift the bar. Quinlin pulls away. After a mile he reaches inside the glove compartment and takes out another watch and puts it on. Yon looks at the gaping compartment and sees half a dozen more.

"Now you've seen the weak spot," says Quinlin. He reaches under his seat and pulls out an old gun, a revolver with a rotating chamber. "And if that doesn't work—"

"Wait. You can't use that. Promise me you won't use that."

Quinlin looks surprised. "Take it easy. I won't use it . . . unless I have to."

"Unless you absolutely have to. Promise?"

"Promise."

* * *

They pull over to sleep in the car. Yon, on the back seat, hears something way off in the distance, the sounds of wailing.

He sits up. "What's that?"

"Just a pack of wild dogs. We're okay if we keep the window up."

He sleeps fitfully.

They drive all the next day through the backcountry. They encounter few cars, and as the road narrows, they have to skirt around deep potholes and wide gashes. From time to time the road transforms into the main street of a small town. People sit on front stoops or the porches of stores and stare at them. Soon the town disappears.

The landscape changes into something resembling an empty battlefield. The trees are stunted and mostly leafless; some are only stumps. Dust covers the ground and drifts onto the roadside; the car raises it in tiny whirlwinds. When they reach a hilltop the view unfolds for miles and miles, desolation as far as they can see.

At one point they come to a wall. Behind it is a line of tall evergreens. When they pass Yon sees they form an arch over a well-tended approach road next to a brook. The entrance is flanked by stone pillars and blocked by a gate. On one side is a guardhouse. Way off in the distance is what looks like the top of a castle.

"An oasis," says Quinlin. "A gated community for rich people. You try to drive there and you're liable to get shot on sight."

* * *

Yon asks Quinlin when he was born and what things were like back then.

"More than fifty years ago. In 2039, in Missouri. That was the height of the horrors."

"The horrors?"

"When storms raged every day and oceans rose and trees fell and houses were demolished."

"So it was dangerous?"

"Yes, it was dangerous. People were killed, hundreds of thousands

130

of them, maybe more. The Great Cull, they came to call it—as if it was a natural thing."

"I've heard of the Great Cull. My grandparents used to talk about it."

Quinlin stares at the road ahead in silence.

"I mostly remember being afraid," he says at last. "Afraid that we wouldn't survive. That my family would perish. That I would die. Like being carried along on floodwaters and seeing everyone you love sinking away from you until they disappear."

"And what happened?"

"*That's* what happened. The flood came, took our house. My father figured this might happen so he built a boat and we all went on it. It rained and rained. Winds blew, tempests. The waters swirled and bucked and my parents fell off, first my father, then my mother. I was strapped down so I stayed on board. Two days later the raft ran aground somewhere south of Chattanooga."

"No brothers? No sisters?"

"No. In those days lots of people didn't want to have *any* children. I was a mistake."

"So what did you do?"

"I got as far away from that river as I could. And when I looked around and realized I didn't have a chance in hell of surviving—I was seven years old—I sold myself. To a man named Hardy."

"*Sold* yourself?"

"Yes. That's how slavery began again. People so weak and scared they signed themselves away, just to live. This man Hardy had a farm in Georgia. A plantation was more like it. It was on hills and the rains mostly washed off so the crops could withstand them."

"What did you do?"

"I worked like a dog. Planting, weeding, harvesting. For five years. Got not a penny, just lodging and three meals a day. Sometimes not even that. He was a miser. I hated him.

131

"One day I looked up. I was alone in a field. My back hurt. I said to hell with this. And I took off. I had squirreled away some things—extra shoes, a shirt. I took that bundle and I got the hell out of there. I was twelve years old."

"Where'd you go?"

"The closest city. Atlanta. Stayed there a couple of years, then bummed around. Years passed. I survived. I did some things I'm not proud of. But like I say, I survived, and *that* I am proud of."

"How did you live? What work did you do?"

"Just about everything, mostly construction—or reconstruction is more like it. The storms were still raging. Houses collapsing. Then things got rough—politically. The government tightened its grip. Emergency decrees—you couldn't do this, couldn't do that. All that crap. Pissed me off. I fell in with some people who felt the same. Over time we joined the Resistance and that's it—you saw the results in New York."

"My grandparents . . . the people who raised me . . . said the world was more advanced way back when."

"It was. We had phones you could carry around, call anywhere in the world. Computers you could find out anything you wanted to know. Lotsa stuff that's no longer around."

"How could they let all that disappear?"

"Bit by bit. Storms wreak havoc, you don't repair the cell towers. Lines go down, you don't fix 'em."

Quinlin is quiet for a moment, then continues.

"People don't have the get-up-'n-go to do much of anything anymore. In the old days, people used to *do* things. They'd invent things, accomplish things, try to learn things. They'd work hard. Sometimes they'd make art. You ever see any art?"

Yon shakes his head.

"Nope, all gone. People just drag themselves along one day after another. Trying to survive. Like zombies. Like they've had lobotomies.

"Good thing they produced gen-modified food and agri complexes or we'd all starve to death."

Yon wants to talk more but sees Quinlin concentrating on the rearview mirror. He turns. Behind them is an old car from the 2070s.

Quinlin pulls to the side of the road, leaving the engine running. He reaches under the seat, pulls out the gun, takes the safety off, and slips it back.

The car stops too. An elderly woman on the passenger side looks at them warily, and a lanky man gets out and walks slowly over. He has a floppy wide-brimmed hat, a beard that reaches his chest, and a weather-beaten face.

"How do you do?" he says, looking down. "Wonder if you can help us out."

"Maybe," says Quinlin.

The man explains. They are trying to find their son who's being held captive by a sheriff in a town not far away. But they have little money and—here he looks down again—they're running low on gas. Now his wife comes over. She has gray hair pulled back in a bun and wears a cotton dress with a faded pattern of flowers.

"Please," she begs. "Do you have any gas? We're desperate."

Yon goes to the rear and opens the hatch, where there are two jerry cans. Quinlin gives him a look but Yon says they're welcome to one of them. The man pushes his hat back on his head. The woman clasps her hands. "We can't thank you enough," she says. "We didn't know what we were going to do."

While Quinlin fills their tank, they chat. Their name is Evans. They haven't traveled much—in fact, this is the farthest they've ever been from home. Quinlin looks up at the gathering dusk.

"This is the worst time," he says. "All kinds of characters out and about. Roadblocks are dangerous. You should stop for the night, maybe join us. We can find a good place to bed down."

The Evanses eagerly agree. They drive on in convoy. Quinlin

knows the area and he takes the lead. They follow him down a dirt road that leads behind a cliff where they find a cave to sleep in.

They dig into their supplies, eat a few bites, then drift off to sleep.

* * *

When Yon awakes, the pale haze of day outlines the mouth of the cave. The others are bustling about.

The Evanses are anxious to be on their way, but Quinlin wants to scout out the terrain. The couple packs up and leaves after a round of awkward handshakes and well-wishes.

Quinlin and Yon follow the path to the top of the cliff. From here they can see for miles. There, down below, they spot the Evanses' car, raising dust as it leaves the road and turns onto the tarmac. It looks tiny.

"God damn!" Quinlin yells.

He grabs Yon's arm and points off into the distance. A mile or so ahead is a roadblock, a tree downed across the road. Yon can see two men leaning against it, wearing gang colors.

"Bangers," says Quinlin.

They watch, unable to do anything, as the car approaches, then slows down. The men motion it forward. It stops. Car doors flung open. The woman is yanked out and thrown to the ground. The old man rushes over to his wife, bends down, lifts his head to say something to the men. They point blast guns at them and fire. Flashes light up the barrels. The man crumples to the ground, the woman writhes. Bits of tarmac fly up around her.

The drama plays out quickly and silently. But soon the sounds of the guns reach Yon, standing helplessly next to Quinlin on the cliff, the *Ka-voom, Ka-voom, Ka-voom* that haunted his childhood.

16

YON IS IN THE DRIVER'S SEAT, PLYING THE ACCELERATOR, WOR-
ried that the noise of the engine will carry to the men around
the bend. He's scared. This is the first time he's driven a car. Quinlin
insisted that he do it, after scouting the roadblock. He came back
with what he said was a perfect plan, laying it out while giving Yon
a rudimentary lesson in shifting, steering, and using the brakes.

"Nothing to it," he said. "Except of course keep your head
down."

Yon is to give him a fifteen-minute start. By the clock in the
dashboard, he waits twenty just to be sure, his hands sweaty on the
steering wheel, going over and over the sequence: go around the
bend, take your foot off the accelerator, put it on the brake and
press down slowly, so slowly that you cruise to a gradual halt. Then
keep it on the brake and shift to neutral. Oh yes, and duck down
below the windshield.

He checks the clock again. Twenty-one minutes. He shouldn't
delay any longer—that'll increase the chances they'll spot Quinlin
sneaking up behind them.

He puts the shift in "drive" and feels the strong tug of the engine.
It jumps ahead faster than he thought. A flutter of panic. How do

135

you control this beast? He drives on, gathering speed, swerving from side to side on the road. The bend is upon him in no time. He slowly turns the wheel and feels the car respond, moving to the right—a little too much. He's almost off the road, corrects with a yank to the left, and gradually straightens out. The roadblock is ahead.

He's so preoccupied with driving that he scarcely looks up. When he does, he sees the bullet-riddled car in the middle of the road. One man is standing out in the open, hands on his hips, staring at him curiously. The other is half hidden behind the car, looking around the open trunk.

Yon drives closer, going too fast. Sixty feet away, now fifty, forty He takes his foot off the gas, but the car keeps going. He slams his foot down but scuffs the brake with the side of his shoe. The car lurches ahead—it slows a second, then lurches again and starts to turn. His foot finds the brake and he shifts to neutral. The car finally stops. He's way too close—maybe twenty feet.

He can see the men clearly, even read their expressions. The one behind the car has a rifle leveled at him, his head cocked as he peers through the scope. The other is walking toward him, casually, as if he were out for a stroll.

Yon ducks. No sooner is his head down than he hears a crack. It's distant and doesn't echo and sounds somehow too soft. A second of silence. Then another crack, this one louder, and an answering crack and then a fusillade so rapid it's impossible to tell who is firing at whom. Now a long silence. He lifts his head and looks over the dashboard.

The gunman is huddled on the ground no more than ten feet away. Not moving. He's hunched over, lying on one arm, apparently in a last-ditch attempt to grab his gun. He's on his belly and his head is wrested upward, his chin resting on the tarmac. His eyes are wide open.

Yon looks anxiously for the other gunman. He doesn't see him, not until Quinlin appears, bounding down and kneeling over the second body. He turns him on his back. Making sure he's dead.

Suddenly!—a flicker of movement. Yon sees it off to the left where the scraggly bushes are. A third man appears, walking stealthily, an exaggerated spring to his step to avoid making noise. He has a gun drawn and he's sneaking up on Quinlin.

Yon shifts and hits the accelerator. The car leaps forward, thrusting him back against the seat. He grabs the wheel with both hands. It's vibrating but he picks up speed so fast it's easier to control. The man looks up in alarm. He spins halfway around, takes a step to the side, then stands firm and fires. The bullet strikes the front of the car with a metallic thud. The man fires again. Into the windshield. Yon bears down upon him. He sees the man fling up his arms and then roll backward below the hood.

The car bounces up to the left. It hits a hump—tossing Yon almost to the roof—then another hump, until it rides down, balancing but still moving, off the road and hits a tree. Yon's head strikes the steering wheel.

Quinlin runs behind to check the body, then comes over. "You alright?"

Yon nods his head. He gets out of the car. His hands are shaking and he is ashamed of it.

"Good job," Quinlin says, putting one hand on Yon's shoulder. "You saved me." He touches his forehead. "How does that feel?" When he takes his hand away, Yon sees blood on his fingers.

"I don't even feel it."

"We got to wash it out. It'll be okay."

They go around the front of the car to inspect the damage.

"Hard to tell," says Quinlin, fingering a hole in the front. He tries to raise the hood but it's smashed tight. He gets in, starts the engine, backs up, and leaves the car on the side of the road.

"Let's clean up and get out of here," he says. "Maybe more of these guys around. But something we got to do first."

As they cross the road, Yon turns away to avoid looking at the body. The man he killed is just a heap of clothing in his peripheral vision. He feels a pounding in his ears. They pass the boulder and follow a path to a small clearing, a campsite. Quinlin rummages among the packs until he finds a canteen of water. He uses it to clean Yon's forehead. It doesn't hurt.

"Follow me," Quinlin says.

He picks up a shovel and leads him down another path to a dry riverbed. The Evanses are sprawled face down, blood visible on the back of their necks. Flies are buzzing above the two bodies.

Yon feels vomit rising in his throat and fights to keep it down. Quinlin starts digging on the bank where the soil is soft. They take turns. It takes a long time to make the graves four feet deep. The hard work calms Yon a bit.

Back on the road, Quinlin glances over at the three bodies. "No time to tend to these. Anyway, they don't deserve it," he says.

They drive in silence for most of the day. That night they reach the river that will take them south. Quinlin puts a rock on the accelerator and sends the car shuddering down a hill, where it disappears into a grove of trees.

They walk to the water. The river is wide here—so wide that in the dark they can't see the opposite bank. The current rushes by, lapping at the shore. There's a dock and tied to it are a dozen boats of all sizes and shapes. No one is around. They choose a wooden raft at the end of the dock, untie it, and push off.

17

THE RAFT CATCHES THE CURRENT OF THE MISSISSIPPI AND floats downriver. The flooding has widened the river so much the far bank is not visible. The water moves in swirling eddies, rising in bubbling arcs whenever it goes over a submerged tree.

Yon steers the rudder pole as best he can. After a while he gets the hang of it, moving it to one side and then the other, surprised at how quickly the V-shaped bow responds. He looks around the raft. At the rear end is a small green tent, hammered down.

"Just keep going," mumbles Quinlin. "Don't look back."

They drift for hours.

At times the water squeezes through gaps and speeds up. Once it sends a splash of spray over Yon's face. It takes him back to stories his grampa used to tell of rain—not the grayish fog-mist of the Cocoon, but a full-on deluge. He described lightning and thunder—a jagged slash of electric bolts followed by a fearful rumbling sound to make you think the heavens were breaking apart. Yon couldn't imagine it.

Grampa, he thinks, *if you could see me now*.

The Cocoon takes on the mournful rust-red color that portends evening, and the raft enters an area that was once a town. The tops of trees and roofs and lampposts rise above the water. It's deserted and silent except for the lapping of the water.

Yon maneuvers through the labyrinth until he reaches the top floors of a factory. He poles behind it and secures the raft, tying it to a metal window frame.

Quinlin stirs and stretches. Yon goes into the tent.

"We're in luck," he exclaims, emerging with a few cans of beans. Rummaging around some more, he finds some papers including a permit for ferry service that has a mug shot of the owner—a back-country man with a full black beard, a dirty cap pulled low, and dark sullen eyes.

That night, nestled inside the tent, they sleep soundly.

* * *

They leave at the Cocoon's first faint hazy light. By now the raft's owner—his mug shot keeps dancing before Yon's eyes—must have found it missing. They have to keep going.

At midday they come to an open-air market set upon a jumble of piers. They dock and climb up, threading their way through narrow rows of vendors selling cans of gasoline, rope, and tools. Sellers ply their trade sitting cross-legged before trays heaped with eggs, nuts, dried corn, and other foodstuff. The smell of smoke and oil is everywhere.

An old man stands in the door of a small shack, turning strips of chicken on a grill and bending down to blow on the embers. They hurriedly buy four pieces, feeling themselves watched a little too closely by two rough-looking men hanging around the dock. One is stocky with shoulder-length matted black hair; the other is wiry and muscular, a sleeve of tattoos covering one arm. As Yon and Quinlin eat and start back to the raft, they hear something at the end of the pier, a rustling disturbance and angry murmurs. Coming toward them is a pair of Black Guards. Both are small but their uniforms make them look foreboding. They're stopping people, demanding identification papers and handing out leaflets.

Quinlin whispers to Yon, then sidles over to place a thousand-dollar bill in the hands of the old man, who accepts it without a flicker of expression. Yon slips into the shack and lies down in a corner and the man tosses a blanket over him. Impassively, he continues grilling chicken.

The Black Guards arrive and stand over them.

"Papers," one demands.

Quinlin and the two dock men produce ID cards. The Black Guards hold them close, looking at the cards and then at the men, back and forth several times. They throw the cards down. One hands over some leaflets and they move down the line.

Quinlin grabs a leaflet and so does the man with the sleeve. It's a wanted poster: two fugitives, a man and a boy. No photos, only vague descriptions. Quietly he summons Yon from the shack. They wait several minutes until the Black Guards are far away, then return to the raft.

They're untying the rope to cast off when a thud sends the raft bouncing, followed by a second thud, even louder. The two men from the dock have jumped aboard.

"We're booking passage. Free passage," the one with long hair says. He looks around the raft, surveying the contents. "You can refuse. But you'll have to take it up with the Black Guard."

They hurry away down the river, the market on the pier getting smaller and smaller behind them.

* * *

Two hours later the river narrows and they come to a bend.

Quinlin steers the raft close to the right bank. The trees are bigger here, the branches hanging over into the water, forming a green tunnel.

The two men, lying down, suddenly look up.

"Hey," says the first, beginning to stand. He looks over at Quinlin, who is pointing a gun at him, and freezes.

"You swim?" asks Quinlin.

"No."

"Time to learn."

He walks over to him, spins him around, and gives him a push. The man tries to leap to the shore but falls short. The second man wordlessly dangles his feet into the river and slides in with barely a splash.

They pound and paddle, sending up spray, their shirts rising up on the water, and make it to shallow ground, then scramble ashore.

"You're finished!" shouts one, stamping his feet. "You hear me! You're dead! They're gonna be on your ass so fast."

Quinlin raises his gun and fires. He shoots up in the air, nowhere near the men, but the sound sends them scurrying for cover.

Only ten minutes later Quinlin and Yon come to another river town set out on a pier.

"Damn," says Quinlin. "If I'd known we were this close, I would have shot them. They'll report us in no time."

They make a plan. Yon will stay onboard, hiding inside the tent, while Quinlin goes in search of transport. Then they'll ditch the raft. Quinlin climbs a ladder to the pier and is gone.

Ten minutes go by, fifteen, half an hour, more. Yon feels drowsy. He's just drifting off when he's startled by a heavy footfall on the raft. He hears cursing.

He lifts a flap on the tent and peers out. A large barrel-chested man with a beard. The raft's owner! He's bending down, examining the bundles left by the two men. He lays down a shotgun while he tosses clothes into the air.

Quietly, Yon raises the back edge of the tent and lowers himself into the water. He feels it mounting to his waist and chest. He reaches back for his knapsack, then slowly pushes off and floats away backward, swimming with his free hand.

He fights to keep off panic. Above one or two people look down at him. He moves into the dappled half light under the pier where no one can see him. Behind, he hears the man, still cursing, rip open the tent flap and bang around inside.

Reaching the far end of the pier, Yon comes to a steep bank, grabs a root, and pulls himself up.

He must find Quinlin—stop him from going aboard the raft.

He stations himself behind a vegetable stand near the entrance to the pier. He waits an hour, then another. The owner on the raft doesn't stir. Yon walks out onto the pier and sees the man's boots peeking from inside the tent. Ten minutes later the two intruders hurry past. At the edge of the pier they climb down the ladder, out of view. Yon doesn't hear a thing but a few moments later he sees the raft moving out onto the river. The man with the tattoos is steering and the owner is seated on a barrel next to him, his shotgun across his knees and trained on the man's belly.

It's evening, growing dark. By now the raft is far away and barely visible.

Quinlin comes up.

"We've got a ride," he says. "A truck."

Yon points to the raft. As Quinlin peers into the gathering darkness, they see two white flashes. A second later, they hear the sounds. *Boom. Boom.*

First the light and then the sound—just like lightning and thunder, Yon thinks.

18

THEY ARRIVE ON THE OUTSKIRTS OF NEW ORLEANS AFTER FOUR days on the open road. The man who contracted to carry them in his pickup tried to rob them. From the start they were suspicious of him, so they took turns at night, pretending to sleep.

On the second night Quinlin saw him sneak into the truck's cab and emerge with an axe. He laid it on the ground as he rifled through their backpacks. Quinlin slipped out of his bedding, pulled his gun, and jammed it between his shoulder blades. They tied him up.

In the morning they threw him in the back of the pickup and drove all day and most of the night, arriving at their destination midmorning. They untied the man, tossed the keys in the bushes, and left the agreed-upon six thousand dollars on the dashboard. Then they walked to town.

* * *

New Orleans bears no resemblance to the city Quinlin described. It's relocated fifteen miles up the Delta, a shantytown of dirt streets, two-story shacks, and bars jammed in cheek by jowl.

"I'll be damned," he says, pointing to a sign reading BOURBON STREET. "They couldn't let that one go."

Passing a back alley they see three muscular men beating a skinny boy no older than Yon. They're shouting curses at him. He falls to the ground and they start kicking him.

"C'mon," Yon says to Quinlin.

"There're three of them."

"You got your gun. That makes three of us."

They move down the alley. One by one, the men spot them and the gun and they trot away down the other end of the alley.

Quinlin pulls the boy to a sitting position and props him against a wall. Yon buys a glass of water from a nearby bar. With a trembling hand, the boy drinks it. He breathes heavily, wipes a smear of blood off his forehead, and looks up.

"*No hice nada,*" he gasps. "*Ellos me han atacara sin razon.*"

"What'd he say?" asks Yon.

"They just attacked him out of nowhere."

"Ask him where he's from."

The boy understands the question.

"Colombia," he says.

They help him up and lead him to the bar, where he goes into the bathroom to check his wounds and clean up. He comes out to find three glasses of tequila lined up on a table. A thin boy with coal black hair, he smiles, revealing a gold tooth, and lifts a glass. They each down one.

His name is Pedro. More drinks. A toast, to helping one another. A third round, a toast to Colombia.

"Why you want to come here?" asks Quinlin.

"*Dicieron que la vida esta mejor.*"

Quinlin turns to Yon. "For a better life."

He says to Pedro, "We want to go there."

"*Donde?*"

"*Al sud.*"

Pedro looks puzzled. "*Pero . . . porque?*"

"For a better life."

They laugh but Yon stops abruptly. "We are serious," he says. "We want to go . . . right away."

Pedro looks down, also suddenly serious. "I can . . . help you. You want *El mercado de cabras.*"

"Goats market," says Quinlin. "Years ago they were called *coyotes.*"

Half an hour later, they follow him into the bowels of the slum. Yon sees Quinlin pat the small of his back where his gun is hidden.

Pedro's pace slackens. He approaches a courtyard, a small patch of barren earth, and stops in the shadow of a nearby building, jerking his head to indicate they have reached the right place. Quinlin presses a wad of bills into his palm.

"*Vaya con Dios,*" Pedro says, disappearing around a corner.

In the center of the courtyard two picnic tables have been pushed together, littered with bottles. Around the tables, in various postures of inebriation and stupor, sit eight or nine men and two women.

Quinlin puts a hand on Yon's shoulder.

"Stay here. I'll be right back."

He retreats into the darkness. Five minutes later he reappears, a bottle in his hand.

They approach the men. Two of three smugglers look up, expressionless. Quinlin puts the bottle down on the table and looks around.

Some of the men don't even stir. Others accept the offer mutely and examine the two interlopers with cold eyes. Quinlin explains: they are looking for a *cabra* to take them to the South. They're willing to pay handsomely.

"Let's see the money," says one.

"We don't have it with us."

"Where d'ya wanna go?"

Quinlin says, "Deep south. Ecuador."

Three men shake their heads. One whistles.

"Mister, you're going the wrong way," says one. "Everyone wants to *leave* the south." He spits. "Only three men can make such a trip."

"Who are they?"

"I can set it up for you . . . for a price. Pay me $2000 each— that'll be $6000 altogether—and you can talk to them. Hold a fucking auction for all I care."

Quinlin agrees to return tomorrow precisely at noon. He offers an outstretched hand to seal the deal but the smuggler just stares at it.

"Don't forget my commission or the whole fucking thing's off."

* * *

Quinlin and Yon turn up at noon on the dot. The courtyard seems less intimidating in daylight.

The fixer is there with three men. Quinlin pulls out six bills. The fixer grabs them and leaves.

There's no small talk. Quinlin sets down the requirements. He and Yon need to reach Ecuador as soon as possible. They'll pay a fair price.

"And how about coming back?" demands a heavyset man with a scrubby beard. "You won't be wanting to stay."

"We'll come back. But not right away. We've got to go inland. I don't know how long."

"So you expect me to wait for you, cooling my heels there?" His voice takes on a wheedling tone. "No fucking way. Count me out." He leaves without a backward glance.

The remaining two are interested. One is older than the other, with a worldly air. The young one is less quick to answer.

They turn to cost. The old one tells the young one to make a proposal first. He does. He'll do the entire trip, both ways, for fifty thousand. The old one steps in quickly.

"I'll do it for forty-five."

They turn back to the younger one. He pulls out a piece of paper and writes down various sums, calculating. It takes a couple of minutes.

"C'mon, for shit sake," says the other.

"*Hombre*, there're a lot of expenses. Give me time. It's important," he says. Finally, he quietly shakes his head. "I can't go any lower. It's a long and dangerous trip. Any lower and I can't guarantee your safety."

On the spot Quinlin decides. They'll go with the younger man. The older one leaves in disgust.

"What's your name?" Quinlin asks.

"Luther. Yours?"

"Brewsters," says Yon. "Father and son."

They discuss arrangements. They're to leave the following day and talk about transportation, supplies, and the route.

Yon can't help staring at Luther's cheek. It has a scar, deep and red, in the shape of a perfect X.

"Mind saying how you got that?"

"Snake bite. When I was young I used to camp out. One night I rolled over into a nest of copperheads. My brother cut my cheek and sucked out the venom. Saved my life."

He spits, a glob that lands in the dust. "My line of work, it's an advantage. Makes the fuckers think twice before jumping you."

19

THEY SLEEP IN THE HAYLOFT OF AN OLD BARN ON THE OUT-skirts of New Orleans. Luther found it last night after stealing a pickup truck and driving them to an abandoned farm.

In the morning Yon looks over at Luther, still sleeping, his mouth thrown open, surrounded by stubble. Not a companionable man for a long trek. But they need him to guide them across the No Man's Zone between North and South and to their destination, a city named Esmeraldas on the eastern coast of Ecuador. Last night Quinlin showed it to him on a soiled map he pulled from his pocket. Luther just grunted.

Yon plied him with questions. Where is he from? How did he get into this business? How does he know about crossing the border? He ran into a wall of resistance. The final brick was put in place when Luther remarked, "You stick your nose in other people's business, you're likely to lose it."

By way of answer, Quinlin patted his revolver and said, "His nose has a good friend who protects him."

They drive the pickup to the center of town. There, perched on the bank of the river, is a long, squat structure made of cinderblocks.

"Black Guard headquarters," explains Luther. He parks behind a junk-filled lot and tosses the keys to Quinlin.

"If I'm not back in an hour, leave. If anyone comes, beat it. Just drive away and don't look back. Go back to the farmhouse. I'll join you there—if I can."

He rubs a thumb and forefinger together. "Hombre, this part's gonna cost. A shitload."

Quinlin hesitates.

"You gotta trust me."

"Trust runs both ways."

Reluctantly, Quinlin hands him a wad of bills. Luther flips a forefinger though them, counting, but stops halfway. It's enough. He pockets the wad and leaves.

They wait. Fifteen minutes. Half an hour. After forty-five minutes, Quinlin stirs and looks out the window.

"We may be screwed."

An hour passes.

"Damn it. I should have followed my instinct."

An hour and a half.

Two hours and Quinlin reaches down to start the ignition.

"Wait," says Yon.

At that moment, a figure rounds the corner, walking rapidly. Luther is carrying a large package. He tosses it into the rear of the pickup and jumps into the back seat, a big smile on his face.

"Success," he says.

* * *

They rise in early morning darkness and head for the airstrip to catch a six-hour flight to the heavily patrolled Zone. Yon and Quinlin wear the flight engineer overalls that were inside the package.

"All you have to do," Luther says, "is look like you belong. Look bored. You've done this dozens of times."

150

Luther's uniform is a Black Guard border patrolman with a blast gun strapped to his waist. He caresses it from time to time.

They board a wide-bodied military transport jet. A dozen other passengers, most of them Black Guards, are already inside. Nervously, Yon takes a seat up front.

"Hey, shitface," yells a Guard with red hair and a face spotted with freckles. "Engineers to the back."

As Yon walks down the aisle, the Guard extends his legs and he has to step over them. As he does, his foot brushes the man's shin.

"Sorry," he says quickly.

The Guard starts to rise but a man on his left grabs his elbow and says, "Not worth it. You don't want another fight on your record."

The passengers strap themselves in along the plane's rib cage. Some close their eyes and rest their heads back. No one speaks. Yon is hopeful. All they have to do, he figures, is play out this charade without giving themselves away and then cross the border to Ecuador.

The plane lands with a series of skipping-stone bounces and they step out into what looks like a military base. Khaki-colored wooden buildings set back from tarred roads trimmed in luminous white paint. Luther sticks with the Guards and Yon and Quinlin follow the flight staff to a barracks. They toss their gear down on bunks and file off to a cafeteria.

Sitting across from one other, the two eat in silence. They eavesdrop on a nearby table where the Guards are ranting about "Southies"—who are dirty, lazy, and violent.

"Man, I'd love to shoot 'em—just one, at least," says one. Yon recognizes the voice—the man who accosted him on the plane.

"No chance," says another. "I hear they've stopped coming. They've given up. Or maybe . . . what some say, there's no one left down there. Place is all fucked up."

Finishing his meal, Yon watches another engineer bus the table. He does the same, carrying his tray to a conveyor belt in the corner.

On the way he passes his nemesis. The redhead glares at him as he scrapes his plate into a garbage can and stacks his dishes.

"Hey, shitface," the man shouts. He gets up and approaches Yon. "You're fucking it all up." Yon feels his face redden. "You put the small plates inside the big ones. Keep the knives and forks separate. Turn the cups upside down. Get it?"

Yon knows he's riding him. No one else has done it like that. He starts to leave. The man steps into his path.

"You a slow learner?" He cocks his head at his table. "Take mine." Yon hesitates, sees his right fist is clenched.

A figure rises up behind the man. It's Luther. He comes around and shoves his tray at Yon. "Take *mine*," he commands.

Yon places the dishes on the belt. Luther derides him, cuffs him on the back of the head and throws a dish at his feet. It smashes on the floor, spraying his shoes with shards. "Get the fuck outta here and don't come back until you learn how to clear your damn dishes."

Yon beats a hasty retreat as the men laugh.

Luther meets them an hour later behind a recreation hall. Daylight is waning.

"Thanks for saving me back there," Yon says.

Luther shrugs it off. He looks worried.

"It's gonna be a nightmare trying to cross," he says.

"I thought we're almost there. The plane landed in the southernmost section of no man's land, right? We're near the border."

"That's the problem."

Luther explains that the only sure way to cross the border is to go under it. For years now smugglers have been using a three-mile tunnel—but the entrance lies farther north in no man's land. To reach it, they'll have to travel by foot, moving *away* from the border.

"Everything you see, the alarms, the traps, everything, is set up to stop refugees going in that direction. So we'll have to take a roundabout route. We'll begin as soon as it's dark. I'll come to you in an hour."

As it turns out, he comes sooner. He rushes into the barracks, grabs Yon, and drags him into a closet. Quinlin stays on his bed. The door slams open. Four men charge in.

"Where's your buddy?" demands the redheaded Black Guard. Three others stand behind him. They're pumped up.

"Not my buddy," Quinlin insists. "Matter of fact, he's headed for the cafeteria." He laughs. "Maybe clearing more dishes."

They leave quickly. Luther and Yon leap out of the closet.

"Gotta leave right away," says Luther. He picks up a knapsack. "Grab what you can."

They race out the door.

* * *

They walk for hours through a terrain of tangled undergrowth and spreading kapok trees, more verdant than anything Yon has ever seen. From time to time they stop to listen; all they hear are bird songs. At some point their absence will be discovered and a general alarm will likely sound. After three hours they turn north and walk until it begins to turn light. They stop at the edge of a wide meadow.

"A minefield," says Luther. "It's seeded with anti-personnel mines. Step on one, you'll hear a click. Don't move. The moment you take your foot off, you'll be blown sky high."

He goes ahead, taking a slow step forward and placing his foot delicately on the ground. He is trying the impossible feat of making himself lighter, as if walking on thin ice.

He takes a second step. A third. He starts moving more quickly, careful to keep his balance.

"I'll go next," says Quinlin.

He sets out, searching for the footprints. He bends low but can't make them out exactly. The two move slowly farther into the field. Then it's Yon's turn. He places each foot carefully, like crossing a stream on stepping-stones.

They're about halfway across the field when it happens. A loud sound, undeniable.

CLICK!

They freeze. They know where it comes from. Quinlin. He stops like a statue, not moving a single muscle, slightly bent over like a runner ready to dash away.

Yon catches up to hold him steady. Luther turns around.

"It's your right foot. That's the one holding your weight. Pick your left foot up slowly and bring it forward. Whatever you do, don't move your right foot. And don't fall."

Quinlin's face is ashen. His skin feels alive and quivering—he can feel a breeze across the hairs on his forearms. Every cell in his body is on alert, seems to cry out. *Don't move! Don't move!*

"Relax!" shouts Luther. "I know it's hard but you got to. Relax."

Quinlin strains with the effort of willing his muscles to loosen. It's no good. He can't.

"Here's what we're going to do," Luther says. He turns fully around now to face Quinlin.

"At the count of three, leap up. Jump straight up, as high as you can. Don't think about anything. Just go for it. If you get high enough . . . well, maybe we can limit the damage to one leg. Understand?"

Quinlin nods. His jaw is set.

Yon sees Luther tense up. He lowers himself as he begins to count: "One . . . two . . ."

Luther lunges ahead, rushing at Quinlin, somehow turning his body to one side in midair. He hits him straight on with his hip against the midsection, just as Quinlin is rising up. They tumble in the air, tangling up, and they fall on the grass in a heap of legs, hands, heads.

There is no sound. Not even a click.

"A dud," shouts Luther. "The fucking thing's a dud."

They laugh, all three of them—hysterical laughter. Quinlin has tears running down his cheeks.

They get up slowly and resume the careful march across the meadow until one by one they reach safe ground. They collapse and lie there, until their heartbeats slow down.

They travel for another two hours, turning east. They spot military buildings ahead and walk casually on the cement pathways, trying to blend in.

Luther leads them to a large empty hangar at the rear of which is a hidden trapdoor. Below is a wooden ladder extending down into darkness. He motions them in.

The tunnel is dimly lit. Water drips down the sides and forms puddles on the bottom. They hurry awkwardly, not slowing down for twenty minutes. Then they walk at a fast pace, breathing with difficulty.

In less than an hour, they see light up ahead and, getting closer, catch their first breaths of fresh air. Yon is so elated he feels an urge to run toward the light. He can't hold himself back. Clumsily, he gallops and slips, sliding into Luther, almost knocking him down.

"Take it easy," says Luther, reaching to a wall to regain his balance. Quinlin barks a short laugh that echoes behind him.

They burst into the light.

"We made it," yells Yon. "We're in the South!"

PART IV

THE EXTINGUISHING

2045
(PAUL)

20

PAUL MESSIAN, NOW TWENTY-TWO YEARS OLD, SAT ON A COUCH in the living room of a two-bedroom brick house on Forty-Sixth Street in the northwest section of Washington, DC. Next to him was his new wife, Agnieszka—Aggie. She was lying down, resting her stocking feet on his lap.

In the dim room the television screen cast a ghostly glow over them.

They were watching the Launch. It was April 10, 2045—ten years after Besermann's conclave at the Metropolitan Opera House, which Paul didn't remember but which Lesley had told him about; four years after the founding of UNCLE at the WHO headquarters in Geneva, and also four years after Lesley's death.

The State set the scene for the Launch of the jet that would save the world with a slick public relations campaign. It was a full year past the internationally agreed-upon deadline for the flight. Pundits explained that the severity of the warming had skyrocketed—more than twice what had been predicted. It was not anyone's fault, and now the warming would be reversed.

On the screen, a parade marched down Pennsylvania Avenue, a lengthy succession of military bands, high-kicking marchers in

159

skimpy costumes and performers acting out historical tableaus on floats of red and white bunting. It was well into its fourth hour.

Paul thought the hoopla was pathetic. To him the smiles of the officials behind the bulletproof glass of the reviewing stand looked forced, rictus-like. And the enthusiasm of the announcers, pumped up by the State's ever-enlarging cadre of public relations specialists, seemed to be deflating by the hour.

"How many different inflections can you give to the words 'History is being made today'?" he said.

Aggie, without taking her eyes off the screen, smiled and dug a big toe into his rib. He swatted her foot away.

"Don't tell me you don't want to be there," she said.

"I don't. I promise."

He was only half lying.

Aggie sat up, nestled in his neck to give a kiss, and went into the kitchen to return with two cold beers.

True, Paul was of two minds. Of course he wanted the Launch to succeed, for the sake of humanity, but on a personal level, which he recognized as petty, he wouldn't mind seeing the damn thing blow up in midair. He and Besermann had had a falling-out. He hadn't seen him for three years.

He peered at the screen, searching for him in the reviewing stand. He spotted him, standing tall in the center. He was wearing a black suit—it looked to be the same one he wore to Lesley's funeral four years ago.

Paul almost shuddered. He recalled sitting in the first pew at All Souls Episcopal Church. The pipe organ played snatches of Mozart's *Requiem*. Alicia, his nanny, sitting to his left, reached over to touch the back of his hand. Earlier that day she had told him, in a flurry of tears, that she had decided to return to Australia.

A preacher got up and made some remarks. It was clear he didn't know Lesley. Gesturing extravagantly, with his hands making circles and swallowed up in the wide sleeves of a black robe, he spoke in generalities of her love and compassion. Others talked about her career, her brilliance, her work with volcanoes, and her passion to save the Earth.

Paul barely listened. Something was happening to him. He felt he was wearing some kind of helmet pressing in on his skull. His sight was fading—his vision narrowing on all sides until he was looking through a tunnel. Words and sounds became remote, like echoes.

At the end he sat there without moving. He couldn't move. Then he felt someone next to him on his right, a man, holding a handkerchief. The man wiped his cheek. Paul had been weeping, unaware. He turned. It was Besermann.

"Don't worry, son," Besermann said minutes later, guiding him down the church steps into a warm afternoon, through the crowd milling about. "Lesley and I, we had our differences, as you know. But we loved each other. And now that she's gone, I'll look out for you."

At that moment he hated him.

* * *

For months after Lesley's death Paul stayed in their apartment. He didn't touch her clothes, her high-heeled shoes and practical sneakers lined up on the closet floor. At first he tried not to think of her. Then he did an about-face and went over his memories one by one like a miser counting coins.

He replayed their fights. The more hurtful the argument, the more he obsessed in calling up all the details—where she stood, the angry words, how her lower lip quivered. How ironic that so many arguments were about Besermann. She had been right all along. She had seen the man for the preening martinet he was.

Her death was veiled in mystery. Was it really an accident? The stories about a secret tryst with a man named Anderson—a man he had never even heard of—infuriated him. It was impossible. It was out of her character. If she fell for someone she wouldn't run off to a cheap hotel.

Six weeks after her death he went to the mountain house road and examined the spot where she had gone off it, measuring the distance from the shoulder to the cliff—a full eight feet. He went home and marked the distance on the floor with tape, pacing it. How could she—so competent in everything—veer off the road by eight whole feet?

He found himself drawn to photos of towns and cities being flooded—Miami, New York, London, Istanbul, Buenos Aires, Sydney, Yokohama. He fixated on time projection sequences of peninsulas turning into islands—how when the water rises the land shrinks down at its lowest point until it loses contact with the mainland.

Like me, he thought.

During this time he still worked for Besermann. He performed backup computer calculations of the Cocoon—he resisted the term, calling it "the shield."

He had no friends among his co-workers and didn't think much of them. At meetings he stayed mostly quiet, slumped in his chair, his elbow on the table, his cheek resting in the cup of his hand.

The money was pouring in; ICCA had government backing and morphed into the Consortium, the American branch of UNCLE. Besermann was constructing a brand new building on the Mall with a penthouse floor reserved for his own office. He had no fewer than four deputies.

The day arrived when Paul ran the final numbers and found his calculations differed from everyone else's. They showed the aerosol density of the sulfur particles was insufficient to maintain the shield. He was convinced his were right.

He brought it to the attention of his manager and got nowhere.

He insisted on a hearing; the team convened around a large conference table to listen to his findings. Everyone disagreed.

It took him two days to obtain a meeting with Besermann. He took the elevator up twelve flights and found the man already installed in his half-completed penthouse office, looking a bit ridiculous with construction workers banging away around him. Besermann was polite but distant and made it clear that he was busy with other matters.

Paul presented his calculations, laid them all out on spreadsheets on his desk—a breeze through an empty window frame rippling the corners of the printouts—but Besermann paid scant attention. Paul had thought the figures would speak for themselves, but it turned out he had to do the talking for them and he knew he was too urgent, too insistent, losing ground.

"For god's sake," Besermann finally exclaimed. "Join the team." He wiped his mouth. "You're just like Lesley. Stubborn."

That day, Paul left.

He withdrew his modest inheritance from Lesley and bought a motorcycle. He packed up, closed the apartment, sent the keys to the landlord, and set out across the country. He had no plan other than to have no plan.

For two years he wandered the country, picking up odd jobs, talking to everyone he encountered, and avoiding the police and thugs.

He was surprised by how many people had seen families and friends dying. Sometimes quickly, burned to death in an unstoppable fire or buried in an earthquake. Sometimes slowly, languishing on a bed with bleeding sores from a new disease.

The official death toll was in the low tens of millions, but almost everyone he talked to believed it to be higher.

Cultists, doomsayers, and wild-eyed fanatics roamed the land. They preached a grab bag of gospels: the resurrection of souls in the stars, the Rapture, intergalactic mind travel, fifth dimension

End Days. They collected disciples and holed up in deserted towns in the mountains and abandoned farms in the valleys.

Paul made his way to a commune on the outskirts of Yakima, Washington, that was reported to engage in a serious study of cosmology. He arrived to find it had set down stakes in a former apple orchard. The leader, a charismatic physicist from Berkeley, welcomed him as a like-minded student of the skies. Paul noticed on their first meeting that his face seemed pale and drawn. The leader fell ill and within a week was bedridden in his small cottage on a bluff overlooking the apple trees. A week after that, he died.

On his first day Paul met Agnieszka Wychowska, the descendent of Polish great-grandparents who had immigrated to the West Coast. She had grown up in Seattle and was his age—twenty-one. Her face was broad, her blond hair hung to the center of her back, and she was unlike anyone he had ever met. Her inhibitions were nil, her curiosity relentless, and her insights sharp.

Their second night they went drinking at all three bars in the block-long dusty town. Between the second and third bar she pulled him into an alley and kissed him. That night they made love, easily and naturally.

When the leader died, they buried him in a graveyard on a small hill outside town. Most of the commune members had drifted away, so there were only half dozen people at the graveside.

They disinfected his cottage and moved in. It was basic with a small stove, one sink for dishes and washing up, and bunk beds. They put two mattresses side by side on the floor and bought canned groceries from a general store. Evenings they would sit out front, looking at the rounded volcanic hills in the distance and the decaying orchard below. The air was filled with the sweet smell of rotting apples.

She plagued him with questions: his interests, his ideas, his background, his parents, his fears, his dreams. She made fun of his remoteness. "Your shell is showing," she'd say, leaning over to touch it two inches from his chest. "Uh oh, a small crack here."

And he *did* begin to talk, slowly, choosing his words as if each one cost him. He talked about Washington, DC—how much he hated it—and about Lesley, who saved him, and even his father. That surprised him. He described his father's work, his studies on global warming, his defiance of the scientific establishment, and his mysterious death in Greenland.

"I don't know really know much about him," he admitted, suddenly feeling a hole inside he had never noticed before.

"Maybe not. But your voice is different when you talk about him. It sounds like . . . pride. You're proud of him."

That was a new thought for him, too.

He told her about Besermann and his own work on SAAM. Hour after hour he described the complexity of the plan and the intricacy of the research, until finally she pulled him close and said into his ear, "I don't get it. Everyone talks about the climate disaster. You're in a position to do something about it. And you throw it away."

"Their plan was wrong. It wouldn't have worked."

"All the more reason to stick with it."

Little by little, he came to a decision. He would return to Washington and try to resume work on the Cocoon. He asked her to come with him.

On the way back, crossing the Clearwater Mountains on the motorcycle, they took shelter from a thunderstorm in a rundown cabin. Thunder crashed overhead, and lightning bolts streaked across the black sky and singed the pines below. Rain pelted the tin roof. They clung to each other and fell asleep.

When they awoke and went outside, the clouds had disappeared. The world was painted fresh. The sun was setting. He felt something stirring in him, rising up from his tightened chest—a memory, the arousal of a deep emotion. What was it?

An image shot into his mind's eye. They were standing on some kind of ridge, he and Lesley. He was young. She was holding him

165

in her arms. Together they watched the setting sun as it sent out fingers of red, orange, and yellow. The colors played upon the bowl of the sky—a brilliant azure that faded into black. Aggie stood next to him and slipped an arm around his waist.

They returned to Washington. She was good to him and demanded that he be good in return. At times he felt his loneliness lessen. One morning, watching her wake up next to him—her limbs slowly coming alive—he felt he cared for her, perhaps even deeply. Two months later they were married.

* * *

At last the Launch parade ended. Paul and Aggie watched as the plane emerged from a large hangar. It was called *Le Sauveur*, the Savior—the name emblazoned on the sides of the nose—as a sop to the French who built part of the engine. A wide-bodied hulk, it was pulled onto the runway by trucks and sat there for two hours while tankers pumped in aerosol sulfur.

Paul got a glimpse of the black tarmac runway. It was straight as a ribbon and wide as a battleship—probably the only part of the project that was completed properly and on time. He remembered the arguments when it was first proposed for the center of the Mall. The idea, to promote it as key to national pride, seemed far-fetched at first. But now he realized the site—smooth, level, and empty— turned out to be ideal from an engineering standpoint.

From time to time the TV camera turned up to the stratosphere. The commentators noted that it was a perfect day with a bright, luminescent sky.

Finally, the moment of truth arrived. The countdown. The cameras zoomed in as the ungainly vehicle lumbered down the runway. It lifted off, almost as if reluctantly, clearing the trees and heading into space. Long-distance cameras caught it high in the sky as a white contrail streamed from its rear.

"Now, at long last, with the Cocoon in place, we will see a change," pronounced the anchor of USA TV, seated behind a desk in the studio. "Now, temperatures will drop. We have finally taken control of our planet and made it once again into a safe, sustainable home."

The camera switched to a woman in a sundress standing uncomfortably near the runway with the hot wind blowing her long blond hair.

"Over to Tracy," said the anchor. "Tracy, how long do you think it'll take until the temperature goes down?"

"Good question. I've talked to the engineers here at the Launch. As you might expect, they're not keen to give a specific date. But they say in general we can expect to see that thermometer dip down pretty soon now."

"And when it does, we'll be back to the good old days?"

"That's right."

"Good. Thanks, Tracy."

There followed self-congratulatory speeches, panel discussions on science and the cosmos, and ads mostly from the oil companies, interspersed with replay shots of the liftoff of *Le Sauveur* disappearing into the void.

"So," said Aggie, turning to Paul on the couch, "it's happening." She examined his face. "How do you feel?"

"Like another beer," he answered.

The TV scanned the reviewing stand one last time, zeroing in on the leaders and particularly on Besermann, who was sweating profusely in the hot sun, accepting handshakes and pats on the back.

"There he is—in close-up," Paul said. "You can really see what he looks like now."

She got up and bent close to the screen, then reached out a finger to touch Besermann's image. She reflected for a moment.

"All those times you described him, I thought he'd have the

face of a monster. He's just ordinary looking. He looks sort of harmless."

She was right. He was older now, fifty-five, with wisps of white hair clinging to his narrowed head. No longer fearsome. Paul took a long second look. With all these people saluting him and the fate of the world hanging on the enterprise he commanded, Besermann's face was flushed with pride. But Paul knew him well enough to spot the worry lines around his eyes.

Paul went to the refrigerator, came back with a bottle of chilled champagne, and poured two glassfuls.

"I guess you're right," Aggie said. "We should celebrate."

"We're not celebrating that."

"Oh, no. What—"

"Stay there," he said. He went to the front closet and returned with a large box.

"All my computer files and notes on the shield. I stashed them in the basement of my old place. I was afraid someone might have taken them but they were there."

She raised her glass and peered over the rim.

"You might as well call it the Cocoon," she said. "Everyone else does."

21

PAUL SUSPECTED THAT THE COCOON DIDN'T WORK, THAT THEY were "juicing" the temperature numbers. He waited for the call, confident that it would come—and it did. Could he stop by, say hello, take a look at the new facilities.

"And what do you mean coming back into town without getting in touch?" Besermann crooned.

Just hearing his voice thrust Paul back; he felt a rush of familiar resentments against his former mentor. For holding a whip hand over his studies, for denigrating him at work, and, above all, for driving that wedge between him and Lesley.

He showed up the next morning carrying a bulging briefcase. A guard at the entrance examined the contents, took his photo, checked it against a computer file, and showed him to a special elevator that whisked him to the twelfth floor. The outer office was resplendent—titanium chairs with deep rose cushions and the silence of a monastery. Three receptionists sat at bare desks and seemed at pains to look busy.

One, a slim young man in a tailored suit, showed him to a couch and offered him coffee, which he declined. Besermann kept him waiting ten minutes—the exact amount of time Paul had

169

predicted—before emerging from his inner office, his arms already extended.

"The prodigal son," he exclaimed, attempting to pull him into a hug. Paul resisted and Besermann let his arms drop, stepping back.

"Let me look at you. You're totally grown. It's been what, three years? Impossible. And how about me? Just the same, right? Maybe one more inch around the gut."

Paul looked at him. He did look older. And those worry lines— the wrinkles around the eyes—they were for real. When Besermann turned, he saw the smile fade and they came out in force.

The inner office was immense and palatial, centered on a mahogany desk that dominated on a six-inch platform. A bright Persian rug lay on the floor and two crystal glass chandeliers hung above. Gigantic abstract paintings decorated the walls except for one wall featuring the obligatory photos of Besermann and various luminaries—with him always smiling broadly for the camera.

Besermann guided him by the elbow to a wraparound window. He made a take-it-all-in sweep of the arm, clearly proud of the view, and studied Paul's face. The sight was indeed impressive: the hangars as large as movie studios, the air controllers' tower, and right in the center of everything the shaft of the sleek runway. It cut at a diagonal through what used to be grass and the reflecting pool, skirting to the left of the Washington Monument and heading toward the Potomac.

"We did it," Besermann said.

"Not we. *You.*"

"Come. It was a communal effort. Everyone did his part. Even you . . ." His voice trailed softly. "Or you tried."

Paul did not follow up the remark.

Besermann insisted on a tour. Leave the briefcase with my receptionist, he suggested, and when Paul demurred, he gave a slight rise of the eyebrows. They descended a glassed-in staircase.

On the floor below were the lesser offices of his deputies. On the floor below that, a cafeteria.

They walked through a passage to the cavernous operations center, which was empty, six desks sitting before an array of computers and banks of instruments and a large screen on one wall.

"You have to see the Launch from here to appreciate it," Besermann said. "Very exciting. Everyone pitches in to make sure it runs flawlessly."

A red electric sign above the screen displayed a countdown: SEVEN MONTHS, THREE DAYS, FOUR HOURS, TWENTY-SIX MINUTES. As Paul watched, the "twenty-six" changed to "twenty-five."

"The next Launch?" Paul asked. "Already scheduled?"

"No. We're just running some tests."

They took an elevator down and visited a third structure that was accessible by an underground passageway. This was the Security Center. Young men and women, in various uniforms, sat at rows of desks, working computers. Views from surveillance cameras covered three walls—sharply etched images of people walking on sidewalks, picking items off store shelves and placing belongings on conveyor belts at checkpoints.

An annoying yellow light flashed from a rotating disc in the ceiling. Besermann caught the question in Paul's glance.

"A warning that a stranger's on the floor," he said. "You."

Only then did Paul notice that the agents close to him had swiveled their computer screens out of view.

They went through another walkway to what Besermann called "our coming attraction." It was a vast chamber under construction. Workers were fitting compressed timber into the walls and laying concrete for banked tiers of seats.

"The new center of governance," pronounced Besermann. "The chamber of the new Inner Council of the Consortium, the ruling body."

Paul had heard increasing references to the Inner Council on State news broadcasts.

"Who's on the Inner Council?"

"Representatives of all the major interests."

"And what does it do, exactly?"

"It sets national priorities. Not all the duties are spelled out. We're still feeling our way—the whole thing's so new."

"Is it more powerful than the White House? Congress?"

"Well, not exactly. They're both represented on the Council. But to be frank, they have been a bit subsumed lately. With things going the way they are, somebody has to be in a position to make decisions, and those decisions have to be enforced.

"You know why it took me ten years to get this off the ground? The presidents dragged their feet. Couldn't come to a coherent position. Couldn't say yes or no. Couldn't even say maybe. And Congress . . . forget it."

He stopped as if he had a spontaneous idea. "Tell you what. We've got a roof garden. Lovely view and a little coffee bar. Let's go there."

The view *was* lovely—panoramic. Paul could see the Capitol dome and the flag on top of the White House hanging limp in the breezeless evening.

Above he saw bits of the Cocoon, a vague grayish haze blanketing the sky. It appeared thicker in some places than in others. Through it the sun burned orange and yellow.

Paul stirred his coffee. He wondered if Besermann was going to bring up Lesley.

Besermann asked him how he had spent the past few years.

"Getting to know the country," he replied. "It pays to get out once in a while. You should try it. It's a learning experience."

"What have you learned?"

How to answer? How to say it all?

"For one thing, the country is falling apart. Physically. Cities are underwater. Farms failing, crops wilting. Stores are poorly stocked. The damage from storms hasn't been fixed. In some places trees aren't even cleared off the roads, and the streets are buck-ling. Rivers have flooded everywhere. They consume whole towns. Tornadoes come through like avenging giants. Believe it or not, they do sometimes leave cars in trees.

"This chaos—it's dangerous. I've seen dead bodies lying around—not many, but no one bothers to pick them up. Dogs are turning wild. They roam in packs.

"Crime is up everywhere. In Oakland, in Piedmont, I first saw houses that had front yards inside cages. Fencing on all sides, even the top. Now those house cages are appearing in other cities.

"Things don't work. Cell phones don't—the towers are mostly down. Computer networks go in and out—I noticed some of your surveillance screens downstairs were dark—I'm sure you've thought about that. It's because those cameras are down, too, in lots of places.

"People are fearful and resentful. They don't get any real news—the papers are long gone and the State news is crap. No one believes it. All kinds of stories and rumors circulate.

"One thing is certain: They don't think much of you people here in Washington. Know what they call you? *The Power.* Just those two little words—they sum it all up. Don't take the nick-name as a compliment."

Paul stopped talking. He could have gone on—there was a lot more to say—but he wasn't sure how much of it was registering. Besermann seemed a bit deflated, sitting there with his head down, but he also seemed somewhat distracted, as if he had something else on his mind.

A full minute passed in silence.

"So when are you going to ask me?" Paul demanded.

"Ask you what?"

"For help."

Besermann lifted his cup and took a final sip. He exhaled, lifted his head, and looked off into the distance, over his domain.

"Perhaps you *could* lend a hand."

"What's the problem?"

"Not a problem exactly. We just need a readjustment."

"Readjustment?"

"Yes. The liftoff went perfectly. The jet performed reasonably well—it carried the large payload easily, which was a concern. The aerosol formed particles, which was an important part of the whole plan."

He paused. "The problem seems to be something else. The temperature has not dropped. The particles are dispersing . . . *without doing their job.*"

He emphasized the last part of the last sentence, as if unburdening himself in a confession, then fell quiet.

"I could have told you that," said Paul. "In fact, I did."

"I know."

"I warned you."

"I know. But no need to hash over the past."

Besermann looked depressed. But Paul felt no sympathy for him. He opened his briefcase and pulled out stacks of charts and calculations and computer printouts and placed them on the checkered tablecloth one by one, like a poker player laying down a winning hand.

Besermann considered the batch of documents, stared at Paul for a moment, and said, "I remember it." He looked up at the swirling blur of the Cocoon, then back at Paul. "What do you want?"

"First of all, an apology."

"For what? Not listening to you?"

"For openers, yes."

"Okay, you have it."

"Where? Why don't you say the words?"

"I'm sorry."

"For what?"

"For not listening to you, for not supporting you, for not backing you. For letting you leave."

The words were right but they didn't really satisfy. Paul thought of raising the issue of Lesley, the way Besermann had treated her. But he let it go. He remained silent for several minutes, enjoying watching Besermann squirm.

"I'll help," he said finally.

They worked out the terms. Paul would come on as project manager. He would have total control over every aspect of the next Launch. He refused to get involved in the management side—overseeing personnel, budget, public relations, security, or liaison with government figures. That was fine with Besermann.

Paul began to put the documents back in his briefcase. He read in Besermann's manner—a slight reddening of the cheeks—that something else remained to be settled and stopped and looked at him.

"Just one thing," Besermann said in a soft voice. "My office—I want to keep it."

Paul couldn't help but give a short laugh, which sounded more like a snort.

"You like your office. I don't wonder." He paused, as if considering the request. "You can keep it." He added in bitter mockery, "It's a penthouse. How could I possibly kick you upstairs?"

* * *

Paul drove a hard bargain and he got what he needed from Bessermann: funds, ample working space and personnel. Besserman even lent him what he insisted were his two most effective deputies—Jeffrey Slatter and Maximus Dodd.

To Paul the two looked like bureaucrats. He didn't think much of their technical abilities but he soon discovered they were able to deliver something more important: whatever he demanded in the way of infrastructure and equipment. And he demanded a lot.

He set up office in the floor below Besermann, combining the physical space that belonged to the two other deputies, who were fired.

He revamped the Control Center, dispensing with the six interconnected workstations in favor of a single command pod. It would have all the data displayed in one central location and access to the most advanced computer. That was where he would oversee the next Launch.

He assembled a team of six flight engineers to overhaul *Le Sauveur*. He ordered them to take it apart and rebuild it from scratch. They were to include improvements, which he designed himself—notably to enhance the complex sulfur release mechanism.

Finally, he ordered the construction of an experimental chamber to conduct aerosol tests. It was to be an enclosed globe three stories high. It would replicate in miniature the planet's weather and cloud formations, with all the attendant temperature variations, in altitudes ranging from four miles to twelve.

This last item prodded Besermann to meet for another cup of coffee. Was it really necessary? It wasn't the cost—"hang the cost," he said—so much as the delay. "It's bound to hold things up. We're in a race against time."

"Time is not the only factor," replied Paul archly. "Quality control is more important." He drew on a napkin. "Envision a graph. Time is the Y-axis. And Quality is the X-axis. Anything less than a 75-degree increase in Quality is unacceptable."

"Unacceptable?"

"Yes. You're lucky people didn't revolt at the first failure. If there's a second one you'll lose all control."

22

"I HAVE TO SAY," SAID AGGIE, "THESE PR PEOPLE DON'T SET A LOT of stock in telling the truth."

They were having evening cocktails on the porch of their new apartment on Dupont Circle.

The vodkas at the end of the day had become their routine, almost a ritual. It was a time to shut the world out, to talk, now that Paul was responsible for the Cocoon. Two and a half years had passed since Besermann had asked for his help.

Paul turned to face her as she continued. "I don't know if I ever mentioned this, but I was told that some people there . . . a lot of them, actually . . . proposed insisting that the first Launch worked, that the temperature was really going down. That no matter what it felt like, the world wasn't as hot. Imagine." She popped an olive into her mouth. "Proponents of 'the Big Lie.'"

Paul had never doubted that his first Launch, fourteen months ago, would be a success. The results of the testing globe made him confident that he could create a sulfur band with properties stable enough that it would endure for at least two years.

He had prepared meticulously. Every detail was referred up the chain of command to his desk. At his insistence the flight was to be performed quietly, with none of the glitzy celebration that had attended the first one. On Launch day, June 20, 2046, he sat in his command pod and guided the operation as coolly as if he were flying the aircraft himself. It worked.

Right away the sky clouded over. One week later the temperature began to drop. In a month it went down a full degree Celsius, 1.8 degrees Fahrenheit. The PR division of the Consortium cheered. They constructed a thermometer two stories tall on the edge of Lafayette Park to dramatize the success. State workers were recruited to crowd around it while a pretend ball of mercury continually dropped down.

Besermann tried to take credit for the success—he pretended he was calling the shots. But Paul undercut him. He would expose his ignorance by posing arcane questions—"tell me, what's the velocity of the jet as it reaches the cruising point?"—in front of a group of co-workers.

Paul didn't court publicity but his stature was high in the corridors of the Control Center. No one really knew much about him. He liked being the power behind the scenes. He liked people deferring to him. The word went around quickly: If you want something done, go to him. Did you know he was the son of the great Harry Messian?

Meanwhile, Aggie took a job with the new Office of Public Information. She explained she wanted to do her part and was interested in learning the techniques of gauging public sentiment. It was important to know what people were thinking. She was naturally curious and good at striking up conversations. She took the job in her maiden name.

At first, Paul had not wanted Aggie to work for the government, but he soon realized her work could be useful to him. It was critical to know the public sentiment and to shape it. That was true for any leader who wanted to accomplish great feats. She would be his eyes and ears.

With the disintegration of digital networks and the collapse of social media, the authorities were rendered deaf. They no longer had their collective finger on the pulse of the nation. The old techniques, like going to meetings and planting agents and eavesdropping on strangers, were back in vogue.

Everything that Aggie heard at work and overheard on the streets convinced her that her husband should be concerned about public opinion. There seemed to be a barely perceptible undercurrent of anger that could rise or fall but never go away completely.

"Sometimes I think people are perpetually enraged," she told Paul. "They demand to know *why*. *Why* has this disaster happened? *Why* was nothing done to stop it? *Why* did the first *Le Sauveur* fail?"

And oddly, she continued, the success of the Launch and the drop in temperature seemed to have done little to assuage the anger.

"Paul, you're not listening," she said. "I bet you didn't hear a word."

"No, I did," he said.

"Well what do you think?"

"I think if the next one doesn't work, we're in deep shit," he replied as he went to fetch another vodka, neglecting to ask her if she wanted a refill.

* * *

Six months passed. The next Launch was held and it, too, seemed to work. It went off without a hitch, but the success didn't bring Paul much solace. He was nagged by a new doubt, as he sat in his office and gazed out over the Launch site.

As he had expected, the Cocoon had cleaved the world's weather pattern in two, separating the hemispheres. In the North the temperature dropped a cumulative 2.1 degrees Fahrenheit. In the South—well, that was not his problem.

Of course State media played the improvement for all it was worth. TV showed testimonials from everyday people—families picnicking under trees, construction workers resting on the job, children racing after a jingling van for ice pops. Their smiling faces almost seemed genuine.

But Aggie told him that the wave of gratitude was only a blip. The poison of disillusionment was leaking back into society. For one thing, the extreme storms hadn't fully stopped. An occasional forest fire or hurricane still rose to send people scurrying for shelter. Droughts lessened but nothing could make the land bloom. For another thing, the damage already caused by the weather dislocations was so vast it couldn't be easily rectified.

"In lots of places houses and office buildings have collapsed. Streets, wires, electrical lines, they're a mess. Look at the Washington Monument. It's got a big hole at the top. You don't think people notice? Life is still miserable for most of them."

Paul didn't like her tone—insistent, as if he himself were somehow responsible. She had no appreciation of his work and the strain he was under.

No wonder their evening tradition of drinks on the terrace had begun dropping away after only six months. So had their lovemaking.

But there was a bigger problem that dwarfed everything else and was so serious he didn't confess it to anyone. This was the kernel of doubt that was eating away at him—the timing of the Launches. His second Launch had been necessary twenty months after the previous one, not twenty-four months as his calculations had insisted. Would they need to send up a plane seeding sulfur more and more often to keep the Cocoon functioning? And if so, what would happen?

As he looked out the window he could see it hanging in the air, a large yellowish-gray bulbous haze that dimmed the sun. He kept wondering: *What happens if the haze keeps getting thicker?*

On the spur of the moment he decided to go for a walk. He took the elevator down and told his security guards not to accompany him. He could walk unimpeded because so few people knew who he was—his photo never appeared in the State media.

He felt a brief moment of freedom. He looked closely at the faces of the people he passed. They were hard to read. Most were not smiling—but when did people really smile?

He strolled along the edge of the Launch site until he came to the bit of the Mall that remained. The heat was oppressive. The grass was gone, replaced by parched brown earth.

He looked up at the Cocoon. It was not the thin hair-like cirrus cloud that Besermann used to invoke so poetically. It seemed more of a mass, a ceiling that was pressing down. Psychologically, it seemed to be holding the heat in instead of bringing relief.

He came upon an elderly couple sitting on a bench. The man wore a thin suit with a fake rose in the lapel. The woman had a elegant dress and waved a fan in her right hand.

"I just miss it terribly," said the man. The woman agreed. "I swear, sometimes I feel such a longing"—she put her left hand on her bust—"I feel my heart could break."

Curious, he took a seat on a nearby bench.

They were recalling places they'd been, islands during their travels, beaches and sunsets. Their reverie made them seem lost in the past.

Paul listened avidly but he couldn't quite grasp the reasons for their nostalgia, the thread that made their commiserations hold together. He didn't understand until the end, when they rose to leave. With a sigh, the woman tilted her head back and closed her eyes. A momentary look of contentment bathed her features, then stole away as she opened them.

"You know what I miss even more than the sun," she said. "The color of the sky—that thrilling, glorious color. It seemed to go on and on forever and it made you glad to be alive."

Paul continued walking until he reached the monument. It was cracked and pocked by dark rectangles and at the top there was a gaping hole where slabs of marble had fallen off. Aggie was right. It *was* ugly. But so many things needed repairing; it wasn't even at the top of the list.

His eavesdropping confirmed his fears. There was a growing sense of restlessness. The public mood was turning sour. No one ever criticized the Power openly. But how do you know what people are really thinking? What signs do you look for?

The media fought to keep up an optimistic front, extolling the Cocoon and explaining that it would take time for the climate to settle down. But the message didn't seem to take. People felt something was wrong. Something was missing from their lives. A vague listlessness was seeping into everyday existence.

Paul stopped in his tracks. He didn't doubt the public mood, because at times—like right now—he himself felt it. Where did it come from? Could it be the sky? Did people miss the sky?

He would ask Aggie.

* * *

She was waiting for him in their apartment. She met him at the door with a kiss that struck him as perfunctory.

He sank into an easy chair, fatigued from his unsettling day, and said he would like to ask her a question. She looked at her watch and said, "Can it wait?" She was eager to show him an encounter she had had that day in her opinion outreach, an interview with a couple she thought might be eye-opening for him.

"Shit," he mumbled.

A screen descended and she switched on a projector.

A couple was sitting in a restaurant, leaning close to one another, talking.

They were identified in a caption as Suzanne and Kurt Zeger.

Aggie was interviewing them, drawing them out. They were remarkably unguarded about their past. They were both academics from Toronto who had decided to give up "the ivory tower" to work the land on a farm Kurt had inherited in Nova Scotia, but had found it impossible to make a living as the crops withered or flooded. They had come to Washington some years back—the date remained vague, as did many things about them—as passionate advocates to do something about global warming.

"We wanted to be freelance lobbyists, to try to reach someone in the government. To knock sense into their heads," explained Kurt.

"We figured somebody in power had to be told what was going on," said Suzanne. "Somebody had to do something."

"But we couldn't get a hearing," put in Kurt. "Unless you count a low-level receptionist at the Department of Agriculture, who took down our names and interviewed us in a room that probably had a hidden microphone."

"You can see how naïve we were," she added. "For weeks afterward a relay of gray vans parked across the street from our rented condo. Talk about surveillance."

Over coffee Aggie asked them, "How about now? The temperature's dropping. Do you go back and see the result?"

"We've been. Not good at all," said Suzanne. "This so-called Cocoon is a travesty."

"The crops are worse than ever," said Kurt. "The blueberries are tiny and the vegetables tasteless. The surrounding forest is dying. Trees are losing bark, branches cracking off, and new shoots grow in small. Some say animals are shrinking."

Paul was shocked that they were so openly critical. Even Aggie seemed nonplussed.

"So why are you still here?" she asked.

They responded in general terms about "pursuing an educational campaign" and "laying the groundwork for change."

The screen went dark. Paul was in a bad mood. That couple was dangerous. They would bear watching. How many people thought like them?

Aggie, on the other hand, seemed excited, glad that she had presented him with some unorthodox views. She turned to him and said, "Wait. You were going to ask me something, weren't you?"

Paul shrugged. "Nothing important."

* * *

Eight months later another Launch, his third, was held. The moment the jet lifted off Paul turned to the TV with the thought that it might give him an insight into the public mood.

He didn't have to wait long for an answer. At the earlier Launches, people used to gather on a public square near the site, a crowd of four or five thousand. This time, he could tell from a surveillance camera, few showed up. The State broadcasters kept the gaze of the TV cameras averted from the nearly empty plaza.

But down a side street came a small group, walking quickly. A camera turned on them as they reached the square. A woman hurriedly pulled a banner from under her coat and held it in outstretched arms. Another held the other side. It read DOWN WITH UNCLE. Four police officers rushed over and lunged at her. She collapsed under a rain of batons and was dragged off.

Other protesters fought back. The camera swerved away but it was too late. Millions saw the melee of fists and police batons.

23

S IX YEARS LATER, THE INNER COUNCIL HAD BECOME THE MOST powerful institution in the country and Paul Messian the most powerful person. Now, as the body of twenty-one officials was meeting in an emergency session to deal with public unrest, he looked around at his fellow councillors. Like most days, he was filled with scorn for his colleagues. He sat slumped in his chair, just like the old times when he was a junior researcher on Besermann's team. Now Besermann sat in the center of the Presidium, wielding the gavel of Chief Councillor.

The year was 2056. With the sun's blazing rays dulled, the temperature in the Northern Hemisphere was under control. The Cocoon was more or less stable, but to keep it that way they had to schedule more and more flights, and its mass was growing ever thicker.

Paul still could not confess his fears about this to anyone, not even Aggie. Their nightly talks were long since past. She no longer shared her thoughts on the public reactions to the Inner Council dictates, and they no longer had drinks on their balcony.

This session was critical. From the time Paul first spotted the abortive march after his third Launch, public unrest had not gone

185

away. It would seem to disappear for a while but then resurface in a new guise—a demonstration in an unexpected place or a sudden plague of graffiti on city walls.

The persistence of the protests had led to the downfall of the presidency and the houses of Congress. It was obvious that the elected bodies lacked the will or the means to deal harshly with subversive elements that threatened the life-saving Cocoon. The Inner Council of the Consortium assumed more and more power, arguing force majeure. It prevailed upon the Supreme Court to change the Constitution to permit it to take "swift and actionable decisions" without the checks and balances of the legislative and executive branches.

Paul was now famous—or infamous. He had joined the majority two years ago in promulgating emergency decrees to push through the changes. His declaration—"freedom is like pocket money; you have to save some to be able to spend it later"—was often cited to back some proposition or other.

This session was called after a dozen protesters had broken through the perimeter of the Launch site, smashing four windshields on black Range Rovers and tossing a Molotov cocktail onto the runway before escaping. The damage done by the masked protesters was negligible—it was their brazenness that was upsetting.

Speaker after speaker voiced the fear that the public unrest would grow and, as one so-called "hard head" put it, "metastasize into a full-blown cancer. We must recognize the resisters for what they are: germs on the body politic. We must wipe them out before they unleash a monstrous epidemic."

He sat down to nodding heads and resounding applause.

Paul was wary of the "hard heads." They were closely allied with the Security Forces. Paul had heard the rumors that the troopers were getting ever more heavy-handed, that "enemies of the State" were taken to the basement of the old Hoover building on Pennsylvania Avenue for rough interrogations.

But Paul wasn't loyal to the opposing faction either, the "traditionalists" who were more reluctant to crack down and spoke of the need to loosen State controls and to appease the public by improving living conditions now that the temperature had stabilized.

They were noticeably subdued during this session, except for one former senator who had been appointed to the Inner Council when he turned against the then president.

"We must use our power wisely," he intoned. "History is not kind to dictators."

Finally Besermann banged his gravel and announced he would advance proposals to deal with the crisis. Paul leaned forward intently. *Let's see what he can come up with,* he thought.

Besermann began in a low key. In dry tones he read a lengthy police report on the protest. It concluded with the admission that so far the authorities had no idea of who had tried to vandalize the Launch site.

"And what's worse," he said, raising his voice, "we assume the vandals must have been seen by some of our citizens. And no one—absolutely no one—turned them in to the police."

"What do you suggest we do?" shouted out a member of the Council.

Besermann summarized a recent research paper entitled "To Restore Public Security." Its critical point was that the police alone could not be expected to maintain order. What was required was the creation of an elite paramilitary force with expansive powers to "suppress demonstrations and disorderly outbreaks." It would be called the "Black Guard."

Besermann threw himself into a sales pitch. He thrust his chin out and deepened his voice as he read out the fine points of the proposal. He proposed placing the Black Guard under the aegis of a security thug named Oswald Magus, who stood up in the gallery to a round of applause.

Then, to drive home the need for action, Besermann showed

a brief film clip of the demonstrators at the Launch taken from a surveillance camera.

"The danger," he summed up as the lights came on, "is not anarchy. We can deal with anarchy. The danger is that public discontent will grow in the shadows and at some point turn into organized resistance and come into the open. That, we must avoid at all costs."

The councillors applauded. His proposals seemed set to sail through and a self-satisfied mood was settling on everyone.

Paul, leaning back in his seat, loudly cleared his throat. All eyes turned toward him.

"One point," he said languidly. "Suppressing demonstrations is fine as far as it goes, but wouldn't it better to anticipate them? Your special corps—and Black Guard is not a bad name, by the way—must be an intelligence agency. It must investigate subversive activities and ferret out anti-State elements *before* they have a chance to act. Would you agree?"

A quick show of nodding heads indicated most of the delegates did.

Paul continued: "One more point. Would you mind playing that clip again?"

The lights dimmed and the tape rolled until it reached a point near the end where Paul yelled out, "There! Freeze it! Did you notice that young demonstrator off to the right? The one carrying a small banner."

They stared.

"I'll take that as a *no*. I'm assuming that you also did not notice that the banner consists of a particular color—am I correct?"

"A particular color?" repeated Besermann.

"It is a color we've seen at other demonstrations. Do you have any idea why the protesters have chosen it?"

Besermann looked confused.

Paul didn't wait for a response. "What is it about that particular color that makes it an emblem of resistance? What does it *mean*? What does it *signify*? Why does it appear to stir their hearts?"

He paused to let his words sink in. The chamber was silent. He spoke with the sarcasm of a teacher addressing a class of dolts. "Do you think that it has anything to do with the fact that that color was once the color of the sky?"

Besermann shrugged. Murmurs ran through the chamber.

24

THE ANSWER FELL TO PAUL. HE INSISTED ON DOING THE SCIEN-
tific analysis of the color's existential essence himself and
hired a staff of five assistants.

They took over what had been a laboratory on the former
campus of Georgetown, the bottom floor of a brick building once
covered in ivy. A water tank was constructed on the roof and a
generator was set up in the back to ensure a continued supply of
electricity.

Paul began by announcing that they would not call the color by
its given name. Instead they would refer to it as "Color X." Doing
so would strip it of its character and reduce it to a subject fit for
objective study and analysis.

He sent a group of researchers to delve into the recorded history
of X. They scattered to the few remaining archives, dug up long
forgotten scientific studies, and reported back within a week.

Intriguingly, they discovered that X did not exist in ancient
times. Other colors—browns, ochres, reds, black—had been found
in primitive cave paintings, but no X. There was no pure X in
ancient Greece and no word for it. The writer who called himself Homer, for example, never used it in descriptions; instead he

190

wrote of the "wine-dark sea" and invoked tints ranging from gray to black.

There was no word for X in other ancient languages, not in Chinese, Japanese, or Hebrew. It did not exist in the original Bible. Nor did it exist in Icelandic sagas, the Koran, or Hindu Vedic hymns. It did not appear on the stage of history until the Egyptians, using azurite and then lapis lazuli from Afghanistan, invented a dye to propagate it. But it was so evocative and mysterious that they confined it to their tombs.

That was intriguing.

On top of that, of all the colors in the world, X was the most rare. It did not occur naturally as often as yellows or reds or oranges. It was found in very few plants and birds and minerals. You could list them on a single piece of paper.

They *did* list them: the eggs, the jays, the river kingfish, the indigo mushroom, the cornflower, the hyacinth. Also a certain forget-me-not flower, seeds of the Ravenala tree, a butterfly, a common berry, a body feather from a peacock, a poison dart frog from Brazil, and lapis lazuli. Not a long list, all things considered.

It only *seemed* to be everywhere. Before the Cocoon, the sky of course was X and, reflecting the sky, so was the ocean. At least people perceived them that way. But, as Paul knew, that was a trick of Nature in which color depended on wavelength within sunlight.

When natural sunlight disappeared because of the Cocoon, X disappeared. Far above the Cocoon, extending into the planets and stars, if people could ever get there, which was doubtful, they would see the universe in its true essence—unending eternal blackness.

They sat around a table discussing the findings. One researcher voiced a question. How about eye color? "If X is so rare, how do you explain the fact that so many people have it for an eye color?"

Paul smiled condescendingly and explained. That, too, was an illusion. Eyes that were hazel or brown or black contained pigment that was either brown or black. But eyes that looked to have the color of X contained no pigment whatsoever. Just as with the sky, the light that entered was scattered back to create the *appearance* of X.

"It's not a color," he said. "It's an absence of color."

The next task was to define X scientifically. The superficial definition was easy; it took no time to place it on the optical spectrum of visible light. It had a wavelength of 470 nanometers, residing at the lowest end of the scale.

"So low you might almost think it could fall off," he remarked.

Following that calculation, he derived a theory to explain the absence of X in the ancient world. Was it possible that X didn't exist long ago for a singular reason: not because it wasn't there but because people were unable to perceive it? After all, the perception of color among humans is fluid and highly variable.

He had established that some people had an innate ability to perceive many more shades than the bulk of the population—in effect, they could see more colors. To convince the assistants of this, he had discovered old experiments in perception with subjects chosen at random. The results astounded them: some people, a rare few, could see over ten gradations of a color that looked indistinguishable to most people.

It was a fact that the ability to perceive colors also varied considerably from species to species, he pointed out; dogs, for example, could see far fewer colors than humans.

The human eye is not uniform throughout history, Paul noted. It is an organ that evolves continually and rapidly. Could it be that long ago almost no one could see X because the eye had not yet evolved sufficiently to be able to detect it? That would explain why it simply didn't exist for the ancients. It may have been there, but they couldn't see it.

One old experiment supported this view. It concerned the

perception of colors by newborn babies, establishing that the last color they could see was X. All the other colors—red, orange, yellow, green—the babies were able to see within a week or two of birth. X took longer.

The conclusion was striking: If X was the last color an infant could see, perhaps it was the last color humans *as a collective species* could see. It required a higher state of evolution for the human eye. In effect, X was there all along but only *appeared* to have come into existence long after all the others. That explained its absence up until about two thousand years ago.

His theory had a significant corollary. If humans took so long to see X, perhaps they would quickly *unsee* it. If it had taken so many generations to see it, perhaps, once it was removed from the field of vision, people would lose the ability to perceive it. In other words, it was vulnerable to extinction. It would drop out of the visible spectrum after only a generation or two.

Paul's research into Color X became his primary fascination. He dove into it with a focus that eclipsed all else, the cold single-mindedness of his upbringing. What obsessed him the most was that the color was known to have powerful emotional properties. It was the hottest part of the burning flame. It contained a multitude of evocative shades: azure, cerulean, cobalt, Prussian, robins-egg, sapphire, indigo, aqua, turquoise. One for every mood. It was inextricably tied to culture; to cite only one example, the discovery of ultramarine propelled painting in the Renaissance.

There was a reason it was used in flags, uniforms, and religious paintings and to describe a melancholy genre of music. It had the ability to enthrall and inspire like no other color. Paul's mind roiled ceaselessly over this idea: how could a color—just a color—have the power to make people feel emotions?

Perhaps the answer was right in front of him. Perhaps that special quality came from contemplation of the sky and the unfathomable cosmos above it. Now that the Cocoon had banished X

193

from the sky and the seas, its ability to cast a spell was enhanced. Maybe it was a reminder of the sky, a conjuring up of the world humans were forced to abandon for the sake of survival but for which they still yearned.

In short, perhaps by its very nature, X was subversive.

The conclusion was clear. For the sake of public safety, it had to be eradicated.

* * *

Paul's study was submitted to the Inner Council and met with acclaim. The body called for immediate action. It established a special branch of the Black Guard—the Color Guard—to wipe Color X from the face of the earth.

It was another triumph for Paul and it was pleasing. He felt power accruing like a current. It was so easy, so natural. It was like water rising around him or invisible threads falling into his hand that, when tugged, made things happen far away.

25

PAUL SAT AT HIS DESK AND STARED DOWN AT THE DOSSIER THAT had been placed there by Oswald Magus. He looked over at Magus, a gnomish man, who sat back in his chair with a sly smile playing on his lips.

Paul knew he had struck a deal with the devil—he was sitting across from him. Over the past four years Magus had consolidated his control over all Security Forces, including the Color Guard and the Black Guard. He had constructed a formidable apparatus of repression and fear.

The Color Guard had made great strides in eradicating Color X. They arrested people who wore the wrong color clothing. They raided museums to demolish paintings and Chinese porcelain, and ransacked stores and offices to ferret out "illegal artifacts." They ignited weekly bonfires in every city and ordered people to toss in items from home that carried the prohibited color.

The Black Guard increased surveillance and amassed files on political dissidents. Paul knew that the interrogation sessions in the basement of the Hoover building on Pennsylvania Avenue had turned into torture sessions.

The crackdown meant the Inner Council was feeling secure.

The signs of political resistance that had so worried it in 2056 were not visible by 2060.

Two months ago Paul had decided to forgo his willful ignorance of Magus's methods in order to satisfy a long-buried craving: to solve the mystery of Lesley's death. And now the answer lay in the dossier on his desk.

The moment he read it, he knew what he would have to do. The conclusion was incontestable. He wondered if on some level, deep down, he had suspected all along that it was Besermann who had ordered Lesley's murder those many years ago.

He and his henchmen had engineered a plot to lure her to the Tiger's Nest mountaintop lodge along with the fall guy, Anderson, and used a remote guidance system to steer her car off the cliff. Cold-blooded murder—done at a distance, without fingerprints.

"Besermann saw her as a roadblock on his path to power," Magus said. "He killed her without a second thought."

Paul asked, "And his two accomplices, Jeffrey and Maximus. They were—I assume—your sources. Did they confess?"

"Yes."

"Under torture?"

"Under *duress*, I'd say."

"And what's happened to them now? Where are they?"

"Hanged."

Paul nodded. Magus was taking on too many decisions independently. He would have to be watched. Paul placed his hand upon the dossier. It included a detailed account of conspirators from the oil companies extending way back to the previous century—how they opposed the idea of man-made global warming and then reversed themselves to embrace it with their own "solution."

He wondered suddenly about his father, whom he had never known. His death while studying the ice melt in the Arctic was said to have been suspicious. Once, in a confessional moment, Lesley had described how he had been swallowed up in a moulin when the cable snapped. Paul asked: Was it an accident? She dodged the question and, when pressed, had replied simply: "Enough said." He had taken that to mean that it might *not* have been an accident.

Chances are, he reasoned, *if they killed her, they killed him.*

He banged his fist on the table, hard enough to startle Magus.

"Prepare a bill of particulars against Besermann," he ordered. "No mention of the conspiracy—we don't want to alert any others. Failure of leadership, dereliction of duty . . . serious charges, enough to warrant serious punishment. Present them to the Inner Council. I won't attend. When he's judged guilty, bring him to me."

* * *

When Paul got home Aggie was already there. She was mixing drinks and proposed they go out on the balcony.

He didn't feel like it but she had a determined look in her eye.

They stepped outside. The sun, barely perceptible through the Cocoon, was going down and sending out the usual fan of red and orange rays—the effect of the light hitting the profusion of sulfur particles at an angle. It happened every evening. It was monotonous and made it feel even hotter than it was.

His mind was elsewhere. He was consumed with Besermann— how he was going to deal with him. Why of all times did she now insist on a drink?

She seemed to be searching for something to talk about. She asked him about his day, the preparations for another Launch. He described some of the problems with the improvements in flight controls. Halfway through he wondered: why are we talking about this?

He suspected she had something on her mind and hoped it was not some new "atrocity" she had heard about. He hated it when she put him in the position of defending all the actions of the State, as if he were the perpetrator.

197

He felt the unhappy contrast with the earlier years, when things were simple and everything was subordinate to his goal of getting a fully functional jet plane into the stratosphere. He had been a hero back then.

Still, whenever she was feeling estranged because of some new rumor, he could tell. She showed it in a false tone of voice, an abruptness in her movements, her eyes never meeting his. None of this was happening now.

She was smiling.

"I've something to tell you," she said. "I'm pregnant."

His mouth dropped open.

"How far along?"

"Three months, almost."

He looked at her directly, the first time in a long time. He noticed a slight swelling of the belly. Why hadn't he seen it before? His mind was trying to catch up. He had not thought about having a child for years.

"I thought you'd be happy," she said.

"I am."

"It's going to be a girl."

He tried to disguise his disappointment. He had always assumed, back when he was thinking about such things, that he would have a son—someone to carry on the name, the dynasty.

That evening, while in bed, they looked up at the ceiling where a fan circled with a murmuring sound. They ran through contingencies—she wanted to continue working, he didn't want her to. They postponed that discussion to another time, and then they came to the subject of names.

She had already come up with one. He thought he would let her have her way—after all, it would be a girl. She said she wanted to name her after a favorite long-dead relative. The name was Sessler.

* * *

Paul was sitting in the penthouse office, in Besermann's own chair, when the prisoner was brought before him. The two Black Guards who escorted Besermann, dressed in black uniforms, took seats in the corner.

The full-length windows were open top to bottom, which was unusual and threatening; it suggested defenestration.

To his credit, Besermann seemed calm. Paul gestured to him to take a seat; he pulled one up before the elevated desk and sat in it, his head a full foot lower than Paul's.

Paul swiveled in his chair, facing the lights of the city, and swiveled back. "Do you know why you're here?"

"I've an idea," replied Besermann. "I knew this was going to happen after that phony bill of particulars this morning."

Paul patted the dossier on the desk. "I want to know why you did it," he said, staring at him. "Why you killed Lesley. I think I know but I want to hear it in your own words."

Besermann wasn't shocked.

"You *do* know," he said emotionlessly. "The world needed saving and she stood in the way."

"How so?"

"It's not complicated. She was against the Cocoon. She was smart and articulate and poking holes in our plans. People would have followed her. She could have derailed the whole project."

"You didn't have to kill her. You might have silenced her."

"You and I both know she was not the type to be silenced."

They were silent for a moment, then Besermann said, "Just so you know—I loved her too. It wasn't an easy decision."

Paul slapped his desk. "How about my father? Did you kill him too?"

Besermann sat upright. "I had nothing to do with that."

"Why should I believe you? If you killed her, you might have killed him."

"I was trying to *solve* his murder, for God's sake. I was working with Lesley. But we could never get anywhere."

"So who do you think did it?"

"I have no idea. Nothing was clear back then; just that it wasn't an accident. We had suspicions but nothing we could prove. And after a while, once I took on the project, I had other considerations."

"Other considerations!"

"Yes. Like the Cocoon."

Another pause. Paul swiveled to look out the window for a full minute, then turned back to look Besermann in the eye. "Do you ever think maybe Lesley had a point?"

"What do you mean?"

"That maybe the Cocoon wasn't the answer."

"Do you think so?"

Paul didn't respond.

"You shouldn't. We saved the damn planet."

They talked for many minutes more. At one point, Besermann asked him how he planned to dispose of him. Humanely, Paul replied.

He handed Besermann a piece of paper.

"Here's a news item that will accompany your death. And you'll have a state funeral."

As Besermann was reading it, one of the Black Guards slipped behind him like a shadow. He raised a gun and dispatched him with a single shot to the back of his head. The two wrapped the body in a cloth and carried it out.

Besermann's death was put down to coronary thrombosis brought on, no doubt, by the stress of his responsibilities. He was cremated and—Paul being true to his word—was memorialized at a state funeral in the lobby of UNCLE.

Paul set out to attend it but once there changed his mind. He spun around and abruptly left, the click of his bootheels echoing over the marble floor and encouraging a handful of subordinates to follow suit.

PART V
BRAVE NEW WORLD

2091
(YON)

26

Emerging from the tunnel in the South, Yon is bathed in tropical heat. It delights him, this torpid, pulsating warmth that turns his skin wet and makes him feel alive.

New sounds strike his ears, a constant humming mingled with high-pierced shrieks—a chorus of birds and animals, calling, scolding, threatening.

The trees are bigger than back home. They're thick and draped with twisting vines. Overhead is a canopy of green. Fig trees dangle roots to the ground like ropes.

He catches a glimpse of the Cocoon through the trees and is bitterly disappointed that it's still there.

"Don't worry," says Quinlin. "I was told about this. It doesn't stop all at once. It'll drop away gradually the farther south we go."

Quinlin has told him everything he knows about their mission—which is precious little. They are to make their way to a coastal town called Esmeraldas. There they will meet a guide who will take them across the mountains to a thriving village, a precursor of a "new world," and the mysterious figure presiding over it. Her name is Soledad.

They have told nothing but their initial destination to Luther, who leads the way and keeps a brisk pace, stopping from time to time only to check a compass.

They come to a fast-moving stream. They fall on their knees, cup their hands, and pull up mouthfuls of fresh water.

They walk for hours as the jungle darkens, then stop for the night, eat some beef jerky, and lie down close to a crackling fire that sends up a spiral of smoke.

Soon—only a few minutes later—Yon and Quinlin hear Luther snoring.

"You up?" Yon asks Quinlin.

"Yeah."

Yon stands and motions for Quinlin to follow him a short distance away. He speaks softly. "So what do you think?—Is he for real?"

"I don't know, but we need him."

"Something's weird. He's going through all this, it's probably more than he bargained for. And he hasn't asked for more money. That doesn't strike me like a smuggler."

"We'll watch him closely."

Yon walks back and lies down, settling on his stomach, using his jacket as a blanket. The fire burns low and the darkness seems to move in close. But Yon can't drift off. The sounds of the jungle seem louder now.

Suddenly, he hears a whining that comes and goes, at times so close it could be inside his head. And then—*ouch!*—a pinprick in his neck. He slaps it and bolts up.

"Damn!" he exclaims. "What the hell?"

"What's the matter?"

"I don't know, I just—I heard something weird, this high-pitched sound, and then pow! I felt something in my neck. I can still feel it."

"Well, I'll be damned." Quinlin starts chuckling.

"What's so funny?"

"Be quiet and tell me if you hear the sound again."

Yon holds his breath. There it is. "I do," he says. "I hear it."

"So do I. And it's something I haven't heard for years. It's a mosquito."

"A what?"

"Mosquito. An insect."

"Is it poisonous?"

"Hell, no. You'll itch for a while. You can't stop scratching but it won't do any good. It'll go away in a day or two."

A moment later he speaks up again. "Actually, it's a good sign."

* * *

They walk all the next day. Luther says they're headed southwest and aiming for an old mining camp that leads to their destination. At the day's end he sits against a tree, his hat pulled over his eyes, and says, "This is a bitch." He raises his hat. "I figure I get you there, I got more money coming."

"I'm sure we can work something out," Quinlin says.

Yon wonders: Is Luther's demand genuine? Or did he eavesdrop last night and figure he better act more like a smuggler?

An hour later they hear a rustling close by, an animal approaching. A long snout protrudes from the bush. Luther pulls out his knife but Quinlin shoots it just as it darts away. He smashes through the trees and yells out, "Got him!" He returns carrying the body of an armadillo. They roast it over a spit.

* * *

The next afternoon, they leave the forest. In the open, light is everywhere. Yon sees something he's never seen before: apparitions that appear on the ground, mimicking everything above. So this is what they mean by shadows! He moves his hand and a mirror image moves below. It's as if everything has a secret double.

He looks up. The Cocoon is thinner, half gone, but the residue still filters out much of the sun.

* * *

They reach the old zinc mine. The camp is deserted and bears the scars of destruction from ferocious storms. Trees are down, fences obliterated, and objects of all kinds are scattered around the ground.

But the railroad tracks appear intact, disappearing into the open mouth of the mine. There is a barracks, almost falling down, and a mess hall and a barn. Inside they find a handcar.

"Hombre, we're in luck," says Luther.

They give it a push. It slides on the tracks, out the door, and comes to a stop in the center of the camp.

"The wheels are rusty," Quinlin says. "I saw a can of oil back in the shed. We'll grease it up, spend the night here, and get an early start."

Luther slaps him on the back.

"Next stop, Esmeraldas."

* * *

The next day they ride the handcar. They take turns pumping the walking bar, one man on each side and the third sitting in the seat up front. The uphill stretches are exhausting but going downhill they fly, the thick air rushing past.

They stop at dusk when they arrive at a treeless hill. They walk to the summit. The Cocoon is almost gone and so is the red and orange evening haze. They see the top of a huge yellow disk sinking down—the sun! It's setting, and as it sets it sends out dazzling colors—red, yellow and orange streaks. They stare until it sinks into the water and the display fades into darkness.

206

Yon has never seen anything as beautiful. So this is what his grampa was talking about!

"I was six years old when the Cocoon went up," Quinlin says. "I haven't seen the sun since then. God, it's grand."

"Tell me," asks Yon, "you ever see stars?"

Quinlin's brow furrows. "I can't say I did. But I must have. I mean, if they were there. But maybe they had gone by then."

"Maybe they were never there," says Luther. "The whole thing is far-fetched. How would stars get there? How would they stay there? I figure that's propaganda."

Quinlin says, "You have no idea what you're talking about."

They find a hollow and settle in for the night around a fire. They have nothing to eat, just hot water drunk in swigs by passing around the canteen. Yon's stomachs feels like it's shriveling up.

In the morning, when Yon wakes, his skin is damp. He feels the ground around him and it's wet, too, covered with a thin coating of moisture. He wipes some off a leaf and brings it to his mouth. No taste.

"What's this?" he asks Luther. Quinlin is away, back on the summit.

"I have no damn idea. Quinlin says it's called dew. Water that comes out at night. Comes from where? He doesn't know. Another one of his cockamamie notions."

"So how do you explain it?"

"I don't."

By early afternoon, they ascend the crest of the last hill. The ocean spreads before them. A band of white, the surf, follows the curving coastline. Yon stares at the water. It looks slightly different down here. It has a kind of depth to it. A hidden sense of color.

Yon notices that Luther is looking at it, too. He seems flustered, preoccupied. He stares at it, looks away, and in another moment stares again.

They spot the railroad tracks winding down toward the coast.

The tracks lead to a jumble of shapes. They scrunch their eyes and focus. The shapes assume recognizable forms—roofs and walls and winding streets. It's a town.

"Esmeraldas!" exclaims Quinlin.

* * *

They leave the handcar on a siding and walk into the ruined town. The pavement is heaved up and most of the buildings are just heaps of rubble. Many trees are down, some split and splintering. No one is around. Quinlin takes out his revolver and checks to see that it's loaded.

They come to shops. The doors are open and they peer inside. They don't look as if they've been looted. Three blocks down they enter a grocery store. The shelves are neatly lined with canned goods and boxes and bins are filled with fresh fruit. Luther picks up a melon, tosses it onto a counter, and slices it clean through with his knife.

"*Tienes que pagar por eso.*"

They whip around to see an elderly woman stepping out of a rear door. She has thin strands of gray hair hanging around her craggy face and an Indian shawl around her shoulders.

Quinlin says, "*Claro. Vamos pagar.*" He pulls out his wallet as a show of good faith.

He talks to the woman—she has ushered him into a seat at a wooden table—while Yon and Luther stare at the food. Quinlin and the old woman are deep in conversation. Soon she goes to a stove and puts on a kettle.

"She says Esmeraldas was pretty much destroyed," Quinlin says. "Flooding and hurricanes and you name it. About three-quarters of the people died. It was like the wrath of God, she said.

"It went on for years. Some people starved to death. Others left by boats, heading out anywhere, just to get away. She lost her husband and two daughters. One grandson survives.

"But now slowly, bit by bit, things are getting better. The storms have stopped. The people are rebuilding the center of town. Crops are planted in the valley and fruit is sweeter than ever. The soil is improving. The weather's not so bad. The sky is clear."

As Quinlin talks, the woman comes over and pours out three cups, holding the kettle high so that it falls hard upon the tea leaves, sending up waves of steam.

"*La esperanza esta volviendo*," she says, with a smile on her wrinkled face.

"Hope is coming back," translates Quinlin.

The tea is so hot they have to wait a few minutes. While they drink the woman cooks furiously, chopping meat and vegetables, banging pots on the stove, pouring in oil. She serves them, and they eat ravenously.

Yon tells Quinlin to ask the way to the main plaza. The woman says her grandson will show them, claps her hands loudly, and a small boy appears from the back.

He leads them to the town center and disappears. There's a surprising bustle to the place. At the center palm trees line the gravel pathways in a small park. An old colonial-style city hall with a clock tower sits across from a towering Spanish church. At one end boys play soccer. At the other mothers sit on benches, rocking baby carriages and talking.

"I never expected this," says Luther. "I thought it'd be a kind of a dump. I mean, you hear so many stories of the South, how wrecked it is. But this . . ."

"I thought you knew the South," says Quinlin.

"Not here. Like I said, I never been here before."

Quinlin points to a small hotel on the corner. "We can stay there tonight," he says. "Just the two of us. Luther, we'll settle up with you. You got us here. But now's the time to split up."

Luther nods slowly. "So what do you do now?" he asks. "How you going to get back?"

"We'll figure that out."

"I can help. Same deal. Not much money."

"We'll think about it."

"You cross over the mountains. There's a town to the south of the equator. On the other coast. Maybe I'll meet you there."

Quinlin hands over the money and Luther stuffs it in his front pocket, shakes their hands, and walks out. Quinlin stares after him. "Can't say I'm sorry to see him go."

They sleep for three hours. When they awake they feel refreshed. It's time to find their contact. They go back out into the square. Now the cafés are crowded and noisy and filled with smoke and laughter. Young men and women promenade around the park.

Yon wears his amulet outside his shirt. After a little less than an hour, a man in jeans and a leather jacket comes by. He admires it.

"Beautiful, isn't it?" agrees Yon.

"Shall I sit down?"

"By all means," says Quinlin.

Yon notices something. He kicks Quinlin under the table and motions with his head to the other side of the café. Luther is sitting there, sipping from a bottle of Club beer and looking out over the plaza.

The man at their table orders a coffee. He's about thirty, with thick black hair that hangs down to his chin.

"My name's Paco," he says.

Quinlin and Yon introduce themselves.

Paco asks, "When do you want to leave?"

27

F OR FIVE DAYS PACO LEADS THEM ON HORSEBACK ALONG NARROW paths and through twisting gullies.

On the way they pass meadows filled with birds and insects and amber grasslands waving in the breeze. They do not see much of the sun—it is mostly cloudy—but once they are above the tree line, they encounter snow.

Yon can't believe the shimmering whiteness that covers the landscape. Snow is everywhere. When they dismount he reaches down and takes a handful. It's soft and light and cold. He tastes it and it melts to water in his mouth. Suddenly—*thwack!*—something crashes into his neck. It's wet and cold. He turns around in time to see Quinlin making another snowball. They toss them back and forth, then wrestle and roll around until they are gasping in the thin air.

On the sixth day they descend, their horses picking their steps carefully among the rocks and riverbeds. The air turns warm, and on the eighth day it turns humid and heavy. Vines and foliage surround them as they enter the jungle canopy.

At noon on the ninth day they come to a river. Across it is a footbridge, a twenty-yard span with cables of twisted vines and palmetto slats to walk on. They dismount.

"See there," Paco says, pointing across the river. "In the distance. Nueva Loja. "

Yon looks ahead. He sees the tops of a line of wind turbines, their blades spinning rapidly.

Paco shakes hands with them both, then mounts his horse and, with the mule and two riderless horses tethered behind, turns and disappears into the jungle.

As soon as they cross the swinging footbridge, a delegation arrives to greet them. Leading it is a dark-haired man about fifty wearing a crisp white shirt and shorts laden with tools. He thrusts his hand out.

"Welcome, welcome to our little enclave of civilization," he says heartily in a British accent. "We've been eagerly awaiting you. I do hope your trip wasn't too arduous."

"Not at all," replies Yon.

They are surrounded by a knot of people, handshakes and smiles all around, a chattering in Spanish, English, and a language they can't understand.

"My name is David Cutler," the Englishman continues. "I'm a general factotum around here." He talks as the group moves forward on the path, gathering people along the way. "Let me take you to your quarters—nothing fancy, I hope you'll understand. Freshen up. And then perhaps a look around, if you're up for it."

Now the crowd is so large it can't fit on the path, with people jostling, children running up to gawk, and dogs barking.

"Guess you don't get too many visitors," remarks Quinlin.

Cutler laughs. "Quite right. You're an event. But not to worry— things will quiet down after a spell."

Abruptly the path turns into a road that widens and leads into the center of town. One- and two-story buildings of whitewashed stone line both sides of the street. Ahead they see a roundabout and more streets and tile roofs extending up a slope. Everywhere there are crowds of people. At the top are the spinning windmills. A beehive of activity.

Cutler glances at Yon and Quinlin. "I know, it's remarkable. It never loses its effect. Sometimes when things seem a bit much, I stop and look around and I'm struck again by what we've done here. We're returning the land to what it was before the catastrophe." He waves his hand at it all. "And that's no easy thing."

"But returning it how?" Yon asked.

"Trees, my boy. Trees. We're rebuilding the rainforest."

They arrive at a central plaza. On all sides are ancient structures, towering walls made of three-foot wide boulders that fit together perfectly.

"If you were on the hill you'd see that on each roof are solar panels. Between that and the wind turbines, we're energy self-sufficient. In fact, we could export electricity if we had transmission cables."

He approaches a massive wall and gives it a hard slap. "This was built so perfectly three thousand years ago it didn't collapse in the storms." He smiled. "But forgive us. You must be exhausted. Let us show you to your quarters for a rest."

He claps his hands. Several children rush forward, pick up their knapsacks, and lead them to a small house made entirely of the ancient stone. The room is whitewashed and clean with two beds of thick wooden frames, a heavy table, and four chairs.

They rest but they are too keyed up to sleep. Children gather outside their window, peering in and pushing one another to get a better view.

Dinner that night is in a communal lodge with wooden beams, long tables, and blazing ovens set inside one wall. Cutler introduces them to a score of people, both indigenous and outsiders, including a meteorologist, several doctors, a chemist, and a number of naturalists.

He reads the puzzlement on Yon's face. "Yes, we are an unusual mix. But it works well. We learn from one another's disciplines and cultures. We are constantly exchanging ideas. I think we've benefited especially from the indigenous peoples in evolving a philosophy."

"And that is?" asks Yon.

Cutler smiles. "Mies Van Der Rohe declared *less is more*. That applies to more than architecture. It's a good credo for living."

Everyone crowds the tables. Yon and Quinlin are handed plates heaped with flatbread, goat meat, and vegetables.

"I regret that Soledad is not here at the moment," Cutler adds. "She's way off in what used to be the rainforest, supervising the replanting."

They finish eating and the dishes are cleared away.

"I'll take you on a real tour tomorrow. You'll see what I mean about the old and the new. We even have a pyramid—it's small but impressive."

They return to their room and this time, despite the murmurs of people talking in the street outside, they fall asleep.

* * *

After breakfast Cutler shows Yon and Quinlin around. As they walk the streets some people stare, but most just go about their business.

"You see, you're no longer novelties," Cutler remarks.

They visit a school, a modern clinic, an engineering office, a library, and a warehouse. They come to the administrative center, a series of passageways and cloistered gardens reminiscent of a medieval monastery. Framed maps and bookshelves line the walls.

Coming to the main office, Cutler grins and gestures toward a door.

"Someone's here you'll want to know," he says. "The reason for your visit."

214

At that moment, the door swings open. Standing there is a woman in her thirties, tall and statuesque. Her skin is brown and her black hair flows down her back in waves. She wears bracelets on her left wrist and a necklace of white stones. But her arresting feature is her black eyes, the color of onyx. They draw Yon in. He has to look away.

She shakes hands and introduces herself.

"Soledad."

Her English has a slight, lilting accent. She apologizes for being away yesterday, invites them into her office, and arranges them around a table. She orders coffee and asks them questions about their trip until it's served.

Yon has the sensation that she is directing much of the conversation at him. He finds his voice and asks about her background and how she came to be here. She replies easily, openly.

Her parents were academics from coastal Peru, she says. Her father was a philosopher and her mother a geomorphologist studying the origin of the Earth's topography. Early on they became alarmed by climate change and tried to figure out how to combat it, or at least survive it. Peru, on the ocean, was badly hit, lashed by storms of nightmarish intensity. Lima lost half its population.

She was born in 2055. "That was ten years after you deployed the Cocoon. For you it was a temporary respite. For us down here, it was unmitigated disaster. It made everything worse and we were left alone to contend with the consequences."

She gave a sharp laugh. "*Cocoon.* What a euphemism. But it has a kernel of truth. Who knew that the creature it would birth would turn into such a monster?"

As a child she was "a climate refugee." Her parents and several like-minded families trekked inland to escape the storms, crossing the mountains to find safe harbor. Their horses hauled cartloads of books and scientific implements.

215

When they arrived at the village, the indigenous people took them in. The villagers followed an ancient religion. As their shaman explained, it centered on the sun as the giver of all life and upheld a belief in animism. Every living thing was sacred. The jungle was bountiful and not to be destroyed in any way.

"I've read of the native people in your land," she says, boring into Yon with her intense eyes. "They treasured and honored the land. They made use of it for their needs but always in moderation and always with respect. When they killed animals they honored them and thanked them. It was like that here."

Her parents became moral leaders along with the shaman.

"This building was their religious center. You can derive a sense of their beliefs just by walking around. It's contemplative and highly spiritual, almost mystical."

Her parents both died of natural causes, as did the shaman. She and her colleagues carried on their work.

"My parents had a defined goal. They wanted to build a storehouse of knowledge and a center for translations and learning. It was going to be a beacon for the future like Andalucia in southern Spain during the Middle Ages, carrying ancient knowledge forward. That's what they hoped."

"*Hoped?*" Yon replies. "Have you given it up?"

"There's no need now. We thought all of civilization was under threat, but after massive destruction the urgency lifted—gradually. Industry was ruined, so pollution stopped. We had no gasoline. The Earth—our hemisphere at least—is slowly righting itself."

As she talks, her voice takes on a proselytizing urgency and she gestures with her hands so that her bracelets jangle.

"We've learned the primacy of Nature. From this simple principle stems a host of other principles. What you take, you replenish. If you cut timber, you plant new forests. You grow most of what you eat. If you kill animals for food, you raise more animals. You use renewable energies, moderate your needs, live more simply, and look for ways to save air, soil, and water. Do not dig into the earth to rob its resources. No coal, ever.

"We've taken that elemental message and modified it by adding Science. A positive Science, not a negative one. A Science dedicated to renewal and natural growth, that will figure out how to reduce the carbon in the atmosphere. How will we do without cars, for example? Or without airplanes? We can't turn the clock back centuries. But we have to allow Science to teach us how to act responsibly, without pumping the chemicals from fossil fuels into the air we breathe.

"Your problem, up North, was you chose the easy way. You didn't take the carbon out of the air, you just covered it over with a blanket of new chemicals and kept on polluting. In doing so you changed the entire equilibrium of the planet's weather system. And now you're stuck. The Cocoon has turned from a solution into the problem.

"Down here we faced the ravages of the weather change. It knocked out our refineries, our generating plants, our airports and harbors and mines. Life as we knew it came almost to a halt. But in retrospect that was something of a blessing. It's given us a chance to start over."

"If the North is stuck," asks Yon, "how do we get it unstuck?"

"That's what you're here for," she replies. "We are going to give you our latest technology.

"It may—if it works—allow you to get rid of the Cocoon—gradually. If you do it all at once, your temperatures will go skyrocketing. Your land will turn into a furnace, your oceans will boil, and you'll undergo horrors that make ours look like child's play. But if you don't get rid of the Cocoon, you're equally done for."

Quinlin clears his throat and says, "It's good of you to help us."

"It's not altruism. We're working with you because we have to. The North must change. You must get rid of the Cocoon. The planet can't survive cut in two, one half poisoning the atmosphere and the other half controlling pollution. Your arrogant ways don't stop at the border. They're hurting us."

She turns her piercing gaze directly at Yon.

"Technology alone is not enough. It will not do the job. You . . . you must carry our revolution North. You must overthrow the leaders. You must restore sanity in the seat of government for the sake of the planet's equilibrium."

She stands up, towering over the table, and looks at Yon again, this time softly. "It'll take a while for us to prepare your package. While you're here, I suggest you visit the library, read a lot, and talk to people and listen. You might also take martial arts training. It's my experience that no one in power willingly gives it up."

* * *

After lunch she drives them through the jungle to view the vast reforestation program. They go thirty miles on a dirt road, in a rattling truck whose engine drowns out conversation, until they come to the burn zone—a lifeless desert of rain-soaked ashes.

They pass newly planted green shoots and reach the work site. More sprouts are unloaded from the back of the truck, their roots bundled in sacks of burlap. Two workers wield post-hole diggers in the ground and others gently slide the sprouts into the holes.

They walk off to one side, careful not to tread on the plantings. Soledad points out the different varieties of the palms.

"We can't recreate all the trees of the original rainforest," she says. "That's impossible. There were something like sixteen thousand species. The idea is to get the canopy growing so the lower growth will be protected and fill in quickly. Then we'll add back new species. Diversity is the key.

"Luckily, burnt soil is good for regeneration. The ranchers intentionally burned the forests. Now our problem is rain. We get some but we don't know if it's enough. How do we reestablish the replenishing rain cycle that made the forest thrive?"

She pauses for a moment. "That's where you come in." Again, her eyes flash. "We think the world needs to restore a unitary weather system. We need you to save us as well as yourselves."

On the ride back, one of the workers drives while they sit in the rear of the truck where they can talk. Settling in—her hair streaming behind her whenever they go fast enough—Soledad leans toward them.

"Something I want to ask. The Power . . . how strong is it? How solid is its hold on things?"

"Anyone who says they know is either lying or misinformed," says Quinlin. "But it's not losing control, that's for sure."

"How strong is the Resistance? Will it ever topple the dictatorship?"

"We exist. We have a presence in some cities—in New York a whole underground group. But the Black Guard is everywhere. They infiltrate us and have surveillance cameras all over the place. They have vast files—they probably know most of us by name and photograph."

He points to Yon. "Except for him. He's been off the grid for years. That's the reason he was chosen for this mission."

"Will there be an uprising any time soon?"

"People aren't happy. They complain and moan. But are they ready to take action? If we come into the daylight, would they support us? That's what we don't know."

"That's what we hear. But the reports are sketchy."

"How do you get reports?" Yon asks her.

"We've got some people up there. And we've got a line of communication with the Resistance—with Sessler. It's a ragtag operation. It takes forever but a message usually gets through."

She grips the side of the truck as it bounces along. "Traveling is harder. Let's hope you can deliver the package."

28

At dusk the following day Soledad comes for Yon. He follows her on a path out of the village and they walk for almost an hour. He hears a stirring in the leaves and vines, movements of small animals.

Eventually the path leads to a large clearing. In the center of the meadow is a pyramid so immense it looms over the trees. It looks as if it's been dropped fully built in the middle of the meadow.

It's made of boulders four and five feet wide and two feet high, stacked into a monumental structure soaring sixty, seventy feet into the air.

"Remarkable, isn't it?" she says, enjoying his amazement. "We've never dated it but it's at least two thousand years old."

They walk to the base. The blocks rise up in geometric perfection to a distant summit. Running up the center is a succession of smaller blocks—a staircase.

She starts to climb and he follows her. The steps are short and steep and as he climbs he begins to feel dizzy. The stone blocks are pockmarked by age and splotched with lichen, their black edges rounded. He keeps going and the higher he goes, the dizzier he feels.

He reaches the summit. She's there waiting, sitting upon an immense flat rock. He sits beside her, hugging his legs. A breeze riffles his hair. He looks around. The dark treetops extend around for miles. Above, clouds rip a veil across a half moon.

He looks down. They're sitting in the center of a circular bowl carved into the rock. It's caked with dark matter, a shallow vessel with residue at the bottom. She strokes it with her hand.

"For human sacrifices," she says. "Young girls, virgins. They had their throats slit. The blood flowed down here." Her hand traces indentations leading to a shallow basin.

"All to appease the angry gods." She smiles. "Not everything was better back then."

He feels a slight chill.

"Can you conceive of the belief, the fervor that motivated them to build this thing?"

"Because the gods were in the sky."

"Yes. That's what I think."

He looks up. It is getting dark. The vastness of space fills him with a different kind of dizziness. He sees pinpricks of light. The more he looks, the more he sees—scores and scores of them, thousands, millions.

Stars!

She points out the constellations: Orion, Sagittarius, Andromeda, Pegasus, Centaurus, and many others. She tells the myths behind them. He can't make the figures out—a few stars somehow depicting a horse or a bow and arrow—but he marvels at the human imagination that gave them shapes.

She talks of nebulae and star clusters and supernovas and distant galaxies and glowing blisters of interstellar gas.

He swoons in the mystery of limitless outer space. Other suns, other planets. What is this Earth—a tiny speck hurtling through? And what are humans? Specks upon the speck.

He feels the way he did when he was young in Canada, lying on

221

the outcropping of rock—that same sense of floating upward. His senses come alive. He hears the heart throbbing in the breast of a bird, the whoosh of insects' wings, the digging of a rodent, and the slithering of a snake.

They sit there for a while, not talking, then climb back down and head toward the village.

"Now you see it," she says, her bracelets jangling softly. "Now you see what the Cocoon has robbed you of."

* * *

Yon and Quinlin stay in Nueva Loja eight weeks. Quinlin is interested in the forestry project and spends days on end working with the replanting team away from the village.

Yon likes to meander around the broad avenues, chatting with people. He goes with others on hunting forays into the jungle and learns how to identify animals by their spoor and how to track them.

Gradually he begins to see the elusive color that so attracted him. It is more majestic than anything he could imagine. He lounges about in the meadow near the pyramid, luxuriating in the sky and the contrast with the billowing clouds that take on so many shapes—everything so different from the deadening Cocoon.

He undergoes a regimen of martial arts training. Every morning he rises early and meets his instructor, a forty-five-year-old Colombian, for two hours. The course is basic jujitsu and it quickens his aggressive instincts. Toward the end, he is able to throw his instructor to the mat.

But soon enough, he wants to return to the North. He's mindful of his mission and he knows that Sessler and others are waiting for him. Soledad tells him that the package he is to deliver is not yet ready. It has to be continually refined, she explains. If it works, it will allow them to dismantle the Cocoon.

"It's not a solution. It's not a panacea," she declares. "It's only a stopgap, and it might not even work." Her eyes flash. "But it's worth a try—it's all you can do."

In the evenings, the two sometimes climb to the top of the pyramid. There, they gaze at the sky at twilight, the setting sun and the emergence of the stars. Each time he is transported.

On a night when the stars are particularly luminous she says, "This sky will be your guide. You must learn to read it. It will take you back home." The next day he reads a book: *Navigating the Seas by the Stars*.

* * *

The day finally comes when she tells him the package is ready. He must leave immediately and take it to Florida, where a runner will be waiting. That evening, there is a goodbye feast and almost the whole village turns out.

The fire reaches almost to the trees. The food is excellent. There are toasts and hugs.

Cutler stands with a full glass of spirits and drinks to their health. "Who knows? Maybe someday you will return. Maybe someday the North and the South will be united again." His voice drops. "But I wouldn't count on it. Not everyone below the equator forgives you, you know."

Soledad speaks last. She hands over a metal canister ten inches tall and another one with liquid inside.

"You need them both," she said. "Get them to Sessler. She knows what to do with them. You must destroy the Cocoon and build something to come after it. When you build that something, that bridge, remember: You cannot strong-arm Nature. You cannot overcome Her by force. You must find other Natural forces, benevolent ones, and let them do their work."

Shortly afterward, the sky darkens and a black cloud rolls in to cover the moon. The branches shudder and the air is enlivened by an electric field. With a clap of thunder—so loud that Yon jumps in his seat—a deluge falls. The heavy drops pound the roofs and make tiny explosions in the dust.

They run for shelter, but Soledad stays out in the open, turning her face up and lifting her arms. The water pours down her hair and bounces off her shoulders. Soon, everyone joins her. They laugh in the rain.

Yon stands beside her. To his surprise the water is warm. He raises his head, opens his mouth and swallows. It is thirst quenching.

Quinlin comes running up, holding a blanket over his head.

"I didn't know it could rain like this. It's like the end of the damn world."

She laughs. "Not at all. It's the beginning."

* * *

The next morning Yon and Quinlin leave. The villagers accompany them to the river, where a raft is waiting. Soledad is nowhere in sight. Yon looks for her until Cutler pulls him aside and tells him she's off planting trees.

"I sympathize," he says with a slight laugh. "Sometimes I think she loves trees more than people."

They step onboard. A young North American named Todd, who knows the river, has been delegated to go with them. The raft is large but basic. Rugs cover the logs bound together by cables. A tent of canvas sheet covers one end and a mountain of provisions are stacked inside. Yon places a knapsack with the canisters next to them.

As Todd poles away, the crowd waves and claps. The raft reaches the center of the river, finds the current, and begins to move downstream. Yon watches the people get smaller. Then they go around a bend and there is nothing ahead and nothing behind but the sun shining down like a sword and the banks of palm trees leaning languidly over the water.

PART VI
THE SOLACE
OF ARTIFICIAL
STARS

2070
(AGGIE)

29

AGGIE SLIPPED OUT THE BACK DOOR OF THE MANSION AND KEPT a watchful eye for the plainclothes security guards who were always around now that her husband had become so powerful.

The din of the construction workers blotted out the sound of the door closing. The incessant hammering and sawing was not unusual. Ever since they had moved into the former Naval Observatory—the stately residence on a hilltop in northwest Washington—Messian had been building grand additions.

But this one was different. It was a whole new wing, costly—she couldn't even venture to guess how much—and secret. Large wooden crates arrived in a truck with New York license plates and were carefully carried inside. Messian wouldn't say what the addition was, only that it was a necessity, not a luxury.

She hurried down the steps to the garage, hopped into her car, and pulled out on Wisconsin Avenue, heading for Alexandria, Virginia. As she crossed the new extension bridge over the ever-widening Potomac, she glanced several times at the rearview mirror. It was a nervous reflex; she didn't really think she was being followed.

* * *

She thought how much Messian had changed since their days on
Dupont Circle, how much his ego had blossomed—if that was the
right word—in the ten years since Besermann's death. She hadn't
known Besermann well and hadn't liked him, but after he was
gone she thought he had at least been a check on her husband.

Messian didn't talk much about his work, but when he did it
was revealing. He'd complain about the Inner Council, how both-
ersome it was having to balance the competing interests and worry
about the shifting alliances. She knew his position had changed.
Before, he was the first among equals; now—in 2070—he had no
equals.

He had adopted the perks of high office, of which the splendid
mansion was only one example. He had dispensed with anonymity,
had even adopted a new title: Chairman of the Consortium. When
she visited him in his office—which was an increasing rarity—she
could tell he enjoyed having underlings jump to his commands
and nod their heads in agreement before he finished speaking.

At his insistence his advisors had produced a hologram of him,
a glowing figure named "Amicus," that was trotted out for pronouncements and public occasions like the graduation ceremony
at the Color Guard academy. It was important, he explained, for
the Power to be personified. That way people could feel a personal
loyalty.

If Messian's life had changed over the decade, so had Aggie's.
When Sessler was born, Messian had demanded that she stop working in order to personally raise the baby. He didn't want any "outside influence" to shape his daughter. For four years she resisted,
but finally when the issue turned into a daily struggle she gave in.

Now Sessler was ten. She had a small circle of friends from families that had been cleared. They always came to her house; she
never went to theirs.

Messian's control was a stone lodged in Aggie's chest. Every day
she searched for something meaningful to do, to avoid lounging

around the pool or in the artificial "sunroom." She needed to get out of the house, to escape, so she hit upon a stratagem: she paid the security detail a monthly bribe to look the other way.

* * *

She drove to the Old Town, protected by a ten-foot levee. The red brick sidewalks were cracked here and there and the ancient two-story houses were missing some shutters but there was still a timeless aura about the place. She parked on King Street next to the car she was looking for.

Suzanne Zeger was sitting in the driver's seat.

"Right on time," she said, coming out to give her a hug.

Suzanne was going to introduce her to her "discussion group." No need to use your real name, she advised. We can let them know who you are later.

Aggie had continued to see the Zegers off and on, even though it meant putting up with a stream of negative comments about the Cocoon and the Consortium. The stream of talk turned into a river once they acknowledged they knew to whom she was married.

Suzanne often went off on a rant that Sessler knew well.

The Power had become a bloated beast. It couldn't muster the will to fix the landscape, still littered with debris. It couldn't maintain civil peace. All it could do was send up more and more Launches, sometimes two or three a year, to achieve the temperature equilibrium.

After each one the opaqueness and thickness of the Cocoon grew. But did the drilling of oil and gas stop? No. Did the emission of fossil-fueled carbon? No. Why not? Because the imperative to stop polluting was gone. Since global warming had been "solved," there was no impetus to search for alternative energy sources. And the main option—solar energy—had been eliminated.

Meanwhile, the forests continued to disappear, along with their carbon-capturing foliage. And with the permafrost melting, the anaerobic bacteria in the north produced huge quantities of methane with its even greater heat-trapping properties. The flora and fauna were dead or dying.

"They used to call it the greenhouse effect," Suzanne said once. "But I don't see anything growing in the goddamned greenhouse."

They entered a house on King Street. A dozen people were gathered in a living room on the second floor, deep in discussion. They continued talking as Suzanne introduced Aggie around. Quick handshakes, nods of hello, some smiles.

A pale young man with sunken cheeks, a black mustache, and large rimmed glasses straddled a chair, resting his arms on the back. He was in the midst of a diatribe.

"You can't see the sun—right? It's barely visible, like the wattage has been sucked out. You can barely feel it. When was the last time you just sat on a bench soaking it up?"

"But it's still fucking hot. Maybe the temperature is lower, nominally. But it feels stifling. Like you're in a perpetual sauna. I sweat all the time. Sometimes I have trouble breathing."

Others joined in. A young woman with cropped hair complained about the "mind-numbing monotony" of "the so-called weather." She spoke loudly. "It's the same day after day. Nothing happens. Shadows have disappeared. Snowfalls are long gone. Rain never falls, just an occasional mist. It's like there are no seasons—the only difference is in winter the glow above is a little less and in summer it's a little more."

An older woman with speckled gray hair said, "The calendar doesn't make sense. And it's not just the calendar. It's time itself. Dawn or high noon or dusk . . . They're meaningless. All we've got are two phases: grimy light and outright darkness."

"And these sunsets, night after night, always the same," said the young woman. "The same red glow. I detest it even more than daytime."

"I miss the sea," said a fourth person.

"I miss the sky," said a fifth.

The young man with the black mustache cleared his throat to speak. He had been introduced to Aggie as Thomas. She noticed that when he talked people paid special attention.

"The stars. Above all, I miss the stars." He pushed his glasses back up to the bridge of his nose. "We see no stars, no Milky Way, no planets, no comets, no meteors, no exploding novae. No majesty above. Nothing to inspire awe or fear. What are we without them?" He shook his head sadly. "We are solitary. We are alone. We are orphans."

The group fell into a moment of silence, then the talk turned to human behavior, how it was changing in reaction to this new environment. The lethargy of some years back had given way to something else, something deeper and more dangerous—a kind of communal despondency. Creativity was dying out. No one studied art or produced it. There was less poetry, less literature, less theater or dance. Music had died except for a few lone, odd instrumentalists. Science fell by the wayside and laboratories closed.

Violence and vandalism increased. It was as if society were breaking apart at the seams. Altruism and empathy were disappearing as violence increased. People were out for themselves. To some in the group, it heralded a return to barbarism.

"You know what it's like?" said Thomas. "It's as if evolution has gone into reverse. The worst of us are going to survive."

* * *

Aggie didn't linger after the meeting. She said she had a lot to do. On the way home, on impulse, she pulled into the National Cemetery in Arlington.

She passed the front gate, then followed the main road past the perfect geometrically aligned rows of white crosses and Stars of David. She parked at the main lot and walked along a path until she came to her favorite spot, the old Sawtooth Oak with its gnarled branches reaching high. The uppermost ones had stopped growing and were leafless.

She sat on a bench.

Her husband had made the Cocoon possible. These horrible repercussions she had just heard about, she knew them, too. Did he? Did he ever consider the unintended consequences of what he had made possible?

When Thomas had talked of Earth as a planet that had lost its sun and sky, hurling through space blind and forlorn, he put into words something she had been feeling for quite a while.

After half an hour she rose to leave, but her mind was still preoccupied and she ended up taking the wrong path. It led over the crest of a hill and toward a dark glen.

Two men stepped in front of her to block her way. They were not wearing uniforms, but they stood stiffly. One held up a hand, palm outward.

"Ma'am, You can't go here."

She looked up, startled. "But why—"

"Ma'am. We'll have to ask you to turn around."

She tried to look ahead over the man's shoulder. Some kind of business going on down below, a bulldozer heaving up dirt. The man shifted to one side, blocking her view.

"Please leave. Now."

She thought he was about to step toward her, so she turned and quickly walked away. As she retraced her steps to the car, she realized her heart was racing. She felt fear but she couldn't say exactly why.

* * *

She heard Messian's key in the lock and positioned herself on the couch. She opened a book and left it open on the coffee table.

Messian looked at her. She thought she saw him stiffen. She imagined him thinking: *Has she just been out? Where did she go?*

Sessler rushed in from an adjoining room and leapt into his arms.

"Daddy. You've been away so long."

"Not so long," he said, laughing.

They sat down to dinner. The meal of bioengineered protein patties and greenhouse vegetables felt both slow and rushed at the same time. Conversation was awkward. They did as they always did in this situation—each one talked mainly to Sessler.

He asked Sessler about her lessons—she had tutors come to the house. Mathematics was her favorite. He quizzed her on algebraic equations. She got all the answers right, pausing sometimes before delivering them and searching his eyes to be doubly sure.

"Don't push her," said Aggie.

"What do you mean?"

"She's only ten. She should learn at her own pace."

"She needs to know this. All of it. Backward and forward. If she's going to follow me."

"Maybe she shouldn't."

"What do you mean by that?"

"We shouldn't talk in front of her. Sessler, go to your room."

The child pursed her lips and left the table. She closed the door quietly behind her.

Aggie was quiet for a moment, then looked squarely at Messian and said, "What kind of life is it? The life you lead."

He recoiled. "A life of leadership."

"God knows what you really do."

"I do what I have to do."

"Do you ever stop to think about it?"

"What do you mean?"

"That you might be wrong. That maybe you're not saving the world after all. Or not the way it should be saved."

Messian stood up and dropped his fork on the table. He left without another word. Downstairs, his bodyguards, lounging in chairs, stood up quickly and snapped to.

He went out the back door to the new wing. The workers were gone for the day but it looked as if the construction was almost completed. Dirt was piled against the foundation of cinder blocks. The structure was windowless.

She watched him from a window. He stepped halfway and stood in an empty doorframe. She saw him look up to where there was a network of metal scaffolding reaching to the top of a domed ceiling.

She knew what it was. It was something he had talked about visiting years ago, a day in his youth that held special significance. The Hayden Planetarium in New York. He was dismantling it piece by piece and installing it at home.

30

FIVE YEARS PASSED. FOR AGGIE THE MONTHS RUSHED BY, NOT because they were exciting but because they were so uneventful; she felt trapped in the stasis of the day-to-day.

Sessler, now fifteen, was in the throes of adolescence. She directed much of her anger at her mother. She was quick to take offense whenever Aggie told her she could not leave the house whenever she wanted like other teenagers. Arguing with her was a losing battle. Her eyes blazed and she spit out words like venom.

Messian was usually in his penthouse office the entire day. When he was home he was a stranger. He often retreated to his private planetarium, immersing himself in his imaginary cosmos. Sometimes Aggie looked at him, now fifty-two but appearing older, a white-haired man quietly picking at his food, and she thought: *Who is that man? What do I really know of him?*

She could no longer attend the meetings of the dissidents group. They had reacted in shock when they learned who she was and abandoned the apartment in Alexandria because she had been there. But Suzanne and Kurt kept her informed of its activities and arranged for her to meet every so often with one or two of them, including Thomas.

Their litany was simple and unchanging. Totalitarianism was evil. UNCLE was a sham. Far from saving the world, the Cocoon was dehumanizing the planet and placing it on the path to destruction. When the proselytizing got hot and heavy, Thomas would wave his hand to stop it and smile at her.

It struck her that the country, too, was in a kind of suspended animation. It was recovering, albeit slowly, from "the Great Cull." There were problems, certainly; infrastructure was in shambles, crime rampant, and enterprise scarce. But at least, she thought, people were no longer just waiting to die. Food production was improving with genetically modified variants and fenced-off cultivation zones.

The northern countries coordinated their autocracies under the auspices of UNCLE. China, Japan, Russia, and Europe all marched to the same band. The embargo against the Southern Hemisphere was complete. The border was heavily guarded and refugees trying to cross it—she had learned to her horror—were killed on sight.

Aggie also opposed the Color X eradication campaign, which was well along in eliminating birds, butterflies, plants, and other condemned flora and fauna. The color was actually dropping out of the spectrum. Young people, who underwent "decolorization tests" every two years, could not see it, and even some older people had trouble distinguishing it.

At first she had defended Messian when the diatribe turned personal. At least he wasn't involved in any of the civil rights violations they spoke of. He had nothing to do with the Black Guards, she insisted. Suzanne and Kurt and Thomas disputed this, and she soon stopped.

Her husband's power, once held so close to the chest, was now visible for everyone to see. She could sense it in the deference people showed her. His alter ego, Amicus, spoke to the nation on national holidays, including the anniversary of First Launch Day, and the shimmering, remote nature of the hologram made it seem that the Power was half invisible, half human and would go on forever.

Aggie and Messian rarely made love but somehow, against the odds, especially considering her age, when she went for a routine physical she learned that she was pregnant. The baby was to be a boy. When she walked out of the doctor's office, she almost fainted.

The news upended the household. Messian was happy. At times he was even affectionate. Sessler said she yearned for a baby brother.

To Aggie's surprise, father and daughter increasingly spent more time together. Messian appreciated Sessler's intelligence and they had a common bond in science.

One evening, when the wine with dinner had relaxed them, Aggie proposed that Messian show them the wonders of the planetarium. To her amazement, he agreed. He leapt up, led them to the entrance, and punched in an access code.

Once inside the three sat side by side in reclining chairs. He turned on a machine in the center, a monstrous-looking thing with metal appendages and rotating lights for eyes.

They were about to see something no one else was allowed to see. Over the past twenty years the Color Guard had destroyed all pictures of the heavens and all references to the stars and the night sky. Descriptions of the old solar system and the universe beyond were censored.

Under the concave dome Aggie settled back in the chair and looked over at Sessler, staring up wide-eyed. The machine began its magic. She let the gathering twilight engulf her. There was the sky! It took on the bright hues of sunset, reds and yellows and oranges streaking across the great vault miles above.

Then the unearthly silence of evening set in. She thought she heard cicadas. The sky above seemed to deepen and almost vibrate. Then the Color X appeared. It shook her to her core. She felt it deep in her retina, flowing into her brain like a balm. Her throat tightened and her eyes filled with tears.

Quietly, the evening darkened and the sky turned to purple and then black. The stars came out, silent as fireflies—at first a few, then a handful, then scores upon scores, then thousands, millions. They sparkled in the sky like bits of mirrored glass. And then the full moon rose, slicing high like a discus over a silvery field, bathing everything in its flaxen glow.

Aggie fell into a trance, buoyed by waves of calm, and almost fell asleep. When daybreak came with a white that quickened into an indigo color and then to a sapphire and then to pure sunshine, she roused herself.

They left the chamber. As she heard the automatic lock slip into place behind them, she understood why he went there so often. He needed it to remain sane. But it was unjust, since others could no longer experience it. She vowed she wouldn't go there again.

When Sessler emerged she could hardly speak. It seemed the infinity of the universe made her mind spin. Then she talked excitedly about the infinite stream of galaxies and the possibility of life on other planets.

But she wasn't able to see the special color. She had no idea what her mother and father were talking about. They took her into their bedroom, opened the bedroom closet, and showed her an inlaid wooden box that opened like a puzzle, by sliding four sides in the proper order. Inside were two precious rocks.

"Lapis lazuli," Messian said. "Probably the only ones left in the country. Perhaps in the entire North."

"What's so special about them?"

"Their color."

"They're white."

"No. Their true color is hidden. It's magnificent. I'll take you to the planetarium until you can see it—as many times as it takes."

He did.

And she did.

* * *

Sessler became obsessed with the special color. She asked Aggie how a color so powerful, so vital, could just disappear. She wanted to find out everything about it, to discover its special properties.

Messian sympathized with her quest. He bragged to Aggie that Sessler, in addition to being headstrong, was a deductive thinker—two qualities he deemed essential for a scientist.

He gave her access to his private library. Soon she was surrounded by stacks of books, scribbling notes and looking up research papers on the effects of color on human emotions. She came across a German author named Goethe, whose treatise on color captured the mysterious thrall X cast upon the human heart. "We love to contemplate it," he wrote, "not because it advances to us but because it draws us after it."

She took notes. Perhaps the secret of X, she thought, is that it brings us to a new place—that it's able to convey and enhance so many profound emotions that are opposites, from melancholy to tranquility, from hope to despair.

She wrote: "This particular color is the only color that has contradiction as its very essence. It is ethereal but also earthy, it evokes the sky above and the ocean beneath. It conveys serenity and beauty but also sadness and loss. It opens the door to our own contradictory nature.

"Why else was it used to describe a certain kind of music? Or an emotional mood? Why was it so prized by Renaissance painters? Why chosen by Christians for Mary's cloak or by Muslims for Mohammed's garments? Why the color of choice for both wealthy kings and folklore paupers? Why the color not only on both shields of battle and coats of arms and police uniforms but also on flags of unity and emblems of peace?"

But there was a more obvious explanation for its power, she concluded. "Ultimately it derives from the singular fact that it clothes the sky. It is the gateway to the mystery of the universe."

For her sixteenth birthday Messian gave her what she most wanted: a passenger seat on the next Launch. She suited up in the bulky white flight uniform and crammed into a space behind the pilot and copilot as they circumnavigated the globe releasing the sulfur particles.

When she returned, she confessed to Aggie, she was disappointed that she had not been able to fly above the Cocoon to see what lay there. The Cocoon extended all the way to the top of the stratosphere. She wanted one more thing, and she was going to pester her father until he promised to give it to her.

What? asked Aggie.

Flying lessons.

* * *

Aggie's labor lasted twelve hours and was beyond painful. The baby was a breech, and to get him out the doctor had to dose her to oblivion and cut her open and lift him out. When Messian saw his son he grabbed him and raised him above his head.

"Just like Caesar!" he exclaimed.

He insisted on naming him Yolander—Yon for short. He said the name had come to him in a dream. Something in the way he handled him, almost like a prince, implied the boy was born for greatness. Maybe he was to be a continuation of the scientific dynasty that had begun with his own father.

31

To a mother's eyes, Yon *did* seem extraordinary. At two and a half, he was always on the move and into everything. When presented with a new object, he scrunched his face in concentration and repeated the word, sometimes mangling it but often mimicking it perfectly. He knew what he wanted and he sized up strangers and consigned them to one of two groups: friend or foe.

Physically he resembled his father. She noticed, when Messian balanced the boy on his lap, how much alike they looked: the same flashing eyes—the Color X—and the same unruly hair centered on a cowlick. They both had thin, wiry bodies.

Messian liked to bounce him on his knee and play an old game—"This is the way the baby rides"—and Yon would laugh, a surprisingly low, throaty laugh, and throw his head back in joy and utter his favorite word: "More, more, more."

At times like these Aggie smiled, but it would be followed by a pang of sadness. She grieved for Sessler, now seventeen. Sessler had not had many such moments when she was a child, and now that Yon was a toddler, after a brief period when Paul was close to her, he seemed to cast her aside.

Now that her pregnancy and the birth were over, Aggie felt

a growing estrangement from Messian. His work had hardened him, changed him from the man she once loved. Back then he had wanted to save the world. Now he ruled the world.

When Yon was old enough to spend part of the day in "school" with a nanny, Aggie resumed regular contact with the Zegers. They welcomed her back with open arms. As a sign of trust, they gave her tasks to perform for the Resistance and told her the actions would prove her bona fides.

* * *

Aggie walked down the block three times, brushing her belly with her thumb to make sure the envelope was still there. She walked past the doorway, trying not to look at it and trying not to look conspicuous. The more times she passed it, she knew, the more suspicious she looked, making the drop-off that much more dangerous.

She was perspiring with fear. The first time, she told herself she was just going to reconnoiter it. The second time, she was about to open the red door when a car pulled into a space; she walked to the end of the block and waited for the driver to leave.

Now she resolved to do it. She approached the red door, glanced quickly around—a mistake, but she couldn't restrain herself—and gave it a shove.

Inside, five mailboxes on the wall. She found the one with the name in black, slipped her hand inside her blouse at the midriff, and extracted the envelope that had been tucked into the elastic of her panties. She dropped it in the box and quickly left.

Walking down the street, her footsteps sounding loud to her ears, she felt a lightening relief that came in waves the farther away she got.

The Underground had a primitive communications system, relying on couriers called "pigeons," but it seemed to function reasonably well. She had been told it extended all the way into the South. This was her fourth drop and the only one to a fixed address, which she took as a sign that the dissidents were coming to trust her.

The Zegers had promised that if she proved her revolutionary credentials, they would persuade the others to admit her back into the cell, which met in a safe house in Georgetown. It was good timing, they said, because exciting things were beginning to happen and she could be a big help.

There was an upsurge of graffiti on the walls. The authorities quickly painted the slogans over in white, and the rectangles of white soon dotted the city like signposts of dissent. Suzanne and Kurt told her about other actions: A group had climbed up the Washington Monument and tossed out bundles of anti-State leaflets. Others put the leaflets in balloons and released them into the wind.

Aggie could tell when public acts of disobedience had occurred by Messian's moods. One night he confessed to being perplexed. On his way home he had passed by the Treasury Building and spotted a splotch painted in the Color X.

"First time I've seen that," he said. "I can't imagine how they got hold of it."

But soon the splotches of X were everywhere.

The Zegers continued bombarding her with diatribes against the Cocoon. From time to time Aggie would test their ideas, in much muted form, with Messian. Didn't he think in some ways things were better in the old days before the Cocoon? Didn't he worry that it was doing something to people?

"Like what?"

"I don't know. Making them feel sort of purposeless. Isolated, less human."

"The Cocoon has kept us alive. That's the first order of existence. Without that, there's nothing. The rest—even if what you say is true—can be fixed."

"I'm not so sure."

"Science can fix anything over time. That's its sole raison d'etre."

He retreated into a sulk. When she tried to talk more, he lashed out at her. She knew she had struck a nerve. He didn't want to listen to what she was saying. Perhaps he had even had the same thoughts himself.

* * *

Aggie took more risks. She agreed to deliver a package to a location in southeast Washington and when she handed it over—to a woman she recognized from the discussion group—the woman opened it, revealing a stack of anti-State leaflets.

Soon Aggie was disseminating the leaflets herself. She placed them in doorways after dark, jumping at every sound. When cars passed, her heart hammered in her chest. But each time she continued until all the leaflets were gone. They were headlined:

DOWN WITH UNCLE!
DOWN WITH THE CONSORTIUM!
DOWN WITH AMICUS!

She began to take to the intrigue. It brought an adrenaline rush and afterward the sense that she had accomplished something important.

* * *

Arriving home one afternoon, she was startled to find Messian there. He was seated at a table across from Sessler, deep in conversation, their heads leaning together. She listened in.

He was telling her stories of how he and Aggie had met in

Washington state, the untimely death of the cult leader, and the evenings of deep talk overlooking the old apple orchard. Then he recounted their early years on Dupont Circle, the drinks on the balcony, when no one even knew they were a couple.

His tone was warm and affectionate, and Sessler was drinking it in.

"How could no one know about it?"

"You'd be surprised. Once you know about all the surveillance, you know how to avoid it."

Sessler tossed her long hair and laughed softly, a laugh Aggie hadn't heard in quite a while. Suddenly her daughter appeared older. She was talking to her father like an equal.

Aggie coughed to make her presence known. The two looked up and invited her to the table.

The three had tea and continued to reminisce. Once, Messian even reached over to put his hand on Aggie's arm.

She felt a rush of tenderness for him, the first in a long time.

Sessler went to her room. Messian looked at his watch and stood up. Time to go. He walked to the door. Out of his coat pocket he pulled something, a piece of paper, and placed it on the table. She looked at it and barely suppressed a gasp. One of her leaflets.

"I know," he said. "I know what you're doing."

And now he turned those searing eyes on her. He shook his head sadly. "You know, if you get caught, there's not much I can do. I can't protect you. Things have gone too far."

She didn't know what to say.

"Everyone's nervous. You'd be surprised. The security people, they're more than nervous. They're scared. That makes them dangerous."

"I . . . I won't get caught."

"You don't know that. The more actions you undertake, the greater the chance you will." He paused a beat. "I can't say I blame you." Again, he gave a small smile—this time one of sadness. He gestured toward the leaflet. "And if I were free to do what I want, who knows? Maybe I'd do what you're doing." A pause. "But I'm not. We're on different sides."

He sounded weary and burdened, a man who had made his bed and must lie in it. He turned to leave, gave her a long look, then came back and kissed her, softly, on the forehead.

"Just be careful," he said, his hand on the doorknob.

"I will. I promise."

He left.

A figure stepped from the shadows. It was Sessler.

"Mom," she said. "Do what he says. You're not good at this cloak and dagger stuff."

32

ONE EVENING AT DINNER, ON A RARE OCCASION WHEN ALL four of them were at the table, Aggie saw a telltale spot on the back of Sessler's neck. Messian had to leave to take a call over the special line used by the authorities. Yon was in his high chair, eating bits of food and throwing some on the floor.

Aggie leaned over and touched the spot on her daughter's neck. "You better fix this—*right away*."

Sessler excused herself. When she returned from the bathroom her neck was clean. The spot of paint was gone.

The next morning Aggie found the workshop tucked away in the back of an old shed on the edge of the property. There were tubes of colors, beakers of pigment, the smell of turpentine. Under a bench were shelves that contained small, portable tubes of paint.

While she was looking at them, Sessler came in. Aggie turned toward her and said, "Are you crazy?"

"No more than you."

"But right here, right under his nose—"

"Safest place in town."

"Do you paint it . . . alone?"

"A bunch of us."

"They cover it up right away. With white paint."

"I know. It's so stupid. People see the white and they know what's underneath. We were saying the other day we should just cut corners and go straight to the white."

Aggie laughed and drew her daughter into a hug. They sat on the bench and talked for almost an hour. At one point Sessler held her mother's hand and asked, "Mom. How did Dad get to be this way?"

She thought for a good five seconds before answering. "Little by little."

* * *

Later that day Aggie dressed in a black suit and rounded the look off with a bright red scarf. She was examining herself in the mirror when Sessler appeared behind her.

"I know where you're going," her daughter remarked.

"You do?"

"To meet a certain couple."

Aggie drew back and stared at her. "What makes you say that?"

"C'mon, Mom. I know the signs. The scarf, for one. And you're nervous. You only get nervous when you go to meet them. The babysitter says you'll be away three hours." Sessler leaned over to pick some lint off her mother's shoulder. "You *had* promised to be careful, you know."

"I know, sweetie. I just feel I should. I mean, everything is so horrible. He keeps saying it's going to get better and it never does."

"They say things are heating up. The Guards are out in force. A lot of rumors flying around."

"You'll stay home—promise?"

"I will."

Aggie went to the door, then turned back and said, "Don't worry. I won't be long."

* * *

Aggie drove toward Georgetown. On Reservoir Road she passed walls scrawled with graffiti: "UNCLE SUCKS" and "BRING BACK THE SKY" One that puzzled her read "AUNTIE"—until she realized it was the homonym of a wordplay on UNCLE: "ANTI."

On P Street she saw a lineup of armored personnel carriers, their motors humming loudly, but she saw only a dozen or so Black Guards standing around outside, smoking and talking.

She looked for splotches of the Color X and spotted two of them on the old Dumbarton Oaks Museum, though there were plenty of white paint-overs. The penalty for anti-State graffiti was severe—ten years in prison, and even then who knew when you'd get out. But painting the Color X, that was such brazen defiance. What would be the penalty? She wondered how many people could discern it and what their reaction was.

She drove to Georgetown and parked the car, then walked to the townhouse on Thirtieth Street. The Zegers had given her the address. They would not be there; they had to bring materials to an underground printing press. But Thomas would. She looked forward to seeing him.

She thought of Yon back home. When she left he was sitting in his room, contented, being read to by the babysitter.

It was important to look natural, as they had counseled her. She spotted the address over the door and walked up the stoop. Across the street repairmen wearing yellow hard hats were mounting an electrical pole. That was unusual, she reflected; things were rarely fixed these days.

She knocked. An eye appeared at a peephole. A man in his thirties with shoulder-length hair admitted her. She went down the stairs to the basement, to a large windowless room. It was hot. More than two dozen men and women were seated on chairs and benches or leaning against the wall.

She recognized some from the earlier discussion group. They waved. The woman with cropped hair smiled. The Zegers had told Aggie that the group had warmed to the idea of her rejoining them; it would be a strategic advantage to include someone so close to the epicenter of power.

A young man in a T-shirt was standing in the center, talking easily and looking down at notes. She took a seat on the bottom step and listened carefully. It was a report on their activities, which he said were expanding. He read a list of the "actions" over the past two weeks that went on for several minutes.

He said they were about to start their own underground newspaper and needed volunteers. Ten people raised their hands and signed up on a sheet that was passed around. The young man said the movement was expanding. He called upon the head of a membership committee to speak.

The woman who had smiled at Aggie rose.

"I don't want to give numbers," she said. "I'll just say a lot of people are joining up. Especially young people. The graffiti campaign is working. People know we're there."

A woman with braided hair interrupted. She wanted to know how new recruits were vetted to weed out government agents and police spies.

"Each recruit needs two members to vouch for him or her. They won't be allowed to attend meetings until we're convinced they're clean. We'll put them through a series of actions that'll serve as loyalty tests."

With that, the membership head called out the names of four new recruits—Aggie's among them—and asked them to stand. They did and met with a round of applause.

The young man took the floor again. He said they were opening chapters in a number of cities where "safe houses" had been set up, including one in New York on West Twelfth Street. A major problem was establishing means of communication, especially from one city to another, given the collapsed infrastructure. So far they had a relay system of runners and half-working phone lines.

The question was how to move the struggle to the next level. For almost an hour they talked and debated, sometimes loudly, and the same questions went round and round. What was the next step? How should they grow? What is the most effective form of resistance? When should they reveal themselves?

They took a quick break. Aggie sat next to the woman who spoke and reintroduced herself. They chatted. Aggie told her that the Zegers weren't coming. She looked around and didn't see Thomas and asked about him.

The woman's face fell. "You didn't hear?"

She said he had been arrested—or at least that was the rumor. The Black Guard was seen entering his apartment house two nights ago and he hadn't been seen since.

Aggie felt herself go numb. What would happen to him?

"If it's true," the woman said, "and they have something on him, he's in for it. He's been taken either to the basement of the Hoover building, to be tortured, or to the Arlington National Cemetery."

Aggie remembered her trip there, the two men who turned her away.

"The cemetery?"

"That's where they execute people. There's a mass grave. They shoot them and dump them in."

Aggie needed to get out. She needed to go up the stairs and get some fresh air, but she could hardly move.

Then there was a distant thud upstairs. It could have been anything, a chair accidentally knocked over, a picture falling from the wall. But an alarm sounded, a buzzer set off by the lookout. It rang steadily, then cut off abruptly.

The people in the basement heard the door crashing in, the sound of wood splintering. The young man with shoulder-length hair ran down the stairs.

251

"Get out!" he shouted. "They're here! Everybody out!"

They panicked. Chairs were knocked over. They ran away from the stairs, bumping into one another. They didn't know where to go. A young woman ran to the far end of the basement.

"Follow me!" she yelled. "This way. This way! Quick!"

She mounted cellar steps and threw herself against sloping double doors. Two others helped her heave them open. They ran out and turned to pull out others crammed into the concrete passageway. Behind them was a view of the Cocoon. Those who got out found themselves in a narrow backyard.

Aggie had been close to the stairs so she was at the back of the crowd. Without thinking she followed the others toward the cellar doors. She heard the door above the stairs splintering and then a crash as the doorknob smashed against the wall.

She had no time to think and was just following instinct. Then her mind abruptly focused. She heard boot steps above, measured the size of the crowd at the cellar door; she wouldn't make it.

A figure dashed back to the stairs—the leader who had been speaking. He carried something, a board or a bar. She watched as he lunged up the steps and turned a corner. Sounds of a struggle erupted and a gunshot blast resounded loudly in the basement. His body came tumbling down. She turned away to avoid looking at it.

The crowd was mostly out now. She ran into the passageway and stumbled up the cellar steps. She was outside. People were running in all directions, looking for a way out. The townhouse was attached to houses on either side and there were no alleys between them.

They were in a long rectangular yard. Stunted shrubs lined the sides. At the rear was a six-foot-tall chain-link fence that had a gate. Two people were shaking it. The gate was padlocked. Three or four began to scale the fence, their feet racking against the metal. Others crowded around, reaching up, gripping the fence.

The back door of the townhouse flew open and uniformed men

leapt out onto a small porch. They carried blast weapons waist high and planted their feet firmly. Shots pounded out like jackhammers.

A rain of explosions sprayed the yard. She heard other sounds from the roof and looked up. Black Guards were there, too, firing down. Everywhere people were screaming. Tufts of grass flew up, branches exploded, bodies collapsed. Blood was pouring into the ground.

Aggie was among the last to flee toward the fence. She ran quickly with her red scarf streaming behind her. She zigzagged like a frightened hare, dodging bodies on the ground.

She felt a bullet enter her thigh. Another in her back. She stumbled. She broke her fall with her arms, then spun onto her back. Her body twitched as more explosions tore into her. One entered her skull. She had no time for thought, only a blinding whiteness that seemed to spread from within.

Then darkness fell as quickly as a curtain.

PART VII
THE TURNING
2092
(YON)

33

AFTER SIX WEEKS QUINLIN AND YON AND THEIR GUIDE TODD reach the eastern coast and the harbor town of Macapa. They pull up to a quay of stacked white boulders and tie up to a line of boats.

The town is teeming. So many people, doing so many things—at first it feels overwhelming. As on the western coast, the signs of destruction are everywhere but a number of buildings have been reconstructed with scaffolds and cranes. As they walk from the pier they see windmills on the hills and solar panels on the roofs.

They come to the main square. Todd peels away—he has his own place to stay. They check into a modest hotel, take long baths, and fall into bed for the night. Yon keeps the canisters under his bed.

In the morning they awake early and go outside to hunt for breakfast. Todd is waiting for them. His eyes scan everyone around. Yon is struck by a realization: he's more than a guide, he's a bodyguard.

The three stroll around the square, past cafés that line the periphery. In the center are market stalls where customers push and shove and barkers hawk their wares.

They come to a stall where fish are frying on a blackened grill. Quinlin bargains with the seller and arrives at a price. Yon reaches into his pocket for cash when an arm from behind rudely pushes him aside. An excited voice yells into his ear.

"Hombre, let me buy that for you!"

They stare at Luther, too amazed to speak.

"I told you I'd wait for you. Sooner or later, everyone from the Amazon ends up here." Luther is grinning so widely his scar turns red. "Though you sure took your time. I was beginning to worry I missed you."

They sit at a café, and Luther pulls up a chair.

"So good to see you," he says over and over. More than once, he asks about their travels and what they did.

"We did what we had to do," says Yon.

"And what's that?"

"We crossed the mountains."

"But why?"

"Like the bear. To get to the other side."

"Very funny, hombre. I think you are not dealing with me like a friend. You are very secretive."

"Even friends have secrets," puts in Quinlin.

"Can you tell me if you got what you wanted?"

Quinlin shrugs.

Luther sips his coffee slowly, puts his cup down, and looks intently from one to the other.

"I know you want to get back North," he says, lowering his voice. "I've been busy. I figured it out—with help from dockworkers here. And smugglers—there're one or two. Luckily there is a tunnel on this side, too. We'll take a boat to get there. It's all arranged."

"And once we're through, then what?"

"Then we grab another boat—a sailboat. And we sail all the way to the US. It's the fastest way. And the safest. Otherwise we cross Panama on foot. Lots of Guards there.

"You'll see. This is easy. We'll hug the coast. Only thing is, I arranged it for three people." He raises his eyes to look at Todd. "These guys who set it all up . . . I don't know. They want you to stick to the plan."

"Tell them it's four," says Yon.

"I don't know how to reach them now. It's all set up."

"Then no problem. Once we're through the tunnel we'll pay you and you can go your own way. The three of us will take the sailboat."

Luther shakes his head. "You'll need me. Trust me. You'll need me."

"We'll manage."

They finish their coffees with the issue unresolved. They agree to meet at the boat the next morning. Luther has checked the tides—the boat is hidden in a marsh and can only make it out at high tide. They must leave by 6:00 a.m., he insists. He hands them a map and wanders off to buy supplies.

Before he's lost in the crowd, Todd stands, too. He hastily copies the map onto a napkin. "I haven't been here in years," he says. "Think I'll look around." He follows Luther, his eyes fixed on his back.

* * *

Yon and Quinlin arise in the thick of darkness. They follow the map through deserted streets, using a flashlight to read the signs, reversing direction two or three times. Dogs bark as they pass, leaving the town behind.

They walk for almost an hour and arrive at a secluded harbor. Luther is sitting on an overturned rowboat, smoking—that's odd, they've never seen him smoke before. He greets them, leads the way to a twelve-foot motorboat, and helps put their bags between the seats. Yon holds on to his knapsack. Luther looks at his watch.

"Almost six o'clock," he says. "Your friend's not here."

They wait twenty minutes, then ten more. The sky is beginning to lighten, the rays of the sun reaching across in a red arc. They can see a gray storm cloud gathering in the east.

"We gotta go," Luther says. "Weather's changing. Now or never."

Quinlin and Yon look at one another. Silently, with misgivings, they nod their agreement.

The three push off in the boat.

34

THE TRIP TAKES A FULL DAY. WHEN THEY LAND FAR UP THE coast, Luther lets them off, rides the boat twenty yards off-shore, and smashes the anchor through a floorboard to sink it.

"Cover our tracks," he explains.

Yon and Quinlin are convinced that he's responsible for Todd's disappearance but don't challenge him. They need him to reach the North.

They come to a tunnel, which Yon thinks doesn't look promising. The entrance is narrow and barely hidden behind a clump of bushes. It looks as if it was recently built.

"When was this thing dug?" asks Yon, touching the entrance and releasing a tiny avalanche of rocks and sand.

"How the fuck would I know?" Luther replies. "All I know is it works."

"And where did you hear about it?"

"Back in Macapa."

"Who told you?"

"Colleagues. Smugglers."

"You trust them?"

"Hombre, trust is our currency." His tone isn't sardonic. "Without it, we are nothing. What's the matter? Don't you like it?"

"I don't."

"Well, you got no alternative. Unless you want to spend the rest of your life here."

Luther opens his backpack. There's not much in it. He pulls out three boxes of matches and hands one to each of them.

"If you have to see for some reason, if it's really important, strike a match. We can't use candles cause that'll eat up the oxygen. There's not much as it is."

"So how do we breathe?" asks Quinlin.

"Every so often, like a couple of hundred feet, you'll come to a pipe. It protrudes down from the ceiling. Stop and take a couple of breaths. More if you need it. Move quickly but not too quickly. That wastes oxygen."

"How long is this thing?" asks Quinlin.

"Like I say, I never been through it. But I reckon it's got to be at least two or three miles to go all the way under the border. Depends of course where it comes out. One other thing, it's tight. Room for only one at a time. Every so often there're turn-arounds in case you meet someone coming the other way. You can use it to move ahead or behind someone else."

"This is sounding worse and worse."

"There'll be wooden supports and crossbeams and stuff like that. Be careful of them. Don't dislodge them. Try not to even touch them." Luther affects a disarming smile. "How are you about rats?"

"Shit." Quinlin shakes his head and walks away.

"And if you gotta piss, I suggest you go now," Luther adds.

Yon and Quinlin step to a nearby clearing and turn their backs.

"I don't trust the bastard," murmurs Quinlin.

"Let him go between us," says Yon. "I'll start and you bring up the rear. That way we can keep an eye on him."

When they come back, Yon announces he's going first.

"I'm smaller. I don't want to get stuck behind your big ass."

"Okay. I'll go next," Luther says.

"Fine," declares Quinlin.

Yon kneels before the entrance and crawls in. He can see five feet or so ahead. The opening is low and narrow. He lifts his head and bumps it on the ceiling, dislodging a rain of sand.

He moves ahead some more. Now he's in total darkness. He feels the walls on both sides and his backpack brushes against the top. He labors to squirm through and swings it around under his belly.

"What's the matter?" yells Quinlin from the entrance.

"There's not even room to wear the pack."

He crawls ahead and the air around him feels clammy. He hears someone behind him entering the tunnel. It's got to be Luther. He can hear his knees scuffling the dirt, the sound of his breathing.

Even without seeing, he can tell the tunnel is shoddily built. Rocks stick out on the sides and the walls are uneven. He comes to a prop and a crossbeam and reaches up to touch it. There is a sheet of wood, maybe plywood, lining the ceiling for about three feet. A small mound of dirt lies below. Someone must have plugged a small cave-in.

"How you doin'?" comes a voice behind him, sounding distant. Quinlin's.

"Okay," he lies.

The blackness is total. He holds his hand an inch before him and can't see it. His knees ache. He fights hard to suppress a growing feeling of claustrophobia. How far behind him is Luther? Was he joking about the rats?

Slowly, he advances. How far has he come? Hard to tell—his sense of distance is off. But it can't be far. Maybe twenty, thirty feet. He stops for a moment to catch his breath. He notices something: even when he takes air deep into his lungs, he needs to breathe again right away. Luther was right. Oxygen is low.

263

He crawls with one hand, holding the other over his head to protect it from rocks in the ceiling. He touches something—a thin, round pipe. He lifts his head, holds the pipe in his mouth, and sucks to fill his lungs. He does it four times. His head clears. Reluctantly, he leaves the pipe and moves on.

He hears something ahead. He stops, searches in his pocket for the matches, and strikes one. Light explodes before him. He peers ahead. A small dark hump of black fur and two yellow eyes staring back. The rat scrambles away. The match goes out.

The passage widens—a turn-around. He crawls past and the passage narrows again and he feels even more confined.

He pushes on, all his senses on alert. He moves from pipe to pipe, grabbing gulps of oxygen. He hears another rat and lights a match and shoos it away. Then he decides not to light any more matches. Better to scare them with noise than stare into those yellow eyes. One scurries by. He feels the paws bouncing off his pants leg.

"*Shit!*" yells Luther, smacking at it.

He passes a turn-around and another. He figures he must be halfway through, maybe more. It's gone on so long. Will it ever end? He passes another crossbeam, a series of logs and planks propping up the ceiling. Something's on the floor, to one side. It feels like a wire. He moves on. Goes another twenty feet.

Abruptly, from behind, comes a creaking, then a loud rumbling. His stomach knots in fear. He knows what it is, even as the noise builds and he feels a shaking. More shaking, thunderously loud. His body pitches forward. The air filled with dust that swirls around, making breathing even harder. He coughs.

Something's prodding behind him. He feels a hand on his foot, his leg.

"Hurry. Hurry. Get a move on!"

Luther's pushing him from behind.

"What happened?" yells Yon. But he knows. He can't bear to even put the thought into words. He just keeps it unnamed.

"Quin. Where are you?"

"Keep going. We'll find out."

Yon stops. Turns as much as he can. He lights a match. It shows the muddy air, swirls of dust. He sees Luther as a dark outline.

"We have to find him." He yells *Quin* over and over. No reply.

"Not now," says Luther. "Move ahead. We're in danger. Damn thing could collapse some more."

"No."

"Get the hell out!"

Yon moves ahead quickly. Ten feet down the tunnel is a turn-around. He moves to one side.

"Come on," he yells back. "Hurry up."

"What're you doing?" yells Luther.

Yon doesn't answer. Luther pulls up next to him.

"Listen to me. You can't go back there. You do and you won't get out alive."

"Get out of the way. *Now.*"

Luther moves ahead. Yon turns and crawls back quickly. He feels the dust against his face. As he gets closer to the cave-in it's thicker. Breathing gets harder. He lights another match.

And there it is. A solid wall of dirt and rock, right ahead.

The brown air swirls, moving like tidal eddies. The wall of rock and dirt starts at the ceiling and reaches the floor, slanting toward him. Impassable. No one could survive that.

And then he sees something—a hand protruding out from under the wall. The palm is turned upward, the fingers curved. Pale white.

He reaches out and touches the hand. Rubs the palm and cradles it. It's warm. He searches for a pulse. There is none.

The match goes out. He lights another.

With his free hand he tries to push the debris away from the hand. It's impossible. Every time he digs around it, more dirt and pebbles tumble down. He tugs the hand. It doesn't move.

The match goes out. He lights yet another and digs at the pile until he comes upon something hard. Slowly, carefully, he excavates it. A knife—Quin's knife. He must have been holding it when he died.

Why? Did he need to defend himself?

He feels his grief welling up. He can't believe it.

He's gone. Gone. Gone.

He takes the knife and stays there a long time. The dust settles around him. He forgets how difficult it is to breathe and thinks: *What now? What do I do now?*

Can he bury Quinlin? Impossible. How would he even get the debris off the body? It pours down like an hourglass. As soon as one spoonful is taken away, another would take its place.

A voice is yelling to him, echoing through the tunnel. Luther must have reached the exit. Yon doesn't answer. But he moves. He backs away toward the turn-around. He has to go on, somehow.

As he retreats, he lights a match for a last look. Then he sees it—the wire, coming down the side of the wall and disappearing into the wall of dirt and rock. Connected no doubt to the crossbeam now crushed on top of Quinlin.

He knows what happened. It was no accident.

35

YON CAN'T FORGET THE IMAGE OF QUINLIN BURIED ALIVE. HE can barely look at Luther. His heart is teeming with revenge. Why did he do it? But for the moment he has to dissemble, pretend he doesn't know Luther killed him.

They've walked up the coast and they're searching for the sailboat. For two days, after emerging from the tunnel shaken and caked with dirt, they've been following a path that is supposed to lead them to it. They've barely spoken and are running out of food.

Overhead, the farther north they go, the Cocoon is beginning to settle in. In place of that vast open sky, there's a stultifying grayness pressing down like a weight.

Luther stops, pulls a small compass from his pocket, consults it, and points straight ahead.

"We should have been there by now," he says. "But I'm sure we're going right."

"You're always sure."

Luther shrugs. He heads out between two trees, pushing aside branches that whip back. Yon drops behind. He feels Quinlin's knife in his right pocket smacking against his thigh. He stares at

267

a spot between Luther's shoulder blades where a circle of sweat spreads on his khaki jacket.

It would be so easy—just walk up and stab him.

But then how would he find the boat? How would he get his precious package to Sessler? He berates himself; he should have seen the betrayal coming. All those times when Luther acted strangely. Why hadn't he acted on his instincts? Maybe for the same reason he doesn't kill him right now.

But what's his game? Who is he working for? If he's an agent for the Power, why is he helping me return to the North? Or is he? Now that he's disposed of Quinlin, will he come after me?

The questions and fears go around endlessly, while the circle of sweat on the back of the man ahead keeps spreading.

* * *

They reach the shore and walk north for an hour along a path that veers into ankle-deep water. The mud sucks at their shoes and they slow to a snail's pace.

Luther yells "Aha!" and points to a building at the water's edge. It's a boathouse. Inside, the far wall is open to the sea. In the center, bobbing gently, is a sleek sailboat twenty feet long.

"Right where I thought," says Luther. He steps onboard. "You know how to sail?"

Yon nods. It has been years since he sailed alone as a boy in Canada, but he remembers it well. "I'll captain," Yon says.

They move straight out, riding the soft waves. Fifty feet offshore, Yon kills the engine and they hoist the sails. They are blazing red—a strange color for a smuggler's boat, thinks Yon.

He checks the telltale on the mainsail. The wind is up, steady and strong. They can make good time. With his hand on the tiller, he takes the boat a mile out, then turns north, following the coastline.

Luther comes to the stern and sits across from Yon, staring down his nose at him, his head tilted. *He's appraising me,* Yon thinks.

"You're quiet," Luther says.

Yon shrugs off an answer and stares back.

"You upset about something?" Yon shakes his head. "Quinlin's death?" persists Luther. "Can't say I blame you. He was a good man."

"Look. I don't want to talk about it."

"Suit yourself." Luther points to the tiller. "Why don't I take over? You get some rest."

Yon nods agreement. As Luther stands, there's a sudden lurch—the boat shudders and the boom swings round, almost catching him in the small of his back. He ducks quickly as it passes overhead.

"Hey! Watch it!"

"Not my fault. Sudden shift in the wind."

"It coulda knocked me over."

"But it didn't."

"No thanks to you."

Yon goes below deck and rests on a bed. He places the knife under his pillow. Soon the rocking of the boat and the soft creaking of her wood lull him to sleep.

Hours later he wakes with a start. He's rolling on the bed and dishes are sliding along the galley. The boat is bucking wildly. He leaps up, goes up on deck. A squall.

"Came up suddenly," Luther says. "Look at that." He points to the east, where a swirling blackness has set in. "You don't usually see this up north."

The waves begin to swell and fall. They grow—six feet, eight feet, ten.

"I'll take down the sails," Yon says, moving cautiously along the side deck toward the bow.

When he returns, Luther is wearing an orange life jacket and tosses another one to Yon. The wind whips his clothes and the waves are growing bigger. The boat heads into them bow first, breaking the crests. They're soaked with spray and rain. Darkness descends. They fight the storm all night, riding out the ten-foot waves. The cabin floods, the pump fails, they bail frantically.

Morning comes and with it, dim light. But the waves and the rain beat on for another four hours, until gradually the storm relents and the rain gives way to a foggy mist.

Luther goes below and Yon lingers for a while, raising the sails. He bends down and through a window catches a glimpse of Luther inside, lying on the bed. He sees him move the pillow, lift it, discover Quinlin's knife. He reads fear on Luther's face and thinks, *He knows I found it and mean to use it.*

Yon makes his way toward the cabin door. As he slides it open, Luther comes lunging out. He's holding the knife outstretched, the blade aiming for his chest.

Yon dodges, fends off the knife with his elbow. Spinning, he slams his arm down to lock Luther's forearm. Luther wriggles free and wields the knife. Yon's life jacket rips, he feels a slash in his shoulder, sees a spot of blood.

They tumble on the deck, rolling and thrashing. Luther drops the knife. He grabs Yon's neck and squeezes. Yon gasps, hugs him, and falls backward, knocking Luther's head on the gunwale. They wrestle, awkward in their life jackets.

Luther falls away, swings a roundhouse, and misses. Yon reaches down, finds the knife, and slashes the air wildly, moving toward Luther, who leaps up and runs to the bow. He turns and backs away with Yon in pursuit, flailing the air, until there's no place left to go.

Luther swings his fist wildly, delivering a glancing blow off Yon's arm. Yon plunges the knife into his elbow. Luther screams and half falls, half jumps into the water. He plunges down, rises up, his head two feet away. His orange life jacket keeps him afloat, bobbing up and down, as the boat rapidly moves ahead.

Yon watches as Luther recedes farther and farther into the distance. He watches while Luther's head gets smaller and smaller, until he's just a dot on top of an orange dot that gradually disappears.

Yon goes below, lies down, exhausted. He removes his life jacket. He finds a first aid kit and bandages the gash on his shoulder. Then, when his adrenaline-fueled rush slowly calms down, he falls into a heavy sleep.

* * *

When he wakes, the sea is as calm as a sheet of smoked glass. He bails the water out of the cabin. A breeze picks up and he lets out the sails. All that day he rides the wind, using Luther's compass as a guide.

He makes his way north, far from the coast, unseen, aiming toward Florida. From time to time he thinks of Quinlin with a heavy heart. He tries to steel himself for what's ahead and for facing it without the protection of his older friend and companion.

He also thinks, without a moment of regret, of Luther meeting his watery grave. Good riddance. If only they had dispensed with him earlier, Quinlin might still be with him.

The farther north Yon goes, the heavier the cover of the Cocoon, until once again the repulsive layer of yellow-gray haze spreads across everything. Once again there's that smothering sense of living under a suffocating blanket that cuts the planet off from outer space.

PART VIII
THE RAID
2092
(SESSLER)

36

FIFTEEN YEARS HAVE PASSED SINCE THAT HORRIBLE DAY WHEN Sessler saw her mother alive for the last time.

She has dedicated those years to the Resistance, rising steadily in the leadership ranks until she reached the top, where she is now, hiding in the half-built water tunnel of what once was a great city.

Now they may have to abandon their hiding place. Bevin, the runner who first encountered Yon and brought Quinlin to him, has fallen into the clutches of the Black Guard. A source high up in the Power told them that his initial interrogator was Vexler Tigor, the notorious sadist with the telltale scar on his cheek. After the first day Vexler apparently disappeared on some kind of mission.

Now Sessler is reconnoitering the far end of the tunnel where no one has been before, searching for an escape in case of a raid.

She stops to rest among the tumbled rocks and dripping walls. There, by her feet, is an unlikely object lying next to broken glass. She picks it up. It's a red bandana next to a pair of broken glasses. She holds the bandana in her hand and sits down on a boulder, experiencing a cascade of painful memories. She makes no effort to fend them off—she succumbs to them, letting them wash over her like scalding water.

She arrived at the townhouse moments after the massacre. She went around the block to an apartment building in the rear and raced up the stairs to the roof. From there she watched the Black Guard in the backyard. They were taking photos, collecting shoes and other articles and searching the pockets of the two dozen dead.

A slash of red cut across her vision, the scarf. She stared, focused on a body in the middle of the yard. It was her mother. She laid in a contorted position, face up. Her hair was spread out like a halo. Sessler could see the dark stains of blood on her bare arms and her temple.

There was no question. She was dead.

Sessler fell to her knees on the rooftop. She was trembling. Her mind seemed to leap around of its own accord. She didn't move, didn't do anything. Minutes passed. Slowly, her mind wound down and she returned to herself.

She wanted nothing more than to hug her mother, to smooth her hair and clean the blood off her temple. She stood abruptly and turned her back on the yard and went home. She dismissed the babysitter, packed a few things, and woke up Yon. She took him into her parents' room, looking for money, jewelry, anything of value.

Suddenly, there was a sound. The front door opening. Someone moving about. It had to be her father—no one else would dare to walk in without being admitted. She stepped into the closet, hugging Yon close. She put a finger on his lips. He mustn't make a sound. She closed the door into the darkness.

She recognized her father's tread. She opened the door a noiseless crack. Steps entered the room. He stepped into the narrow band of light. He looked wild, anguished. She saw him, for just an instant, not as her father but as someone else.

He left. The sound of the front door closing. She waited minutes, then stepped out, tripping on something in the closet. The wooden box. Yon started to say something. She ordered him to be quiet, set him on the bed, put the box on the dresser, and opened it by sliding the sides. She reached down and pocketed the two stones.

Years later she couldn't say how she reached the Zegers' apartment in Maryland. She must have driven but she couldn't say for sure. She remembered only the sight of Suzanne and Kurt opening the door, how scared they were. They waved her inside.

Where are you going? she asked. They looked at one another, seemed to be thinking: Should we tell her? Up north, Kurt said. Back to Canada. Stay there a while. See how things turn out.

She thrust Yon at them. Take him, she said. You must. It's the only way to save him from Messian—it was telling, she thought later, that she said "Messian," not "my father." Suzanne squatted down to his height and held him. Her shoulders sheltered him. The transfer was done.

And you? they asked. I'll be fine. Don't worry. Sessler felt in charge, older than seventeen. On a piece of paper she scribbled the address of a safe house in New York, the one she had heard about. Kurt took it gratefully.

She went to the door but then turned back on impulse. She approached them and pulled out one of the stones from her pocket and handed it over.

"Take it," she commanded. "For him."

Then she was gone. On the way down stairs an image wouldn't leave her, her father in the bedroom standing in the band of light. He *was* somebody else. He was a man she barely knew, a monster who had brought horror and bloodshed to the world and to his own family.

* * *

After handing Yon off to the Zegers, she lived a vagabond existence, seeking out groups of similarly disaffected people and staying with them, moving from one town to another, relying upon word of mouth to find compatible souls. She never told them her real name.

She ended up in a commune on the South Carolina coast, young people trying to make a go of it off the grid. They lived in a strip of six abandoned houses within five minutes' walk to the ocean, which had flooded a grove of hackberry trees. They foraged for hours every day for food and talked endlessly about the deteriorating world and its corrupt leadership. She didn't tell them who she was.

And then one day, this dark-skinned, willowy rebel—Gabriella—walked in. She was dynamic and seductive. She carried a cane but didn't need it for walking. She pulled out the handle and showed off the dagger.

On the first night, with the whole group eating a communal supper, Sessler felt Gabe's presence like a beam of light. She kept an eye on her without looking at her directly. Whatever Sessler did—picking her plate from a stack, ladling out her beans, sitting cross-legged on the blanket—she knew exactly where Gabe was and what she was doing.

The group talked about the sky; some were old enough to remember it. Sessler talked knowledgably about the constellations and planets. She was talking for Gabe's benefit, sounding brilliant, careful not to look at her. When she cast a sidelong glance she saw Gabe sitting quietly with her arms folded behind her head, looking at her.

On the second night the two fell into bed. Their lovemaking was slow, deliberate, elevated by suppressed passion. Sessler had never felt like this with anyone. She didn't confess this right away.

For weeks they fed each other ideas and the discussions turned political. One night at 3:00 a.m., over endless cups of coffee, Sessler admitted her identity. She wept. Gabe hugged her and assured her she detested her father almost as much as Sessler did.

They realized that in their separate wanderings, they had encountered a wide range of people who despised the Power. If they could only bring them together in a network they would have the kernel of a Resistance movement.

They moved to New York, a more propitious place for recruiting. The city was wild in those days, lots of crime, misfits and anarchists roaming the streets.

They squatted in a former factory in Brooklyn, called in their contacts, and accumulated converts. Their numbers grew. Dispossessed workers joined, including a former sandhog named Templar. One evening, when they were discussing where to move "the operation," he laughed and said, "I got the perfect place." The next morning he introduced them to the water tunnel.

* * *

Sessler stands up to resume her search for an exit. She feels crushed by worries—the Resistance, the possible raid, and Quinlin and Yon. What are the odds that they'll reach the mountain village, meet Soledad, and make it back, bringing the essential package? The mission, which once seemed difficult but achievable, now strikes her as a desperate gamble.

And the gamble is not on her own life. It's on her younger brother's.

And at home, how long did Bevin hold out? Probably not long. The question is: How much information did he have? Did he know the location of the water tunnel? She asked everyone who knew him; no one could say for sure.

She has had strategic talks with Gabe, going over the possibilities. They've spent three years building the Resistance headquarters underground and now the whole enterprise is in jeopardy.

"Listen," Gabe says. "As a runner he knew the drops. We haven't heard that any of them have been rolled up. Maybe he's not talking. Or maybe they're not asking."

"Look me in the eye and tell me you believe that."

Gabe shrugs and gives a small confessional smile.

Sessler walks over and plants a grateful kiss on her lips. "But thank you."

* * *

She pockets the bandana, leaves the glasses on the tunnel floor, adjusts the light on her miner's helmet, and keeps walking north, where none of them has ventured before. She knows the tunnel has been constructed in segments; the workers must have left access points along the way.

This part of the tunnel has deteriorated. In places she has to wade through water a foot deep and work her way around boulders fallen from the roof, some of them half as large as she is.

She comes to a storage room blasted out of the wall. Inside are old tools covered in granite dust, coiled hoses, a small drill, two folding chairs, and two lanterns. She picks up the lanterns and shakes them—still some kerosene inside. She lifts the lid of a bin in a corner and sees explosives. They could come in handy.

She walks on. Farther up she sees a shaft and a thin beam of light shining down. It's another elevator, this one with a manual crank to raise and lower it. She steps in and tries it. Slowly she ascends, gets out, and looks around. She is above ground, in a deserted alley next to abandoned railroad tracks. A sign reads 49TH STREET.

She returns underground and retraces her steps to the headquarters.

Gabe is waiting for her. They go into Sessler's office.

"Well?" says Gabe.

Sessler replies she has found the exit but that it is a long way away and the elevator is manual.

"It'll take a long time to get everybody up."

"So, what do you think? Should we just leave now?"

Sessler thinks it over. If Quinlin and Yon succeed in their mission, she and Gabe and everyone else will have to move quickly to strike the Power. They'll need a functioning headquarters to coordinate the complicated plan.

She reaches a decision. "We'll stay here but we'll run evacuation drills. We may be able to devise a way to give us more time to get out. We can plant explosives to cover our retreat. And meantime we should scout out other places in the city as a fallback. That's for you to do."

"Great," says Gabe. "I was getting antsy here anyway."

37

SESSLER IS IN HER OFFICE WHEN THE ALARM GOES OFF. IT'S A piercing sound, activated by one of the lookouts in the shed above ground.

She runs to the tunnel entrance. Templar is standing in the bucket, looking up. Several others are close to him. At that moment a Black Guard comes rappelling down. The heel of his boot strikes Templar on the forehead and he falls to the ground. The Guard leans down, pulls a knife out of a leg sheath, bends over, and slits his throat.

"Quick," yells Sessler to her shocked troops. "Get weapons."

Another Guard rappels down the elevator cable and lands squarely on the back of the first one, who cries out. The two collapse at the bottom of the shaft, slipping in the widening pool of Templar's blood. A third Guard comes down, this one with a blazing helmet light.

The melee gives precious time to the Resistance. Two members of the security team take positions behind an outcropping of rock. They fire at the Black Guards as more and more of them come down the shaft, a tangle of arms and legs. They're enmeshed in the growing pile of bodies.

"Hold them off as long as you can," Sessler shouts. She leaves to order the evacuation.

More defenders arrive and fire from the darkened tunnel. They have an advantage: the shaft is so narrow that the attackers have to come down one by one. The beams of light from the Black Guard helmets make them easy targets.

Sessler looks back to see the bodies piling up, so many that they form a barrier. Behind it the Guards are more protected. They rest their blast guns on the heap and shoot back.

The Resistance members know what to do: report immediately to assigned stations. They've recently practiced an emergency escape, but even so, some are confused. The gunfire sets off panic. Others run to their rooms to retrieve belongings they think are essential.

The designated defenders rush toward the entrance to fight the attackers at the elevator.

Sessler directs the evacuation, telling people where to go. She checks each emergency station to make sure that everyone has turned up. When they have, she waves the group down the tunnel, away from the fight.

"Go quickly," she orders. "Watch your step. If you fall and hurt yourself you'll endanger everyone."

Group leaders have miner's caps to light the escape route. They've practiced this during drills and know not to face backward to avoid signaling the way for their pursuers.

The leaders leave as soon as everyone is there. Young people help the older ones, putting their arms around them to steady them and occasionally lifting them over cracks in the floor. Others carry the few children piggyback or on their shoulders, shushing them as they hurry forward.

One group lingers anxiously at its station, awaiting its missing leader. "Where is he?" asks a sixteen-year-old girl.

Sessler has seen the man among the defenders. She appoints the girl as the new leader for the group.

"Wait here a moment," she says. She rushes to her office in the shed, opens a locked file, pulls out a raft of documents, and stuffs them into her knapsack. She comes back and hands it to the girl. "Save this at all costs. Whatever you do, don't let the Black Guard get it."

She sends the group on, watching the figures fleeing down the darkened tunnel, their lights flickering ahead on the walls. Soon they will enter the part of the tunnel they've rarely seen, where the floor is littered with boulders and flooding and the footing is treacherous.

She buzzes the tunnel entrance on the walkie-talkie. A woman's voice comes on. It's Gabe.

"What's going on?" Sessler asks.

"We've constructed a barrier and we're behind it. But more and more Guards are coming down. They're grouping. They're going to charge soon."

"If they do, retreat."

"Okay."

She looks around. The tunnel is all but deserted and clothes and other belongings are scattered everywhere. She rushes to her office and into the makeshift laboratory, where she smashes the beakers and chemicals. Nothing can be left to shed light on her experiments.

* * *

In the distance, toward the entrance of the tunnel, the sounds of fighting are louder. They can't hold out much longer, not against a full assault. Not much time left.

What else must be done? She goes to the meditation room and smashes the controls—no point in letting them know they were able to recreate the forbidden color. She goes to the generator and extinguishes the lights in the tunnel. Total darkness engulfs her.

She calls Gabe, who says they're pinning them down, but Sessler can tell she's lying.

"Hold on. I'll be there soon."

She pulls out a revolver and runs back through the tunnel toward the elevator. She arrives as the Black Guards are ready to charge. They vault over the barrier and rush toward the resisters.

The only light comes from the Black Guards helmets and the resisters fire at them. Their bodies fall to the granite floor in a heap.

Sessler grabs Gabe by the arm and pulls her away. They lead the six other defenders back through the tunnel. They know the terrain and make good time, rushing past the dormitories, the shed, the meditation room, and the supply depot.

Here they stop and retrieve lamps. They pour out the kerosene and set it alight, leaving a wall of fire behind them. This gives them some time to negotiate the unknown passageway north.

Another fifty yards up the tunnel, Sessler stops the group. She shines her light on the sides and roof of the rock. They see the charges planted in crevices—the handiwork of Templar, who planted the explosives the day after she found them. The dynamite is their last best hope.

She stops at a hollow in the rock and sends the others on ahead, waiting until they're almost out of sight—all but Gabe, who stops and waits. Sessler connects the wire to a timed detonator and quickly joins her.

They run together, jumping over the boulders and splashing through the ankle-deep water. Every twenty yards or so the tunnel veers to one side, giving them a sense of protection from the blast.

But when it comes, it's powerful. They feel the concussion of air at their backs, an ear-splitting noise, followed by the long low roar of a cave-in. They can take their time now, but they don't. They can't be sure that the debris has formed an impenetrable wall.

After another forty-five minutes they make it to the exit. They crank their way up the elevator to the alleyway under the railroad tracks.

No one else is there. They've split up and gone to their assigned hideouts.

38

SESSLER STANDS AT THE EDGE OF BRYANT PARK, BRINGING IN THE
last of the resisters to the old public library on Fifth Avenue. It
was Gabe who found the new headquarters. Already, two months
after the raid, it's up and running.

In the hours after the bust, luck favored Sessler. She felt strange
above ground; the light hurt her eyes. One by one, she and Gabe
tracked down the groups at their assigned hideouts. Among the
first was the sixteen-year-old girl who had escaped with the knapsack, which contained contact information for Resistance groups
across the country—a huge relief.

Sessler leads the last few stragglers through the shantytown in
the park. The denizens are tough but for the most part friendly.

"Where you been, Sis?" inquires an old man sitting on a stool.

"Here and there." Sessler smiles.

"Still causing trouble?"

"My middle name."

"Naw. Your middle name's *gorgeous*."

She has three or four amiable encounters like this. Though
pressed, she takes the time to stop and chat. Neighborliness is the
price she pays to have five hundred friendly people sitting on her

287

doorstep. They're against the Power and would raise the alarm the moment the Black Guard entered the settlement.

She reaches the west wall of the library. It's crowded with huts of plywood, cardboard, and metal sheets. They enter a shack with a wooden door and a long tarp hanging down from above. Inside is a ladder tilted against the wall under the tarp.

One by one she sends her charges up the ladder. They climb through a broken window into the building. She follows them and leads them along a darkened corridor. At the end she finds a lantern and lights it with a match.

"Here's the deal," she says. "There are almost fifty of us. We've got the run of the building. The Power closed it decades ago.

"We've no idea how long we'll be here. It depends on a lot of things. Meanwhile, make use of it. We've got a decent kitchen upstairs but getting food is hard, so your rations are limited. You can use the main lobby for exercise. It's got grand staircases on both sides.

"But make sure the windows are covered and for God's sake don't make noise. Nothing must be seen or heard on the outside, both during the day and at night. Do you understand?"

They say they do.

"Down that way"—she points to the end of the corridor—"is a staircase. The elevators don't work. So we've come up with a way to reach the stacks below ground."

She leads them to a chute. The floor and the ceiling have four-foot wide holes and two thick cables hang between them, disappearing in the darkness above and below.

"This is our elevator. You thought the one in the water tunnel was dicey, check this out."

"What is it?" asks a young woman with tattoo sleeves.

"The dumbwaiter that used to carry books up from the underground shelves. Down below are the subterranean stacks. Up above is the old reading room."

She pulls on a cable until the box comes up, steps on top of it, grasping the cable tightly, and gently lowers herself down. She passes one tier of shelves and another and another.

One by one, the group follows her. As they descend they feel a slight chill and are struck by the smell of molding paper and disintegrating leather. They go down seven levels to the very bottom.

Here, by the light of lanterns, is an underground habitat. The metal shelves have been cleared away, opening up an area for sleeping quarters and living space. Dozens of people are there.

She leaves the group in the hands of the quartermaster to obtain cots and supplies. She finds Gabe standing next to a blackboard with a cluster of young people seated before her.

They go to a corner and sit at a small table. Coffee is brewing nearby and they each take a cup.

Gabe lowers her voice excitedly. "I couldn't wait to tell you. We got word yesterday that Yon and Quin reached Macapa. That's on the east coast. So presumably they came from Nueva Loja. They must have already met Soledad. Maybe they're returning."

Sessler feels a rush of joy but has an immediate question. "How did you hear this?"

"From our source in SAAM."

"Did Yon get the package?"

"He didn't say."

Sessler sips her coffee slowly, thinking about their source inside SAAM. So the Power knew of Yon's mission—but how much did they know? "It'd be good to learn if they didn't report spotting a package because there wasn't one or because they didn't know to look for it."

"I agree."

"How long ago were they spotted in Macapa?"

"Not clear. Maybe a week. Maybe more."

"So odds are, they're well on their way. If they come by land, it could be a month or more. If by boat, what?—three weeks?"

"Depends. On winds, currents. We don't know what it's like down there."

Sessler's quiet. Gabe interrupts her train of thought.

"Just because the Power spotted them doesn't mean they know their route. I mean, it's a huge ocean and a huge continent."

"Maybe. I hope you're right. I'd feel better if I knew how they tracked them down."

Gabe finishes her coffee in one gulp. "I guess we'll find out one way or another when our contact meets them in Florida."

"I think one of us should go to meet them. It's dangerous now."

"I'll do it," says Gabe. "You should stay here and prepare so as soon as we have the package we can get moving."

"That makes sense."

"Where exactly is the rendezvous?"

"Ocala. The first settlement on the Gulf coast of Florida. There's an old hotel, the Statler. We told Quin before he left."

"Nothing is more important than this mission," says Sessler. "Everything rides on it."

Gabe strides off. "Of course. I know. Stop worrying."

Sessler didn't voice her real concern. How did the Power manage to conduct surveillance in the South? Did they have agents down there? A whole network of informers? What if they had somehow infiltrated an agent to shadow Yon and Quinlin?

She shakes her head. Not likely. Quinlin is street smart. He'd spot an agent right away.

She rides the box elevator to the upstairs reading room. It's her favorite place. The heavy wooden desks are there, though many of their green lamps are broken. The filthy windows don't let in much light and some of the chandeliers have crashed to the ground.

But on the ceiling, inside the elaborately carved wooden moldings, are the frescoes. Luminous clouds are depicted in whites and pinks, and behind them is the sky. The sky makes her want to gasp with pleasure. It's painted in the color she loves.

She believes that the painting survived only because the Power assumed that once they sealed the building, no one would ever see it.

She walks to the far end of the room, where she keeps her books on the molecular make-up of minerals and the cellular structure of marine plants. She sits down and reaches for the small stack of old scientific periodicals she had come across last time. They were called "CRI Reports," published by the Climate Research Institute. She vaguely remembers hearing her father talk about the Institute, which was run by that woman named Lesley Kyserike, who raised him.

The last issue is dated April 12, 2040—more than fifty years ago.

She opens it and turns to an article entitled, "Is SAAM Lethal?" It focuses on a potential problem with stratospheric spread of sulfate particles.

She is riveted and reads it again. Is it possible? Could this woman have detected a possible fatal flaw in the Cocoon half a century ago? If she was right, Sessler thinks, it is more important than ever that the resisters' plan succeed.

* * *

Two hours later Sessler is driving down the old, cracked New Jersey Turnpike. She takes an exit south of Trenton, heads into deep backcountry, takes an old county highway, then turns onto an isolated dirt road leading to a large concrete factory. On it is a faded red and white sign: ATLAS METAL WORKS. She looks around the yard. Stacked beside the fence are iron rods, steel beams, and piles of other metals in all sizes and shapes. In the back corner is a towering heap of wrecked cars.

She unlocks the door and goes inside. The first thing she sees are four massive tanks, each one twenty feet in diameter. They are filled with salt water that circulates gently. Suspended above are banks of heat lamps, turned off.

Along one wall are four long worktables and benches and two furnaces, currently shut down. Nearby is a wall of tools and storage cabinets for chemicals, metal filings, and various additives.

To one side are the kitchen galley and living area, including two bunks. One is messy. In the other—she startles as she sees him—is a man lying on his back. It's Frankie, the caretaker. He's asleep with his mouth open and his boots crossed.

She shakes his bed. He stirs, lifts one arm, groans, and sits up, rubbing his neck.

"When d'you get here?" he asks.

"Minute ago. Where's Sam?"

"Food run. He'll be back."

"So how you guys doing, Frankie?"

"Not bad. Bit of cabin fever, that's all."

"You've done a lot."

"I wouldn't know. Sam says we're all set. Just waiting to get the stuff. When's it coming anyway?"

"Soon. Soon as we get it, you'll get it. Tell Sam."

They talk for half an hour and she leaves. At least that part's all set, she thinks as she drives back down the dirt road. She didn't tell Frankie that there is a firm deadline—the Launch is set to take place in nine days.

PART IX
THE RISING

2092
(VARIOUS)

39

YON REACHES FLORIDA AND SAILS UP THE EAST COAST. THE
Everglades are flooded and the deserted skyscrapers of Orlando
are half submerged. He comes to Ocala, the place Quinlin mentioned. Hopefully a contact will be waiting for them—for him.

He guides the boat through lagoons until he finds dry land,
arrives at a pile of logs serving as a ramshackle wharf, ties up the
boat, and steps ashore. The street is swarming with open-air shops
and sidewalk hawkers—reminiscent of the towns he saw on the
Mississippi months ago.

He motions to a cluster of street kids. They giggle and shove
one another until a small boy, braver than the rest, steps forward.

What's your name?" Yon asks.

"Martin."

"Martin, keep an eye on my boat for me, will you?"

He hands him a coin. The boy nods solemnly and runs back and
sits on the top log.

Yon follows the main street and has the unnerving sense that
others are staring at him—a grocer piling tin cans, a barber cutting
hair under a tree, a man tinkering under the hood of a car. They
don't get many strangers, he figures.

295

He walks through a shantytown. Garbage lies in ten-foot-high mounds and sewage runs along open drains. Ragged children play next to chickens pecking at the mud.

He arrives at the Hotel Statler. There's a commotion out front, people shouting and shoving. Those on the edge of the crowd jump up to get a look.

Yon joins them and pushes his way to the center.

A Black Guard is straddling a thin young man, beating him with the butt of his blast gun. Another Guard is holding a woman from behind, squeezing her arms together. On the ground is a torn sign, SHUT IT DOWN! Behind them is an old Exxon station. A manager stands in the doorway.

A protest.

The man on the ground is injured. The Guard steps aside and kicks him in the head. His eyes are rolling back and blood and spittle stream out of his mouth and congeal in the dust.

The woman is squirming to break away. The Guard holding her slips in front of her and swings his gun at her abdomen. She doubles over.

"Stop!"

Yon yells the command without thinking.

The effect is electric. The crowd surges, engulfing Yon, who is pushing his way toward the man on the ground. The Guard stops kicking to scan the crowd, looking for the perpetrator. His head is turned when Yon punches him hard, knocking him off balance.

No one moves. The other Guard lets the woman go and swivels to Yon, raising his gun. He points the gun at Yon's stomach and moves closer. Some of the people behind Yon fan away out of firing range but others remain. Someone yells "No!"

Then everyone is silent. Yon stands tall, staring steadily at the Guard, who moves toward him with a look of pure hatred on his face. He is so close Yon can smell his sweat. The gun touches Yon's side. Without thinking, he slams his arm down, smacking the gun to one side. Startled, the Guard drops it. Yon strikes him with a blow to the chin and he falls backward.

The other Guard scrambles to point his gun at Yon, but the crowd surges around him, pressing him in so tightly he can't raise his weapon. There is a blur of movement behind him, someone pushing their way in. An object comes crashing down and strikes the Guard on the neck. Yon sees a knife. Blood spurts out.

The Guard makes a gurgling scream and grabs his throat, dropping the gun.

Yon looks at the assailant—a woman, tall and dark-skinned. Something about her is familiar. A rush of recognition. *It's Gabe!* The crowd, emboldened, turns on the first Guard lying on the ground, punching and kicking him. Gabe grabs Yon's arm, cradles him close.

"Come," she says, pulling him away. She slides the knife back into the handle of her cane.

Yon bends over the wounded protester, but the woman demonstrator is already there. Several men pick him up gently and carry him toward a nearby house. The front door is already opening, a white-haired woman gesturing them in quickly.

"We have to get out of here," says Gabe.

"But *you* . . . how did you get here?"

"I've been here a week. Waiting for you."

She glances around. "Where's Quin?"

"He . . . he didn't make it."

"What?"

"He's dead."

A look of horror flits across her face, but she collects herself. "I need to hear it. All of it. But not right now."

They start to leave. The two Guards are lying motionless on the street.

"We should help them," Yon says.

"Too late for that."

People are pulling off their uniforms.

The manager of the Exxon station has closed it down, the shade on the door drawn and the pumps hooded.

"How about their guns?" asks Yon.

"We'll keep them. They're valuable. So are the uniforms."

They hurry through the slum. After ten blocks they slow to a walk. Yon has the feeling that people are looking at him—the same feeling he had before his confrontation with the Black Guards, only now it's fraught with foreboding.

"You're walking too fast," whispers Gabe. "You're drawing attention."

They hear police sirens coming toward them. Gabe opens a door and they're in a darkened hallway of an apartment building. As the sirens whiz by, their eyes adjust. At the far end of the hall a small boy looks up at them wide-eyed. Gabe smiles and holds a finger to her lip. The boy imitates her.

They leave and walk another ten blocks.

"Not far now," says Gabe.

They come to an alley. She gives a quick look around and tugs his sleeve. At the end is a small door that leads to the basement of what was once a church. In a corner, behind a pile of pews that reaches to the ceiling, is a small living space—a stove, sink, table, four chairs, and two cots.

She nods toward a cupboard. "Coffee there, if you want it."

He sits on a cot, beginning to calm down.

"First things first," she says. "What happened to Quin?"

Haltingly, he tells her everything, ending with the cave-in. She is quiet for some moments. "We had started to think he was indestructible," she murmurs, shaking her head sadly. Then, pulling herself together, she gestures toward the knapsack. "Is that it?"

He reaches in and hands her the two canisters.

She weighs them up and down with her hands. "Seem small for such a big job."

"How's it getting there?"

"Plane. Sessler's flying down in her old prop Beechcraft."

"Flying? Isn't that risky?"

"Can't avoid it. Time's not on our side."

They share a meal of pasta and beans. Yon eats ravenously. Across the table he looks at Gabe, thin and intense, with dark penetrating eyes.

"Okay," he says abruptly. "Tell me. What the hell was I carrying?"

"Afraid that's over my head."

They talk for another hour. She fills him in on the raid in the water tunnel and the regrouping of the Resistance in the library. She sees his eyes beginning to close and turns out the light.

* * *

Yon awakens in the dead of night, his heart pounding so loudly he thinks he can hear it. He is panic stricken. He had a nightmare. He was in a labyrinth, just like in one of his grampa's stories. He had to solve the maze and reach the end—it was extremely important, a question of life or death, not just for him but for many people—though he didn't know exactly why.

The labyrinth was ancient, made of giant rectangular stones and dimly lit, but it turned into modern, long steel hallways lighted by neon with passageways opening everywhere. And then comes a monster—a ten-foot-tall Minotaur, his lower half human, his gigantic hairy head rising up with blazing eyes and horns curling above.

The monster chases him, up one passage and down another. Just when he thinks he's lost him, he appears around a corner right before him. He can feel his hot breath against his chest. He can't move his feet. He's riveted to the ground. At that moment he's handed a sword—by whom? A woman. He raises it up but the bull

299

is too close. It turns its head, the corkscrew horn inches away from his neck—

And he sits up, awake, gasping.

40

MESSIAN, SO TROUBLED HE CANNOT SLEEP, IS UP AT DAWN. HE is walking across the Mall, followed by his security detail of six Black Guards, when on impulse he enters the Washington Monument. Two watchmen are startled to see him. He orders them to use the generator to power the elevator and take him to the top.

The gaping hole there is like an open sore. It happened years ago. Something must have struck the wall or perhaps a hurricane dislodged the marble slabs. Walking over to it, he looks at the capital lying before him.

The city is slowly coming awake. There are a few cars moving, trails of smoke, some trees bending over the rippling water. Only a few people are up and out. A dash of color here and there. Nothing much.

The sight moves him; the city where he has spent the better part of his seventy years. The city as far as he can see, all of it, depending on him, relying on him to keep it safe. And he has done that, to the best of his ability. His city. His country.

A black cloud crosses his mind. Sessler. Where is she? His agents haven't been able to locate her since the raid on the tunnel. She's in hiding somewhere. Plotting against him, no doubt.

He followed the raid in real time on a video hookup. Before the Black Guard plunged down the shaft he had wondered, fearfully, if she would be there. Years ago intelligence reports had said she was in a politically suspect commune. And then reports came in that she was a member of the underground somewhere in New York and that she was rising up the ranks of the anti-State agitators. He never told anyone she was his daughter.

As he watched the screen from Washington, he urged his troops on. But at the same time he was plagued by another feeling, a confounding one. He was looking for her, searching the screen.

He dreaded seeing her like this, when she'd be fighting for her life. But also, on some level he could hardly admit, he *wanted* to see her. He hadn't laid eyes on her since the day before Aggie died.

And sure enough—there, underground, behind the barricade, that figure with long hair, moving quickly and giving orders—could that be her?

He froze the image and magnified it. The lighting was so poor the white and black pixels blurred into one another. He couldn't be sure. But when he unfroze it and the figure burst into action again, he was almost certain—something about the way she moved.

He couldn't tell what he was feeling.

He perceived at once the Guards were ham-fisted and the raid poorly planned. There were only half a dozen defenders behind that barricade; their objective was clearly to allow everyone else to escape. What was needed was to locate the tunnel's plans and set up an ambush at the closest exit.

He could have ordered this, but something stayed his hand. And when he heard the explosion and the cave-in that thwarted the attack, his anger was bound to another sensation, one that he didn't want to name but couldn't help but recognize. A sensation that felt suspiciously like relief.

She's alive.

302

* * *

He takes the elevator to his penthouse office.

"Good day, Mr. Chairman, sir," chirps the young man at the receptionist's desk.

Messian nods perfunctorily and commands: "My calendar."

"Right away, sir." The young man punches a code into a desk computer. "Your first appointment is in ten minutes. An interview with STANA. The State News Agency."

"I know what it is." Messian adds sharply, "I created it."

The young man gulps and looks down.

The office curtains rise automatically. Messian peers down at the gigantic walled complex of SAAM and then turns to his desk. On it he recognizes the thick yellow files from State Security. More and more reports of public unrest.

More and more reasons for the Inner Council to get nervous.

The intercom buzzes. The reporter from STANA is ready.

"Five minutes. Send him in."

He goes into the bathroom. He's surprised at the reflection of the old man there. He realizes he's shrunk, a full inch, maybe more. There are certain things the anti-aging regimen can't help. They can repair his skin blemishes, his yellow teeth, his balding, his frequent urination, the hair growing out of his ears.

But not his shrinking height. At times like this he feels it's the burden of responsibility that is crushing his spine, like that statue of Atlas he once saw in an old photo of New York's Fifth Avenue.

He splashes water on his face, sucks in his stomach, and tightens his belt.

* * *

"And so," continues the young reporter, "do you ever feel it's time to relax, to give it all up and enjoy life?"

303

He's surprised at the audacity of the question. It's not quite a direct challenge, but it does imply that there may be leadership after him and perhaps even a successor in the wings.

In fact, Messian is surprised at the way the interview is going. It's supposed to be a straightforward exercise in image management, a bit of puffery to show he is physically fit and in command. It doesn't feel like that.

The reporter is a woman, dressed in the power suit that young people favor. Something about her—her tone of voice, her cavalier self-confidence—lacks the diffidence he has come to expect.

"No," he lies. "The people, the country, the world . . . still need me. As long as there's breath in this body, I'm ready to answer the call."

A mistake, he thinks immediately. An admission that I'm mortal. "Of course," he adds, "I'm in perfect health. I'm not going anywhere, much less to a rocking chair on a porch somewhere."

She doesn't smile or nod, as he thought she might.

"And Amicus," she persists. "He, too, will remain with us for quite a while?"

"Of course." Now he's irritated. As a hologram, Amicus is expected to live forever. This interview is cutting too close to the bone.

He looks at his watch. "Perhaps we should wrap this up."

"Certainly," she says, a bit surprised. "One last question, if I may."

He nods. "Go ahead."

"These rumors of a raid on resisters—"

"Rumors?" he cuts her off.

"Well, perhaps more than rumors. Stories. Reports."

"Yes?"

"Of resisters. Living in an underground cave. What is being done to find them?"

He stands, towering over his desk.

She continues. "And what about the rising public discontent? What are you going to do about that?"

He points to the door and orders her to leave. The cameraman looks ashen as he packs up the equipment and slips through the door.

With one phone call Messian will quash the story if it crosses the line. But where did she get her information and how did she have the guts to cross the line herself?

* * *

One of the security reports—written by Vexler—grabs his interest. Messian immediately summons the man to his office. Half an hour later, out of breath, Vexler waits in the reception area.

From his desk on a raised platform, Messian waves him to a chair. As Vexler settles back his head is six inches lower than the commanding figure across from him.

Coffee? Vexler shakes his head and stammers, "No, thank you."

Messian pats his personnel file, which is lying on his desk next to the "after action report."

"Impressive career," he says. He looks at the scar on Vexler's cheek—a perfect X. "That's dashing. How did you get it?"

As a youth, Vexler relates, he was poor. He was in a gang, they tangled with another gang and decided to settle the matter with a one-on-one contest between the two best fighters. He was cut.

And the other man?

He was killed.

"Even more impressive," says Messian, who knows it's a lie. "I'm glad to have such a man in the Black Guard, especially in counterespionage. Your story reminds me: Have you heard of 'bragging scars'?"

Vexler says no.

"They were popular in the eighteenth-century dueling societies of Austria and Germany. Badges of honor. The fencers used to rub salt in the wounds to deepen them."

He gives Vexler a searching look, then gets down to business. Could he kindly describe his recent assignment to the South, every significant detail, from start to finish?

Vexler does. He tells of his interrogation of the young runner named Bevin, how he first got an inkling of some kind of anarchist mission to the South and broke off the interrogation to follow up on it, how he used bits of surveillance and snippets of reports to track the two perpetrators and managed to meet them in New Orleans.

He describes—a bit laboriously, but Messian doesn't want to interrupt the flow—the long trip to Ecuador, the parting at Esmeraldas, and his cleverness in reuniting with the perpetrators at Macapa on the Brazilian coast.

"And on the return," says Messian, tapping the report on his desk, "all did not go well, I understand."

"Not go well?" Vexler can't help blurting out.

"You killed one of them. This man we now know was called Quinlin."

"They got suspicious. It was him or me."

"And the other?"

Vexler describes the fight on the sailboat in the storm, how he ended up in the water and how, after a perilous hour treading water, he was picked up by the security craft that was tracking them and flown home.

Messian tries to keep his voice calm. And did you ever discover the purpose of their mission and whether or not they had succeeded?

Vexler looks down, the first time. "Not exactly."

"And one of them is dead and the other, the young man, is missing. We have no idea of where he is or what he is up to."

"That's not entirely accurate, sir. I got this close to him"—he holds up two fingers side by side—"and I know how he thinks. I can find him again."

"Which is the reason you're here before me now. That is precisely what I want you to do. Find him. Bring him to me."

"I will, sir."

"I am raising you two grades, to commander. You will have whatever resources you require and you will report directly to me."

Messian waves him out but before Vexler reaches the door, he calls him back.

"One more thing. This person, the young one. You called him a boy."

"Yes."

"Was he?"

"I'd say he was about seventeen."

"Ah. Seventeen. More of a man than a boy. What's his name?"

"They called themselves the Brewsters, but I didn't believe it. They're phony names. They also said they were father and son and I didn't believe that either."

"What's the boy's first name, his real one?"

"I heard Quinlin use it once. When they thought I was asleep. An odd name. I never heard it before. Yon."

Messian's head snaps toward him. "What did you say?"

"Yon."

Messian sinks back into his chair. He holds his head in his hands, suddenly so preoccupied he doesn't notice when Vexler quietly opens the door and slips out.

41

WHEN YON WAKES IN THE MORNING, GABE HAS BEEN OUT AND is back with food. She takes her cane and extracts the dagger from the handle, using it to cut thick slices of bread and cheese.

She pours them coffee and leans back to inspect him.

"Have you seen yourself lately?"

It's been many weeks. He shakes his head no.

She goes to the bathroom and returns with a hand mirror. "Take a look."

He is surprised by the rugged visage looking back. His stubble has become a small beard. His skin is darkly tanned—that never happened before. But most of all, his eyes look different, deeper somehow. Perhaps it's a trick of the light. Or perhaps they've changed. For they have a new color—the color of the sky in the South.

"My eyes," he says.

"The supreme color."

"You see it, too?"

"I've been able to see the color for years. They're just like Sessler's."

Noises come down from the street side. A few people are there, inexplicably waiting for something. One of them is Martin, the boy Yon commissioned to look after his sailboat. There's a rap on the door. Sessler steps in. Speak of the devil, says Gabe. Sessler hugs her tightly and then Yon and steps back to take a full look at him.

She congratulates him on the success of his mission. They commiserate over Quinlin's death. She wants to hear every last detail, painful as it is, and he tells her the whole story. He assures her that Quinlin died quickly. And that man who killed him, Luther—he's gone too. Sessler asks what he looked like.

In his forties, an ugly mug. His most distinguishing feature was a scar on the cheek—it was in the form of a perfect X.

They both turn to him in shock.

"That's Vexler," Sessler says. "Vexler Tigor. You were in the company of the top counterespionage man in the Black Guard—and a bloodthirsty bastard. All that time. You sure he's dead?"

"I saw him with my own eyes, dropped in the ocean miles from the shore. Not a chance he'd survive."

Sessler wonders how Vexler had managed to infiltrate them. He'd obviously gotten wind of the mission from Bevin. But how had he gotten so close? She had thought Quinlin, with his street smarts, could detect a spy a mile off.

Yon recounts their meeting in New Orleans, the seedy guides bidding for their services, how the man called Luther won by not overplaying his hand. As he talks, Sessler observes him closely.

When he's done she says, "You look different."

"Everyone's telling me that."

She doesn't tell him what she's really thinking: that he *is* different—she can tell immediately by the way he holds himself—not superficially different but deeper; he's older, tougher, confident, the smooth edges taken off the innocent boy who stepped into her underground office so many weeks ago.

* * *

They go outside for some air. Gabe knows of a safe place, deep in a swamp. They come to a lagoon where she has hidden a canoe. She paddles in the back while Sessler sits in the front, steering with her paddle.

Yon brims with questions. As so often in Sessler's presence, he has the odd feeling that she is holding back, not telling him the full story. First of all, what's in the canisters and how's it supposed to save us?

"It's secret," she says. "Because it's a long shot. But if anyone has the right to know, you do." She takes a breath and dips the paddle into the water, raising it slowly. It's covered with mossy strands of green seaweed that stands out as the water drips over the sides.

"See this?" He nods. "We hope to use something like this to help regenerate the sky.

"There are two containers. One has a mixture of metals, mostly magnesium and iron but with a few other minerals from the South mixed in. It took forever to get the mixture right but it's not the main thing. It's the catalyst. It's job is to speed up the reaction. The other canister is the critical one. It contains a kind of plant."

"A plant?"

"Genetically altered algae. That's what Soledad was able to produce."

"And what does that do?"

"Ocean fertilization. The idea, in principle, is simple. Phytoplankton absorb carbon dioxide from the air. When they die, they sink to the bottom, taking the carbon with them. You've heard of bad algae. This is good algae.

"So we spread a bloom of benign algae on the oceans. We use the metal filings as micronutrients. If the algae engulf the carbon in large quantities and sink quickly enough, that might just do the trick—deplete atmospheric carbon. That's been the dream of scientists for a hundred years: don't solve global warming with some cockamamie scheme to reduce sunlight; solve it by cleansing the world of the gook that's actually causing it.

"I got the idea from rogue experiments that were done in Canada seventy years ago. But will it work on a massive scale? The super-algae hasn't ever been tested. Will it get rid of the carbon fast enough so we don't all burn up while the Cocoon disintegrates?"

"Sounds dicey."

"It is. There are other potential problems, a lot of them. But we have to try."

"How do you spread the stuff around the world?"

"We steal a leaf from the playbook of SAAM. We use a plane."

"But this one little container—"

"No. We'll be making tons of it. We have a lab in New Jersey to test it and if it works, we'll replicate it. Once a sufficient mass is in place, it'll replicate itself. And one planeload won't be enough. We'll have to do it over and over again and just hope that we can get it in place in time—and that it works, obviously."

Yon is skeptical. *A clump of algae is going to save the world?* Not to mention all the practical problems: Getting a plane. Filling it with the stuff. All this under the watchful eye of the Power.

Sessler senses his reservations. She is quiet for a long time, paddling in silence, until they return to the shore. Then she looks him square in the eye.

"Now comes the hard part. And that's where you come in."

"Me?"

"If you're willing, of course."

Listen, she says. We have people all across the country, resisters. It's not like an underground army or anything, and there are obvious problems of communicating, but they tell us things. And what they tell us now is that people are fed up, they've had enough, they're angry at the Power and what's happened to the world. All these years there was an unspoken agreement: you'll cut back on our freedoms, run a police state, okay, but in exchange you'll save us from extinction. And now that bargain doesn't hold up anymore. It's not worth it. They're fed up with the violence and decay and depression and everything else that makes life not worth living. They're ready to act. It's an explosive situation. What it needs is a spark to set it off.

"And what is that?" Yon asks.

"That's you. You've come back from the South. You've seen another world. You know how it is. You have to figure out how to get that message across. To light the spark." Her voice dropped. "Without, of course, getting caught."

Yon is struck dumb. *Me*, he's thinking, *why me?*

Again she seemed to read his mind. "Somebody's got to do it. I wouldn't ask you except that I think you're ready. You *are* different. You have the moral authority of a leader. What you need is to figure out the tactics. I'll leave Gabe here to help you. Meanwhile, I've got to get back. We've only got a week before the next Launch.

"A *week*! You're giving me a week to somehow set off some kind of uprising, some general chaos, that will somehow create a distraction so you can somehow do this?"

"Basically, yes."

* * *

Two hours later Sessler steps into the cockpit of the single prop plane parked on the side of a meadow that had made for a bumpy landing. She cradles the two canisters in her arms and secures them in the seat behind her with a seat belt. Gabe is seeing her off. She steps up to the cockpit.

"Why didn't you tell him?" she yells above the sound of the engine.

"You mean why didn't I tell him that he's my long-lost brother and we have a monster dictator for a father?" Sessler yells back.

"I thought about it. But I figure he's got enough to deal with right now."

Gabe casts her a doubtful look, steps down, and waves goodbye.

As she ascends into the miasma of the Cocoon, Sessler wonders about her motive in keeping Yon ignorant. She remembers how shaken he was at their first meeting when she told him the people who raised him weren't his true grandparents. How many of these long-buried secrets can he handle without losing his footing, his newfound confidence?

Strange. All those years ago when they were young and she felt pushed aside by him—he who did nothing other than being born a boy. And now here he is again, back on the scene, effortlessly about to become the center of the action—after she's done so much groundwork for the Resistance.

She's ashamed of these feelings. The cause they're fighting for is so much larger than personal jealousies. Why do we never outgrow our childish fears and resentments?

She will tell him everything. She owes it to him. But she'll do it when she needs to. In the meantime, she'll hold it in reserve.

* * *

For hours Yon has been pacing inside the safe house, subsisting on coffee and adrenaline. A plan gradually forms in his mind. He goes outside where Martin is sitting and motions him indoors.

"I want you to gather your friends and come back here. I've got a job for them."

Martin nods his head solemnly and dashes away.

"What are you going to do?" asks Gabe, coming downstairs.

"*We.* What are *we* going to do?"

"Okay. What are *we* going to do?"

"First we need paper and ink. We're going to make some leaf-lets. And then, I want you to find a good place for a mass meeting."

"Okay, but why?"
"To strike a match."

* * *

The meadow was once a high school football field. A scoreboard with faded lettering still stands. The two bleachers facing each other have half their seats intact, the others retaining only the metal armrests. On the field a rusting bulldozer lies near two stumps that once were a goalpost.

The street kids have done their job. They've spread the news like town criers about the stranger who beat the Black Guard—come and hear him speak.

For an hour a smattering of people have been arriving, mostly in ones and twos but sometimes entire families. Altogether about twenty or thirty people sit in the bleachers, waiting. There's an electric current in the air. The sense that something extraordinary and dangerous might happen.

Gabe has organized a band of five marshals wearing armbands. Discreetly they eye the spectators as they enter, looking for suspicious bulges under clothing that might be weapons and trying to spot undercover Black Guards.

Yon approaches the microphone and the audience falls silent. The only sounds are the occasional crying of a baby and, way off in the distance, the barking of a dog.

For a moment, a long moment, Yon collects himself. He stands before the mike, breathing deeply. He thinks back to his night lying at the top of the pyramid looking up at the stars with Soledad's voice filling him with knowledge, with conviction. There are a few resounding squawks, feedback from the loudspeakers. He taps the microphone. It bangs like a gunshot.

And then he speaks.

Slowly at first. Calmly, but with authority. He starts with the history. How we got to where we are. The years of polluting, the powerful fossil fuel industry, the coal interests, the automobile companies, the corruption and ineptitude of the governing bodies. The warnings that went ignored.

The crowd is spellbound. More and more people arrive.

He talks of the men and women who came up with a scheme to end global warming and put the world on a path to perdition. Geo-engineering. So obvious, so straightforward, so efficient, and so cheap, it was bound to happen.

Except of course that it was a mistake, a dreadful mistake.

And now his voice begins rising, getting louder.

He describes how the authorities drew more power to themselves, had to do this to jam their project through. They became the dictatorial *Power,* set up the Black Guard and then the Color Guard, and devised that odious term: The Cocoon.

"They sold us a bill of goods, and we bought it. We gave away our power because we were scared. But did we know the Cocoon was going to be forever? Could we have imagined that the polluters would keep polluting, and they would just keep pumping more and more sulfurous particles into the air we breathe?"

The crowd is stirring, aroused. They've never heard anything like this.

He attacks the Power, the Consortium, and, most of all, the Chief Councillor and his alter-ego. Gabe has filled him in on the background and make-up of the dictatorship, including Amicus.

"What kind of person is this to rule us? Not a person at all, but a quivering illusion. A shadow. A nothingness. All these years we've been prostrating ourselves before an empty shell."

By now his voice is loud, powered by the depth of his conviction, and it resounds through the meadow.

"And what's the result of all this? We've lost our world. We've lost our sky, the sky that used to extend forever upward, our doorway to the universe. And we've lost the sky's partner, the ocean brimming with marine life and adventure. We've lost the sun that warms us, the moon that inspires us, the stars that guide us."

He's yelling now and gesticulating wildly. The people are spellbound.

"And most of all—we've lost ourselves. Everything that made us human. Our creativity. Our imagination. Our dreams. Our very souls."

The crowd stirs in anger. Here and there people yell out. He is speaking the blunt power of truth.

He pauses for a moment, then speaks again, lowering his voice.

It doesn't have to be like this. There is another way. He's seen it himself. He's been to the South. And the South is regenerating! Equilibrium is returning. Nature is overcoming human transgression. She is cleansing Herself.

"I've seen it. That's the truth. I've seen the sun. It's extraordinary. It lights up the whole sky. It bathes you in warmth. And guess what. There is no Cocoon. The sky is a splendid color. A magnificent color. Some of you . . . most of you . . . have never seen it. Believe me. It reaches right down and stirs your soul. And to think: that color used to be everywhere."

He turns up the volume.

"It's time to rid ourselves of those who outlawed the sky. We must destroy those who put us on the wrong path. We must overthrow the Power. We must do away with SAAM and UNCLE and the Inner Council and"—his voice rises so high it cracks—"the Chairman.

"But there is one condition, one basic vow. We must help Nature recover. We must stop all pollution—right now—all pollution of air and water and earth. We must change the factories and do away with gas-powered automobiles and stop the industries that ruin our soil, foul our streams, and blacken our air. We must stop fouling our own nest!"

The crowd stirs in anger. Here and there people yell out. They stamp their feet. They want action.

A young man near the mike yells out "What do we do?" so loudly that it carries through the sound system. It starts a chant. "What do we do? What do we do?"

Yon holds both arms up. The chant breaks off.

"We rise up!" he declares. "*That's* what we do. We carry the message. Nature is the Power and Earth its domain. Respect it. Defend it. Bow down before it. And beg Nature to forgive you.

"We rise up to overthrow the Power! To get the sky back."

He repeats the message, word for word. He does it again, a third time. People send his words back in chants. "Rise up! Sky back!" Over and over.

He steps away from the microphone and surveys the crowd, which is uplifted, inspired, and angry—mirroring back his rage. The crowd streams out of the stadium, ready for action.

While speaking, Yon was so swept up in the moment that he barely noticed what was going on around him. He failed to register a plump young man circling around him and pointing something at him. It was an old device that Gabe had pulled out of a storage cabinet, something that the authorities had long ago deemed illegal for private use—a video camera.

Two hours later, in a house on the edge of town, the video is edited into a three-minute segment. It begins with Yon's first words and follows him throughout as his voice swells, interspersing shots of the swirling crowd. It ends with his message and the people thundering back the chant.

No one has ever seen anything as dramatic or as dangerous. The fingers of the plump young man doing the editing are shaking. Philip is his name. He's overcome with the palpable sense that he is on the cutting edge of history.

The video is delivered to Gabe shortly after midnight. Two hours later Yon and Gabe and Philip and two others, still wearing their marshal armbands, slip aboard Yon's sailboat. They carry the two blast guns taken from the Black Guards the day before.

Quietly, except for the purr of the engine, they drive way out beyond the harbor. In the growing morning light they see their destination, a deep-sea offshore drilling rig no longer used to bring up oil. Now it has another function, housing a government broadcast center.

The mission is quickly accomplished. They ascend the platform climbing up a ladder. The skeleton staff is ushered at gunpoint into a cafeteria. Gabe pulls the dagger out of her cane. Yon levels a blast gun. They enter the production room, surprising a broadcaster who has his back to them and is deafened by his earphones. He almost jumps out of his skin when he sees the weapons. He tears off his earphones.

Convincing him is easy. He will do what they demand. They wait for the start of the first morning "news."

Then Yon's words are broadcast. They are cut off after two minutes—when an alert producer in the mainland control room cuts a switch—but that's enough for the gist of his message to reach across the nation.

42

NOBODY KNOWS HOW MANY PEOPLE ACTUALLY SEE YON'S SPEECH. Only a few tune in to the propaganda-laden STANA news, but word of mouth gets around and soon people are talking about it. Overthrow the Power! How is that even possible? Wouldn't the world burn up? And who is this young man who is ready to stick his neck in a noose? He's foolhardy but persuasive. He seems to know what he's talking about.

The next morning Yon and Gabe start their trek north. They decide to head out in the sailboat. Half a mile out to sea they hear a noise down below. Gabe goes to investigate. She returns shaking her head and holding a small figure by the arm. Martin pleads with them to let him stay. They confer and reluctantly agree.

"But you've gotta do whatever we tell you," Yon says. "You can't go off and do something crazy."

Martin is so excited he jumps up and hits his head on the boom. They all laugh.

The seas are rough. Yon sticks close to the coast, because he fears satellites above. Gabe has told him that the Power doesn't have cameras that can penetrate the clogged atmosphere—the one positive feature of the Cocoon is that it defeats aerial surveillance—but he's not convinced. He feels vulnerable out of sight of land.

They sail all day and into the night, taking turns at the tiller. At dawn a squall suddenly comes up, the waves growing larger by the minute and the wind pushing the sails like a giant hand. Yon decides to head for land. It's hard to see in the driving rain. Abruptly, he hears a grinding noise and the boat jams to a stop. They've hit a rock.

Gabe peers over the side. "The hull is smashed," she says. "A hole as big as my arm. Water coming in fast."

The three abandon ship and wade ashore, stumbling in the surf, carrying their few belongings on their heads. When they arrive, they're fully soaked. What now?

Gabe gently pulls a piece of paper wrapped in a plastic bag out of her breast pocket. It is, she explains, a list of the Resistance safe houses. All they have to do is find out where they are and go to the nearest one.

"That's all, is it?" says Yon, but he's grinning.

* * *

The safe house is in Georgia, in an abandoned plantation manor with Spanish moss dangling from the encircling oaks. A group of squatters has occupied it, sleeping on mattresses on the floors, cooking over outdoor fires, and preparing for political action.

They welcome Yon and Gabe as celebrities. Excitedly, they recount reports they've heard of growing unrest everywhere: protests in the streets, anti-State graffiti on the walls, the venerated color painted on government buildings and security installations. The resisters have maintained a communications network—a patchwork of ancient phone lines, long-distance runners, a couple of old illegal radios. The network is buzzing like never before. There's electricity in the air.

Word of the visitors leaks out and soon a string of locals turns up, many of them bringing bread and heaps of vegetables and dried beef. They all move outside and gather around the fire. They feast as sparks fly up into the enveloping darkness, talking softly. They look over at Yon from time to time, anticipating something.

Gabe pokes him in the ribs. "You have to say something to them."

"But what?"

"You'll think of something. Look at them, can't you see? They want to hear from you."

Yon stands on a tree stump not far from the fire and the townspeople form a circle around him. He begins talking extemporaneously, at first slowly, then more and more animatedly, and finishes on a high note.

Cheers fly up. Arms with clenched fists shoot into the air. The chants start up. "We want the sky!" "Give us our sky!" The words echo back from the darkness.

Much of the group stays up late, talking excitedly, but Yon and Gabe, exhausted from their trip, go inside and sleep in an attic. The next morning, more people arrive. An elderly man with cracked leather boots and a military jacket arrives on horseback and demands to see Yon. He hands him a package wrapped in brown paper.

"Not many people seen one of these," he says, spitting on the ground. "And there's some can't see it right before their eyes. But God willing, and with your help, they will again."

Yon unwraps it—an old American flag, the Stars and Stripes. In the upper left-hand corner, underlying a spread of fifty stars, is the mysterious color that's been outlawed, that has turned the flag into a renegade totem. Yon hands it to Martin, who has been dancing around with excitement. He wraps himself in it.

A jalopy comes down the old approach road, raising dust. At the steering wheel, grinning widely, is Philip, the videographer.

"Thought you might need a lift," he says.

"How'd you find us?" Gabe asks.

"Been driving around for hours. Word gets around. You're a celebrity," he adds, "thanks to this." He lifts up his camera.

They decide to leave immediately. The crowd of supporters has now grown. Many among them vow to make it to Washington. They give the trio a rousing send-off as they step into the car. A few even sing a long forbidden song, "The Star Spangled Banner."

Yon, riding in the passenger seat, turns to Gabe in the back and says, "You know, I'm beginning to wonder just how good the State's security system really is. Here we are, out in the open, followers gathering from all over, and we haven't seen a single Black Guard."

43

THE FIRST INKLING OF THE CATASTROPHE COMES AT 12:16 A.M. Messian knows the exact time because he happened to glance up at the clock as he entered the multi-locked doors of the Launch Control Center.

Inside is the beating heart of the system that monitors the health of the planet. Every current, every wind, every beam is captured from hundreds of locations in the Northern Hemisphere and funneled into the central computer. It analyzes and contextualizes every iota of information and pictures the result on a giant screen.

It'll tell of any problems. As he told the assembled throng when this room was built forty-five years ago, "Once you start mucking about with Mother Nature, you'd better be damn sure to keep a close eye on her." They laughed, knowingly.

The machines are silent but pulsating with lights, and the air, purified, is sterile. He wanders up and down the aisles, looking at the machines and even stroking some of them, the ones he invented. He marvels: many of them are replacements but some are original. They function smoothly, effortlessly, with little human oversight. A team comes in twice a day to make sure they're running okay.

The room usually thrills him, but this time he has a disturbing sense of foreboding.

What could possibly be wrong?

Then he sees it.

He looks up at the giant simulation of the Earth composed from real-time photographs from an army of satellites; they are above the Cocoon and so they are not hampered by the haze. The simulation on the screen spins in hyper-time, so that the entire globe can be seen over the course of a single minute.

There!

What is that? Up there above the Arctic Circle, not far from the North Pole. A spot. An opening.

The Earth spins. He waits. Thirty seconds, forty, fifty.

There it is again!

No question. It's a lacuna, a hole in the stratosphere.

He has to sit down to steady himself.

This is the fear that lurked in the back of his mind all these years. The one flaw that could not be ruled out. The breakdown in the system.

* * *

He avoids the Control Center until the late afternoon.

He's given orders to keep it off limits to everyone except for the maintenance crew, whose ministrations are necessary to keep the air 100 percent sterile. And just in case—in case there's a prying eye—the giant screen simulator showing the Earth's atmosphere is turned off.

Now he's back, about to enter. He punches in the code to open the multi-locked doors and—nothing happens. How is that possible? He feels a moment of panic. He tries again and it works; he feels relief at the sound of the bolts retracting. He must have put in the wrong code. A sign of his mental confusion.

He enters and flips on the bright neon lights. He walks past the humming machines and goes to a console and presses a button to charge up the screen. Yet he doesn't glance at it, not yet. He wants to sit down first. He finds a swivel chair, moves it to the center of the room, and looks up.

Just what he feared. He scoots over to the console and types on the keyboard, hitting a command button to shift the angle of viewing. The image of Earth rotates smoothly from the bottom up. Antarctica moves up front and center, no longer white with ice as in the old days but a brown landmass.

Then the Arctic. He hits a few more keys to decipher the atmosphere far above it. Colors leap in, a large orange blotch, surrounded by a bright green. The orange blotch is the problem; it shouldn't be there at all and it has spread so that now it covers the top cap of the continent.

Messian picks up a phone and summons his deputy and project manager, Sylvan Brea. Despite his youth and shoulder-length hair, the manager is knowledgeable and adept with the controls. He arrives quickly and pulls up a chair beside Messian. Instantly, he looks up.

"What am I seeing?"

"The ozone. A hole in the ozone."

Sylvan Brea whistles softly. He lowers his voice. "So that's what's happened. The accumulation of aerosols have caused a spontaneous negative chemical reaction. Resulting in ozone depletion—a lot by the looks of it."

"Precisely. And the rate of change has accelerated."

"You may remember we talked about this possibility many years ago. We said this might happen."

"Of course I remember. But it was highly theoretical. We computed the odds and they were deemed acceptable. One out of twelve for minimal spread, as I recall."

"This is not minimal."

"No." Messian rises and walks around. "This has happened before. Over a hundred years ago, back in the 1980s. Caused by man-made chemicals from refrigerants and various solvents and propellants. Caused an outcry, fears that the ultraviolet light would cause skin cancers, cataracts, and other things."

"What happened?"

"They banned them. The Montreal Protocol of 1987. It worked, slowly but surely."

"Hardly an option here."

"Hardly. We can't reduce the sulfur seeding or we burn up. The next Launch is in four days. And that will widen the hole in the ozone."

"So what are you going to do?"

Messian shrugs—he isn't accustomed to displaying his irresolution. He forces a commanding tone. "I want you to compute the minimal payload to keep the temperature rise within acceptable limits."

It's a ridiculously impossible demand. The payloads have been getting heavier for years; there's no way to lighten them without sending the temperature soaring.

Sylvan Brea looks uncertain. "What's acceptable?"

"That's part of your calculation. It should be noticeable but not too noticeable. We want people to pay attention but not panic."

"Hmmm."

"What?"

"That's a subjective measurement. It's political, not scientific."

"Dammit, figure something out."

"Perhaps we should mobilize a public response? Maybe institute restrictions on fossil fuels."

"It's a little late for that."

"Like seventy years."

Messian doesn't care for Sylvan's tone. He points toward the door and tells him to get busy. The manager walks out, shaking his head.

44

WHILE PHILIP DRIVES, GABE PLANS THE ROUTE, AN OLD MAP spread across her legs. She aims for them to stay over in safe houses, which delays their progress. They come to one, a ranch house. It is suspiciously empty and they see right away it is in shambles—the front door smashed, chairs overturned and anti-State pamphlets scattered on the floors.

Yon is shaken. "What do you think happened?" he asks.

"Probably they were arrested," Gabe says.

"Yes, but what'll happen to them?"

"Not clear. They'll go on trial. They'll be found guilty. Then in all likelihood they'll be executed."

"How?"

"Probably hanged."

He's quiet for a long time, looking out the window. She knows something's bothering him. "What?" she says finally.

"If the Black Guard knows about me and Quinlin going to the South, then they were looking for us. We led them to them." His voice drops almost to a whisper. "If it weren't for us, they'd still be alive."

"You can't think that way. Everyone in the Underground knows

327

they're taking a risk. That's a calculation they've already done—that it's worth it to stand up for what they believe."

Yon remains silent.

* * *

A dozen miles to the north they come to a semi-abandoned coal-mining town along a river. Half the doors are hammered shut and the windows covered in plywood. The silence broken only by the remote chorus of locusts. At the edge of town the road leads past rusted railroad tracks and broken-down coal silos overgrown with kudzu.

In the distance they hear a commotion. As they come down a hill they reach the coal mine and see a mob of protesters. Forty people or so, gripped by anger, have apparently seized the mine.

The marchers stop and sit on the hillside while Yon and Gabe walk down to meet the protesters, who are dazzled to see them in the flesh. They crowd around and pump their outstretched hands. The leader, a bearded man with the build of an ox, invites them to sit at a picnic table in the center of the yard.

He says they've cornered the foreman inside the office and planted explosives in the mine itself.

"This mine has the worst safety record in the whole county. Two years ago we had a cave-in that killed twenty miners. The company didn't give a shit. They paid the families almost nothing."

Another miner interrupts, pointing to the rickety wooden building with a sagging porch. "That foreman up there is an old bastard. He docks our pay if we come up short." He raises a shaking finger at a knot of six men standing off to one side below the hill. "And those guys are sellouts. They're as bad as the bosses."

"We want to blow the whole thing up," says the leader. "You're our guy. You tell it right. This mine and all the other mines are killing the planet and doing us no good. We want to dynamite the

fucker and forget it ever existed." He shares a look with the ten or
so men around him. "And we'd like you to do the honors."

He points to a T-bar plunger sitting on the porch, attached to a
wire that snakes across the dusty yard into the mouth of the mine.

"Press that down and watch the pieces fly!"

Gabe pulls Yon to one side. "Give us a minute," she says to the
miners. They walk twenty yards away. "I'm not sure about this,"
she says.

"Why not?" he asks.

"Think about it. So far the Power has left us alone. But this
might be the provocation they're waiting for."

"This might be the provocation *we're* waiting for."

Yon walks off alone, completes a wide circle around the wooden
office building, and goes back up to the hill to the marchers. He
returns with Philip, who follows Yon with the camera running.
Slowly, almost casually, Yon walks over to the plunger. The miners congregate around him, leaving a gap for the camera to take in
the scene. It starts rolling.

Yon squats and reaches forward, places his right hand on the
plunger. His other hand raises his lapis lazuli amulet in the air.
He pauses for a dramatic second, then with a powerful thrust he
pushes the plunger down.

For an instant nothing happens. Then there's a thunderous
explosion deep within the Earth. The ground shakes. A cloud of
rocks and dust comes shooting out of the mouth of the mine. The
sound echoes off the hillside.

The workers cheer and thump one another on the back. They
hoist Yon up on their shoulders and carry him back to the table.
The company miners run off.

After some minutes of celebration, Yon and Gabe walk back up
the hill.

Before they move on, the office door swings open and a man
with a ripped white shirt comes barreling down the steps shouting

something. He's carrying a pickaxe and he charges the miners. He strikes the first one he comes to across the brow and the man crumples to the ground.

The miners turn on the foreman. He runs but they catch him and he disappears beneath a rain of blows and kicks that send up a cloud of dust. Another man comes running out of the building, a coil of rope in his hand. He runs over to a tree and tosses the rope over a branch. The miners carry the foreman over and hold him, squirming, while the man ties a hangman's knot. The miners place the noose around the foreman's neck.

Yon and Gabe stand motionless, aghast. It all is happening too fast.

"My God," Yon says. He starts to run down the hill. He's too late, too far away. He'll never get there in time. He stops.

Three miners pull the rope to hoist the foreman up and tie it around the tree trunk. He's suspended in air—his body spasms and twitches and then stops moving. A woman comes screaming out of the building. She stops on the porch, sees the body, puts the back of her hand to her mouth, and collapses.

Yon and Gabe don't speak. They see Philip down below, still kneeling and whirling the camera around to take in the whole scene.

Later that day, the two argue about the video. Yon wants to destroy it—he's guilt stricken over the man's death—but Gabe says it should be aired. What happened, happened, she asserts. You can't start censoring things now. That's what the Power does— and look where it got them.

They look for Philip to get his opinion, but he's already gone to the nearest pirate broadcasting station to send the video.

* * *

The protests across the country set off alarm bells in the higher realms of the Power. Dozens of Black Guard agents and informers have been sending a cascade of reports to the Security office. From there they go to top councillors and—even though marked "ultra classified"—they filter down to lower staff. They're often accompanied by videos, which feature the chants: "Rise up! Sky back!"

Soon members of the Inner Council can talk of little else. A delegation is formed to demand a meeting with Messian to hear how he plans to handle the situation. They ask that he appear at Council headquarters, but he counters that instead they should assemble in his penthouse office. He wants a home-ground advantage.

But he is preoccupied by a more serious matter: the destruction of the ozone. Already the Cocoon appears to him less stable. From his balcony he thinks he can sometimes hear a strange, distant rumbling.

The councillors are too dim-witted to realize what's happening, he mutters to himself.

Seven of them crowd into his special elevator. He watches through a hidden camera as they gather in the reception area. He deciphers the power dynamic; as expected, the most conservative "hard head" is the leader. Messian calculates how long he'll keep the delegation waiting. Twelve minutes, he decides—long enough to demonstrate that he's occupied with a pressing matter and short enough to suggest he's eager to hear their concerns.

The wait infuriates them. Finally they file in and sit without prompting. Messian stands and circles the room, shaking their hands. One of them, a councillor representing the Department of Energy Investment, wastes no time in small talk.

"So what are you doing to stamp out this rebellion?"

"*Rebellion?*" Messian sits behind his desk. "That may be a bit of an overstatement."

"What would you call it?"

"More than a trifle, less than a calamity. A nuisance, perhaps."

The "hard head" leader speaks up. "A *nuisance*. I would say it's more than a nuisance. These people are in open revolt."

"I can see why you might say that," agrees Messian.

His cavalier attitude astounds them. Is he covering something up? Is there even more cause for alarm?

"So what are you going to do about it?"

He sits back and lets their questions fall like brickbats: Why doesn't he arrest the troublemakers? Why not shut them down? What if they encourage others to rise up? What if more and more do?

Finally, he stands, goes to the window, looks out briefly, then whirls around.

"Believe me, we have the situation well in hand. We can move in at any time but for the moment we choose not to."

"You choose not to—"

"Because it's useful to refrain." He now stares at them, one after another. "You catch more fish with a wide net than a single line."

He cautions that what they are about to hear is highly secret. Not a word must be breathed to anyone. They promise.

"What you don't know is that we have penetrated the Underground thoroughly. Our security has penetrated their communications system. We intercept their messages at will. We are building an invaluable map of the loci of anti-State resistance. We are reaping a bonanza of actionable intelligence. We know the protest leaders and the protest followers. And when the time is ripe, we will strike. We will apprehend them all."

"And when will that be?"

"That's for me to decide. You won't learn about it until it's over."

"Why not?"

"This place leaks like a sieve."

"Well, are you making *any* arrests?"

"Certainly. Just yesterday we broke up a cell in Alabama. We apprehended ten anarchists. They are awaiting secret trials."

The councillors appear impressed.

One final question, says the hard head. "Who is this leader we hear about? Somewhere down south. He came out of nowhere. There're all these wild stories about him."

"We know all about him and we'll stop him dead in his tracks when the time is ripe. We have infiltrated his ranks. In the meantime, he is useful as a Judas goat."

They adjourn the meeting. In the lobby the delegation confers. He presses a switch to eavesdrop and is satisfied. For the moment they are mollified.

He wishes that what he told them was true, even just some of it. But anyway, he has something vastly more troubling on his mind: the continued existence of human life on the planet.

45

YON AND THE OTHERS DRIVE FROM GEORGIA TO CHARLOTTE and then to Raleigh. At each stop they address gatherings. Yon's confidence is growing rapidly. He enjoys being in the limelight.

They take a zigzag route, mostly on back roads and mostly at night. Still, they're amazed that they're not arrested. At each stop they fear a trap but it never materializes.

Maybe the State has too many other problems to contend with, Gabe offers. From what they hear from fellow conspirators in the safe houses along the way, the clandestine video of Yon at the coal mine and the hanging of the mine manager has circulated widely and, as Gabe predicted, it is taken as a call to violence. Acts of sabotage are breaking out across the country, and small insurrections are rising up here and there.

Protesters turn their rage on gasoline delivery trucks. They slash the tires and smash the windshields. Some set the vehicles on fire. Others hurl firebombs at gas stations. The explosions are dramatic, resounding booms that shake the Earth and send red flames and black smoke twisting up into the air.

A few guerrilla bands go after bigger game. In Galveston—the sandbagged enclave for oil processing that is all that remains of that once thriving city—saboteurs break into a refinery and smash the pipes. In Oklahoma, they drop explosive charges down the shafts of a dozen oil wells. In Nebraska they sever a cross-country pipeline, sending oil gushing onto the parched earth like blood from a wound.

Boston activists sneak into Logan Airport at night and chop up the runways. They break into a passenger jet, smashing cockpit instruments and snipping the tubing of the oxygen masks.

In Los Angeles a Black Guard captain orders his troops to dispel demonstrators with tear gas and, when that doesn't work, with bullets. The mayhem is captured on camera: images of a Guard smashing his truncheon on the head of a boy, another kicking a woman in the face, and a third shooting a man in the back. The death toll is twenty-three. STANA shows the video—to quell more protests, no doubt—but the tactic backfires, bringing more angry people into the streets.

* * *

The four have set up camp for the evening at a hidden spot on an embankment of the James River. A dry, dusty plain extends from the half-filled riverbed to a withered grove of stunted saplings half a mile away. Their car is well camouflaged.

From time to time people approach to join them but when it is explained that a large entourage will surely attract the attention of the Black Guard, they leave, quickly and apologetically.

Sessler has flown in. She opens the tent flap. Only Gabe is inside. There's a problem, Gabe says.

"What?"

"It's Yon."

"What about him?"

"For one thing his ego is growing. For another he's worried about the violence. He doesn't see what it's going to accomplish and he feels he alone is causing it. You have to talk to him."

"Where is he?"

At that moment, Yon appears. He sees Sessler and smiles, but it's a weak smile and he looks distracted. He clearly hasn't slept for nights.

They sit at a table outside the tent, a street map of Washington, DC, open in front of them. Yon looks at it and shakes his head. What's the matter? Sessler asks.

"What do you hope to accomplish? Do you expect us to take over the whole city? Do you think the security forces are just going to lay down their arms? They're not going to give up without a fight."

Sessler looks him in the eye. "No. It won't be easy. But ask yourself why they haven't already come down on us. Why hasn't the Black Guard stomped in to crush us?"

"Why do you think?"

"*Something* is stopping them. Okay, there are uprisings all over the place. They're rushing around putting out fires. But maybe there's something deeper, a reluctance, a paralysis of spirit. There's a void and we have to take advantage of it by mobilizing the masses."

"I don't know. It's turning brutal."

The people hate the Black Guard and the Color Guard and the State. They're finally standing up to them, and this is what we need. We'll overwhelm the Power with sheer numbers."

"But don't they have the firepower," Yon points out. "What if they use it? It'll be a massacre."

"That would be awful," Sessler admits. "But ultimately, we'll triumph. The people will block the streets. The Security Forces will refuse to shoot. The Inner Council will panic."

"That's not a plan. That's just a hope."

"A well-founded hope," Sessler insists.

"I disagree."

They fell silent for a moment, staring at each other.

"There's something else," she says. "We've got a source high up in the Power. We believe the Cocoon is unstable, maybe even breaking up. And the Launch is in two days. That means we have to act."

"Yes, but how? With what?"

"With the brute force of numbers. With a revolution that we direct. We can't stop now."

"I'm not asking you to stop. Just to—"

"Just to what?"

"Be sensible. Think things through. Listen to reason."

"You mean listen to *you*."

He snapped back quickly: "Yes, me."

She looks at him. He continues: "I am the leader. I am the head of the Resistance."

"Well—"

"I *am*."

"I know that. And I respect you and value your opinion. But—"

"But what? You're not the one who went to the South. You're not the one who met Soledad and brought the word back here. You're not the one who's mobilized all these people. I am!"

Sessler and Gabe exchange looks. Sessler nods calmly and takes his arm. "Come with me. Let's take a little walk."

They go outside, following a trail along the river bank. She leads with a determined stride, not talking, and makes her way to the edge of a large hill. She doesn't stop until she reaches the top, where there are two boulders. She sits on one and directs him to sit on the other.

She looks away over the meadow and the river and finally speaks. "You know, there is something I've been meaning to tell you for some time. I just didn't know how."

"What?"

"It's hard. I don't know where to begin."

"I'm listening."

"Do you remember when you came into my office? When we first met."

"Of course."

"And you showed me your amulet. And it matched my rock. There was a reason for that." She takes a deep breath. "I gave it to you."

Yon stares at her, confused.

"I got the rocks from my father. Lapis lazuli. The prohibited color. And—this is the difficult part—my father is Paul Messian. The dictator. And he is also your father."

Yon is stunned.

"Messian . . . my *father!*?"

"Yes."

"And you . . . you're my *sister?*"

"Yes. I was sixteen when you were born. I held you in my arms when they carried you home from the hospital."

"How is that possible?"

"It's the truth."

"But I don't know you. You didn't recognize me."

"You were a toddler when I last saw you."

"But how did it happen? How did I—how was I separated?"

She explains the long story to her brother—their father's megalomania, their mother's death, the Zegers.

He holds his head in his hands.

"My father, a dictator. A mass murderer. You sure?"

"You remember that first day in the tunnel? You handed me that scrap of paper with the New York address on it. That's how I knew who you were."

"How?"

"It was my own handwriting. I wrote it down and gave it to the Zegers."

He doesn't speak for a moment, then says, "How is that—" He doesn't finish the sentence.

She knows he needs time to take it all in. He starts up from the rock, sits back down. His eyes open wide. He looks over at Sessler again, says in a soft voice, "Is there any doubt?"

"None whatsoever."

"I was raised so alone. I always felt lonely. To think I had a sister all along. I feel like I should hug you or something, but I don't want to."

"I understand." She has tears in her eyes. "Yon, I was there when you were born. I babysat for you. I watched your first steps. I fed you. I watched you grow those first years."

He's quiet again.

She continues. "You must believe me. I did it for you. You went up to Canada. You were supposed to be out of the whole thing. And you *were* out of it . . . until that day you appeared at our safe house in New York."

Yon looks out over the meadow and abruptly stands up. He walks in circles, lost in thought. He turns his head to look up. Above is the detested, never-changing underbelly of the Cocoon. He sits back down on the boulder.

"So it all fits together," he says finally.

"What?"

"All this." He makes another sweeping gesture with his arm. "Everything. Everything that's happened to me. My childhood. My coming to you. My journey to the South. Meeting Soledad. It's all part of some larger plan." He rises again and takes a deep breath.

"I have no choice. I *must* go on. It's destiny. I always knew I was destined for something larger."

He doesn't say anything more but turns and goes down the hill. She stares after him, worried.

* * *

That night, in his cot in the tent, he has the nightmare again. He is in a maze, a modern one this time, with gleaming corridors and tables of stainless steel, searching for a way out. Behind him, the pounding of hooves. Hot breath on his neck. He turns just as a shadow looms over him. A horn twists in the air. The Minotaur! A woman comes from somewhere, bearing a sword. She unsheathes it. He sits up, drenched in sweat.

46

MESSIAN PACES UP AND DOWN IN THE CORRIDOR, TRYING TO work off some of his anger before entering the Inner Council chamber. His attempt to assuage the fears of the councillors hasn't worked. He's been summoned to attend an emergency session.

That word alone—"summoned"—raises his ire. And they are keeping him waiting—*him*, who used to be the one sitting behind the desk while they cooled their heels outside. He's told he won't sit in the exalted chair from which he usually presides but in a seat in the well of the chamber, as if he were on trial.

He is feeling his age more than ever. His bones ache and he is stooped and his steps are short and uncertain. But at the moment his rage lends him a short-term energy. He swings a cane from side to side before him, like a minesweeper.

The morons! Not one of them can come within a mile of his intelligence. Yet they presume to question his judgment—he who saved the Earth by creating the Cocoon. The cowards! Here they are, worried about civil unrest. The ignoramuses! They know nothing about the infinitely greater threat, the one that means the very existence of life on the planet is hanging in the balance.

Only forty-eight hours to go before the Launch. Should it go ahead? The hole in the ozone is even larger and it's bound to affect the Cocoon. He can't bear to look at it on the screen. When he walks out of doors, he can almost sense this giant rent up above. He imagines burning up alive.

And there is nothing to do about it. Sylvan Brea, the project manager, said as much this morning—or he would have if he had been more articulate. He just sat there across the desk with his pile of papers filled with scribbling, shaking his head and mumbling, "I don't see it."

What he meant was there was no way out: no way to calculate a reduction in the Launch's sulfur particles sufficient to keep the Cocoon in place while at the same time stopping the destruction of the ozone.

And this lot of phony councillors! All they worry about is their own necks! Will they be tossed out on their ears by a mob chanting slogans and led—and here is the irony, so perverse it almost makes him laugh—by none other than his very own son? If only they knew.

Black Guard undercover agents had managed to send him a few photos of Yon and Sessler. His shock when he saw them was almost a physical blow. There she was, Sessler, by Yon's side—so close, so intimate. How did they come together to lead an uprising against him, *their own father?*

He examined his son, scrutinizing every feature: the wide lips, the large brow, the eyes—most of all the eyes. And he had to admit the resemblance was uncanny. No question, Yon was his progeny.

What did he do to deserve such children? He had once hoped to hand them the keys to the kingdom, had even saved two rocks of lapis lazuli to initiate them into the secret color.

And meantime Resistance everywhere is growing. Underground presses produce leaflets that are dropped from rooftops and stuffed under doors, revolutionary posters are plastered on walls. Long-banned books about dictatorship are hawked from house to house. That damned Orwell.

Some of their tactics are almost laughable. In a dozen cities, people lean out their windows at night to bang pots and pans into the darkened streets. The din is often accompanied by chants— "Rise Up, Sky Back."

The daytime protests often end at the local office of UNCLE. Chants of "Down with UNCLE" and "Down with SAAM" morph into the catchy combination: "Down with UNCLE SAAM."

At first the government doesn't mention the protests in its STANA news reports, then it shifts signals and carries a flood of propaganda against them. Commentators condemn "violent anar-chists," and anchors interview actors pretending to be protest lead-ers who admit they're in it for fame and money.

But reports on Messian's desk indicate many people do not believe the disinformation. Media people and public figures asso-ciated with the regime are being shunned. In Boston the mayor, an apologist for the Power, is to give a speech in North Hill. When he reaches the dais the audience applauds. He breaks into a grin. But the applause continues; it doesn't end. He is unable to speak over the din. Realization dawns on him. Shamefaced, he ducks away.

In San Francisco a pirate radio station issues news bulletins. One night it decides to test the size of its listening audience. If you hear us, flash your lights five times, the announcer says. An instant later, the whole city is ablaze and then dark, ablaze and then dark—five times.

Messian is a student of history. He knows that collective action can breed everyday heroes and when heroes act, their courage can be contagious. He has read about the intoxication that beset the *sans culottes* in the French Revolution, that invisible sense that power is flowing into their own hands, that they're the spear tip of history. It makes them want to cut off heads and put them on spikes.

* * *

He's called into the chamber. The room falls silent when he enters and takes his seat in the well.

The deputy chairwoman of the Inner Council presiding over the meeting, an officious councillor in ash blond curls, pounds a gavel once, then stops. It's a ridiculous thing to do since the room is as silent as a tomb. Messian glares up at her.

She calls upon another councillor, who stands, clears his throat, and summons up a prosecutorial demeanor. He demands to know why the security forces haven't stopped "the rabble rousers."

The councillors pile on. They attack the "anti-State agitators," the protesters, the anarchists. They even know about the destruction of the coal mine.

"You're aware what they're shouting?" demands one indignantly. "They're shouting *Give Us Our Sky*. As if we took it away from them!"

Messian interrupts with a bitter laugh. "Technically, we did," he says.

The first councillor whirls around to look at him. "What do you mean by that?"

"Simple. We produced the Cocoon. The Cocoon took away the sky. So technically, yes, we robbed them of the sky."

"But that's absurd. The Cocoon saved them. It saved life on Earth. What would they have us do? Give over power to them?"

"So far the protests have been confined to specific targets. Coal mines. Fossil fuel facilities, producers of carbon dioxide," Messian observed.

"And so?"

"They're saying the enemy is pollution."

"And so?"

"And so perhaps they're right. Perhaps we should have tried to stop it."

Messian's remarks scandalize his fellow councillors. Murmurs of discontent bounce around the chamber.

"You're beginning to sound like the agitators," shouts one, leaping to his feet. He happens to be chairman of the largest zinc-mining conglomerate.

"I move we strike these remarks from the record," shouts another.

The presiding officer bangs the gavel three times. "Order, order," she yells.

The meeting goes on like this for some time, veering between expressions of alarm and veiled accusations against Messian, until the first councillor who spoke rises solemnly and demands to present a resolution. The chairwoman gratefully cedes the floor to him. He clears his throat and reads from a piece of paper.

"Since this so-called rebellion is in violation of the laws of the State and since certain persons are deemed to be leading it, those persons shall be declared enemies of the State. Further that the Chairman of this body"—here he casts an arch look at Messian—"shall bring such persons before this body and after a full and open proceeding to determine the facts of the case, that such persons shall be duly executed."

The reading is met by grunts of approval and quickly passed—unanimously. Messian, alone in the dock, doesn't vote. They seem to have forgotten about him. He walks out, almost unseen in the midst of the self-congratulatory clamor, into the hallway.

"Morons," he mutters once again to himself. "Cowards. Ignoramuses. Let them fiddle while Rome burns."

At home, he retires to his sanctuary, the planetarium. Inside, the light gray dome surrounds him and feels as comfortable as if he's inside an egg. He sits in a reclining chair next to the machine. He turns a switch and it gyrates and comes alive.

Slowly, the sky darkens. One by one, the stars appear, twinkling in the night. And then in the morning, that magnificent color comes, the one he now understands deep in his bones, the one that evokes serenity.

It is balm for an old man, the way a calming sleep may be a prelude to death.

* * *

Hours later Messian has an odd sensation as he stands in his office conferring with Vexler. The sensation is that the two of them are somehow equal. It's disturbing to imagine an equilibrium of power, as if they are balancing each other on a seesaw.

The feeling vanishes. He dismisses it as a momentary fluke. Perhaps it's just that he's not accustomed to such a lack of deference from an underling. Or simply that they're standing side by side, their heads at roughly the same level, as they look down on the maps on his desk.

Vexler is presenting his plan to quash the head of the insurrection in Fredericksburg. The plan is straightforward. He is sure that Yon and Gabe will move through the center of town, as they have before, feeling a false sense of security in numbers. The Black Guard will ambush them with an overwhelming force at a strategic point.

He points with a thick finger to the places where his forces will hide and where the reinforcements will wait. His finger moves from downtown over to the Rappahannock River.

It'll be right here, he says, just as they come up the Jefferson Davis Highway.

"When they cross the river, that's when we'll strike. We'll capture the head of the Resistance."

Separate the head from the body, thinks Messian, like killing a snake. Except that in this case the snake's head is his son.

"And the other one, the woman?" he asks.

"We don't know where she is. We'll question him to get her."

Messian asks some minor questions and makes one or two points, wondering whether he's fully disguising the ambivalence he feels.

"Don't harm them," he says. "We don't want martyrs."

Vexler reassures him. He'll have a select group of Black Guard loyal to him to handle that part.

Messian thinks, *He is looking at me strangely. Is he testing me? Does he think for some reason I don't want to be handed that head on a platter?*

He approves the plan and dismisses Vexler with a wave, but Vexler remains behind and clears his throat. He has something on his mind.

"One more thing. If you agree, would you circulate this plan in advance to the other top security officers and the high councillors?"

Messian looks up.

"Explain."

"Let me ask a question. Why is it, do you suppose, that so many times when we raid a cell, the occupants have just left?"

Messian waves his hand for him to continue.

"It's not chance. It's because someone is tipping them off. They have a mole high up in the apparatus of the State."

"A mole? Close to me?"

"Yes."

"And you want to leak the plan as bait to find him."

"Exactly."

Messian quickly mulls it over. It's not impossible. He gives permission and watches Vexler leave through the reception area, a bounce to his walk. That man is a born conspirator, he thinks. To him, the only thing more thrilling than a well-laid trap is *two* well-laid traps.

47

Sessler is driving to the Atlas Metal Works factory, taking the old dirt road in New Jersey.

Because she had to return north immediately, she didn't have a chance to patch things up with Yon. Their conversation at the encampment troubles her. By the end, in a strange mood swing, he was talking of dying for the cause, almost as if he were courting martyrdom.

Even more she's bothered, even hurt, by his reaction when he learned they were blood siblings. She expected he would be overwhelmed but she thought he might be comforted, perhaps even joyful. Instead he showed a kind of emotional blankness, an emptiness.

Less than forty-eight hours before the Launch, she thinks, and still so much to do. If this part of the plan fails, then nothing else matters. It's the key to everything.

She drives to the locked gate in the chain-link fence and it swings open just as she arrives. They've been waiting for her.

Right away she sees it—a huge trailer truck parked next to the side of the factory. Its side blazes with the red and white logo of the Launch and the words —UNCLE written on the door of the cab.

348

Frankie comes out the door and waves her inside.

"Good to see you," she says. "How you guys doing?"

"Okay," says Frankie. He points at Sam. "Except for his snoring."

She hands over a paper bag with a bottle inside.

"Vodka."

"Thanks." Frankie stores it in the freezer.

"Listen," he says, sitting at the table and motioning her to do the same. "I know I'm only the flunky. But this guy"—he points again at Sam—"Dr. Frankenstein over here, he won't tell me a damn thing."

Sam looks at her.

"You told me not to," he says defensively.

"Okay, I will," she says. "It's simple. You're creating carbon-eating algae." She turns to Sam. She can no longer contain herself. "So tell me. Is it working?"

"See for yourself," he replies, guiding her to the workbench. She grabs the end of a canvas sheeting and pulls it off, revealing a large pile of metal filings. They shimmer in the light. Off to one side is the metal canister Yon brought back, resting on its side.

"You were able to replicate it?"

"One hundred percent."

"And you tried it?"

Sam smiles and points to the four large tanks under the blazing hot lights in the rear. She goes over and her heart leaps up. Floating on top of each one is a thick blanket of green algae.

She puts her hand into the gooey mass and lifts it up. She drops it back in and allows herself a moment of hope.

"You tested it?"

Sam nods. "I've monitored temperature, salinity, and a dozen other variables. Oh"—he gives an impish smile—"and we've tested for carbon dioxide at the bottom, in case that's of any interest to you."

Sessler holds her breath. "And?"

"The concentration of CO_2 is intense. Three to four times higher than expected. The algae sink relatively quickly. And we see no signs of the gas bubbling back."

"How long did it take to grow?"

"No time. Once you add the nutrients."

She hugs them both, to their embarrassment.

"And the fish!—are they affected?"

"C'mere," says Sam. He brushes a forearm across the algae, clearing a small window as it continues to sink. "Look down there."

She sees the flicker of a tail.

"We thought we'd serve you one for lunch. You like sea bass?"

"Especially with vodka."

They laugh. Frankie spreads out the shot glasses.

* * *

Two hours later they lock the door with a padlock and leave, lugging a suitcase.

"What do you think?" asks Sam, pointing at the side of the truck. "A beauty—no? The reproduction of the logo is exact."

"You don't mind if I check the load," says Sessler. "Not that I'm doubting you."

"By all means." Sam throws open the rear doors. Cardboard boxes are piled to the roof. Sessler climbs inside the refrigerated trailer. She has to move the boxes aside, and they're not light. It takes time and effort and it's freezing, so she hurries. She squeezes past. Hidden at the front behind the cartons is a tarp. She lifts it to reveal a pile of bags. She opens one bag and sees the iron filings. Next to it are other bags, waterproof, containing the algae.

"Looking good," she says, jumping down.

"We just gotta hope they don't do what you just did," says Sam. "That they're lazy sons-of-bitches who'll stop at the cartons."

"How you gonna get in?" asks Frankie.

350

"A little help from a friend," she replies. She doesn't want to say more, anything that might reveal their mole.

She tosses her suitcase into the cab and climbs up behind the steering wheel while Sam gets in on the passenger side. Frankie shouts up to her window. "I bet this baby burns a shit load of gas. Hope you don't run into any of those protesters."

They laugh—even though it's not all that funny.

Frankie gets in Sessler's car to return it to New York. They drive out the gate and take the dirt road back to the turnpike and then they part. Sessler and Sam head south toward Washington, DC.

* * *

That night Messian is gripped by an unnameable darkness. He is alone in his mansion, except for the staff below stairs and the guards outside. He paces from room to room with a heavy dread in his heart. He sits at his desk and begins opening drawers. There is one on the bottom that he hasn't looked into in years.

Inside is a packet of photographs. He shuffles through them. He appears so young, he takes a moment to recognize himself. And there are Aggie and Sessler and even one of Yon as a baby, holding on to someone's hand. His tiny fingers are curled around an adult forefinger. And one of Yon standing for the first time, with a look of . . . what? Pride. He puts the photos away and feels a heaviness in his chest.

* * *

Sessler is in an old white clapboard house in Chevy Chase. The safe house is eerily quiet, except for the rhythm of Sam's snoring— Frankie was right, he *does* snore. She is in a little girl's room, with flowered wallpaper, children's books, and a lineup of dolls on a bookshelf. She hasn't been in a room like that, a room that housed a family, in years.

351

It makes her think of her own childhood and everything she missed. She lived with a giant void inside. She has filled that hole with activism and subversion and the Resistance. And now the objective is to topple her father from power and destroy everything he has done. The man who used to hold her on his knee and explain principles of Science. How strange. Is he truly evil? It was a question she never wanted to answer, never even wanted to pose.

* * *

Yon lies in a cot in his tent. He keeps himself awake on purpose. He tries distracting himself—thinking of what might happen when they reach Washington. Where will they go? Will there be a crowd? He tries to think of what he'll do when the Security Forces charge. He keeps awake and keeps trying to distract himself because he doesn't want to sleep. He doesn't want to sleep because he doesn't want to dream. He doesn't want to see the Minotaur tonight.

48

A S THE JALOPY ENTERS FREDERICKSBURG, YON AND GABE DO
something foolish. They get out of the car and parade
through the streets. They've done this before but never quite so
brazenly. Maybe they're overly confident because they've come
this far without an attack. Maybe they want to test their support
with an impromptu march. Or maybe their judgment is impaired
by tiring days on the road.

In any case, a growing number of people fall in step behind
them. Pretty soon there's a crowd moving through the streets, the
buildings echoing back the sound of many footfalls.

It weaves an exhilarating spell. Yon, wearing binoculars around
his neck, strides confidently. So does Gabe next to him, stretching her athletic legs in long bounds, her cane needlessly tapping
the surface of the street. Ahead of them, grinning irrepressibly, is
Martin, waving the illegal flag in wide dips.

A window opens and a woman's voice cries out: "You all are
plain crazy!"

Yon quickly scans the tops of the buildings. He can't see the
Black Guard snipers behind the parapets with their blast guns hidden, the scopes in place and the safeties off. Nor does he have any

idea that two blocks away, behind a line of graceful structures, is a line of troops with heavy weaponry.

He pulls up his binoculars. At the end of the street, at the juncture of Route 1 and Princess Anne Street, is a construction site, with piles of macadam, street barricades, stationary tractors, and dump trucks.

They slow down, then stop. Gabe borrows the binoculars and scans the river on the right and the road ahead leading to the bridge.

"It's the only way to cross the river," she says.

They resume the march and reach the construction site, which extends onto the bridge itself. It will constrict the space to a single lane.

Curiously, no one's working there, but equipment has been left in place. There are barricades and wooden horses with blinking orange lights and yellow tape around piles of paving stones.

Yon and Gabe confer. They'll continue on foot through the passage over the bridge. They'll go first and the others, now numbering several dozen, will follow. Once they reach the other side, they'll get back in the car.

They start to cross. The marchers behind squeeze into the passage onto the bridge. Yon and Gabe reach the far bank.

Then it happens.

An armored car roars down to cut off the marchers. Troops leap out and rush at the leaders. Explosions break out and smoke bombs land around them all, setting off a blinding fog.

Shock and confusion everywhere, people shouting and running. Troops line up across the bridge, cutting it in two. On the near bank, Black Guards attack the crowd, wielding truncheons. Canisters of tear gas fly through the air and a fog of gas rises up.

The marchers flee in all directions. Some fall to the ground. The Black Guard fire rubber bullets. People scream and scramble for safety, turning back and running through the streets.

On the far bank military vehicles roar up to surround Yon and Gabe. Black Guards leap out. Two of them grab Yon, one on each arm. A third holds a blast gun to his temple.

"You're coming with us," he says.

Yon looks over at Gabe. She is in a headlock, forcibly bent at the waist, clutching her cane. A trooper is lying at her feet, bleeding from the forehead.

The Guards bundle them into a gray van through the rear doors, slamming them shut. The van spins a half circle and takes off, careering around a corner, then speeds away on a highway going north.

Eventually the smoke and tear gas lift and the troops depart. Around the construction site are a sprawl of shoes, papers, and items of clothing. A half dozen people lie on the ground, some moving and groaning, a few immobile.

It is all over. The remnants of uninjured marchers mill about, angry and leaderless.

* * *

Sessler and Sam reach the Launch site and pause a moment to collect themselves before trying to drive the truck inside. They need to stash the bags inside the hangar where they can get them for tomorrow's Launch.

They're at the last checkpoint. Sessler hands over the papers, which are impeccable, thanks to the source who provided them.

"Meat delivery," she says.

Sam steps out to meet the Black Guard inspectors and opens the back of the truck. One of the Guards climbs into the trailer, pulls out a knife, and stabs one of the boxes labeled "Geo Sausage." He smells the meat, lifting his upper lip in distaste, and jumps back down. They close the door. That's it. They're in.

Sessler pulls the truck around to the back of the complex and parks near the rear entrance to the kitchen. She checks the hand-drawn map; she's in the right spot. They look out to scout the area. No one is around. They climb down.

"Gotta hand it to you," says Sam. "Smart idea, using a refrigerated truck. He couldn't get his freezing ass out of there fast enough."

Sessler nods. "Now we get to the hard part."

She says that they'll move the iron filings inside while the pilots, mechanics, and support staff attend a pre-Launch briefing at the other side of the hangar. Their "friend" has said he will make it last forty-five minutes. She figures they can do the job in forty minutes.

She sets a stopwatch and stuffs it into a pocket.

They drive to a gigantic structure made of thick steel, the jet's hangar. She parks in the bay of a loading dock where the source has told her the surveillance camera is not working.

She climbs onto the dock and approaches the door, checking a band on her left wrist for the code, which she punches in. The door unlocks and she looks at her stopwatch: thirty-five minutes left.

They move aside the boxes and unload ten fifty-pound bags of filings and ten twenty-pound bags of algae and the tarp onto the dock. They prop the door open, carry them inside, and lug them one by one to the door of a large storeroom located, as the map told her, down a corridor to the left.

She checks the band for another code and opens the door. They drop the boxes inside.

She checks the stopwatch. Ten minutes left—not too bad.

"I'll hide these," she says. "You go and drive the truck back to the kitchen. We can't run the risk of its being spotted here."

Sam leaves. She looks around the room for a good hiding spot. It's dim but she makes out workbenches, long tables, machine tools, and other equipment. In one corner, next to thirty-foot-high closed doors leading into the hangar, suspended from chains, are two jet engines—backups, she figures.

Nearby are ten canisters for gases. She goes over and taps one on the outside, then spreads a hand along the side. It's cold.

So this is it. The sulfur they use to fortify the Cocoon. The stuff that's robbing us of our sky. How I'd love to bury it at the bottom of the ocean.

She stacks the bags of iron filings and algae in a far corner and covers them with the tarp. There's no way to stash them out of sight. Best just to leave them here as if they belong.

She checks her watch. Five minutes. Better scram.

Her heart skips a beat. *What's that?*

A noise coming closer. Footsteps. The door handle turns. She dives under the tarp. The lights go on brightly. She doesn't dare look out. She holds her breath to keep the tarp from moving.

Someone shuffles in. Sounds like two people.

"They must think we're some kind of idiots," says a man's voice. "Every goddamn Launch it's the same thing. I can recite it in my sleep. So why this step-by-step run-through?"

"The countdown," comes a woman's voice, tinged with sarcasm. "They want to make sure we can count backward."

Sessler hears the thumping of a hand striking metal—the same sound she made moments before when she tapped the tank. She feels she's about to pass out. She can't breathe.

The two walk around. She can't figure out what they're up to. The woman's voice says: "Hey, what's this?"

She walks over to the tarp and raises a corner—five feet from Sessler.

"Some bags of something. Who woulda left them here?"

Another sound—the tarp dropping onto the floor.

The footsteps move away and the door opens. At that moment, Sessler's stopwatch rings. She swats it silent.

"What's that?"

"A bell."

"But it came from over there."

"No. Couldn't of. It's the assembly bell."

"Doesn't sound like it."

"It's gotta be. What else could it be?"

"How should I know?"

A beat.

The door closes. All is quiet.

Sessler waits a full five minutes before venturing out of the tarp and opening the door. She sees a group of men working at the far end of the hangar. She walks out, follows the wall, and slips out onto the loading dock.

Once outside, she hurries to the kitchen parking lot, where Sam is waiting, frantic with worry.

"Where were you? What happened?"

"I'll explain later. Let's get out of here."

49

THE GRAY VAN SPEEDS NORTH ALONG INTERSTATE 95 FOR twenty miles. The driver and passenger in the front are in plainclothes but they have the invincible air of top-level Security personnel. In the back, behind the wire mesh partition, two Black Guards keep their guns trained on Yon and Gabe.

Gabe demands to know where they're going. Neither of the Guards answers. They haven't said a single word the whole time.

Yon is sitting on the metal bench across from Gabe, the flag draped around his shoulders, quietly staring ahead.

Abruptly, the van turns, throwing them to one side, and hits bumps that sends them bouncing. They've taken a side road.

"Hey, what in hell—" a Guard next to them protests.

"Pit stop," says the front passenger, turning back to look through the mesh.

Still, the van keeps moving ahead, riding the bumps and swerving to miss the potholes.

The Guard bangs on the partition wall. "How far you going?"

"We're there."

The van stops in a cloud of dust. They hear a scattering of

pebbles strike the sides of the tire wells. A front door opens. They hear a man get out and stand on the side of the road, urinating.

"Me too," says one of the Guards in the back. He unlocks the rear doors, throws them open, and steps outside. The other Guard remains inside, his back to the open doors, swinging his gun barrel back and forth between Gabe and Yon.

He doesn't see a plainclothesman leap into view behind him, pointing a gun. He reads alarm in Gabe's face and starts to turn as the man fires—a loud blast. The Guard pitches forward, smashing against the partition. His blood splashes on the mesh and begins to slowly drip down.

The gunman looks at Yon and Gabe and waves the barrel. "Get out."

They do. They're standing on a dirt road, trees on both sides, no one around. The driver is standing on the roadside, training his gun on the other Black Guard, who is on his knees.

Yon and Gabe share a look.

"What is this?" asks Yon.

The first gunman points his rifle back at the highway. "There's the main road two miles back. Straight to DC." He spins his rifle around, pointing dead ahead. "This is a back road. It goes there, too. Your choice."

Yon asks, "We walk?"

"Of course."

"Who sent you?"

"I'm not at liberty to say. But get a move on. And I'd be careful if I was you."

They choose the back road and set out, Gabe with her cane and Yon still carrying the flag. Not far down the road, they hear a single gunshot behind them. They don't look back.

* * *

Messian's office is bathed in shadows. He is slumped in an armchair watching a video of Yon speaking to a crowd some days ago. The camera scans the crowd and Messian is struck by the way people are looking at him, the adoration on their faces.

"We will stop the Launch. We must do this to save the planet. The Cocoon that encircles our hemisphere was meant to protect us from the sun's heat but it was misconceived and turned into our enemy."

Messian notices that his voice, which began so softly you had to pay attention to make out the words, gathers in intensity.

"It spawned a dictatorship to keep it in place. It allowed the greed that led to our planet's destruction to continue. It must be destroyed, and we shall destroy it.

"This will be dangerous. No one knows what will happen. But even at the risk of extinction we must remove the barrier to the sun. I believe we will survive. Nature will right itself if given a chance. We must help her cleanse the Earth and restore it.

"This means no drilling oil wells, no fracking, no excavating mines, no killing coral. It means no polluting rivers, no burning fossil fuels to foul the air, no leaking pipelines, no burning garbage. It calls for a radical change in how we live. We shall live smaller and slower and purer."

The camera concentrates on Yon, who pauses to see how his words are sinking in. Many of the heads before him nod in assent, but a young man yells out, "But how can we go back a century?"

Yon quickly turns to him. "This is not going backward. I am not talking about giving up cars and using horse-drawn carts. I'm talking about using electric cars and producing electricity without polluting. About scaling back our demands so that only renewable energy is used. I am talking about a new simplicity and, for some, a new spirituality.

"I have seen it work in the South. The change is progress, not regress. It means going forward—forward to a richer, deeper existence. It requires rebuilding society on a human scale.

361

"Three centuries of material progress based on harmful practices will be consigned to the ash heap. But the beneficial advances— in medicine, agriculture, and other enterprises—will be retained. Science will flourish. Our lives will become better.

"How will this be done? Not by fiat or edict, not by autocratic government. It will be done by the communal will of the people once our rights are restored. We've seen what happens when we take the wrong path. We've looked into the abyss and we draw back in horror at what we've seen. We will no longer foul our own nest."

The crowd cheers. Yon holds high his amulet of lapis lazuli, gripping it tightly in one hand. He surveys the throng with fierce eyes and a look of certitude.

Messian clicks a button to shut off the video. The screen goes dark.

He's lost in reflection for a long time, mulling over Yon's words.

* * *

Vexler is shown in to Messian's office. This time he appears nervous, looking down at a sheaf of papers as he sits on the edge of his chair and gives his report on the ambush.

"We captured the two ringleaders who lead the Resistance. As expected, traitors intervened. The van that was transporting them was commandeered by two plainclothesmen who killed the two Black Guards and released their prisoners. We believe they are on their way to the capital. We will find them and re-apprehend them."

The good news, he says, is that the scheme he devised to uncover the mole worked. The plainclothesmen who freed the Resistance leaders were arrested. Under torture they revealed the name of the turncoat.

"We captured him."

Vexler pauses.

"Go on."

"He is Sylvan Brea."

Messian is speechless. His deputy—a *traitor!* Vexler hurries to fill in the silence. He says that Brea confessed to crimes against the State. He admitted having doubts about the Cocoon for years and recently came to believe that it was not merely ineffective but actually dangerous. Something about it was going wrong.

So it was a small step to support a group that was planning to destroy it. There is a plan to hijack the Launch. It involves the trip that Yon and Quinlin took to the South and the material Yon brought back in two canisters.

"I have finally solved that mystery," says Vexler, closely scanning Messian's face.

And the material in the canisters?

One was some kind of mineral, the other a plant. Vexler says he hopes to have more details soon.

Messian tells Vexler to keep Brea in prison. They'll figure out later what to do with him. The immediate step is to find the young leader and apprehend him.

"Find him. Detain him. But don't harm him. I need to speak to him."

Vexler departs.

Ten minutes later Messian leaves, taking a limousine from the underground garage. He tells the driver to take him to one of the unmarked houses he uses when he feels unsafe at home.

Through the darkened windows he sees the streets beginning to fill up with protesters. There are thousands of them. They crowd the Mall and spill over into side streets. No longer a disciplined crowd, they seem to be moving about aimlessly, separate people, energized by rage.

They're like a swarm of bees that's lost their queen.

* * *

Yon and Gabe walk the entire day. The back roads have almost no cars. They pass through the deserted town of Triangle on the flooded banks of the Potomac and follow old Route 1, which has reverted to the wild.

In the evening they come to the outskirts of a hamlet called Lorton, identified by a faded, pockmarked sign lying on the side of the road.

Off in the distance, a light beckons and they approach a handsome white clapboard house in which rectangles of yellow light gleam through the windows.

Gabe knocks gently with the tip of her cane. The wooden door gives way, opened by a large man. He has a shock of white hair, an expansive chest under a flannel shirt, and the thick arms and calloused hands of a farmer.

He welcomes them. Gabe explains that they are on their way to Washington. The man nods graciously.

"I know who you are," he says respectfully.

He leads them into a large kitchen where a dozen or so people are seated around a table. Four of them are children. The others have the indefinable air of strangers. Gabe realizes that they are protesters who've blundered off the beaten track. They look at Yon with wide eyes, awestruck.

The farmer and his wife provide a night's lodging—in their own bed. In the morning, they will give them a car.

50

IN THE CHEVY CHASE HOUSE, SESSLER WAKES AT DAWN. SHE looks out the window as daylight gathers. For a moment everything is still and quiet and surprisingly beautiful.

The good aura doesn't last long. She didn't get more than a couple of hours sleep and even those were fitful. She's plagued by worries.

The Launch will take place in twenty-four hours. She hasn't heard from the mole to verify any last-minute changes in the plan. She has no idea where Yon and Gabe are. She knows about the bloody confrontation in Fredericksburg and their arrest and the subsequent reports of their escape, but that's all. Without them to march on the Power, the whole enterprise will collapse.

She gets dressed and brews a pot of coffee. It's ready just as Sam comes downstairs, looking exhausted.

"I was up late, going over the pilot's manual," he explains. "But that wasn't the problem. The problem was I fell asleep."

"Why was that a problem?" asks Sessler.

"I had a nightmare." He pours himself a cup. "The nightmare was we actually got in the plane and had to fly the damn thing."

* * *

Messian is up shortly after the light gleams in the east. He, too, looks out the window and pauses a moment before starting his day.

He shuffles down the stairs of the manor house in Rock Creek Park to the dining room, where the table is set with sterling silver for his breakfast. A servant comes in and asks him what he'll have.

Boiled eggs.

He tightens his immaculate dressing gown and sits in an old-fashioned easy chair to wait. The TV set across from him flicks on.

He sees himself speaking—or rather his simulacrum, Amicus, moving and talking with ghostlike imitation. His chin jutting out strongman style, his head raised as if peering off into the future, his right hand resting on the back of an armchair, he counsels patience, he demands obedience, he pledges that these difficult days will soon pass.

"I ask this of you," he commands. "I who have saved you from calamity and given you more years of peace and prosperity than you ever thought possible. Stay home. Do not join the protesters, who are anarchists bent on overthrowing your benevolent government."

Messian almost forgets it's himself. The recording was spliced together using some footage from years ago—with what foresight, he now appreciates—when he was youthful and commanding and brimming with confidence.

I was another person, he thinks.

* * *

Yon and Gabe get an early start.

In the initial hours they cover a lot of ground. They arrive at George Washington's Mount Vernon home, where a band of protesters is assembling on the sloping lawn of the mansion. The group begins to grow as word of Yon's presence spreads.

By ten o'clock, they reach Alexandria. With mounting excitement, others march behind. They tread the cobblestone streets past the old wooden townhouses. At each major juncture, more protesters join in. With swelling numbers, they soon turn loud, singing and chanting.

They head north on Washington Street and then follow the George Washington Memorial Parkway. From there they approach the bridge over the Potomac. Their shouts and chants can be heard far across the opposite bank of the river.

Yon and Gabe cross the bridge first. They get out of the car. Now they are followed by thousands of marchers who mix with the marchers already on the far side of the river, converging like tributaries.

Yon walks steadily forward, his face strong and otherwise expressionless. As he moves, the flag draped on his shoulders stirs. The crowd around him is joyous and excitable. They chant, "Down with SAAM" and "Smash the Cocoon."

On the sides of the road, hawkers of food and water thrust their wares into outstretched hands and stuff money into their pockets.

Police and Black Guards in civilian clothes dot the crowd and look down from the roofs of buildings. They carry hidden radios, bending their necks from time to time to speak into them, conveying the latest information on the mood and direction of the marchers.

At 1:00 p.m., the march reaches the Mall. Yon stops to give a quick talk to rally his supporters. They strain to listen but only those around him are able to hear what he's saying. They pass his words on so that they travel to the edge of the crowd.

A boy who's scaled a lamppost yells, "Tell it, Yon." The crowd laughs and roars. Yon turns and waves to him. It's Martin. When Yon's finished, they cheer.

Vexler is at his command post in the Pennsylvania Avenue headquarters and he has five live video screens to choose from. He has drones in the air and thirty agents on the ground, some a short distance from Yon. What he needs is for Yon to move into the right position, for him to step away from the protection of his thousands of followers for just a moment. That's when the agents will strike.

* * *

On Connecticut Avenue Sessler passes three cars on fire and a group of protesters smashing the front gate of a store selling survival equipment. Down the cross street she sees looters running with boxes of stolen goods.

She crosses the Mall near the Capitol, heads for the Washington Monument, and climbs the stairs, stopping three times to catch her breath. At the top she goes over to the gaping hole and peers down. Below, tens of thousands of people move in a continual flow.

She pauses, rubs her eyes, and scans the multitude. She sees one place where the crowd is denser and swirls around a central point, like metal shavings around a magnet. She can hear them shouting and chanting.

She spots Yon in the thick of it. And next to him, Gabe.

She turns to go but not before she sees something she feared— dark objects flying above the mass of protesters, circling like vultures. Drones. And one of them is right above Yon.

* * *

Yon comes to the foot of the Lincoln Memorial. Intrigued, he stops. The crowd stops too, gathering around, expecting him to speak. But instead, he climbs up the mountain of cracked steps. Gabe follows.

"We don't have time for this," she pleads.

But Yon shakes her off. He's drawn by the solemnity of the place, the atmosphere of sanctity it conveys. How they must have adored and revered this man to construct such a temple!

They pass the columns and enter the dim interior. Before them sits the immense statue. The base is chipped and around it litter swirls in miniature whirlwinds. But the man in marble has a wondrous power. His massive arms and hands extend beyond the chair's arms. His knuckles bulge. He sits erect and stares straight ahead. Pigeon droppings cover his hair and beard, but he has a stately bearing.

"Look at him, Gabe. Look at his face. See the pain on it. It's as if he can see the future—the pain to come, the tragedy of it all, but he continued and he prevailed."

He reads the inscription cut into the marble wall: WITH MALICE TOWARD NONE, WITH CHARITY FOR ALL . . . LET US STRIVE ON TO FINISH THE WORK WE ARE IN . . . He turns to leave.

But dark figures step forth from the shadows. They surround Yon and Gabe and train their guns on them. Electric arcs shoot across to strike them in the chest and legs. They quiver and crumple to the floor.

The Black Guards bind them and carry them through an unmarked door and down a rear staircase. They wait at an exit behind the monument.

* * *

A breathless Sessler arrives at the foot of the Memorial, darting past the restive crowd. She mounts the steps two at a time and runs inside. She shouts his name and only an echo answers.

Across the Mall behind her, an explosion blasts. The crowd panics. People shove one another and flee in all directions. Behind the Memorial, a door opens and the Guards carry their prisoners out and toss them into a waiting gray van.

51

THE STAR CHAMBER OF THE INNER COUNCIL IS CALLED IN emergency session in the building on First Street. On the architrave above its sixteen columns is emblazoned the motto, EQUAL JUSTICE UNDER LAW. Already evening has darkened the windows. It's 6:00 p.m.

It took five hours to convene the body because the nine judges were slow to gather, frightened by the unruly mobs in the streets. Only when an escort of heavily armed Black Guard was provided did they consent to appear.

In an underground cell Yon and Gabe are chained together at the wrists. Gabe has a bleeding bump on her forehead—she was thrown bodily into the van and banged her head on the metal bench. Even so, she held fast to her cane.

Yon's wrists are red and swollen. The Guard who attached the handcuffs pressed them especially tight.

For the past four hours they've been confined to the cell without food or water.

Yon demands that the jailers treat Gabe's wound but he's ignored. As for himself, he almost seems to behave as if all this is happening to someone else.

370

Two Black Guards enter the cell. They pull the prisoners up by the chains, place manacles around their ankles, and march them through a tunnel and up a staircase.

Shuffling because of the restraints, they enter a back door to the courtroom, creating a stir. All heads turn toward them as they're escorted to a ten-foot by ten-foot cell in the center of the well. It's shaped like a cube, with iron bars. The Guards enter the cell with them, push them into two wooden chairs, and stand behind them.

Yon looks around. Ahead is a raised dais for the judges, who are leaning forward, staring at him. The chair for the Chief Justice is in the center and unoccupied at the moment. The others fidget and smooth their robes and chat uneasily.

To one side is a table for the defense. To the other is one for the prosecution. At the rear is a gallery for the public that is completely empty.

The Chief Judge enters through a side door. She's a large woman in a wig that doesn't completely cover her ash blond curls. She looks long and hard at the two defendants, then bangs a gavel to open the proceedings.

Messian is watching the trial from his office. Closed-circuit cameras and microphones allow him six different views of the courtroom and surrounding chambers. He sits before the screens, his head swiveling to catch every raised eyebrow and every whispered word.

He has seen the Chief Judge preparing to walk into the chamber, adjusting her wig and hiking her skirt up under the robe. He hears her sit down and intone gravely, "Will the Marshals bring in the prisoners!"

He turns a dial and one screen explodes into a close-up of Yon. He scans the high cheekbones, the strong chin, the broad forehead. It's the face he's come to know from all the photographs.

But the expression! Now Yon tilts his head, an imperturbable look in his eyes. He *does* look like me, Messian thinks. And like his mother, too.

* * *

"Hear ye, hear ye! The High Court is in session."

The deputy chairwoman strikes the gavel. "The clerk will call the case."

A white-haired clerk stands. "Case 46,718. The People versus Yolander Messian and Gabriella Doe."

An invisible current spikes through the air, even with the public gallery empty. It is the surname that has shocked them.

The Chief Judge instructs the clerk to read the charges.

The clerk intones: "Participating in unlawful activities—to wit, leading an unauthorized march, disseminating falsehoods calculated to undermine the State, and fomenting treason against the duly-constituted State Power, including but not limited to the Inner Council of the Consortium of UNCLE."

Again, the buzz.

The Chief Judge says that the last charge—treason—carries a sentence of death by hanging.

Yon listens without reacting. Gabe puts her hand on his arm.

"Did you hear that?" she whispers.

"Yes." His answer sounds remote.

The trial speeds on. The prosecutor mounts a parade of evidence. He holds a device and clicks on it with dramatic flair; a screen descends from the ceiling. On it are projected snippets of video: the judges see Yon dynamiting the coal mine, exhorting his followers to revolt, crossing the Potomac bridge.

"I need hardly spell out for your honors the significance of the words '*Rise Up*' and '*Sky Back*,'" he concludes. "And we all know the effect of these words. All you have to do is to step out on the streets to witness it."

The judges share looks. His summation strikes close to the bone. They can now hear the cries and chants of protesters outside. To them they sound like the howls of wild animals.

372

The clerk calls the case for the defense. A frail-looking man with a wrinkled face approaches the cell and leans down to whisper to the two prisoners. Would they like to say something?

Gabe declines with a barely perceptible shake of her head.

But Yon stands. He clutches his amulet close to his chest. He is handed a microphone, which squawks loudly with feedback. Obviously the cell has another mic hidden somewhere. A technician in a remote room shuts it off.

Yon stares at the officers sitting high up on the bench. He begins slowly but gathers steam as he goes along, marshaling his arguments methodically. He insists that the Cocoon has made life miserable.

"And now, on top of everything else, it has stopped working. The signs are there. Only a blind person, or a person willfully closing his eyes, would fail to see them. Who hasn't been struck by the cracks in the Cocoon? The sudden changes in temperature? The gathering of dark energy far above?

"Face it. The Cocoon is rotting and must be allowed to die. Sending more particles up to reinforce it only makes it worse. Tomorrow's Launch should not occur. It must be stopped at all costs. You must stop it."

Reading the expressions on the judges' faces, Yon knows that the warning is falling on deaf ears.

"And you would act," he ends, his voice rising in frustration, "if this were a true government. A government—in words that I read today—*of the people, by the people, and for the people.*"

He sits just as a Black Guard rushes over to force him to. The Guard places a hand uselessly on his shoulder and presses down. Yon has said his piece. The time for making speeches is over. He has done what he came to do.

The judges deliberate for less than ten minutes before handing down the expected verdict.

Messian doesn't bother to wait. He switches the screens off and sits at his desk in the growing darkness, staring into space.

52

SESSLER BACKS INTO THE TREES TO WAIT OUT OF SIGHT, EVEN though it's dark. She doesn't want him to see her, not before he gets near. She needs to make sure she can talk to him—reason with him, close up.

She stares out at the path that he'll be taking soon—*maybe*. She checks her watch. Two o'clock in the morning. She's not thinking clearly.

Everything that could go wrong has gone wrong. Everything she hoped would happen did not happen. Her plan depended partly on serendipity to succeed, and now it has all turned to dross.

Yon has been sentenced to death. Her younger brother! It's her fault for getting him involved in all this. As if that's not bad enough, Gabe, the love of her life, has been condemned to hang too.

The plan to subvert the Launch and switch the payload is hanging by a thread. There are no protesting crowds to encircle the site and come to their aid, just tens of thousands of people milling around wondering what to do. Their high-up source is inexplicably unreachable. The supersonic plane encircling the Earth will carry the dreaded sulfur instead of the iron and algae.

She checks her watch again. In five or six hours it'll happen. Far from offering a glimmer of hope to escape from the Cocoon and set the Earth on a healing path, it will deepen the disease—and likely doom the planet.

What a litany of catastrophes.

There is only one way out. She detests the thought of abasing herself to her father. But there's no choice. He is the one person who can help her, if he wanted to. Somehow she would have to persuade him.

An hour ago she checked the mansion at the Naval Observatory. She stayed a half hour, looking at the windows, including the one on the second floor that as a child was her own, a portal for her dreams. There were no signs of life.

Like any paranoid ruler, he changes residences to thwart assassination, and her underground network listed this manor house, set in the gorge of Rock Creek Park, as the likely abode for tonight.

Sure enough, she saw the telltale vans of security guards. She also saw a lighted window on the second floor, the shadow of someone moving behind a drawn shade. Perhaps he, too, like her, is too anxious to lay his head upon a pillow. Perhaps he's consumed over the fate of his son—*if he knows that Yon's his son*. That's her last card to play.

She stands outside, looking up at the window. In less than a minute, two guards emerge from a guardhouse. She tells them who she is, pleads with them to take a note to him, and waits a good ten minutes with a gun pointed at her abdomen. The messenger returns and tells her to station herself down the road.

* * *

She waits and waits. Standing still is unbearable, so she walks in small circles in front of the trees. Stops and walks again. Until she hears the sound of boots approaching. Four guards come.

Flashlights beam through the night. One stands next to her while the others search the nearby wooded area.

She sees him. A slight figure passing under the white cone of a streetlight, a ghostly apparition, approaching slowly. He gets closer.

Behind him are two security guards. She sees him speak to them and they drop back ten paces. She steps into his path. He continues, comes closer, and looks at her. He stops.

"I saw it was you back there." He nods toward his house. "I was waiting for you to ring the bell. It's infinitely more convenient to meet in my study, but your note said you wanted me to come outside." His voice is cold, distant. "Here I am."

"I'm sorry," she blunders. "I didn't know . . . " She trails off. Here she hasn't seen him for over twenty years and he's already reduced her to a blubbering idiot. "Do you want to go back?"

"No. We're here. Might as well go on."

She wishes she could see him better. The figure that appeared under the streetlight seemed bent, older than she expected. But she barely caught a glimpse.

They walk side by side on the path, which verges away from the road into the bushes. The guards walk ahead, checking the way.

He clears his throat. "Well. You wanted to see me. Why?"

She tells him everything, lays it all out without attacking him or accusing him of anything. She talks uninterrupted for twenty minutes as they walk. She tells him about the massive support they've attracted, the hundreds of thousands of marchers, about the plan to supplant the sulfur with iron filings, and the need to stop the Launch.

"You know the Cocoon's not working. You know it's deteriorating." she says.

"What makes you so sure?"

"We have an informant in your office."

He's not shocked. That surprises her.

"And anyone can tell," she presses on. "You can see it. Temperatures fluctuate. The Cocoon even *looks* sketchy sometimes."

"Not sketchy. Less dense." He resumes walking but is silent for a while. Then he says, "And if what you say is true—which I'm not confirming—we're talking hypothetically here. But if what you say is true, why should I let you proceed with your crazy plan to drop iron filings over the oceans?"

"It's not a panacea. It might not even work. But we have to try. The Cocoon is destroying the ozone. We believe that one more flight might finish it off completely. So tomorrow's flight must be stopped."

They're walking side by side at the same pace.

He stops and turns his head toward her but she cannot see his eyes in the darkness.

"You can't allow the Launch to go ahead," she says. Her voice rises. "Don't you see? That'll just make it worse. You're giving the patient medicine that's killing him."

He answers curtly. "I expect scientific arguments, not metaphors— from you, of all people. And for God's sake, keep your voice down."

Again, she feels belittled.

He continues, suddenly calm. "What makes you think your plan will work?"

"Algae are the only short-term remedy we know of. We've grown it and tried it out. It works."

"In the lab. Not in real life."

"We have to try."

"What about the long term?"

"Long term we have to stop pollution, all of it. We can look to science, to human ingenuity, to guide us over the transition. That can provide a bridge. But science isn't the ultimate answer. Humans are. We have to be our own saviors. There must be a new land at the end of the bridge. We have to change the way we live. Nothing else will work."

"Quite an inspirational little speech."

Her face flushes.

"You know what they say," he continues, "put your faith in human beings and you're bound to be disappointed."

Time to play the winning card.

"That's where Yon comes in," she says. "That's why we need him to lead the Revolution."

She holds her breath. She waits to see his reaction. He comes to a park bench and sits down. He doesn't talk.

"You know he's going to hang in a few hours," she says. "And so is the person I love—Gabriella."

"That's the decision of the Court. The Council. The whole government depends—"

"Bullshit. There is no government. There is *you*. He's your son. Your blood. She is my love. You cannot let them die."

He looks up at her. It's hard to read his face.

She continues. "At least go see him. Talk to him."

Messian springs up surprisingly quickly and starts off toward his home.

"Are you hearing me?" she shouts.

He keeps going. She wants to yell, *Do it for me. I'm your daughter.*

He turns around.

"Leave me alone," he yells.

The words shoot through her. She sits on the bench. The guards leave. She's surprised at how little she feels from the rejection. It's as if he's someone else, not her father. *Maybe love can actually perish—my love for him, not just his love for me.*

* * *

Sessler drives back to the house in Chevy Chase. The lights are on when she arrives and the door opens before she reaches it. It's the woman who lives there, her silhouette lighted from behind.

"Thank God, you're here," she says.

"Why? What's happened?"

"Sam. He hasn't come back. He went to the demonstration and he never returned."

Sessler's heart sinks.

Now, somehow she'll have to try to load and fly the plane alone. That'll take twice as long—if it's possible at all.

In her room she retrieves two mechanic's uniforms—maybe Sam will turn up—and drives back to the Launch site. It's early in the morning and the streets are alive with marchers milling about.

At the Launch, support staff is beginning to arrive. The man in the guardhouse looks at her papers for a long time but eventually waves her car through.

Too easy, she thinks. Could the source have arranged it? Or— and this would be best of all—has her father finally come to his senses? Did her arguments prevail? Or is it a trap?

She drives straight to the hangar, climbs up to the loading dock, and finds the back door open.

She sees no one inside and slips into the storeroom. The tarp is over in the corner. She goes to it and lifts one end—the bags are there, untouched.

She drops it just as the door opens. In comes ten Black Guards, weapons drawn. They seize her before she has a chance to speak, bind her arms, and carry her off.

53

YON'S CELL IS SMALL BUT CLEAN. HE'S LYING ON WHAT PASSES for a bed—a long metal shelf affixed to the cement wall with metal brackets. He has a gnawing hunger in his belly. He still hasn't been given anything to eat.

He knows Gabe is somewhere near, no doubt in a similar cell. They were brought down together in chains after the sentencing, but he does not know exactly where she might be. He sees and hears no one.

It is his thoughts that are keeping him awake, spurred and darkened by the only sound to reach him through the small barred window out of reach. A sound of hammering and sawing in the courtyard just outside. He knows what it is and tries to picture it from books he had seen long ago in the cabin in Canada. The workers are building a scaffold to hang him.

He does not fear death but he fears the agony of getting there. The rough rope placed under his chin like a heavy necklace—will it snap his neck instantly and mercifully? Or will it constrict his breathing pipe slowly so that his lungs cry out desperately for air?

A rat scuttles by just beyond the bars, startling him. Lying on his metal bed, he thinks back to the tunnel in the South, to the cave-in and Quinlin's death. How would Quinlin stand up to this? He knows that on the raft Quinlin was scared of the water, from his days as a child during the Great Cull. That's why he wanted Yon to steer at first, but he never let on.

Grampa Zeger faced death matter-of-factly in his sickness, without a fuss. For him it was like keeping a long-ago-arranged appointment. All those stories he used to tell of the ancient Greek heroes facing death—even the young boys running from the Minotaur in the labyrinth.

Will I be that brave when it comes to walking up the wooden steps in the shadow of the noose?

He has no religion to console him. But he does have a cause. Earlier, through the window, he heard some distant chants and yells of protesters. That made the prospect of dying more supportable because it reminded him of the cause. But now, in the dead of night, they've stopped.

Wait.

He hears something. A door opening, echoing down the empty corridor. A light pierces the darkness. The sound of footsteps approaching—slow footsteps. A shuffling figure moves into view, lighted from behind so he can't easily make it out. It's a man, an old man.

He knows immediately who it is.

Messian steps out of view for a moment and comes back carrying a chair, which he sets down a few inches from the bars. He sits and examines Yon for a full minute before speaking.

"You know who I am?"

Yon nods. His eyes, Yon thinks—they are like mine, like Sessler's. The rest of him, I recognize nothing. I feel nothing.

Messian falls silent again as if he's waiting for Yon to speak, but Yon says not a word.

"You hear that sound?" Messian asks. His eyes rise up to the window behind him. "Do you know what it is?"

"Yes. A scaffold."

"And do you know what that's for?"

"Of course."

"What does it make you feel?"

"Numbness. Fear. Doubt."

Messian grips a bar with his right hand. "I'm glad you're telling the truth. We must speak the truth to each other—do you agree?"

"I always speak the truth."

Yon can see the wrinkled skin of his father's wrist and arm.

"You will be hanged at 7:00 a.m." Messian looks at his watch. "Three hours from now. Do you know why?"

"Because you—and the Power you command—are afraid."

"Afraid?"

"Afraid of me and what I represent."

"What do you represent?"

"Radical change. The destruction of everything you've built in your foolishness and its replacement by a system of salvation."

"Foolishness!" Now Messian grips the bars with both hands. "You're the foolish one. You and your sister. You have no idea what you're talking about. You have no idea what I've done. You have no appreciation."

Yon remains quiet, searching his face. Gradually, in the silence, Messian calms down. "Listen," he says, "and listen carefully. I can get you out of here. There's a chance but only one chance and it must be done quickly."

"What do we do?"

"Not *we*. You!"

"What do I do?"

"You renounce what you've done. You say you were wrong. You abandon this silly protest and call upon your supporters to leave and go home. You sign an official document saying you were duped. You visited the South and you were taken in. Things there are in chaos."

Yon doesn't move a muscle and doesn't speak.

"You sign such a document saying this and I take it to the Inner Council. I tell them it's a way out of the crisis. They'll listen. They have to listen. They want all this over."

Yon remains quiet. A flicker of hope arises in his breast. He looks at his father and says, "And the Launch?"

"The Launch goes on."

"And the Cocoon."

"That, too."

Yon stands up and approaches the bars. "You don't get it, do you?"

"Don't get what?"

"What we're doing. What we're about. What I'm about."

"What are you about?"

"We're fixing what you messed up."

"That crazy scheme of the oceans—it'll never work."

"You don't know it won't."

"You don't know it will."

"Not for certain. But it's a chance. A chance we have to take."

"Yon, listen. It's not worth your life. Nothing is worth your life."

"Life—as you have made it—is not worth living."

"Son. Please. Listen." Messian reaches through the bars to touch Yon's arm, but Yon pulls away and steps back.

His voice rises, almost bellowing. "You have ruined the planet. You've done it, old man, and now it's time to step aside so that our generation can try to salvage something from the ruins."

Messian stands and knocks the chair back.

His voice quivers. "I *saved* the world."

"You *destroyed* it."

Messian walks back to the door, faster this time.

"I'll leave the light on. I want you to think. I'll station a guard here. If you change your mind, shout for him."

He leaves and the door slams behind him.

54

As Messian steps outside he senses something in the darkness, something different. There's a volatility, a shift in the air that fills him with a heightened sense of alertness. It's a sense he hasn't felt for decades, not since he was a child. He thinks back. The leaves turning their green undersides up, the breezes mounting, the sky darkening.

But it can't be that.

* * *

In bed, he can't sleep. His brain is churning. Memories of his childhood rush in, things he hadn't thought about for years. Things he heard about from others.

His famous father, so brilliant. Ahead of his time. His death up in the Arctic—it used to give him nightmares, the way it was described, being sucked into the mouth of a frozen hole of darkness.

Maria, his mother. What was she like? The stories about her struggles with alcohol. Her suicide. He can't call up a single image of her, not even from a photo.

But he can remember Lesley. He can almost smell her, a warm

384

womanly smell that brings comfort. He remembers sitting in the pew at the funeral. Her death was so horrible, plunging off the mountain. And it was murder!

He drifts on, thinking of Aggie, how much he cared for her in the early days. Sessler running to greet him with open arms. Those were happy times . . . until his wife fell in with the Zegers. And Yon, bouncing him on his knee. Yon whom he never really knew, kidnapped by the Zegers. They must have brainwashed him.

Besermann, Lesley's murderer. A pathetic megalomaniac. In some ways he was smart; he grasped the threat of global warming, but he had no backbone. It was easy to turn everyone against him.

This parade of people—some gone, others grown. An old man's memory is a long corridor. And at the end of the corridor . . . what is there? What counts? What is it all for? How could he allow his only son to die?

* * *

In the early hours, before the first paltry gleam of light, a strange rumbling rends the atmosphere. It is deep and fearsome, like the growling of a jungle beast or the cracking of the Earth. It's a fearful sound— one that must have made early humans fall to their knees, paint their cheeks in streaks of red, and sacrifice humans on the tops of pyramids.

No one under the age of fifty has heard anything like it.

But Messian has. Lying there in his bed, having barely slept, he sits upright. Can it be? After all this time? He can hardly believe his ears.

Thunder.

How can there be thunder when there are no thunderstorms? The Cocoon, the whole stratosphere is out of control. He has no idea what's going to happen. He's frightened.

He rings for his assistant, who appears in a bathrobe, breathless and pale.

"What was that?" the assistant asks.
"Never mind. Get dressed."

* * *

Yon, in his cell, can't sleep either. At a certain point the hammering in the courtyard stops—they must have finished their gruesome task. But then, within the hour, comes that ear-splitting crash that seems to shake the very bars of his cell. He knows what it is from his time in the South.

Now, in the gathering morning light, he stands on a chair and looks out through the small window. He sees the gallows but above it he sees something else.

The Cocoon looks different. Ninety percent of it is the familiar yellow-gray pallor that hangs over everything. But there, way over to the east, is what looks like a hole. A ray of light is shining through it. The blanket of the Cocoon seems to be rising and folding up within itself. It's a dark billowing, as if it's gathering strength or energy for some unknowable purpose. The black is spreading. A storm cloud is brewing.

His life is about to end. He is filled with fear. He has nothing to do but watch and wait.

* * *

Messian finishes his directive and stamps it with his personal seal. He picks up the closed-circuit phone but it isn't working. He hands the directive to his assistant and looks at his watch.

"Deliver it at once," he commands.

The messenger looks at the envelope, which is marked "Most Urgent." It's addressed to the warden of Yon's jail—clearly a stay of execution.

"Do it yourself," commands Messian. "Fast as you can." He looks at the clock. It's 5:30 a.m. No time to spare.

The messenger rushes out. Messian walks over to the window and looks outside. The Cocoon, his creation, is dying. It's outlived its usefulness. What will happen now?

Maybe it doesn't matter. He's old and tired. He's outlived his usefulness, too. What has it all meant now, his life, when all is said and done? What has he left behind of value?

His meetings with Sessler and Yon—he regretted how he acted, saying the things he said. To his own children. Perhaps they're right. Perhaps there is some hope in their scheme to use iron to fertilize the oceans. Perhaps people can be taught to actually change the way they live, with proper guidance.

And Yon. He has to be saved. *He will be saved.*

* * *

Sessler, when thrown into the cell in the basement of the Pennsylvania Avenue building, found Sam there, sleeping in a corner. She woke him and they talked for hours, commiserating over the plan gone wrong.

They were still talking in the early hours when the crash in the atmosphere seemed to shake the building. They take turns peering at the roiling sky through a small window above the bed.

"I think I know what that is," she says. "I heard my parents talk about it when they reminisced about the old days. It's thunder. It precedes a kind of disturbance, an electrical storm. They had a poetic saying about it. They said it sounded like angels bowling."

"I don't believe in angels and I've never been bowling, but I'll take their word for it," replies Sam.

She's pacing up and down their cell, listening to the thunder and trying unsuccessfully to avoid looking at her watch. Last time she did, it was 6:00 a.m., only an hour before the hangings. She can't bear it.

The heavy door down the corridor clicks open. They hear booted footsteps approach uncertainly. A guard stops. He looks panic stricken.

"What is it?" he says, "that sound?"

"Just the Cocoon," she says. "A little hole. You can see it from here." She motions to the window. He pulls out a bunch of keys, opens the cell door, and stands on the bed.

Sam and Sessler knock him to the floor, grab the keys, and lock him in the cell. He barely resists. They run down the corridor. The place is deserted—a phone receiver hangs down a wall. They almost collide getting out the main door.

As they step outside, they look up. Clouds are turning dark loops up above and there is a strange feeling in the thick air, a kind of electrical crackling, as if something fearsome and miraculous were about to happen.

They jump in a police van, find the keys in the ignition, and head for the Launch site.

* * *

As the messenger hurries through the streets to Yon's jail, as the transport carrying Sessler and Sam careers around corners, the downpour begins. It smashes down, ferociously. It's as if billions of gallons of water have been collected in a vast, stratospheric balloon that was suddenly punctured.

The rain comes down in sheets, accompanied by thunder and lightning. The water plunges in a solid wall off the buildings, gushes down the streets in rivers, and floods low-lying areas, turning them into ponds and lakes. No one has seen a deluge like this. It knocks branches off trees, pours down from roofs in a single sheet like a waterfall.

Then, as abruptly as it started, the rain stops.

* * *

Vexler is sitting in a basement office in the cellblock making preparations for the executions, which are to be televised to the nation.

Someone knocks on his door. A messenger is ushered in. He places the envelope holding the directive on the desk and waits. Vexler looks at it. The envelope indicates it's from Messian.

"An order to stay the executions," he says. His voice is flat.

The messenger nods and says they tried to reach him by phone.

"I disconnected the phones," he responds. He doesn't explain.

He rips open the envelope and reads the top page of the directive, his face impassive. He places the directive in the center of the desk, pinching the corner edges with both hands to align it perfectly, and looks down at it with contempt.

He raises his beefy right hand, brings it down, and crumples the paper. He lifts it and places it between both hands and squeezes it into a ball. Then he throws it into a corner.

"You didn't see that," he commands.

The messenger, aghast, takes a step back.

"And you didn't get here when you got here. Roads were clogged with anarchists. Right?"

The messenger, looking frightened, doesn't move a muscle.

"A wise decision," says Vexler. He leans back in his chair, his arms behind his head. "I'd say the old man is getting soft—don't you agree?"

* * *

Sessler and Sam arrive at the Launch. The gatehouse is unmanned and she's able to drive right through the front entrance. Cars and equipment are lying around—the place has been abandoned in a hurry. They drive to the hangar and dash inside to the storage room, where the tarp still lies in a corner.

Sam goes into the hangar and returns.

"It's fueled up and ready to go," he says. "They must have panicked just before the Launch."

They load the iron filings to the spreader, board the aircraft, and check out the payload. They strap themselves in. Sessler runs through the checklist. She starts the engines and guides the aircraft out the door onto the runway. The blast shakes the cockpit. Slowly she starts off down the runway, then goes faster and faster until she pulls up the yoke to raise the nose.

"Here we go!" she yells into her mouthpiece.

* * *

STANA is still working. The camera catches both at once in a split screen, the Launch and the gallows. It shows the jet taking off, the long loop into the air, and then, far above that, the contrail.

The other half of the screen focuses on the scaffold and the ropes. The moment that image appears, Messian spots it on the screen at home. His chest tightens. His stay of execution wasn't delivered—or maybe isn't being obeyed. The hangings must be stopped. He hurries out of his house and into a waiting van. He has a motorcycle escort, sirens screaming through the wet streets.

Protesters scatter before them. But the closer they get to the prison, the more people there are in the streets. They are everywhere, slow-moving bodies that clog the way. Soon the cavalcade slows, then stops. People are wandering around aimlessly on all sides.

Messian lowers the window and leans out, shouting at them to get out of the way. A dozen or so protesters look at him, perplexed. No one pays him any mind.

* * *

Yon, shackled, waits in his subterranean cell. Gabe hobbles by, her hands tied behind her back. She is pushed along by two Guards.

"Let me have my cane," she pleads. "Let me walk to my death with dignity."

The Guards confer. One releases her bonds and ties one arm behind her back while the other fetches her cane and hands it to her. They move on. She has not looked at Yon.

A minute later, the executioner, wearing the black hangman's hood, comes down the corridor and stands before his cell. The hood rises up on both corners—they look like horns.

Yon sees him and shrinks back to a corner. He knows who it is—the Minotaur. The cell door opens. The beast approaches him, looms over him, and leans down. He grabs Yon roughly by the arm and raises him up.

Yon barely stands. The Minotaur spins him around and ties his hands behind him. He shoves him forward out of the cell. Still shackled, Yon shuffles down the corridor, pushed from behind. He is too terrified to turn around. He comes to the stairs and mounts them slowly, both feet on each step. The Minotaur seizes his arm with a powerful hand and pushes him out the door.

They enter the courtyard where the gallows stand. Long wooden staircases have been constructed, one on the right and one on the left. The gallows has two nooses dangling down side by side. There's a drop of twenty feet or so, more than enough to snap a neck. Yon sees Gabe slowly walking toward the left staircase.

The courtyard is draped in shadows, bright light coming down. He looks up. The sky is changing. He can see it, way off to the east, a tiny hole of luminescence.

In the near distance he hears shouts and chants—the protesters. They're coming toward the prison.

He turns to look at his hooded tormentor still holding him by

391

the arm—the fleshy shoulders, the cocked head. He is not a beast at all, not a Minotaur. He is just a man, the executioner. Yon shakes his arm, dislodging the man's hand, and trudges toward the gallows. He's moving slowly.

The executioner orders his leg irons removed. Yon looks over at him again. That voice, it sounds familiar.

Gabe is walking even more slowly, leaning on the cane. She hobbles precariously, her feet barely advancing. The executioner orders her shackles taken off.

She moves more easily now, but one hand is still tied behind her back. The guards prod her to the left staircase and lift her up the steps, one by one. At the top, a guard grabs her cane, struggles with her, and throws it down. She stands tall.

The guard positions her on the trapdoor that will plunge her down.

Yon watches her, his heart flooded with profound love.

The executioner in the hood comes over to him and leads him to the bottom of the stairs on the right. Yon can hear him breathing and sees the hood pulsating before his mouth. He can smell him, his sweat. Something about him is familiar.

The man guides him up the steps. They mount slowly. Yon feels the pressure on his elbow tighten. The man is squeezing it, almost trying to hurt him. Yon almost knows him, becomes more and more convinced of his identity—though how could that be?

They reach the top. Gabe is standing on a trapdoor under the noose on the far side. Both arms are behind her back and they appear to be moving. Yon is pushed onto a platform four feet from her. It feels shaky. A guard places the noose around Gabe's neck. The executioner near Yon gently drapes the noose around his neck. It lies heavy on his shoulders. He is moved onto the trapdoor.

The executioner reaches up and removes his hood.

Luther!

Vexler stands there, grinning wickedly.

Yon feels the revelation strike him physically, like a blow, staggering him. It is beyond explanation. But as he takes it in, an odd sensation overwhelms him. He accepts it. All of it. The strange twist is not any stranger than life itself, the inscrutability of it. Anything can happen. And in the wake of that feeling comes a mysterious comfort. A warm ecstasy floods his body. He's transported back to the top of the pyramid. The sounds of the jungle animals surround him. The stars gleam above.

Is it all meant to happen? He looks around, his senses sharpened to a knife edge. The drops of water dripping from the leaves, the breeze stirring a wisp of Gabe's hair, the fly buzzing off to one side. The sky roiling above.

The connectedness of it all. How is it all here before him? How is it all happening at this very instant?

It's his fate. It's destiny.

He looks at the man standing next to him. For the first time he sees Luther in full.

Vexler is angry. Why is Yon so accepting? He turns away quickly and moves close to Gabe. He places his hand on the lever to open the platform beneath her. Her eyes widen and tighten. She has cut her binds. Her arms fling out and she lunges at him, thrusting the hidden dagger wildly toward him. It sinks in his gut. He spins as he plunges the lever. She's suspended a moment in free fall, then plunges down through the trap door.

The rope tightens but she breaks her fall as she grabs it in one hand and struggles to cut it with the other. There's the sound of her feet landing on the ground.

Vexler turns. He looks down at his hand holding his abdomen. It comes away soaked in blood. He looks over at Yon. He staggers closer, falls against the lever, pressing it down. The trapdoor opens. Yon drops from sight, instantly, plunging down through the gaping hole. A horrible sound—the crack of neck bones breaking. The rope bounces, then hangs taut.

Vexler topples over. He falls the full length of the gallows, past Yon's dangling body, and smacks against the earth. Gabe rises up from the ground, gasping.

Protesters have scaled the walls and run toward the gallows yelling and waving weapons. The guards abandon their stations and retreat to the prison. Gabe mounts the gallows and cuts Yon's body down.

The crowd is aghast. They lay Yon's body down on the grass and stand around for some moments, unsure what to do. Gabe goes into the building and brings out a blanket and covers him.

Paul Messian arrives. The old man is stricken the moment he sees the blanket. He walks over slowly and bends down and lifts it. When he sees Yon he falls to his knees. He sits down next to him and cradles him, moaning almost soundlessly. The TV camera is still rolling. The whole nation sees Messian—Amicus—holding his son.

He closes Yon's eyes with his finger. He raises his son's head slightly and reaches down and removes the amulet of lapis lazuli from around his neck. He stares at it for a moment, then places it in his pocket.

Messian stays there holding Yon for a long time. He hears shouts over the prison walls as more people arrive. Among them is a young boy who throws himself on Yon's body. Overhead a strange light blazes down, rays through clouds that are forming.

A worker comes over. With his help Messian stands up and walks away, leaning on the worker's arm.

55

S ESSLER AND SAM RETURN. AS THEY ROUNDED THE EARTH, reports of the hangings—one successful, one not—were radioed to them. Sessler, in a crossfire of sorrow and joy, gives over command of the jet to Sam while she rests her head on the side of the window and tries to compose herself.

When the jet skids to a stop on the runway, she leaps out to find Gabe waiting for her. They fall into each other's arms and remain there without speaking. She tells Sam to make the next seeding without her—and to keep them going, over and over until the Cocoon disappears. They go to the house in Chevy Chase and stay indoors for a full day.

Then they get down to work.

As the first order of business, they arrange for Yon's burial. They choose a simple grave in Arlington Cemetery. Not far away is the mass grave of dissidents. They make plans to identify as many remains as possible and to lay them to rest in separate graves centered on a memorial.

* * *

Two weeks have passed since Yon's funeral. Difficult, uncertain weeks.

His hanging unleashed a fury that could not be contained. All across the country, people rose up. They stoned police stations and Black Guard quarters. They attacked the offices of mining companies and oil corporations, trashed gasoline stations, and looted stores.

In the capital, angry mobs roamed the streets. They pinpointed their targets: They broke into the Hoover building, burning the secret files. They smashed the Court, STANA, and various State offices, but not the headquarters of UNCLE or the Inner Council chamber.

That's because Sessler and Gabe have brought the Resistance members there. They hold sessions late into the night on how to repair the country and get it moving again. They plan trials of Security and other State officials. They set a date for the founding of a constitutional convention and they order up a program of rebuilding, starting with the Washington Monument.

Every so often, people look to the sky, trying to ascertain what's going on. Dark clouds are pitching and rolling there in a feverish broth.

When most of the stores have been looted and the offices vandalized, the anger burns itself out. The marchers return to their hometowns, the protesters return to their homes, and people everywhere wonder how they are going to restart their lives and what the world will be like.

Scientists confirm that Sessler's flights, still ongoing, have spread a bloom of algae around the world and that it is beginning to consume the carbon in the atmosphere. But not fast enough. Sam is placed in charge of a program to increase the super-plant to the optimal level. The open questions are: What is the proper equilibrium and how will it be maintained?

In the third week a new kind of light appears above—haltingly, uncertain.

There's much discussion of what to do with Messian. One faction is in favor of putting him in the dock, but they decide it is better to start anew in the spirit of reconciliation rather than have a public trial. The shattered old man is allowed to retire to an undisclosed location where he will live out his few remaining days. Sessler is not sure if she will visit him or not.

Then, one day in the fourth week, people freeze in place. Something impossible is happening. The light above, the same light that Yon got a glimpse of from his jail cell, burns brighter. It's as if there is a rip in the fabric of the sky. The Cocoon peels away. Bit by bit, the layers of it break away and shrivel up and disappear.

And still, the light grows.

Sessler and Gabe step out of the penthouse office onto the roof, the very one she used to walk with her father on the way to the planetarium. On the Mall, thousands of people gather. They look to the sky.

Sessler raises both arms up. *If only Yon could see this. If only Quin could see this.*

The light still grows. It's becoming hotter. How hot will it get? When will it stop? Impossible to say. A window in the sky opens and through it they get a glimpse of outer space.

The light mesmerizes the people. They've never seen it before—it's so bright. It comes from the center of the carapace above, taking on form as the Cocoon deteriorates. At last they see it whole, right before their eyes—the sun, blazing down. So brilliant it hurts to look at it.

But you can feel it. You can stand there and feel the warmth streaming down, filling your body with energy. A blinding, fierce whiteness that seems to conjure the dawn of creation.

And there, over to one side—*see it!*—the white rim of a smaller globe, barely perceptible. It's the moon, hard to see it in the flood of the sun's light but at night it will come out, blood orange and yellow, to occupy its own perch of mystery.

And what's that? Far above, everywhere.

It's the sky, the infinite sky. Around the sun, it gleams a luminous creamy white. And then it shades off into other colors, richer and darker and deeper. As deep as the ocean. And the ocean too, now that you look at it, is the same unnameable color as the sky.

Everyone, everywhere sees it. Some gape in disbelief. Others stand stock still, pointing. The young ones have never seen anything like it. The old ones remember it.

It's a color so beautiful it plunges into your soul. It's a color that summons poetry and history, for wolves to howl and lovers to sigh and painters to grab their brushes. It's a color for kings and prophets, lovers and explorers, Odysseus and Poseidon, Viking ships and space rockets, musicians and dancers, Romeo and Juliet, Daedalus and Apollo.

The magnificent color sprung straight from the rainbow, the last and most passionate color on Nature's easel. The color of longing.

Blue

BLUE

BLUE

Acknowledgments

E VERY BOOK IS DIFFERENT IN THE WRITING AND HAS A DIFFER-ent passage to completion. This one, a complicated blend of science and make-believe, was longer than most. It happily found a home in Arcade Publishing, run by Jeannette Seaver, to whom I owe a great debt. I also thank Peter Osnos, who championed the manuscript and was instrumental in bringing it to light. I owe a debt to my nephew, Nicholas Darnton, for planting the seed of the idea of the Cocoon during a long-ago discussion over Thanksgiving turkey. I'm grateful to Jarek Serafin of the Historic Museum of Sanok in Poland for permission to use a painting by Zdzislaw Beksinski as the cover illustration. Phyllis Grann cast her expert eyes on the manuscript. David Ebertshoff made excellent editorial suggestions. Kathy Robbins, my agent, gave hours to discussions of structure and other matters. Dr. Radley M. Horton of Columbia University's Climate School generously shared some thoughts on global warming; any errors in that department are mine, not his. I also thank Katherine Kiger, Nicole Mele, and Stephan Zguta of Arcade for excellent copy editing and supervising the smooth change from manuscript to book. Finally, I am deeply indebted to my wife, Nina, who read every word multiple times, discussed every concept, critiqued every character, and kept my spirits up. And I would be remiss if I did not thank my three children—Kyra, Liza, and Jamie—for reviewing the various drafts and making smart suggestions. I leave it to their children, to whom the book is in part dedicated, to help get the world out of the mess we've created.